D1337813

Fearsome and funny and original, it's requisite reading for fantasy lovers of all ages.

— Libby Hathorn, CBCA Award-winning author of *Thunderwith*

It's a fast-paced read that is sometimes funny and sometimes scary, but always completely magical.

— *Readings*

Townsend's intensely cinematic writing, quirky humour and superior world-building conjure a genuinely fresh take on magical fantasy.

— *The Bookseller*

Unexpected, exciting and funny. Like *Alice in Wonderland*, Harry Potter and *Doctor Who* swirled up together. I loved Morrigan Crow, and I want to check in at the Hotel Deucalion.

— Judith Rossell, ABIA Award-winning author of *Withering-by-Sea*

Jessica Townsend

Nevermoor

The Trials of
Morrigan
Crow

LOTHIAN

A Lothian Children's Book
Published in Australia and New Zealand in 2017
by Hachette Australia
(an imprint of Hachette Australia Pty Limited)
Level 17, 207 Kent Street, Sydney NSW 2000
www.hachettechildrens.com.au

10 9 8 7 6 5 4 3 2 1

National Library of Australia
Cataloguing-in-Publication data:

Townsend, Jessica, author.
Nevermoor: the trials of Morrigan Crow/Jessica Townsend.

978 0 7344 1807 4 (paperback)

For primary school age.

Adventure stories.
Children's stories.
Fantasy fiction.

Cover design by Christabella Designs
Cover illustration by Jim Madsen
Author photograph courtesy Lani Carter
Text design by Bookhouse, Sydney
Digital production by Bookhouse, Sydney
Printed and bound in Australia by McPherson's Printing Group

MIX
Paper from
responsible sources
FSC® C001695

FSC
www.fsc.org

The paper this book is printed on is certified against the
Forest Stewardship Council® Standards. McPherson's Printing
Group holds FSC® chain of custody certification SA-COC-005379.
FSC® promotes environmentally responsible, socially beneficial
and economically viable management of the world's forests.

For Sally, first guest of the Hotel Deucalion.

And for Teena, who made me think I could do anything, even this.

Spring of One

The journalists arrived before the coffin did. They gathered at the gate overnight and by dawn they were a crowd. By nine o'clock they were a swarm.

It was near midday before Corvus Crow made the long walk from his front door to the tall iron rails keeping them at bay.

'Chancellor Crow, will this affect your plans to run for re-election?'

'Chancellor, how soon will the burial take place?'

'Has the president offered condolences?'

'How relieved do you feel this morning, Chancellor?'

'Please,' Corvus interrupted, holding up a leather-gloved hand to silence them. 'Please, I wish to read a statement on behalf of my family.'

He pulled a piece of paper from the pocket of his smart black suit.

'We wish to thank you, the citizens of our great Republic, for your support over the past eleven years,' he read in a clear, authoritative voice honed by years of demanding order in the Chancery. 'This has been a trying time for our family, and the distress will no doubt linger for some time yet.'

He stopped to clear his throat, looking up for a moment at his hushed audience. A sea of camera lenses and curious eyes gleamed back at him. A ceaseless assault of flashes and clicks.

'The loss of a child is difficult to bear,' he continued, returning to his notes. 'Not only for our family, but for the townspeople of Jackalfax, who we know share in our grief.' At least fifty pairs of eyebrows shot upward, and a few embarrassed coughs broke the momentary silence. 'But this morning as we welcome the Ninth Age of the Wintersea Republic, know that the worst is behind us.'

There was a sudden, loud caw from overhead. Shoulders hunched and faces flinched, but nobody looked up. The birds had been circling all morning.

'The Eighth Age took from me my beloved first wife, and now it has taken my only daughter.'

Another piercing caw. One reporter dropped the microphone he was thrusting at the chancellor's face and scrambled noisily to pick it up. He turned pink and mumbled an apology, which Corvus ignored.

'However,' he continued, 'it has also taken with it the danger, doubt and despair that plagued her short life. My . . . *dear* Morrigan' – he paused to grimace – 'is finally at peace, and so must we all be. The town of Jackalfax – indeed, the entire state of Great Wolfacre – is safe again. There is nothing to fear.'

A murmur of uncertainty rippled through the crowd, and the onslaught of camera flashes seemed to slow. The chancellor looked up at them, blinking. His paper rustled in a slight wind, or perhaps it was his hand shaking.

'Thank you. I will not be taking questions.'

CHAPTER ONE

The Cursed Crow

Winter of Eleven
(Three days earlier)

The kitchen cat was dead, and Morrigan was to blame.

She didn't know how it had happened, or when. She thought perhaps he'd eaten something poisonous overnight. There were no injuries to suggest a fox or dog attack. Apart from a bit of dried blood at the corner of his mouth, he looked like he was sleeping, but he was cold and stiff.

When she found his body in the weak winter morning light, Morrigan crouched down beside him in the dirt, a frown creasing her forehead. She stroked his black pelt from the top of his head to the tip of his bushy tail.

'Sorry, kitchen cat,' she murmured.

Morrigan thought about where best to bury him, and whether she could ask Grandmother for a bit of nice linen to wrap him in. Probably best not to, she decided. She'd use one of her own nightshirts.

Cook opened the back door to give yesterday's scraps to the dogs and was so startled by Morrigan's presence she nearly dropped her bucket. The old woman peered down at the dead cat and set her mouth in a line.

'Better his woe than mine, praise be to the Divine,' she muttered, knocking on the wooden doorframe and kissing the pendant she wore around her neck. She glanced sideways at Morrigan. 'I liked that cat.'

'So did I,' said Morrigan.

'Oh yes, I can see that.' There was a bitter note in her voice, and Morrigan noticed she was backing away, inch by wary inch. 'Go on now, inside. They're waiting for you in his office.'

Morrigan hurried into the house, hovering for a moment near the door from the kitchen to the hallway. She watched Cook take a piece of chalk and write KICHIN CAT – DEAD on the blackboard, at the end of a long list that most recently included SPOYLED FISH, OLD TOM'S HEART ATACK, FLOODS IN NORTH PROSPER and GRAVY STAYNES ON BEST TABELCLOTH.

'I can recommend several excellent child psychologists in the Greater Jackalfax area.'

The new caseworker hadn't touched her tea and biscuits. She'd travelled two and a half hours from the capital by rail that morning and walked from the train station to Crow Manor in a wretched drizzle. Her wet hair was plastered to her head, her coat soaked through. Morrigan was struggling to think of a better remedy for this misery than tea and biscuits, but the woman didn't seem interested.

'I didn't make the tea,' said Morrigan. 'If that's what you're worried about.'

The woman ignored her. 'Dr Fielding is famous for his work with cursed children. I'm sure you've heard of him. Dr Llewellyn is also highly regarded, if you like a gentler, more maternal approach.'

Morrigan's father cleared his throat uncomfortably. 'That won't be necessary.'

Corvus had developed a subtle twitch in his left eye that only appeared during these mandatory monthly meetings, which signalled to Morrigan that he hated them as much as she did. Coal-black hair and crooked noses aside, it was the only thing father and daughter had in common.

'Morrigan has no need of counsel,' he continued. 'She's a sensible enough child. She is well acquainted with her situation.'

The caseworker chanced a fleeting look at Morrigan, who was sitting beside her on the sofa and trying not to fidget. These visits always dragged. 'Chancellor, without wishing to be indelicate . . . time is short. Experts all agree we're entering the final year of this Age. The final year before Eventide.' Morrigan looked away, out the window, casting around for a distraction, as she always did when someone mentioned the E-word. 'You must realise this is an important transitional period for—'

'Have you the list?' Corvus said, with a hint of impatience. He looked pointedly at the clock on his office wall.

'Of – of course.' She drew a piece of paper from her folder, trembling only slightly. The woman was doing rather well, Morrigan thought, considering this was just her second visit. The last one barely spoke above a whisper and would have considered it an invitation to disaster to sit on the same piece of furniture as Morrigan. 'Shall I read it aloud? It's quite short this month – well done, Miss Crow,' she said stiffly.

Morrigan didn't know what to say. She couldn't really take credit for something she didn't control.

'We'll start with the incidents requiring compensation: the Jackalfax Town Council has requested seven hundred kred for damage to a gazebo during a hailstorm.'

'I thought we'd agreed that extreme weather events could no longer be reliably attributed to my daughter,' said

Corvus. 'After that forest fire in Ulf turned out to be arson. Remember?'

'Yes, Chancellor. However, there's a witness who has indicated that Morrigan is at fault in this case.'

'Who?' Corvus demanded.

'A man who works at the post office overheard Miss Crow remarking to her grandmother on the fine weather Jackalfax had been enjoying.' The caseworker looked at her notes. 'The hail began four hours later.'

Corvus sighed heavily and leaned back in his chair, shooting an irritated look at Morrigan. 'Very well. Continue.'

Morrigan frowned. She had never in her life remarked on 'the fine weather Jackalfax had been enjoying'. She *did* remember turning to Grandmother in the post office that day and saying, 'Hot, isn't it?' but that was hardly the same thing.

'A local man, Thomas Bratchett, died of a heart attack recently. He was—'

'Our gardener, I know,' Corvus interrupted. 'Terrible shame. The hydrangeas have suffered. Morrigan, what did you do to the old man?'

'Nothing.'

Corvus looked sceptical. 'Nothing? Nothing at all?'

She thought for a moment. 'I told him the flowerbeds looked nice.'

'When?'

'About a year ago.'

Corvus and the caseworker exchanged a look. The woman sighed quietly. 'His family is being extremely generous in the matter. They ask only that you pay his funeral expenses, put his grandchildren through university and make a donation to his favourite charity.'

'How many grandchildren?'

'Five.'

'Tell them I'll pay for two. Continue.'

'The headmaster at Jackalfax – *Ah!*' The woman jumped as Morrigan leaned forward to take a biscuit, but seemed to calm down when she realised there was no intention to make physical contact. 'Um . . . yes. The headmaster at Jackalfax Preparatory School has finally sent us a bill for the fire damage. Two thousand kred ought to cover it.'

'It said in the newspaper that the dinner lady left the stovetop on overnight,' said Morrigan.

'Correct,' said the caseworker, her eyes fixed firmly on the paper in front of her. 'It also said she'd passed Crow Manor the previous day and spotted you in the grounds.'

'So?'

'She said you made eye contact with her.'

'I never did.' Morrigan felt her blood begin to rise. That fire *wasn't* her fault. She'd never made eye contact with anyone; she knew the rules. The dinner lady was fibbing to get herself out of trouble.

'It's all in the police report.'

'She's a liar.' Morrigan turned to her father, but he refused to meet her gaze. Did he really believe she was to blame? The dinner lady admitted she'd *left the stovetop turned on*! The unfairness of it made Morrigan's stomach twist into knots. 'She's *lying*, I never—'

'That's quite enough from you,' Corvus snapped. Morrigan slumped down in her chair, folding her arms tight across her chest. Her father cleared his throat again and nodded at the woman. 'You may forward me the bill. Please, finish the list. I have a full day of meetings ahead.'

'Th-that's all on the financial side of things,' she said, tracing a line down the page with a trembling finger. 'There are only three apology letters for Miss Crow to write this month. One to a local woman, Mrs Calpurnia Malouf, for her broken hip—'

'Far too old to be ice-skating,' Morrigan muttered.

'—one to the Jackalfax Jam Society for a ruined batch of marmalade, and one to a boy named Pip Gilchrest, who lost the Great Wolfacre State Spelling Bee last week.'

Morrigan's eyes doubled in size. 'All I did was wish him luck!'

'Precisely, Miss Crow,' the caseworker said as she handed the list over to Corvus. 'You should have known better. Chancellor, I understand you're on the hunt for another new tutor?'

Corvus sighed. 'My assistants have spoken to every agency in Jackalfax, and some as far away as the capital. It would seem our great state is in the throes of a severe private tuition drought.' He raised one dubious eyebrow.

'What happened to Miss . . .' The caseworker consulted her notes. 'Linford, was it? Last time we spoke you said she was working out nicely.'

'Feeble woman,' Corvus said with a sneer. 'She barely lasted a week. Just left one afternoon and never returned, nobody knows why.'

That wasn't true. Morrigan knew why.

Miss Linford's fear of the curse prevented her from actually sharing the same room with her student. It was a strange and undignified thing, Morrigan felt, to have someone shout Grommish verb conjugations at you from the other side of a door. Morrigan had grown more and more annoyed until finally she'd stuck a broken pen through the keyhole, put her mouth over the end of it, and blown black ink all over Miss Linford's face. She was prepared to admit it wasn't her most sporting moment.

'At the Registry Office we have a short list of teachers who are amenable to working with cursed children. A *very* short list,' said the caseworker with a shrug, 'but perhaps there will be someone who—'

Corvus held up a hand to stop her. 'I see no need.'

'I beg your pardon?'

'You said yourself, it's not long until Eventide.'

'Yes, but . . . it's still a *year* away—'

'Nonetheless. Waste of time and money at this stage, isn't it?'

Morrigan glanced up, feeling an unpleasant jolt at her father's words. Even the caseworker looked surprised. 'With respect, Chancellor – the Registry Office for Cursed Children doesn't consider it a *waste*. We believe education is an important part of every childhood.'

Corvus narrowed his eyes. 'Yet *paying* for an education seems rather pointless when this particular childhood is about to be *cut short*. Personally, I think we should never have bothered in the first place. I'd be better off sending my hunting dogs to school; they've got a longer life expectancy and are much more useful to me.'

Morrigan exhaled in a short, blunt *oof,* as though her father had just thrown a very large brick at her stomach.

There it was. The truth she kept squashed down, something she could ignore but never forget. The truth that she and every cursed child knew deep in their bones, had tattooed on their hearts: *I'm going to die on Eventide night.*

'I'm sure my friends in the Wintersea Party would agree with me,' Corvus continued, glaring at the caseworker, oblivious to Morrigan's unease. 'Particularly the ones who control the funding of your little department.'

There was a long silence. The caseworker looked sideways at Morrigan and began to gather her belongings. Morrigan recognised the flash of pity that crossed the woman's face and she hated her for it.

'Very well. I will inform the ROCC of your decision. Good day, Chancellor. Miss Crow.' The caseworker hurried out of the office without a backward glance. Corvus pressed a buzzer on the desk and called for his assistants.

Morrigan rose from her chair. She wanted to shout at her father, but instead her voice came out trembling and timid. 'Should I . . . ?'

'Do as you like,' Corvus snapped, shuffling through the papers on his desk. 'Just don't bother me.'

Dear Mrs Malouf,
    ~~*I'm sorry you don't know how to ice-skate properly.*~~

I'm sorry you thought it was a good idea to go ice-skating even though you're a million years old and have brittle bones that could snap in a light breeze.
I'm sorry I broke your hip. I didn't mean to.
I hope you are recovering quickly. Please accept
my apologies and get well soon.
Yours sincerely,
Miss Morrigan Crow

Sprawled on the floor of the second sitting room, Morrigan rewrote the last few sentences neatly on a fresh sheet of paper and tucked it into an envelope but didn't seal it. Partly because Corvus would want to check the letter before it was sent, and partly on the off chance that her saliva had the power to cause sudden death or bankruptcy.

The *click-clack* of hurried footsteps in the hallway made Morrigan freeze. She looked at the clock on the wall. Midday. It could be Grandmother, home from morning tea with her friends. Or her stepmother, Ivy, looking for someone to blame for a scratch on the silverware or a tear in the drapes. The second sitting room was usually a good place to hide; it was the glummest room in the house, with hardly any sunshine. Nobody liked it except for Morrigan.

The footsteps faded. Morrigan let out the breath she'd been holding. Reaching over to the wireless, she turned the little brass knob through squealing, static-filled airwaves until she found a station broadcasting the news.

'The annual winter dragon cull continues in the north-west corner of Great Wolfacre this week, with over forty rogue reptiles targeted by the Dangerous Wildlife Eradication Force. The DWEF has received increased reports of dragon encounters near Deepdown Falls Resort and Spa, a popular holiday destination for . . .' Morrigan let the newsreader's posh, nasal voice drone in the background as she began her next letter.

> *Dear Pip,*
> ~~*I'm sorry you thought TREACLE was spelt*~~
> ~~*with a K.*~~
> ~~*I'm sorry you're an idiot.*~~
> *I'm sorry to hear you lost your recent spelling*
> *bee* ~~*because you're an idiot*~~. *Please accept my*
> *deepest apologies for any trouble I may have*
> *caused you. I promise I'll never wish you luck*
> *again* ~~*you ungrateful little*~~.
> *Yours faithfully,*
> *Morrigan Crow*

There were now people on the news talking about the homes they'd lost in the Prosper floods, crying over pets and loved ones they'd seen washed away when the streets ran like rivers. Morrigan felt a stab of sadness and hoped Corvus was right about the weather not being her fault.

> *Dear Jackalfax Jam Society,*
> *Sorry ~~but don't you think there are worse things~~*
> *~~in life than bad marmalade?~~*

'Up next: could Eventide be closer than we think?' asked the newsreader. Morrigan grew still. The E-word again. 'While most experts agree we've one more year until the current Age ends, a small number of fringe chronologists believe we could be celebrating the night of Eventide much sooner than that. Have they cracked it, or are they just crackpots?' A tiny chill crept along the back of Morrigan's neck, but she ignored it. *Crackpots*, she thought defiantly.

'But first: more unrest in the capital today as rumours of an imminent Wunder shortage continue to spread,' the nasal newsreader continued. 'A spokesperson for Squall Industries publicly addressed concerns at a press conference this morning.'

A man's voice spoke softly over the background hum of murmuring journalists. 'There is no crisis at Squall Industries. Rumours of an energy shortage in the Republic are entirely false, I cannot stress that enough.'

'Speak up!' someone yelled in the background.

The man raised his voice a little. 'The Republic is as full of Wunder as it ever has been, and we continue to reap the rewards of this abundant natural resource.'

'Mr Jones,' a reporter called out. 'Will you respond to the reports of mass power outages and malfunctioning Wundrous technology in the states of Southlight and Far East Sang? Is Ezra Squall aware of these problems? Will he emerge from his reclusive lifestyle to address the problem publicly?'

Mr Jones cleared his throat. 'Again, these are no more than silly rumours and fear-mongering. Our state-of-the-art monitoring systems show no Wunder scarcity and no malfunction of Wundrous devices. The national rail network is operating perfectly, as are the power grid and the Wundrous Healthcare Service. As for Mr Squall, he is well aware that as the nation's sole provider of Wunder and its by-products, Squall Industries has a great responsibility. We are as committed as ever—'

'Mr Jones, there's been speculation as to whether the Wunder shortages could have anything to do with cursed children. Can you comment?'

Morrigan dropped her pen.

'I – I'm not sure . . . I'm not sure what you mean,' stammered Mr Jones, sounding taken aback.

The reporter continued. 'Well, Southlight and Far East Sang between them have three cursed children listed on their state registers – unlike the state of Prosper, which has no cursed children at present and has remained untouched by Wunder shortages. Great Wolfacre also has a registered cursed child, the daughter of prominent politician Corvus Crow; will it be the next state hit by this crisis?'

'Once again, there *is no crisis*—'

Morrigan groaned and turned off the wireless. Now she was being blamed for something that hadn't even happened yet. How many apology letters would she have to write next month? Her hand began to cramp at the thought.

She sighed and picked up her pen.

> *Dear Jackalfax Jam Society,*
> *Sorry about the marmalade.*
> *Yours,*
> *M. Crow*

Morrigan's father was the chancellor of Great Wolfacre, the largest of four states that made up the Wintersea Republic. He was very busy and important, and usually still working even on the rare occasions he was home for dinner. On his left and right would sit Left and Right, his ever-present assistants. Corvus was always firing his assistants and hiring new ones, so he'd given up learning their real names.

'Send a memo to General Wilson, Right,' he was saying when Morrigan sat at the table that evening. Across from her sat her stepmother, Ivy, and way down at the other end of the table was Grandmother. Nobody looked at Morrigan. 'His office will need to submit a budget for the new field hospital by early spring at the latest.'

'Yes, Chancellor,' said Right, holding up blue fabric samples. 'And for the new upholstery in your office?'

'The cerulean, I think. Talk to my wife about it. She's the expert on that sort of thing, aren't you, darling?'

Ivy smiled radiantly. 'The periwinkle, dearest,' she said with a tinkling, breezy laugh. 'To match your eyes.'

Morrigan's stepmother didn't look like she belonged at Crow Manor. Her spun-gold hair and sun-kissed skin (a souvenir from the summer she'd just spent 'destressifying' on the glorious beaches of southeast Prosper) were out of place amongst the midnight-black hair and pale, sickly complexions of the Crow family. Crows never tanned.

Morrigan thought perhaps that was why her father liked Ivy so much. She was nothing like the rest of them. Sitting in their dreary dining room, Ivy looked like an exotic artwork he'd brought back from a holiday.

'Left, any word from Camp 16 on the measles outbreak?'

'Contained, sir, but they're still experiencing power outages.'

'How often?'

'Once a week, sometimes twice. There's discontent in the border towns.'

'In Great Wolfacre? Are you certain?'

'Nothing like the rioting in Southlight's slums, sir. Just low-level panic.'

'And they think it's due to Wunder scarcity? Nonsense. We're not having any problems here. Crow Manor has never functioned more smoothly. Look at those lights – bright as day. Our generators must be full to the brim.'

'Yes, sir,' said Left, looking uncomfortable. 'That . . . hasn't gone unnoticed by the public.'

'Oh, whinge, whinge, whinge,' croaked a voice from the opposite end of the table. Grandmother was dressed formally for dinner as usual, in a long black dress with jewels around her neck and on her fingers. Her coarse, steel-grey hair was piled in a formidable bun atop her head. 'I don't believe there is a Wunder shortage. Just freeloaders who haven't paid their energy bills. I wouldn't blame that Ezra Squall if he cut them off.' She sliced her steak into tiny, bloody pieces as she spoke.

'Clear tomorrow's schedule,' Corvus told his assistants.

'I'll pay the border towns a visit, do a bit of handshaking. That should shut them up.'

Grandmother gave a mean little laugh. 'It's their heads that need shaking. You have a spine, Corvus – why don't you use it?'

Corvus's face turned sour. Morrigan tried not to smile. She'd once heard a maid whisper that Grandmother was a 'savage old bird of prey dressed up as a lady'. Morrigan privately agreed but found she rather enjoyed the savagery when it wasn't aimed at her.

'It's – it's Bid Day tomorrow, sir,' said Left. 'You're expected to make a speech for the local eligible children.'

'Good lord, you're right.' (*Nope*, thought Morrigan as she spooned carrots onto her plate. *He's Left.*) 'What a bother. I don't suppose I can cancel again this year. Where and when?'

'The Town Hall. Midday,' said Right. 'Children from St Christopher's School, Mary Henwright Academy and Jackalfax Prep will attend.'

'Fine.' Corvus sighed unhappily. 'But call the *Chronicle*. Make sure they have someone covering it.'

Morrigan swallowed a mouthful of bread. 'What's Bid Day?'

As often happened when Morrigan spoke, everyone turned to face her with vague looks of surprise, as though she were a lamp that had suddenly grown legs and started tap-dancing across the room.

There was a moment of silence, and then—

'Perhaps we could invite the charity schools to the Town Hall,' her father continued as though nobody had spoken. 'Good publicity, doing things for the underclass.'

Grandmother groaned. 'Corvus, for goodness' sake, you only need one idiot child to pose for a photo, and you'll have hundreds to choose from. Just pick the most photogenic one, shake its hand and leave. There's no need to complicate things.'

'Hmm,' he said, nodding. 'Quite right, Mother. Pass the salt, would you, Left?'

Right cleared his throat timidly. 'Actually, sir . . . perhaps it's not such a bad idea to include the less privileged schools. It might get us a front page.'

'Your approval rating in the backwoods could do with a boost,' added Left as he scuttled down the table to fetch the salt.

'No need to be delicate, Left.' Corvus lifted an eyebrow and glanced sideways at his daughter. 'My approval rating everywhere could do with a boost.'

Morrigan felt the tiniest tremor of guilt. She knew her father's major challenge in life was trying to maintain his grip on the affections of Great Wolfacre's voting public while his only child brought about their every misfortune. That he was enjoying his fifth year as state chancellor despite such a handicap was a daily miracle to Corvus Crow, and the question of whether he could sustain this implausible luck for another year was a daily anxiety.

'But Mother's right, let's not overcrowd the event,' he continued. 'Find another way to get me a front page.'

'Is it an auction?' asked Morrigan.

'Auction?' Corvus snapped. 'What the devil are you talking about?'

'Bid Day.'

'Oh, for goodness' sake.' He made a noise of impatience and turned back to his papers. 'Ivy. Explain.'

'Bid Day,' began Ivy, drawing herself up importantly, 'is the day when children who've completed preparatory school will receive their educational bid, should they be lucky enough.'

'Or rich enough,' added Grandmother.

'Yes,' Ivy continued, looking mildly put out by the interruption. 'If they are very bright, or talented, or if their parents are wealthy enough to bribe someone, then some respectable person from a fine scholarly institution will come to bid on them.'

'Does everyone get a bid?' Morrigan asked.

'Heavens, no!' Ivy laughed, glancing at the maid who'd come to place a tureen of gravy on the table. She added in an exaggerated whisper, 'If everyone were educated, where would servants come from?'

'But that's not fair,' Morrigan protested, frowning as she watched the maid scurry from the room, red-faced. 'And I don't understand. What are they bidding for?'

'For the privilege of overseeing the child's education,' Corvus interrupted impatiently, waving a hand in front of his face as though trying to brush the conversation away. 'The glory of shaping the young minds of tomorrow and so on. Stop asking questions, it's nothing to do with you. Left, what time is my meeting with the chairman of the farming commission on Thursday?'

'Three o'clock, sir.'

'Can I come?'

Corvus blinked repeatedly, a frown deepening the lines in his forehead.

'Why would you want to attend my meeting with the chairman of—'

'To Bid Day, I mean. Tomorrow. The ceremony at Town Hall.'

'You?' her stepmother said. 'Go to a *Bid Day ceremony*? Whatever for?'

'I just—' Morrigan paused, suddenly unsure. 'Well, it *is* my birthday this week. It could be my birthday present.' Her family continued to stare blankly, which confirmed Morrigan's suspicions that they'd forgotten she was turning eleven the day after tomorrow. 'I thought it might be fun . . .' She trailed off, looking down at her plate and dearly wishing she hadn't opened her mouth at all.

'It's not *fun*,' sneered Corvus. 'It's *politics*. And no, you may not. Out of the question. Ridiculous idea.'

Morrigan sank down in her chair, feeling deflated and foolish. Really, what had she expected? Corvus was right; it was a ridiculous idea.

The Crows ate their dinner in tense silence for several minutes, until—

'Actually, sir,' said Right in a tentative voice. Corvus's cutlery clattered onto his plate. He fixed his assistant with a menacing stare.

'*What?*'

'W-well . . . if you were – and I'm not saying you should, but if you *were* – to take your daughter along, it might help to, er, soften your image. To a degree.'

Left wrung his hands. 'Sir, I think Right is . . . um, right.' Corvus glowered, and Left rushed on nervously. 'Wh-what I mean is, according to polls, the people of Great Wolfacre see you as a bit . . . er, remote.'

'Aloof,' interjected Right.

'It couldn't hurt your approval rating to remind them that you're about to become a . . . a g-grieving father. From a journalistic point of view, it might give the event a unique, er, point of interest.'

'How unique?'

'Front-page unique.'

Corvus was silent. Morrigan thought she saw his left eye twitch.

CHAPTER TWO

Bid Day

'Do not speak to anyone, Morrigan,' her father muttered for the hundredth time that morning, hurrying up the stone steps of the Town Hall in great strides she struggled to match. 'You will be sitting on the stage with me, where everyone can see you. Understand? Don't you *dare* make anything . . . happen. No broken hips or – or swarms of wasps, or falling ladders, or . . .'

'Shark attacks?' offered Morrigan.

Corvus rounded on her, his face blooming scarlet patches all over. 'Do you think this is *funny*? Everyone in the Town Hall will be watching to see what you do and how it will reflect on me. Are you *actively* trying to ruin my career?'

'No,' said Morrigan, wiping a bit of angry spit from her face. 'Not actively.'

Morrigan had been to the Town Hall on several other occasions, usually when her father's popularity was at its lowest ebb and he needed a public show of support from his family. Flanked by stone columns and sitting in the shadow of an enormous iron clock tower, the gloomy-looking Town Hall was Jackalfax's most important building. But the clock tower – although Morrigan usually tried not to look at it – was much more interesting.

The Skyfaced Clock was no ordinary clock. There were no hands, and no lines to mark the hours. Only a round glass face, with an empty sky inside that changed with the passing of the Age – from the palest-pink dawn light of Morningtide, through the golden bright Basking, to the sunset-orange glow of Dwendelsun and into the dusky, darkening blue of the Gloaming.

Today – like every day this year – they were in the Gloaming. Morrigan knew that meant it wasn't long until the Skyfaced Clock would fade into the fifth and final colour of its cycle: the inky, star-strewn blackness of Eventide. The last day of the Age.

But that was a year away. Shaking the thought out of her head, Morrigan followed her father up the steps.

There was an air of excitement in the normally sombre, echoing hall. Several hundred children from all over Jackalfax had arrived wearing their Sunday best, the boys with their hair slicked down and the girls with pigtails and ribbons and hats. They sat straight-backed in rows of chairs under the familiar stern gaze of President Wintersea, whose portrait hung in every home, shop and government building in the Republic – always watching, always looming large.

The riotous sound turned to a buzzing murmur as Morrigan and Corvus took their seats on the stage behind the podium. Everywhere Morrigan looked, eyes narrowed in her direction.

Corvus placed a hand on her shoulder in an awkward, unnatural gesture of paternal affection while some local reporters snapped photographs of them. Definitely front-page material, Morrigan thought – the doomed daughter and her soon-to-be-grieving father, a terrifically tragic pair. She tried to look extra forlorn, which wasn't easy when she was being blinded by camera flashes.

After a triumphant chorus of the Wintersea Republic National Anthem (*Onward! Upward! Forward! Huzzah!*) Corvus opened the ceremony with a very dull speech, followed by various headmasters and local businesspeople who all had to chime in. Then, finally, the Lord Mayor of Jackalfax brought out a polished wooden box and began to read the bids. Morrigan sat up straight in her seat, feeling a flutter of excitement she couldn't quite explain.

'"Madam Honora Salvi of the Silklands Ballet Company,"' he read from the front of the first envelope he pulled out, '"wishes to present her bid for Molly Jenkins."'

There was a squeal of delight from the third row, and Molly Jenkins leapt from her seat, rushing to the stage to curtsy and collect the envelope that contained her bid letter.

'Well done, Miss Jenkins. See one of the aides at the back of the hall after the ceremony, dear, and they'll direct you to your interview room.'

He retrieved another envelope. '"Major Jacob Jackerley of the Poisonwood School of Warfare wishes to present his bid for Michael Salisbury."'

Michael's friends and family cheered as he accepted his bid.

'"Mr Henry Sniggle, owner and proprietor of Sniggle's Snake Emporium, wishes to present his bid for Alice Carter for a herpetology apprenticeship" – dear me, how fascinating!'

The bidding carried on for almost an hour. The children in the hall watched anxiously as each new envelope was drawn from the box. Every announcement was met with shouts of joy from the recipient and their parents, and a collective sigh of disappointment from everyone else.

Morrigan began to get fidgety. The novelty of Bid Day had worn off a bit, really. She'd thought it would be exciting. She hadn't accounted for the dull, gnawing jealousy that settled in the pit of her stomach as she watched child after child snatch up their envelope, each one containing some shiny future she would never have for herself. Ivy's words echoed in her head: *You? Go to a Bid Day ceremony? Whatever for?*

Morrigan felt a rush of blood to her face, remembering how Ivy had laughed. She tried to resist her sudden, frantic urge to escape the stifling warmth of the hall.

A cheer erupted from the front row when Cory Jameson was bid on by Mrs Ginnifer O'Reilly from the prestigious Wintersea Academy, a government-sponsored school in the capital. It was his second bid of the day; the first was from a geology institute in Prosper, the richest state in the Republic, where they mined rubies and sapphires.

'My, my,' said the Lord Mayor, patting his fat stomach as Cory collected his second envelope and waved it over his head, to even louder cheers from his family in the audience. 'Two bids! This is a turn-up for the books. The first double bid Jackalfax has seen in a good few years. Well done, lad, well done. You have a big decision to make. And now . . . ah, we have an anonymous bid for . . . for . . .'

The Lord Mayor paused, glancing at the VIP section and back to the letter in his hand. He cleared his throat. 'For Miss Morrigan Crow.'

Silence fell. Morrigan blinked.

Had she imagined it? No – Corvus rose slightly from his seat, glaring at the Lord Mayor, who shrugged helplessly.

'Miss Crow?' he said, waving her forward.

A chorus of whispers arose from the audience at once, like a flock of birds startled into flight.

It's a mistake, Morrigan thought. *The bid is for somebody else.*

She looked out across the rows of children; nothing but scowling faces and pointing fingers. Had the Town Hall just grown twice as big? Twice as bright? It felt like a spotlight was shining directly on her head.

The Lord Mayor beckoned her again, looking fretful and impatient. Morrigan took a deep breath and forced her legs to stand and walk forward, each footstep echoing excruciatingly in the rafters. Taking the envelope in her trembling hand, she looked up at the Lord Mayor, waiting for him to laugh in her face and snatch it back. *This isn't for you!* But he simply stared back at her, a deep line of worry between his eyebrows.

Morrigan turned the envelope over, her heart pounding, and there, in fancy cursive handwriting – her name. *Miss Morrigan Crow.* It really was for her. Despite the growing tension in the hall, Morrigan felt lighter inside. She fought the urge to laugh.

'Well done, Miss Crow,' said the Lord Mayor with an unconvincing smile. 'Take your seat now, and see one of the aides at the back of the hall after the ceremony.'

'Gregory—' said Corvus in a warning undertone. The Lord Mayor shrugged again.

'It's tradition, Corvus,' he whispered. 'More than that – it's the *law*.'

The ceremony continued and Morrigan, stunned and silent, sat down again. She didn't dare open her bid. Her father was very still, glancing at the ivory-coloured envelope every few seconds as if he wanted to seize it from her hands and set fire to it. Morrigan tucked it away in the pocket of her dress, just to be safe, and held it tightly as eight more children accepted their bids. She hoped the ceremony wouldn't last much longer. Despite the Lord Mayor's brave attempts to jolly on as if nothing had happened, she could still feel several hundred eyes burning into her.

'"Mrs Ardith Asher of the Devereaux Ladies' College" – never heard of it! – "wishes to present her bid for . . . for . . ."' The Lord Mayor trailed off. He took a handkerchief from his pocket and mopped the sweat from his brow. '"For Miss Morrigan Crow."'

This time, the audience gasped. Morrigan moved as if in a dream to collect her second bid of the day. Without even looking to see if it was really her name on the front, she put the envelope – pink and sweet-smelling – in her pocket to join the other.

Just minutes later, Morrigan's name was called a third time. She rushed forward to collect her bid from Colonel Van Leeuwenhoek of the Harmon Military Academy, hurrying back to her seat as swiftly as possible and staring determinedly at her shoes. She tried to ignore the swarm of butterflies holding a celebration in her stomach. It was hard not to grin.

A man in the third row stood up and shouted, 'But she's cursed! This isn't right.' The man's wife pulled at his arm, trying to shush him, but he wouldn't be shushed. 'Three bids? Never heard of such a thing!' A rumble of agreement spread through the audience.

Morrigan felt her happiness stutter like a dying gaslight. The man was right. She was cursed. What could a cursed child possibly do with three bids? She'd never be allowed to accept them.

The Lord Mayor held out his hands, appealing for quiet. 'Sir, we must continue or we'll be here all day. If everyone could please be quiet, I'll get to the bottom of this most unusual turn of events after the ceremony.'

If the Lord Mayor was hoping for calm to be restored he was to be disappointed, for when he took out the next envelope, it read:

'"Jupiter North wishes to present his bid for" . . . Oh, I don't believe it. "Morrigan Crow."'

The Town Hall erupted as children and parents alike leapt to their feet, shouting over each other, turning various shades of pink and purple and demanding to know the meaning of this madness. Four bids! Two was uncommon and three highly unusual, but four? Unheard of!

There were twelve more bids to announce. The Lord Mayor sped through them, his face dissolving into sweaty relief each time he read a name that wasn't Morrigan's. At last, his hand scrambled around the bottom of the box and came up empty.

'That was the final envelope,' said the Lord Mayor, closing his eyes in gratitude. His voice shook. 'W-would all the children who received bids please move to the back of the hall, and, um, our aides will show you to the interview rooms where you can, er, meet your prospective patrons. Everyone else . . . I'm sure you'll all . . . you know. Doesn't mean you're not all very capable and, er . . . well.' He waved vaguely at the audience, who took it as their cue to depart.

C.———

Corvus swore he would take action, he would sue, he would remove the Lord Mayor from office – but the Lord Mayor insisted on following protocol. Morrigan *must* be allowed to meet her bidders if she wished to.

She very much wished to.

Of course Morrigan knew she'd never be able to *accept* any of the bids. She knew, in fact, that once these mysterious strangers discovered they'd bid on a cursed child, they'd take it all back, and probably run very fast in the opposite direction. But it would be rude not to at least *meet them*, she reasoned. As they'd come all this way.

I'm sorry, Morrigan rehearsed in her head, *but I'm on the Cursed Children's Register. I'm going to die on Eventide. Thank you for your time and interest.*

Yes. Polite and to the point.

She was ushered into a room with bare walls, a desk and a chair on either side. It felt like an interrogation chamber . . . and in a way, Morrigan supposed it was. The idea of the meeting between patron and child was that the child could ask as many questions as they wished, and the patron had to answer honestly. It was one of the few things she'd picked up from her father's boring Bid Day speech.

Not that she would be asking any questions, Morrigan reminded herself. *Thank you for your time and interest*, she repeated firmly in her head.

A man with feathery brown hair sat in one of the chairs, humming a little tune to himself. He wore a grey suit and a pair of wire-rimmed spectacles that he pushed up on his nose with one pale, slender finger. He smiled calmly, waiting for Morrigan to sit.

'Miss Crow. My name is Mr Jones. Thank you for seeing me.' The man spoke softly and in neat, clipped sentences. His voice sounded familiar. 'I've come on behalf of my employer. He'd like to offer you an apprenticeship.'

Morrigan's rehearsed speech tumbled out of her head. A little flutter returned to her stomach. One tiny, optimistic butterfly had just climbed out of its cocoon. 'What . . . kind of apprenticeship?'

Mr Jones smiled. Tiny lines wrinkled the corners of his dark, expressive eyes. 'An apprenticeship in his company, Squall Industries.'

'Squall Industries?' she said, frowning. 'That means you work for—'

'Ezra Squall. Yes. The most powerful person in the Republic.' He lowered his eyes to the table. 'Second most powerful, I should say. After our great president.'

It suddenly struck Morrigan where she had heard that voice. He was the man on the wireless talking about Wunder shortages.

He looked just the way he ought to, she thought – serious and neat. Tasteful. His white, spidery hands were clasped firmly in front of him, his skin so pale it was nearly translucent. He wasn't terribly young. But he wasn't old. There was nothing unruly about him, nothing to mar his immaculately groomed appearance but for a thin white scar that split his left eyebrow clean in half and a splash of silvery hair at his temples. Even his movements were precise and deliberate, as if he couldn't spare the energy for any unnecessary gesture. A perfectly contained man.

Morrigan narrowed her eyes. 'What could the second most powerful person in the Republic possibly want with *me*?'

'It's not for me to say why Mr Squall wants what he wants,' said Mr Jones, briefly unclasping his hands to straighten his spectacles again. 'I'm only his assistant. I carry out his wishes. Right now he wishes for you to become his student, Miss Crow . . . and his heir.'

'His heir? What does that mean?'

'It means that he wishes for you to one day run Squall Industries in his place, to be rich and powerful beyond your wildest dreams, and to lead the greatest, most influential and most profitable organisation that has ever existed.'

Morrigan blinked. 'I'm not even allowed to lick envelopes at home.'

Mr Jones looked amused. 'I don't believe you'll be licking envelopes at Squall Industries either.'

'What will I be doing?' Morrigan had no idea what would make her ask such a question. She tried to remember what she'd been planning to say earlier. Something about being cursed . . . *Thank you for your time* . . .

'You will be learning how to run an empire, Miss Crow. And you will be learning from the very best. Mr Squall is a brilliant and talented man. He will teach you everything he knows, things he hasn't taught another living soul.'

'Not even you?'

Mr Jones laughed gently. 'Especially not me. By the end of your apprenticeship you will be in command of Squall Industries' mining, engineering, manufacturing and technology sectors. Over one hundred thousand employees all over the Republic. All reporting to you.'

Morrigan's eyes widened.

'Every citizen, every household in this country will owe you a debt of thanks. You will be their lifeline – the provider of their warmth, power, food, entertainment. Their every need, every want . . . all reliant on the use of Wunder, and all filled by the good people at Squall Industries. By you.'

His voice had become so soft it was almost a whisper. Morrigan leaned closer.

'Ezra Squall is the nation's greatest hero,' he continued. 'More than that – he is their benevolent god, the source of their every comfort and happiness. The only living person with the ability to harvest, distribute and command Wunder. Our Republic relies on him totally.'

His eyes had taken on the unsettling gleam of a fanatic's. One corner of his mouth curled into a strange little smile. Morrigan shrank back. She wondered if Mr Jones loved Ezra Squall, or was afraid of him, or wanted to be him. Or all three.

'Imagine, Miss Crow,' he whispered. '*Imagine* how it must feel to be so beloved. So respected and *needed*. One day, if you work hard and do as Mr Squall teaches . . . that will be you.'

She could imagine it. She *had* imagined, a hundred times over, how it would feel to be liked instead of feared. To see people smile instead of flinch when she walked into a room. It was one of her favourite daydreams.

But that was all it was, Morrigan told herself, shaking the cobwebs out of her head. A daydream. She sat up straight and took a deep breath, willing her voice not to tremble.

'I can't accept, Mr Jones. I'm on the Cursed Children's Register. I'm going . . . I'm going to . . . well, you know. Th-thank you for your time and—'

'Open it,' said Mr Jones, nodding at the envelope in her hand.

'What is it?'

'Your contract.'

Morrigan shook her head, confused. 'M-my what?'

'It's standard.' He gave a tiny shrug. One shoulder. 'Every child commencing sponsored studies must sign a contract, and have a parent or guardian sign also.'

Well, there goes that, Morrigan thought. 'My father will never sign this.'

'Let us worry about that.' He pulled out a silver pen from his coat pocket and placed it on the table. 'All you have to do is sign. Mr Squall will take care of everything.'

'But you don't understand, I can't—'

'I understand perfectly, Miss Crow.' Mr Jones watched her closely, his dark eyes piercing her own. 'But you needn't worry about curses or registers or Eventide. You needn't worry about anything, ever again. Not if you're with Ezra Squall.'

'But—'

'Sign.' He nodded at the pen. 'Sign, and I promise you: one day you will be able to buy and sell every person who has ever made you unhappy.'

His glittering eyes and calm, secretive smile made Morrigan believe – just for a second – that he and Ezra Squall could somehow see a future for her that she had never dreamed possible.

She reached for the pen, then hesitated. There was one last question burning inside her, the most important question of all. She looked up at Mr Jones.

'Why *me*?'

There was a loud knock. The door swung open and the Lord Mayor stumbled in looking harassed.

'I'm terribly sorry, Miss Crow,' he said, pressing a handkerchief to his forehead. His suit bore sweat patches, and what was left of his hair stood on end. 'Somebody appears to have played a horrible prank on you. On all of us.'

'P-prank?'

Corvus stalked in behind him, his mouth in a thin line. 'There you are. We're leaving.' He grabbed Morrigan's arm, pulling her out of the room. Her chair tipped over and clattered to the floor.

'None of your so-called bidders have arrived,' said the Lord Mayor, trying to catch his breath as he followed them into the hallway. 'I blame myself. I should have realised. Harmon Military whatsit, Devereaux Ladies' thingy . . . nobody's heard of them. Made up, you see.' He looked from Morrigan to her father and back again. 'Terribly sorry for putting you through it, Corvus, old friend. No hard feelings, I hope?'

Corvus glowered at the Lord Mayor.

'But wait—' began Morrigan.

'Don't you understand?' said her father in a cold, angry voice. He snatched the envelopes from her. 'I have been made a fool. It was all somebody's idea of a joke. Humiliated! By my own constituency!'

Morrigan frowned. 'You're saying that my bidders—'

The Lord Mayor wrung his hands. 'Never actually existed. That's why none of them showed up. I'm sorry you had to wait.'

'But I'm trying to tell you, one of them *did* show up. Mr Jones has come on behalf—' Morrigan stopped mid-sentence as she dashed back into the interview room.

His chair was empty. No pen, no contract. He'd disappeared. Morrigan gaped at the empty space. Had Mr Jones slipped out while they'd been arguing? Did he change his mind? Or had he just been playing a prank on her as well?

Realisation sank in swiftly, like a boot to the stomach.

Of course it was a joke. Why would the Republic's most powerful and important businessman want her as his apprentice? His *heir*? The thought was positively ridiculous. Morrigan's cheeks turned pink as a wave of belated embarrassment hit her. How could she have been so gullible?

'Enough of this nonsense,' said Corvus. He ripped the envelopes into tiny pieces, and Morrigan watched mournfully as they fluttered to the ground like snow.

The shiny black coach pulled away from the Town Hall with Morrigan and her father inside it. Corvus was silent. He'd already turned his attention to the ever-present stack of paperwork in his leather case, trying to salvage what was left of the working day. As if the morning's misadventure had never happened.

Morrigan turned to watch the crowd of excited children and parents spilling out of the building and into the street, chattering and waving their bid letters in the air. She felt a sharp pang of envy.

It doesn't matter, she told herself. She blinked fiercely, tears stinging her eyes. *It's all just nonsense. It doesn't matter.*

The crowd didn't seem to be dispersing. In fact, so many people were gathering on the street that the carriage came to a complete stop. A stream of people hurried past, heading towards the Town Hall and gazing up at something in the sky.

'Lowry,' barked Corvus, knocking on the roof to alert the driver. 'What's the holdup? Get those people out of the way.'

'I'm trying, Chancellor, but—'

'It's here!' somebody shouted. *'It's coming!'* The crowd cheered in response. Morrigan craned her neck, trying to see what was happening. People embraced in the streets – not just the Bid Day children, but *everyone*, whistling and whooping and throwing their hats in the air.

'Why are they . . .' began Morrigan, then stopped, listening. 'What are those bells ringing for?'

Corvus looked at her strangely. His papers slipped from his hand and scattered across the carriage floor as he pushed open the door and leapt out onto the street. Morrigan followed and, looking up, saw what everyone had been running towards.

The clock tower.

The Skyfaced Clock was changing. Morrigan watched as the dusky twilight blue deepened to sapphire, to navy and finally to a profound, unfathomable black. Like an inkpot in the sky. Like a black hole, come to swallow up the world.

The bells were ringing for Eventide.

That night Morrigan lay awake in the dark.

The bells had rung until midnight, when they were abruptly replaced by an oppressive silence. They'd been a warning, a signal to everyone that Eventide was coming . . . but after midnight, they didn't need to ring anymore. Eventide was here. The last day of the Age had begun.

Morrigan knew she should feel frightened, and sad, and worried – and she did, she felt all of those things. But mostly, she felt angry.

She'd been *cheated*. It was supposed to be a twelve-year Age. Everyone said so – Corvus, Grandmother, all of

Morrigan's caseworkers, chronologists on the news. Twelve years of life was already too short, but *eleven*?

Now that the Skyfaced Clock had turned black, the experts were all scrambling to say they'd long suspected, they'd read the signs, they'd been on the cusp of publicly announcing that in their opinion this year, *this* winter, was the last of the Age.

Never mind, they all said. We guess this one's an eleven-year Age. Everyone makes mistakes, and one year doesn't make much difference.

Except, of course, it made all the difference in the world.

Happy birthday to me, Morrigan thought miserably. She tucked her stuffed rabbit, Emmett, into the crook of her arm, where he'd slept every night for as long as she could remember, and she squeezed him tight and tried to fall asleep.

But there was a noise. A very small noise that was barely a noise – like a tiny whisper or rush of air. She flicked on her lamp and the room flooded with light.

It was empty. Morrigan's heartbeat quickened. She jumped up and looked around, under the bed, threw open the wardrobe – nothing.

No. Not nothing.

Something.

A small white rectangle stood out against the dark wooden floorboards. Someone had slipped an envelope under her door. She picked it up and creaked the door open to peek into the hallway outside. There was nobody there.

On the envelope, someone had written untidily in thick black ink:

> *Jupiter North of the Wundrous Society wishes to present his bid for Miss Morrigan Crow. Again.*

'The Wundrous Society,' Morrigan whispered.

She ripped open the envelope and pulled out two pieces of paper. One was a letter, the other a contract – typed and official-looking, with two signatures at the bottom. Above the word PATRON was the large, messy signature of Jupiter North. The second, above PARENT OR GUARDIAN, she couldn't read and didn't recognise at all. It certainly wasn't her father's handwriting.

The third space – CANDIDATE – was blank. Waiting.

Morrigan read the letter, feeling utterly bewildered.

> *Dear Miss Crow,*
> *Congratulations! You have been selected by one of our members as a candidate for entry to the Wundrous Society.*
> *Please be advised that your entry is not assured. Membership in the Society is extremely*

*limited, and each year hundreds of hopeful
candidates compete for a place among our
scholars.*

*If you wish to join the Society, please sign the
enclosed contract and return it to your patron
no later than the last day of Winter of Eleven.
Entrance trials will begin in spring.*

We wish you the very best of luck.

Regards,

Elder G. Quinn

Proudfoot House

Nevermoor, FS

At the bottom of the page, in a hurried black scrawl, was a brief but thrilling message:

Be ready

—J.N.

CHAPTER THREE

Death Comes to Dinner

On Eventide night, even the streets of dull, conservative Jackalfax came alive.

The cobbled stretch of Empire Road had swelled from a merry hum of good spirits in the morning to raucous, uncontainable revelry in the final hours before midnight. Street bands played for coins on every corner, competing for the attention of passers-by. Coloured lanterns jostled with streamers and strings of tiny lights, and the air smelled of beer, burnt sugar and meat grilling on the spit.

The blackened Skyfaced Clock loomed above the celebrations. At midnight it would fade to the colour of Morningtide – a pale, promising pink – and Spring of One would bring a fresh beginning for everyone. The night was uncommon and crowded with possibility.

For everyone, that is, except Morrigan Crow. Morrigan's night held only one possibility. Like every other child born precisely eleven years ago on the last Eventide, when the clock struck midnight she would die – the eleven short years of her doomed life complete; her curse finally fulfilled.

The Crows were celebrating. Sort of.

It was a sombre affair in the house on the hill. Lights dimmed, curtains drawn. Dinner was Morrigan's favourite – lamb chops, roast parsnips and minted peas. Corvus hated parsnips and would never usually allow them to be served when he was home for dinner, but he kept a grim silence as the maid spooned a huge mountain of them onto his plate. Morrigan felt this spoke volumes about the sensitivity of the occasion.

The room was quiet but for the soft scratching of silverware against china. Morrigan was conscious of every mouthful of food she swallowed, every cool sip of water. She heard each tick of the clock on the wall like a drumbeat in a marching band, marching her ever closer to the moment when she would cease to exist.

She hoped it would be painless. She'd read somewhere that when a cursed child died it was usually quick and peaceful – just like falling asleep. She wondered what would happen afterwards. Would she really go to the Better Place, like Cook had once told her? Was the Divine Thing real, and would it accept her with open arms, as she'd been promised? Morrigan had to hope so. The alternative simply didn't bear thinking about. After hearing Cook's tales of the Wicked Thing that dwelled in the Worst Place, she'd slept with the light on for a week.

It was a strange thing, she thought, to be celebrating the night of your own death. It didn't feel like a birthday. It didn't feel like a celebration at all. It was more like having your funeral before you die.

Just as she was wondering if anyone would say a few words about her, Corvus cleared his throat. Morrigan, Ivy and Grandmother looked at him, their hands pausing halfway to their mouths with forks full of lamb and peas.

'I, er, just wanted to say,' he began, and then seemed to lose momentum. 'I wanted to say . . .'

Ivy's eyes misted over and she squeezed his hand encouragingly. 'Go on, dear.'

'I just . . .' He tried again and cleared his throat loudly. 'I wanted to say that . . . that the lamb is very good. Cooked to perfection. Nice and pink.'

There were murmurs of agreement around the table, and then a clinking of cutlery as everyone carried on eating. That was probably as good as it was going to get, Morrigan realised. And she couldn't say she disagreed about the lamb.

'Well, if nobody minds,' said Ivy, dabbing her mouth prettily with her linen napkin. 'I've not been a member of this family for very long, but I thought it might be appropriate for me to say something tonight.'

Morrigan sat up straight. This should be good. Maybe Ivy was going to apologise for making her wear that frilly, itchy chiffon dress to the wedding. Or maybe she was going to confess that although she'd scarcely spoken a dozen words to Morrigan since moving in, truly she loved her like a daughter, and she only wished they could have more time together, and she would miss Morrigan terribly and would probably cry buckets at the funeral and ruin her makeup, which would streak ugly black rivers all down her pretty face – but she wouldn't even care how ugly she looked because she would just be thinking about lovely, lovely Morrigan. Morrigan arranged her face in an expression of humble serenity.

'Corvus wasn't sure if I should say anything, but I know Morrigan won't mind . . .'

'Go on,' Morrigan said. 'It's fine. Really, go ahead.'

Ivy beamed at her (for the first time ever) and, emboldened, stood up from her seat. 'Corvus and I are having a baby.'

The room fell silent; then a great smash came from the doorway as the maid dropped a platter. Corvus tried to smile at his young wife but it came out as a grimace.

'Well?' Ivy prompted them. 'Aren't you going to congratulate us?'

'Ivy, dear,' Grandmother said, smiling icily at her daughter-
in-law. 'Perhaps your announcement might have been better
received at a less sensitive time. For instance, the day *after*
my only grandchild is due to leave us tragically at the age
of eleven.'

Strangely, her words made Morrigan perk up a little. It
was perhaps the most sentimental thing she'd ever heard
Grandmother say. She felt an unexpected warmth towards
the savage old bird of prey.

'But this is a good thing! Don't you see?' Ivy said, looking
to Corvus for support. He squeezed the bridge of his nose
as if warding off a migraine. 'It's like . . . the circle of life.
One life may be snuffed out, but another is being brought
into the world. Why, it's practically a miracle!'

Grandmother groaned faintly.

Ivy was relentless. 'You'll have a *new* grandchild, Ornella.
Corvus will have a new daughter. Or a son! Wouldn't
that be lovely? A little boy, Corvie, you said you'd always
wanted a boy. We can dress him in little black suits to
match his daddy.'

Morrigan tried not to laugh at the grim expression on
her father's face.

'Yes. Delightful,' he said unconvincingly. 'But perhaps we'll celebrate later.'

'But . . . Morrigan doesn't mind. Do you, Morrigan?'

'Mind what?' Morrigan asked. 'That I'm going to be blotted out of existence in a few hours and you're planning a wardrobe for my replacement? Not in the slightest.' She shoved a forkful of parsnip into her mouth.

'Oh, for goodness' sake!' Grandmother hissed, glaring down the table at her son. 'We weren't going to bring up the D-word.'

'It wasn't me,' Corvus protested.

'I didn't say "dead", Grandmother,' said Morrigan. 'I said "blotted out of existence".'

'Well, just stop it. You're giving your father a headache.'

'Ivy said "snuffed". That's much worse.'

'*Enough.*'

'Doesn't anybody care that I am *with child*?' shouted Ivy, stamping her foot.

'Doesn't anybody care that I'm *about to die*?' Morrigan shouted in return. 'Can we *please* talk about me for a minute?'

'*I told you not to say the D-word!*' boomed Grandmother.

There were three loud knocks on the front door. Silence fell.

'Who on earth would visit at a time like this?' Ivy

whispered. 'Reporters? Already?' She smoothed down her hair and dress, picking up a spoon to check her reflection.

'Vultures. Trying to get the scoop, are they?' said Grandmother. She pointed at the maid. 'Send them away with your most contemptuous sneer.'

Moments later they heard a brief, murmured conversation from the entrance hall, followed by the fall of heavy boots coming up the hallway, the maid's timid protests echoing close behind.

Morrigan's heart pounded with each footstep. *Is this it?* she thought. *Is this Death, come to take me? Does Death wear boots?*

A man appeared in the doorway, silhouetted by light.

He was tall and slender with wide shoulders. His face was half obscured by a thick woollen scarf, and the remaining half was made of freckles, watchful blue eyes and a long, broad nose.

All six-plus feet of him were decked out in a long blue coat over a slim suit with mother-of-pearl buttons – stylish but slightly askew, as if he'd just come from a formal event and was in the process of undressing on his way home. Pinned to the lapel of his coat was a small golden *W*.

He stood with his feet wide apart and hands stuffed into trouser pockets, leaning casually against the doorframe as if he had spent half his life standing in that spot and couldn't think of a place he felt more at home. As if he himself owned Crow Manor and the Crows were merely his dinner guests.

His eyes locked onto Morrigan's. He grinned. 'Hello, you.'

Morrigan said nothing. There was silence but for the ticking of the clock on the wall.

'Sorry I'm late,' he continued, his voice slightly muffled by the scarf. 'Was at a party on a remote island in Jet-Jax-Jaida. Got chatting to the *dearest* old man, a trapeze swinger – fascinating chap, once swung over an active volcano for charity – and I forgot all about the time difference. Silly old me. Never mind, I'm here now. Got your things ready? I'm parked out the front. Are those parsnips? Lovely.'

Grandmother must have been in shock, for she didn't utter a word as the man snaffled a large piece of roast parsnip straight from the platter and ate it, licking his fingers with relish. In fact, all the Crows seemed to have lost the capacity for speech, not least of all Morrigan.

Several moments passed as their uninvited guest rocked on his heels and waited, politely expectant, until something occurred to him.

'I'm still wearing my hat, aren't I? Goodness me. How rude.' He arched an eyebrow at his dumbfounded audience. 'Don't be alarmed; I'm ginger.'

'Ginger' was an understatement, Morrigan thought, trying to hide her astonishment as the hat came off. 'Ginger of the Year' or 'King Ginger' or 'Big Gingery President of the Ginger Foundation for the Incurably Ginger' would have been more accurate. His mane of bright copper waves could probably have won awards. He unravelled the scarf from his head to reveal a beard that was only slightly less shocking in hue.

'Um,' Morrigan said, with all the eloquence she could muster. 'Who are you?'

'Jupiter.' He looked around the room for signs of recognition. 'Jupiter North? Jupiter North of the Wundrous Society? Your patron?'

Her patron. Jupiter North. *Her* patron. Morrigan shook her head in disbelief. Was this another prank?

She'd signed the contract. Of course she'd signed the contract, because it had been wonderful, *glorious* to pretend – just for five minutes – that it was all true. That there was really something called the Wundrous Society, and that they'd invited *her* – Morrigan Crow, of all people! – to join them. That she would live long enough to start the mysterious trials in spring. That some thrilling future waited for her on the other side of Eventide.

Of course she'd signed that blank space at the bottom. She'd even doodled a little black crow next to her name, to cover up a splotch of ink that had dropped from her pen.

Then she'd thrown it on the fire.

She hadn't for a second believed that any of it was real. Not really. Not deep down.

Corvus at last found his voice. 'Preposterous!'

'Bless you,' said Jupiter as he renewed his attempts to usher Morrigan from the dining room to the hallway. 'I'm afraid we really do have to hurry, Morrigan. How many suitcases do you have?'

'Suitcases?' she echoed, feeling dim-witted and slow.

'Dear me,' he said. 'You *have* packed, haven't you? Never mind, we'll pick you up a toothbrush when we get there. I trust you've already said your goodbyes, but we have time for a quick round of hugs and kisses before setting off.'

Following that extraordinary suggestion (another first for the Crow household), Jupiter rushed around the table, squeezing each of the Crows in turn. Morrigan wasn't sure whether to laugh or run away when he leaned in to plant a loud, wet kiss on her father's horror-struck face.

'That is quite enough!' spluttered Corvus, rising from his chair. It was one thing for a man to arrive unannounced at Crow Manor on Eventide, but quite another to bring the notion of physical affection with him. 'You are nobody's patron. Leave my house immediately, before I call for the town guard.'

Jupiter smiled as if tickled by the threat. 'I *am* some-body's patron, Chancellor Crow. I am the patron of this slow-moving but otherwise delightful child. It's all legal and aboveboard, I can assure you. She signed the contract. I have it right here.'

He whipped out a wrinkled, fold-creased, shabby piece of paper that Morrigan recognised. Jupiter pointed at her signature, complete with the tiny black crow that covered the accidental ink smudge.

But that was impossible.

'I don't understand,' said Morrigan, shaking her head. 'I watched it burn to ashes.'

'Oh, it's a Wundrous contract.' He waved it around without care. 'It creates identical copies of the original as soon as you sign it. That does explain the singed edges, though.'

'I never signed that,' said Corvus.

Jupiter shrugged. 'I never asked you to.'

'I'm her father! That contract requires my signature.'

'Actually, it only requires the signature of an adult guardian, and—'

'Wundrous contracts are illegal,' said Grandmother, at last finding her voice, 'under the Misuse of Wunder Act. We ought to have you arrested.'

'Well, you'd best do it quickly, I've only got a few minutes,' said Jupiter, sounding bored. He checked his watch. 'Morrigan, we really must go. Time is running out.'

'I know time is running out,' said Morrigan. 'You've made a mistake, Mr North. You can't be my patron. Today's my birthday.'

'Of course! Happy birthday.' He was distracted, moving to the windows to peek through the curtains. 'Mind if we celebrate later, though? It's getting quite late and—'

'No, you don't understand,' she interrupted. The words felt heavy and dry in her mouth, but she forced them out. 'I'm on the Cursed Children's Register. Tonight is Eventide. I'm going to die at midnight.'

'My, aren't you a Negative Nelly.'

'That's why I burned the contract. It's worthless. I'm sorry.'

Jupiter was gazing anxiously out the window now, a frown creasing his forehead. 'You did actually *sign* the contract before you burned it, though,' he said without looking at her. 'And who says you're going to die? You don't have to die if you don't want to.'

Corvus slammed his fist on the table. 'This is intolerable! Who do you think you are, waltzing into my home and upsetting my family with this nonsense?'

'I told you who I am.' Jupiter spoke patiently, as if to a senseless child. 'My name is Jupiter North.'

'And *I* am Corvus Crow, the state chancellor of Great Wolfacre and a ranked member of the Wintersea Party,' said Corvus, puffing up his chest. He was on a roll now.

'I demand that you go at once, and allow me to mourn the death of my daughter in peace.'

'*Mourn the death of your daughter?*' echoed Jupiter. He took two deliberate steps towards Corvus and paused, his eyes glittering. The hairs on Morrigan's arms stood up. Jupiter's voice dropped an entire octave, and he spoke with a cold, quiet anger that was terrible to behold. 'Can you possibly mean the daughter standing right in front of you? The one who is demonstrably, superbly, *brilliantly* alive?'

Corvus sputtered and pointed to the clock on the wall, his hand shaking with outrage. 'Well, *give it a few hours!*'

Morrigan felt something squeeze in her chest, and she wasn't sure why. She'd always known she was going to die on Eventide. Her father and grandmother had never kept it secret. It shouldn't have been a surprise that Corvus was so resigned to her fate, but Morrigan suddenly realised that to him, she might as well already be dead. Perhaps in his heart, she'd been dead for years.

'Morrigan,' said Jupiter, in a voice very different from the one he'd just used with her father. 'Don't you want to *live*?'

Morrigan flinched. What sort of a question was that? 'It doesn't matter what I want.'

'It does,' he insisted. 'It matters so very, very much. Right now it's the only thing that matters.'

Her eyes flicked from her father to her grandmother to her stepmother. They all watched her intently, uneasily, as if seeing her properly for the first time.

'Of course I want to live,' she said quietly. It was the first time she'd ever spoken the words aloud. The tightness in her chest eased a little.

'Good choice.' Jupiter smiled; the cloud disappeared from his face as quickly as it had arrived. He turned back to the window. 'Death is boring. Life is much more fun. Things happen in life all the time. Unexpected things. Things you couldn't possibly expect because they're so very . . . unexpected.' He stepped backwards, inching away from the window and reaching blindly for Morrigan, fumbling to take her hand. 'For instance, I bet you didn't expect your so-called death to arrive three hours early.'

Morrigan felt something powdery land on her face. Wiping it away, she looked up to see the light fixtures shaking and cracks appearing in the plaster. The light bulbs stuttered and buzzed. The windows began to rattle. There was a faint smell of burning.

'What's that?' She squeezed his hand automatically. 'What's happening?'

Jupiter leaned down to whisper in her ear. 'Do you trust me?'

She answered without thinking. 'Yes.'

'You sure?'

'Positive.'

'All right.' He looked her in the eye. The floor trembled beneath their feet. 'I'm going to take that curtain down in a moment. But whatever you see out there, you mustn't be afraid. They can tell when you're afraid.'

Morrigan swallowed. 'They?'

'Just follow my lead and you'll be fine. Yes? No fear.'

'No fear,' repeated Morrigan. Meanwhile, fear had set up camp in her stomach and was having a festival. A Ferris wheel of fear spun idly in her abdomen. Dancing circus elephants of fear somersaulted through her intestinal tract.

'What the devil are you talking about over there?' said Grandmother. 'What's he saying to you, Morrigan? I demand to—'

In a rush of sudden movement Jupiter pulled a handful of silver dust from his pocket and blew it towards Corvus, Ivy and Grandmother like a cloudy, starry kiss, then leapt up to the window and ripped down the curtain, dropping it in a crumpled, messy pile in the middle of the floor.

He stood back to gaze at his handiwork and shook his head slowly, mournfully. 'I am *so* sorry. How tragic to have lost her so young.'

Corvus frowned and blinked, looking unsure. His eyes were glassy. 'Tragic?'

'Mmm,' said Jupiter. He threw an arm around Corvus's shoulders and led him closer to the pile of fabric. 'Dear, dear Morrigan. So full of life. So much to share with the world. But taken! Taken too soon.'

'Too soon.' Corvus nodded in shell-shocked agreement. 'Much too soon.'

Jupiter put his other arm around Ivy and drew her into his chest. 'You mustn't blame yourselves. Although you could a bit, if you wanted to.' He winked at Morrigan, who felt a small, hysterical laugh working its way up out of her throat. Did they really believe that curtain was her, lying dead on the floor? She was standing right in front of them!

'She looks so small.' Ivy sniffed and drew her sleeve across her nose. 'So small and thin.'

'Yes,' said Jupiter. 'Almost as if she were . . . made of fabric.'

Morrigan snorted, but the Crows made no sign that they'd heard her.

'I'll leave you to make the necessary arrangements. You'll need to prepare a statement for the press, Chancellor. But before I go, may I suggest a closed casket for the funeral? Open caskets are so tacky.'

'Yes,' said Grandmother, gazing down at curtain-Morrigan. 'Indeed. Quite tacky.'

'What did you do?' Morrigan whispered to Jupiter. 'What was that silver stuff?'

'Highly illegal. Pretend you didn't see it.'

The light fixture swung violently, casting shadows across the room. An unmistakable smell of woodsmoke filled the air. The floor began to shake again, and in the distance Morrigan heard something like heavy rain or rolling thunder or – was it – *hoofbeats*?

She turned to the window and felt a hot, prickling fear all the way down her spine. Panic rose like bile in her throat.

She could see it. She could see her death coming.

CHAPTER FOUR

The Hunt of Smoke and Shadow

Through the sparse woodland and over the crest of the hill, a dark and shapeless form approached Crow Manor.

To Morrigan it looked like a swarm of locusts or a cloud of bats, but it was too low and loud to be either. The sound of hooves became deafening as the dark mass grew closer. Amongst the black were hundreds of specks of fiery red light, getting brighter by the second.

The amorphous figure began to take shape. Heads and faces and legs grew out of the swarm, and Morrigan felt her stomach drop; the glowing red lights weren't lights at all. They were eyes. The eyes of men, the eyes of horses and the eyes of hounds.

Not individuals made of flesh. More like a single living shadow. They were darkness – a pure absence of light. And they moved with purpose.

They were hunting.

Morrigan couldn't breathe. Her chest heaved in and out as she tried to take in enough air to fill her lungs properly. 'What are they?'

'Not now,' said Jupiter. 'We have to run.'

But Morrigan's feet felt stuck to the floor. She couldn't turn away from the window. Jupiter grasped her shoulders and looked straight into her eyes.

'No fear. Remember?' he said, giving her a little shake. 'Save it for later.'

Jupiter led Morrigan away, into the hall. She paused at the door.

'Wait! What about them?' she said, looking back towards the Crows. They were still gathered around the curtain on the floor, oblivious to the sound and sight of a hundred ghostly hunters barrelling towards the house. 'We can't just leave—'

'They'll be fine. The Hunt can't touch them. I promise. Come *on*.'

'But—'

Jupiter pulled her onward. 'It's *you* they're hunting, Morrigan. You want to help your family? You need to get yourself far, far away from this house.'

'Then why are we going *upstairs*?'

Jupiter didn't answer. When they reached the third floor he ran to the nearest window and flung it wide open, sticking his head out. 'This'll do. Ready? We're aiming for the skylight.'

Morrigan looked out the window at the strangest machine she'd ever seen.

As state chancellor, her father had been fetched from Crow Manor in all sorts of vehicles over the years. Corvus still favoured his old-fashioned horse-drawn carriage for daily use, but sometimes the Wintersea Party would send expensive dark-windowed coaches with rumbling mechanical engines, and once even a small piloted airship that needed a special permit to land on the roof. Neighbours had gathered to gawk at it and take pictures.

But Corvus had never, to her knowledge, travelled in a gleaming brass pod standing two storeys high on eight spindly legs like an enormous metallic spider. *What would the neighbours think of THIS?* wondered Morrigan, her eyes like saucers.

'I didn't park close enough,' said Jupiter. 'We'll have to push off a bit when we jump.'

Jump? Surely he didn't expect her to jump out of a third-storey window?

Jupiter climbed onto the sill and levered his body so that

he was mostly out of the window, then held out a hand to Morrigan. 'On the count of three, okay?'

'No.' She shook her head, backing away from the window. 'Not okay. The opposite of okay.'

'Morrigan, I admire your instinct for self-preservation. I really do. But I think if you look over your shoulder, your instinct might tell you to jump out the window.'

Morrigan looked.

Perilously close to the top of the staircase was a wolf-like hound with glowing red eyes, his teeth bared in a low snarl. His pack crept slowly up the last of the stairs behind him. At least a dozen, maybe more. They jostled for position, snapping their ferocious jaws and growling as they stalked Morrigan, frozen at the window.

'N-no fear,' she whispered, and every cell in her body replied, *Yes fear*.

'Count of three.' Jupiter took Morrigan's hand to guide her up onto the ledge. 'One . . .'

The hound was joined on the landing by a second pack member, then a third, all with the same sharp yellow teeth and fiery eyes and the swirling, smoky fur as black as pitch. Their growls vibrated all the way to Morrigan's toes.

'Two . . .'

She stepped backwards and scrambled for Jupiter's support as her foot touched nothing but air. He wrapped his arms around her chest and she felt him lean back, pulling her with him. The hounds launched themselves at Morrigan.

'Three!'

Cold, sharp air whipped around her ears as she fell. There was an almighty shattering of glass and then they landed hard – Jupiter's arms wrapped tightly around Morrigan, his body cushioning her fall – on the floor inside the body of the giant brass spider. Above them, the hounds disappeared from the window.

'Ow,' Jupiter moaned. 'I'll regret that tomorrow. Off you get.'

He rolled Morrigan onto the floor. She winced as a stray piece of glass embedded itself in the heel of her palm.

'Where did they go?'

'Dunno. But they won't be gone for long. Hold on to something,' said Jupiter. He ran to a control deck at the front of the vehicle and began pulling levers. The engine roared into life and the spider lurched forward, pitching Morrigan face-first into a wall. She felt nausea rising in her stomach. 'The first bit's always bumpy. And the last bit. But don't worry; the middle bit's as smooth as silk. Sometimes. Depends, really.'

Morrigan stumbled into the cramped cockpit and held on to the back of an old leather chair, where Jupiter sat at the controls. She picked the piece of glass out of her hand

and threw it away, wiping the blood on her dress. 'What *were* they?'

'The Hunt of Smoke and Shadow.' Jupiter looked darkly over his shoulder as the spider lumbered away from the house.

'The Hunt of . . .' Morrigan clamped a hand over her mouth, trying not to bring up her dinner all over Jupiter's panel of shiny buttons and levers – or worse, the back of his head. She felt like she was in a small boat on a choppy sea. 'What do they want with me?'

But Jupiter was distracted, trying to steer and change gears and stay upright at the same time. 'Strap yourself into the passenger seat,' he said, jerking his head towards the battered-looking chair on his left. Morrigan pulled herself over to it with some difficulty and clicked the seat belt into place across her chest. 'Ready? Hold tight.'

The spider climbed over the gates of Crow Manor in great staggering strides. The woods loomed ahead, but Jupiter steered in another direction, towards the centre of Jackalfax. On the smooth road, the movements of the mechanical spider evened out as it picked up downhill speed.

Jackalfax was awash with the light and noise of the early fireworks show, and a crowd had gathered to see the night ablaze with colour. Morrigan had never seen Empire Road so full of people.

The eight-legged machine scurried through the town centre, skirting the edges of the crowd. Jupiter couldn't have timed it more perfectly – the spectacle in the sky was a brilliant cover for their escape from the Hunt of Smoke and Shadow. Everyone was looking up, their ears filled with whistles and bangs.

'Shouldn't we be heading out of town, not into it?' asked Morrigan.

'We're taking a shortcut,' said Jupiter.

He was steering them straight towards the Town Hall. The vehicle stood to full height with a grinding of its metal joints and stepped delicately through the crowd, looking for all the world as if it were walking on tiptoes.

'What is this thing?' Morrigan asked. 'This spider thing?'

'This "spider thing", as you've indelicately baptised it,' said Jupiter, giving her a pointed look, 'is called an arachnipod, and it is the most exquisite machine ever built.'

A particularly loud firecracker shattered the night sky, leaving a trail of flower-shaped smoke in its wake, the ghost of an explosion. The crowd made noises of delight.

'Beautiful, isn't she? Her name's *Octavia*. One of only two arachnipods ever built. I knew the inventor. Pull that blue lever for me, will you? No, the other one. That's it.'

The arachnipod juddered to a halt. Jupiter frowned. He

stood up and ran to the back of the pod, looking anxiously out of the domed glass walls.

'Is something wrong?'

'Interesting machines like this are out of fashion now, of course,' he continued, as if nothing had happened. 'But I'll never let go of old Occy. She's too reliable. Hoverships and automobiles, they're all very modern and flashy, but like I always say – you can't roll over a mountain, and you can't hover underwater. *Octavia* can go almost anywhere. Which is useful in moments like this. We appear to be rather cornered.'

He returned to the control deck, reached up to the ceiling and pulled down a screen with four split images. Each showed a different view from the arachnipod.

The Hunt of Smoke and Shadow had caught up with them. They were surrounded on all sides by the huntsmen on horseback and their slavering hounds.

'How is any of that helpful in moments like this?' Morrigan's heart raced. *This is it*, she thought. *We're trapped. This is the end.* 'I don't see any mountains or water!'

'No mountains, no,' mused Jupiter. 'But there is . . . *that*.' She followed his gaze to the top of the clock tower.

'The really excellent thing about spiders,' he said, strapping himself into the driver's seat, 'is the way they crawl.

Fasten your seat belt, Morrigan Crow. And whatever you do, don't close your eyes.'

'What happens if I close my eyes?'

'You miss the fun.'

Morrigan had barely managed to check her seat belt when the arachnipod suddenly reared back, throwing her against the chair. Two great spindly metallic legs latched on to the eaves of the Town Hall, and the pod heaved itself upward, lurching higher and higher towards the black, fathomless façade of the Skyfaced Clock.

'It's not ideal, but as an improvised emergency gateway it's not my worst idea ever.'

She had no idea what he was talking about. 'Gateway to where?'

'You'll see.'

Morrigan looked back through the glass dome. The ground swam metres below, and worse than that – the huge black-smoke hunters had dismounted and were climbing the tower.

'They're behind us!' cried Morrigan.

Jupiter grimaced but didn't look back. 'Not for long. The Hunt can't follow where we're going.'

'Where are we going?'

They arrived at the top of the tower as the fireworks

display reached its dramatic climax, explosions of red and gold and blue and purple lighting up the night sky.

'We're going home, Morrigan Crow.'

The arachnipod put one spindly leg right through the clock. The glass didn't break – it didn't even crack. Another leg went through, gently rippling the clock face like a pebble on the surface of a deep black lake. Morrigan stared, open-mouthed. One more impossible thing in a night of impossible things.

She turned back. The huntsmen were so close their breath could have fogged up *Octavia*'s glass dome. They reached out their skeletal arms as if to grab Morrigan through the back window and pull her downward to her death. She wanted to squeeze her eyes shut – but she couldn't look away.

With one final heave, the arachnipod pitched forward and tumbled through the clock face, spinning over and over, throwing Morrigan into the unknown.

The sound of exploding firecrackers disappeared. The world had gone silent.

CHAPTER FIVE

Welcome to Nevermoor

Spring of One

They landed with a thud. Outside the arachnipod, a thick white mist enveloped them. All was quiet and still, as if the chaos of Jackalfax's town square had simply ceased to exist. Morrigan felt sick.

Was *this*, finally, her death? Had they died and crossed over to the Better Place? Taking stock of how she felt, Morrigan thought this was unlikely. Her ears were ringing, she was nauseous, and the cut in her palm still throbbed, crusted in a smear of blood. She peered out the window into the fog. There was no Divine Thing waiting with open arms, no choir of angelkind to greet them. Wherever they were, it wasn't the Better Place.

But it definitely isn't Jackalfax, Morrigan thought.

She heard a soft groan and turned to see Jupiter pushing himself up out of the pilot's seat with a pained grimace. 'Sorry. Not as smooth as I'd hoped. You all right?'

'I think so.' Morrigan took a deep, calming breath and looked around, trying to shake the Hunt of Smoke and Shadow from her brain. 'Where are we? What's all this fog?'

Jupiter rolled his eyes. 'Dramatic, isn't it? Border control,' he said apologetically, as if that explained everything.

Morrigan opened her mouth to ask what he meant but was interrupted by a buzzing, crackling sound that reverberated inside *Octavia*'s walls.

'State your name and affiliation,' boomed an official-sounding voice, amplified through a speaker that Morrigan couldn't see. It seemed to come from everywhere.

Jupiter picked up a small silver device from the control deck and spoke into it. 'Yes, hello! Captain Jupiter North of the Wundrous Society, the League of Explorers and the Federation of Nevermoorian Hoteliers, and Miss Morrigan Crow of . . . no affiliation. Yet.' He winked at Morrigan, and she gave him a small, nervous smile in return.

A mechanical whirring sounded around them. Outside the window a giant eye – bigger than Jupiter's whole head – emerged from the white fog on a long mechanical arm. It blinked in at them, looking left to right, up and down, examining everything inside.

'You've entered from the Seventh Pocket of the Free State through the Mount Florien gateway, is that correct?' bellowed the disembodied voice. Morrigan flinched.

'Correct,' Jupiter said into his little silver microphone.

'Did you have permission to travel to the Seventh Pocket?'

'I did, yes. Scholastic diplomacy visa,' said Jupiter. He cleared his throat and flashed a look of warning at Morrigan. 'And Miss Crow is a resident of Barclaytown in the Seventh Pocket.'

Miss Crow has never heard of Barclaytown in the Seventh Pocket, thought Morrigan.

She watched Jupiter with fascination and mounting anxiety. Mount Florien gateway? Scholastic diplomacy visa? It was all nonsense. Her heartbeat sounded loud in her ears, loud enough to fill the arachnipod. But Jupiter was unruffled. He answered the border guard's questions with gracious calm, merrily lying through his teeth.

'Does she have permission to enter the First Pocket?'

'Of course,' Jupiter said smoothly. 'Educational residency visa.'

'Present your papers.'

'Papers?' Jupiter's confidence faltered. 'Right, course. Papers. Forgot about . . . papers . . . Hang on, I'm sure I've got . . . something . . .'

Morrigan held her breath as Jupiter fumbled through different compartments on the control deck, finally producing an empty chocolate bar wrapper and a used tissue. Smiling placidly at Morrigan, he pressed them up against the glass for the giant eye to examine. Like an actual madman.

The moment stretched out in silence, and Morrigan braced herself for sirens, klaxons, armed guards breaking down the arachnipod's doors . . .

The microphone crackled and buzzed. The voice on the other end heaved a long-suffering sigh and whispered, 'Honestly, you're not even trying . . .'

'Sorry, it's all I could find!' whispered Jupiter in return, looking into the giant eye and shrugging contritely.

Finally, the voice boomed, 'You may proceed.'

'Marvellous,' said Jupiter, strapping himself into the old leather seat again. Morrigan let out the breath she'd been holding. 'Cheers, Phil.'

'Oh, for goodness' sake.' There was a muffled sound from the speakers and a squeal of feedback, as though the microphone had been dropped, and then the voice whispered, 'North, I've told you not to use my first name while I'm on duty.'

'Sorry. Give Maisie my love.'

'Drop round for dinner next week, you can give it to her yourself.'

'Will do. Ra-ra!' Jupiter clipped the silver microphone back in its stand and turned to Morrigan.

'Welcome to Nevermoor.'

The mist cleared, revealing an enormous stone archway with silvery gates that shimmered like heat from a stovetop.

Nevermoor. Morrigan rolled the word around in her mind. She'd seen it only once before, in her bid letter from the Wundrous Society. It had meant nothing to her at the time, just a nonsense word.

'Nevermoor,' she whispered to herself.

She liked the way it sounded. Like a secret, a word that somehow belonged only to her.

Jupiter put *Octavia* into gear as he read from a screen displaying notices. '"Local time 6:13 a.m. on the first day of Morningtide, Spring of One, Third Age of the Aristocrats. Weather: chilly but clear skies. Overall city mood: optimistic, sleepy, slightly drunk."'

The gates groaned open and the arachnipod shuddered into life. Morrigan breathed deeply as they entered the city. Having never been outside the town of Jackalfax, she was unprepared for what lay beyond the gates.

In Jackalfax, everything had been neat and orderly and . . . *normal*. Homes sat side by side in uniform rows – identical brick houses on straight, clean streets, one after the other. After the first neighbourhood in Jackalfax had been built one hundred and fifty years earlier, subsequent boroughs were all built in, if not precisely the same style, similar enough that if one were looking at Jackalfax from above, one might guess the entire town was designed by a sole miserable architect who hated her life.

Nevermoor was no Jackalfax.

'We're in the south,' said Jupiter, pointing at a map of Nevermoor on the screen of his control panel. The arachnipod scuttled low through the darkened, mostly quiet streets, dodging the odd pedestrian here and there.

Evidence of the night's Eventide celebrations was strewn about the darkened streets. Balloons and streamers littered front yards and lampposts, and early-morning street sweepers collected discarded bottles in huge metal bins. Some people were still out celebrating in the bluish predawn light, including a group of young men crooning the poignant Morningtide Refrain as they stumbled out of a pub.

'*Oh, beeeeeee not weeeary, frieeeend of mine—*'

'*While saaaaailing o'er the tiiiiides of time* – Pete, you're flat, that's – no, stop singing, you're flat—*'

'*The New Age greeeets us at the shore—*'

'*Just liiiike the Olden Age before* – no, it goes – it goes down at the end, not up—*'

Octavia sped through cobbled lanes, narrow alleys and sweeping boulevards, some neat and old-fashioned and others flamboyantly hectic. They floated through a borough called Ogden-on-Juro that looked like it was sinking. The streets there were made of water, and people rowed little boats through swirling mists that rose around them.

Everywhere Morrigan looked there were rolling green parks and tiny church gardens, cemeteries and courtyards and fountains and statues, illuminated by warm yellow gaslights and the occasional rogue firework.

She was up out of her seat, moving from window to window, pressing her face to the glass as she tried to take it all in. She wished she had a camera. She wished she could jump out of the arachnipod and run through the streets!

'Check that screen for me,' said Jupiter, gesturing with his head as he steered *Octavia* through a mess of backstreets. 'What time is sunrise?'

'It says . . . six thirty-six.'

'We're running late. Show me some speed, Occy,' Jupiter muttered, and the arachnipod's engine roared.

'Where are we?' asked Morrigan.

Jupiter laughed. 'Have you been asleep? We're in Nevermoor, dear heart.'

'Yes, but where *is* Nevermoor?'

'In the Free State.'

Morrigan frowned. 'Which one's the Free State?' There were four states that made up the Republic: Southlight,

Prosper, Far East Sang and of course Great Wolfacre, outside of which Morrigan had never before ventured.

'This one,' he said, steering *Octavia* into a side street. 'The Free State is the free state. The one that's actually free. State number five, the one your tutors never taught you about, because they didn't know about it themselves. We're not technically part of the Republic.' He wiggled his eyebrows at her. 'You can't get in without an invitation.'

'Is that why the Hunt of Smoke and Shadow stopped at the clock tower?' she asked, returning to the passenger seat. 'Because they didn't have an invitation?'

'Yes.' He paused. 'Basically.'

She watched his face closely. 'Could . . . could they follow us here?'

'You're safe, Morrigan.' He kept his gaze on the road. 'I promise.'

Morrigan's excitement faltered. She'd just seen him lie so skilfully to the border guard, and it wasn't lost on her that he hadn't properly answered her question. But very little about this strange night made sense. A tornado of questions swirled in her head, and all she could do was try to grab at them as they flew by.

'How – I mean . . .' Morrigan blinked. 'I don't understand. I was supposed to die on Eventide.'

'No. To be precise, you were supposed to die at *midnight* on Eventide.' He slammed his foot on the brakes, waited for a cat to cross the road, then hit the accelerator hard. Morrigan clutched the sides of her chair, her fingers turning white. 'But there was no midnight on Eventide. Not for you. Nevermoor is about nine hours ahead of Jackalfax. So you skipped right past midnight – out of one time zone and into another. You cheated death. Well done. Hungry?'

Morrigan shook her head. 'The Hunt of Smoke and Shadow – why were they chasing us?'

'They weren't chasing us, they were chasing you. And they weren't chasing you. They were hunting you. They hunt all the cursed children. That's how cursed children die. Good grief, I'm famished. Wish we had time to stop for breakfast.'

Morrigan's mouth had gone dry. 'They hunt children?'

'They hunt *cursed* children. I suppose you could call them specialists.'

'But why?' The tornado in her head gained speed. 'And who sends them? And if the curse says I'm supposed to die at midnight—'

'I could murder a bacon butty.'

'—then why did they come early?'

'Haven't the foggiest.' Jupiter's voice was light, but his face was troubled. He switched gears to navigate through a narrow cobbled street. 'Perhaps they had a party to get to. Must be rubbish having to work on Eventide.'

***

'I know what you're thinking,' said Jupiter as they locked *Octavia* up in a private parking garage. He pulled a chain next to the vast rolling door and it descended. The air was frosty, turning their breath to clouds of steam. 'Nevermoor. If it's so great, why haven't you heard of it? Truth is, Morrigan, this is the best place – the *best* place – in all the Unnamed Realm.'

He paused to slip out of his tailored blue overcoat and drape it around Morrigan's shoulders. It was much too long for her, and her arms didn't quite reach the end of the sleeves, but she hugged it close, revelling in its warmth. Jupiter ran one hand through his wilting coppery updo and, taking Morrigan's hand with the other, led her along the chilly streets as the sky began to lighten.

'We've got great architecture,' he continued. 'Lovely restaurants. Reasonably reliable public transport. The climate's great – cold in winter, not-cold in not-winter. Much as you'd expect. Oh, and the beaches! The *beaches*.' He looked thoughtful. 'The beaches are rubbish, actually, but you can't have everything.'

Morrigan was struggling to keep up, not just with Jupiter's rapid-fire monologue but also with his long, skinny legs, which were half-skipping, half-running down a street signposted HUMDINGER AVENUE.

'Sorry,' she panted, half-hobbling and half-limping from the cramp that was beginning to seize her calf. 'Could we . . . slow . . . down a bit?'

'Can't. It's almost time.'

'Time . . . for what?'

'You'll see. Where was I? Beaches: rubbish. But if you want entertainment, we've got the Trollosseum. You'll *love* that. If you love violence. Troll fights every Saturday, centaur roller derby Tuesday nights, zombie paintball every second Friday, unicorn jousting at Christmas and a dragonriding tournament in June.'

Morrigan's head was spinning. She'd heard stories about a small centaur population in Far East Sang and she knew there were dragons in the wild, but they were incredibly dangerous – who would think of *riding* one? And trolls, zombies? *Unicorns?* It was hard to tell whether Jupiter was serious.

They turned into a street called Caddisfly Alley, flat-out sprinting now down the twisting, maze-like backstreet. Morrigan thought it would never end, but at last they stopped outside a curved wooden door with a small sign reading HOTEL DEUCALION in faded gold lettering.

'You . . . live in . . . a hotel?' Morrigan puffed.

But Jupiter didn't hear her. He was fumbling with a brass ring of keys when the door flew open and Morrigan nearly fell over backwards.

Looming in the doorway was a cat. Not just a cat. *A giant cat.* The biggest, scariest, toothiest, shaggiest cat she'd ever seen in her life. It sat back on its haunches and still struggled to fit in the frame. Its face was squashed and wrinkled as though it'd run into a wall, and it snuffled and fuffed just like a huge, prehistoric version of the kitchen cats at Crow Manor.

If she'd been shocked by its appearance, that was nothing to how Morrigan felt when it turned its enormous grey head towards Jupiter and spoke.

'I see you've brought my breakfast.'

CHAPTER SIX

Morningtide

Morrigan held her breath as the cat's fist-sized amber eyes scanned her up and down. Finally, it turned and slunk back inside. Morrigan tried to retreat but Jupiter nudged her through the doorway. She looked up at him, panicked. Was it a trick? Had he saved her from the Hunt of Smoke and Shadow only to feed her to his *giant cat*?

'Very funny,' Jupiter said to the animal's hulking backside as it led them down a long, narrow, dimly lit hallway. 'I hope you've got *my* breakfast on, you matted old brute. How long have we got?'

'Six and a half minutes,' the cat called back to him. 'You're cutting it stupidly fine as usual. Do take those disgusting boots off before you go walking mud across the lobby, won't you?'

Jupiter held one hand on Morrigan's shoulder, steering her straight ahead. Gas lanterns in sconces on the wall were turned low. It was hard to see much, but the carpet looked shabby and worn and the wallpaper peeled in places. There was a faint smell of damp. They reached a steep wooden staircase and began to climb.

'This is the service entrance. Ghastly, I know – needs some fixing up,' said Jupiter, and Morrigan realised with a start that he was speaking to her. How did he know what she was thinking? 'Any messages, Fen?'

The cat turned to look at him as they reached a set of glossy black double doors at the top of the landing, and Morrigan could have sworn it rolled its eyes. 'How should I know? I'm not your secretary. I said *take off those boots.*' With a thrust of its big grey head, the cat pushed open the doors and they stepped into the most magnificent room Morrigan had ever seen.

The lobby of the Hotel Deucalion was cavernous and bright – which came as a surprise after the dim, threadbare service entrance (although as surprises go, it wasn't quite in the same league as being greeted at the door by a large talking cat). The floor was made of chequerboard black and white marble, and from the ceiling hung an enormous rose-coloured chandelier in the shape of a sailing ship, dripping with crystals and bursting with warm light. There were potted trees and elegant furniture all around. A grand stair-case curved around the walls, up and up to thirteen floors (Morrigan counted them) in a dizzying spiral.

'You can't tell me what to do. I pay your wages!' Jupiter grumbled, but he took off his travelling boots. A young man collected them and handed Jupiter a pair of polished black shoes, which he reluctantly put on.

Staff in pink and gold uniforms greeted Jupiter with a cheerful 'Good Morningtide, sir' or 'Happy New Age, Captain North' as they passed.

'Happy New Age to you, Martha,' he called in reply. 'Happy New Age, Charlie. Good Morningtide, everyone! Up to the roof now, all of you, or you'll miss everything. You three – no, four – come take the elevator. Yes, you too, Martha, there's plenty of room.'

As a small handful of staff obediently shadowed Jupiter across the vast lobby, Morrigan realised – he didn't just *live in* the hotel, he *owned* it. All of this – the marble floors and chandelier, the gleaming concierge desk, the grand piano in the corner, that resplendent staircase – it was *his*. These people were Jupiter's employees, even the enormous cat that scolded and scowled at him. Morrigan tried not to feel daunted.

'See you up there,' said the cat, leaping onto the curved staircase. 'Don't dawdle.' She bounded up the steps four at a time.

Jupiter turned to Morrigan. 'I know what you're thinking,' he said for the second time that day. 'Why do I let a Magnificat tell me what to do? Well, it's simple—'

'That's not a Magnificat,' Morrigan interrupted.

Jupiter breathed in sharply, arching his neck to watch the cat disappear up the stairs in a receding spiral. He listened to make sure it was well out of hearing distance before turning back to Morrigan and whispering, 'What do you mean, "That's not a Magnificat"? Of course she's a Magnificat.'

'I've seen pictures of Magnificats in the newspaper, and they're nothing like that. President Wintersea has six of them pulling a carriage. They're black and shiny' – Jupiter held a finger to his lips to shush her, glancing anxiously up the staircase again – 'and they wear studded collars and big nose rings, and they definitely don't *talk*.'

'Do *not* let Fenestra hear you saying that,' he hissed.

'Fenestra?'

'Yes!' he said, indignant. 'She has a name, you know. No offence, but your ideas about Magnificats are wildly askew and you'd best keep them to yourself if you ever want to have clean sheets around here. Fen's head of housekeeping.'

Morrigan stared at him. She wondered, at that moment, if it was wise to have travelled through a clock to a strange city to live in a hotel with a madman. 'How can a cat be a housekeeper?'

'I know what you're thinking,' he said again. They'd reached a circular elevator of gold and glass. Jupiter pressed a button to call it. 'No opposable thumbs. How does she do the dusting? To be honest, I've asked myself the same question, but I'm not letting it keep me up at night and you shouldn't either. Ah – here's Kedgeree.'

The elevator arrived and its doors opened just as an ancient but sprightly man with snowy-white hair dashed over to join them. He wore rosy tartan trousers, a grey suit jacket and a pink handkerchief tucked into his pocket, the letters *HD* monogrammed on it in gold.

'Morrigan, this is Mr Kedgeree Burns, my concierge. When you get lost in the hotel – and you will get lost – call for Kedgeree. I suspect he knows this place better than I do. Any messages? I've been out of range.' Jupiter ushered everyone inside the elevator before the doors whooshed shut.

Kedgeree handed him a stack of notes. 'Aye, sir – sixteen from the League, four from the Society and one from the mayor's office.'

'Marvellous. Everything running smoothly?'

'Right as rain, sir, right as rain,' the concierge continued in a thick brogue. 'The gentlemen from Paranormal Services came in on Thursday to see about our wee haunting on the fifth floor; I've sent the invoice to accounting. The Nevermoor Transport Authority sent a messenger yesterday – they're after your advice, something about echoes on the Gossamer Line. Oh, and someone's left four alpacas in the conservatory; shall I have the front desk make an announcement?'

'Alpacas! Golly. Do they seem happy enough?'

'Chewing through the hothouse orchids as we speak.'

'Then it can wait until after.' (*After what?* Morrigan wondered.) 'Is the room ready?'

'It certainly is, sir. Housekeeping done. Furniture polished. Fresh as a daisy.'

The elevator climbed, lighting up floor numbers as outside the glass walls the foyer fell away beneath them. Morrigan's stomach dropped. She pressed a hand to the glass to steady herself. Martha, the housemaid Jupiter had greeted, gave her a reassuring smile. She was young but capable-looking, her mousy brown hair fastened into a neat bun, her uniform immaculately pressed.

'It's like that the first few times,' she whispered kindly. Her smile reached all the way to her big, hazel eyes. 'You'll get used to it.'

'Brollies ready?' asked Jupiter, and there was a flurry of movement as the staff all held up umbrellas in response. 'Oh! I almost forgot. Happy birthday, Morrigan.'

He reached over and produced a long, thin brown paper parcel from somewhere in the depths of the blue overcoat still draped over her shoulders. Morrigan carefully unwrapped the paper to find a black oilskin umbrella with a silver filigree handle. The tip was a little bird, carved from opal. Morrigan ran her fingertips over the tiny iridescent wings, feeling utterly lost for words. She'd never had anything so lovely.

Attached to the handle with string was a little note.

You'll need this.
—J.N.

'Th-thank you,' Morrigan stammered, a lump forming in her throat. 'I've never – nobody's ever—'

But before she could finish, the elevator doors opened to a great roar of celebratory noise, and Morrigan felt as if she'd been thrust into the eye of a colourful hurricane.

The wide open-air rooftop swarmed with hundreds of party guests, shrieking and giggling, dancing wildly, their euphoric faces lit by rows of burning torches and festoon lights. A huge dragon puppet danced among them, carried by a dozen people underneath. Costumed acrobats danced and somersaulted on scarily high platforms. Above their heads spun glittering mosaic mirror balls, suspended seemingly by magic, spraying kaleidoscopic light everywhere Morrigan looked. An older boy laughed as he ran past her, chasing after the dancing dragon.

In the centre of everything was a frothing pink champagne fountain and a bandstand where a group of white-jacketed musicians played swing music. (One of them appeared to be a large, bright-green lizard on the double bass, but Morrigan thought perhaps she was hallucinating due to exhaustion.) Even Fenestra the Magnificat seemed to be enjoying herself, batting a mirror ball and glowering at any dancer who came too close.

Morrigan hung back, her eyes wide, her eardrums assaulted by the wall of noise. In her head, she counted the hazards, tallied up all the many things that might go wrong with this party now that she and her curse had arrived. She imagined tomorrow's newspaper headlines: ACROBAT FALLS FROM PLATFORM AND BREAKS NECK; CURSED CHILD TO BLAME. CHAMPAGNE FOUNTAIN TURNS TO POISONOUS ACID, HUNDREDS DIE GROSSLY.

It was all too much. First the Hunt of Smoke and Shadow, then a giant mechanical spider, the fog-laden mystery of border control and now this . . . this ridiculous party. On a hotel rooftop. In a wild, sprawling secret city she'd never even heard of. With a mad ginger man and a giant cat.

This endless night would surely be the death of somebody, even if it wasn't Morrigan.

'*Jupiter!*' somebody shouted. 'Look – it's Jupiter North! He's here!'

With a squawk of surprised saxophone, the music came to an abrupt end. An excited tremor ran through the party.

'Toast!' one woman cried out.

Others echoed her, applauding and whistling, stamping their feet. Morrigan watched, captivated, as hundreds of shining faces all turned to him like sunflowers to the sun.

'A toast to the New Age, Captain North!'

Jupiter leapt onto the bandstand and held up one hand, reaching out to swipe a champagne flute from a waiter's tray with the other. The party fell silent.

'Friends, honoured guests and my dear Deucalion family.' His voice rang out clearly in the crisp, early morning air. 'We have danced, we have dined, we have drunk our fill. We have bid a tender and triumphant farewell to the Old Age, and now we must step boldly into the New. May it be a good and happy one. May it bring unexpected adventures.'

'To unexpected adventures,' the party guests echoed as one, downing their pink champagne.

Jupiter grinned straight at Morrigan through the crowd, and she smiled back, holding her umbrella tight. Everything about this night was an unexpected adventure.

'Now, if you have the courage, I invite you to join me in the Deucalion's time-honoured Morningtide tradition.' He pointed to the east. Far off on the horizon, a shimmering line of golden light was beginning to show. 'Put out the torches. Dawn has come, and we will see ourselves by its light.'

One by one, the torches were extinguished. The festoon lights flickered out. Jupiter beckoned Morrigan over, and she followed him to the edge of the rooftop.

Nevermoor stretched out for miles in every direction. Morrigan imagined she was on a ship, sailing an ocean of buildings and streets and people and *life*.

A thrill crept down her neck, leaving a trail of gooseflesh. *I'm alive*, she thought, and the idea was so absurd and so wonderful that a laugh spilled from her mouth, cutting through the quiet. Morrigan didn't care. She felt expansive, bursting with a new joy and temerity that could only come from having cheated death.

It's a New Age, she thought with disbelief. *And I'm alive.*

A woman to Morrigan's left climbed up on the balustrade. She held up the hem of her long, flowing silk gown and opened an umbrella above her head. All around, others followed suit, until the rail was packed with people standing shoulder to shoulder, holding their umbrellas high and staring into the sun.

'Step boldly!' the woman in the silk gown shouted. Then without hesitation, she leapt from the roof and floated down, down, down all thirteen storeys. Morrigan turned to Jupiter with alarm, but he looked utterly untroubled. She waited for a cry of pain or a loud splat from below, but neither came. The woman landed on the ground, stumbled a bit, and gave a shout of triumph.

Impossible, thought Morrigan.

'Step boldly!' cried another guest, and then Kedgeree the concierge, then Martha the housemaid – 'Step boldly!' – and another, and another, and soon the air was filled with a chorus of those two electrifying words. They stepped off the rail one by one, until Morrigan was looking down on a sea of umbrellas.

Then Jupiter, without a backward glance, stepped onto the rail and opened his umbrella. The boy she'd seen earlier climbed up on his other side. Together they cried, 'Step boldly!' and leapt from the balustrade.

Morrigan watched them drift gently downward. It felt like an age passed before they reached the ground, but finally Jupiter and the boy landed safely on their feet, laughing and hugging, thumping each other on the back. Then Jupiter turned to look back up at her.

She waited for him to say something, but he was silent.

No words of encouragement. No persuasion or reassurance. He simply watched, waiting to see what she would do.

Morrigan felt a swirl of panic and elation. This was her second chance; the beginning of a new life she never dreamed she'd have. Was she going to ruin it by breaking both her cursed legs? Or worse – splattering herself all over the ground? Had she cheated Death on Eventide, only to hand him an easy victory on Morningtide?

There was only one way to find out.

Morrigan let Jupiter's overcoat fall in a pile at her feet. Climbing onto the balustrade, she opened her new oilskin umbrella with shaking hands. *Don't look down don't look down don't look down.* The air felt thin.

'Step boldly,' Morrigan whispered.

Then she closed her eyes.

And jumped.

The wind caught her in its arms. Morrigan felt a powerful rush of adrenaline as she fell to the ground, the cold air whipping her hair around her face, and at last landed firmly on both feet. The impact sent a jolt up her legs and she stumbled, but somehow – miraculously – stayed upright.

Morrigan opened her eyes. All around, party guests were celebrating their triumph over gravity, jumping into the fountain with loud splashes and drenching their party clothes. Only Jupiter stood still, watching Morrigan, his face a mixture of pride, relief and admiration. Nobody in the world had ever looked at her that way.

She marched over to where he stood, unsure whether to throw her arms around him or push him into the fountain. In the end she did neither.

'Happy New Age' were the words Morrigan spoke.

But the words in her heart were *I'm alive.*

CHAPTER SEVEN

Happy Hour at the Hotel Deucalion

Morrigan dreamed of falling into darkness, but she woke to sunshine, a tray of fried eggs and toast, and a note.

> *Come to my study after breakfast.*
> *Third floor, two doors down from the Music*
> *Salon.*
> *—J.N.*

On the back, Jupiter had drawn a little map with arrows pointing the way. The clock on the wall said it was one o'clock in the afternoon. *Well past breakfast*, Morrigan thought. How long ago had he left the note?

Eyeing the tray, Morrigan realised she hadn't eaten since her lamb chop birthday dinner at Crow Manor – when was that, a hundred years ago? She wolfed down two eggs, a thick piece of buttered toast and half a cup of milky, lukewarm tea, taking in her surroundings as she ate.

Compared to what she'd seen of the hotel, with its gilded mirrors and oil paintings, lavish carpets, lush green plants and crystal chandeliers, her bedroom came as a surprise. It was . . . a room. A perfectly fine room. But a *normal* room, with a single bed and a wooden chair and a little square window and a tiny bathroom through a door to her left. If it hadn't been for Jupiter's note on the side table, and her silver-handled umbrella hooked on the bedhead, waking up in here Morrigan might have thought she'd dreamed up the Deucalion, and Nevermoor, and the whole thing.

Barely stopping to swallow her last mouthful of tea, she changed into a clean blue dress (the sole item of clothing hanging in the wardrobe) and ran all the way to Jupiter's study on the third floor, following his directions. She paused to catch her breath before knocking.

'Come in,' called Jupiter. Morrigan opened the door to a small, sensible room with a fireplace and two worn leather armchairs. Jupiter stood behind a wooden desk, leaning over a mess of papers and maps. He looked up, smiling broadly. 'Ah! There you are. Excellent. I thought I might give you a little tour. Sleep well?'

'Yes, thanks,' said Morrigan. She suddenly felt shy. It was all this smiling at her that Jupiter kept doing, she thought. It wasn't natural.

'And your room is all right?'

'Y-yes, of course!' she stammered. 'At least it was when I left it. I swear.'

Jupiter looked at her for a moment, his brow knotted in confusion. Then he closed his eyes and laughed as though she'd said something achingly funny. 'No – no, I meant . . . I meant do you *like* it? Is it all right . . . for you?'

'Oh.' Morrigan felt her cheeks turn warm. 'Yes, it's lovely. Thank you.'

Jupiter had the good grace to wipe away the last of his grin. 'It's, uh . . . it's a bit boring, I know, but it's only just met you. You'll get acquainted. Things will change.'

'Oh,' said Morrigan again. She had no idea what he meant. 'Okay.'

The walls of Jupiter's study were lined with bookshelves and framed photographs, mostly of strange landscapes and people. Jupiter himself only popped up in a few of them – younger, gingerer, skinnier, less beardy. Standing on the wings of a biplane in mid-flight. Giving two thumbs up as he rode on the shoulders of a bear. Dancing on the deck of a boat with a beautiful woman and, for some reason, a meerkat.

On his desk, the photograph in pride of place was one of Jupiter and a boy sitting together with their feet propped up on that same desk, arms folded, grinning ear to ear. The boy had straight white teeth, warm brown skin and a black patch over his left eye.

Morrigan recognised him – it was the boy she'd seen at the Eventide party, running after the dancing dragon and jumping off the rooftop at Jupiter's side. She hadn't noticed his eye patch at the party. But then, he had rushed past her in an instant, and she supposed her brain had been busy trying to make sense of lizard musicians and giant cats and so on.

'Who's that?'

'My nephew. Jack. There he is again – see? Last year's school photo.' Jupiter pointed at a photo of a group of boys standing in uniform rows. Across the bottom it read: *The Graysmark School for Bright Young Men. Winter of Eleven, Age of Southern Influence.* The boys were dressed in black morning suits with white shirts and bow ties.

Morrigan read through the list of names beneath the photograph. 'It says here his name is John.'

'Mmm, John Arjuna Korrapati. We call him Jack.'

Morrigan opened her mouth to ask about the patch, but Jupiter cut her off.

'You'd best ask him yourself. Might have to wait until spring holidays, though, I doubt he'll be around much during first term. I wanted you to meet him today, but I'm afraid he's had to go back to school.'

'Isn't today a holiday?'

Jupiter sighed with his whole body. 'Not according to our Jack. He's just started third year and he insists that all his classmates will be back at campus over the Eventide break, already studying for their first exam. They keep them busy over at Graysmark.' Jupiter led Morrigan into the hallway, shutting the study door behind them. 'I'm hoping you'll be a bad influence on him. Shall we visit the Smoking Parlour?'

'So.' Jupiter rocked on his heels, hands in pockets, as they waited for the elevator to arrive. 'Morrigan . . . Morrigan.'

'Yes?' She wondered if he was about to tell her about the Wundrous Society at last.

He looked up. 'Hmm? Oh, just thinking about what we can do with Morrigan. You know, for a nickname. Morrie . . . Morro . . . No. Moz. Mozza. Mozzie?'

The elevator doors pinged open. Jupiter ushered her inside and pressed the button for the ninth floor.

'Definitely not,' Morrigan said, bristling. 'I don't want a nickname.'

'Course you do, everyone wants—' He was interrupted by a squeal, a crackling sound, and the clearing of a throat coming from a horn-shaped amplifier mounted in the corner.

'Good morning, ladies, gentlemen and Wunimals. Could the guest who left four alpacas in the conservatory please collect them at his or her earliest convenience? Please call for Kedgeree if you require assistance. Thank you.'

'Everyone wants a nickname,' Jupiter continued after the announcement. 'Mine, for example, is the Great and Honourable Captain Sir Jupiter Amantius North, Esquire.'

'Did you make that up yourself?'

'Bits of it.'

'It's too long for a nickname,' Morrigan said. 'Nicknames are, like, Jim or Rusty. "The Great and Honourable Captain Sir Thingy" takes about a year to say.'

'That's why everyone calls me Jupiter for short,' he said. The elevator shuddered to a halt and they stepped out. 'You're right, shorter is usually best. Let's see . . . Mo. Mor . . . Mog. Mog!'

'Mog?' She wrinkled her nose.

'Mog is a *great* nickname!' Jupiter insisted. He rolled the word around in his mouth as they walked down the long hallway. 'Mog. Moggers. The Mogster. It's so *versatile*.'

Morrigan made a face. 'It sounds like something an

animal vomits up and leaves on your doorstep. Are you going to tell me about the Wundrous Society now?'

'Soon, Mog, but—'

'Morrigan.'

'—first, the grand tour.'

The Smoking Parlour wasn't a room where guests were allowed to smoke pipes and cigars, to Morrigan's relief, but in fact a room that emitted great rolling clouds of coloured, scented smoke that seemed to pour from the walls themselves. This afternoon it was a murky green sage smoke ('to promote the art of philosophisation,' Jupiter told her), but a schedule on the door informed her that later that evening the smoke would change to honeysuckle ('for romance') and, late at night, to lavender ('to aid the sleepless').

Sprawled dramatically on a love seat was a very small, very pale man dressed all in black, wrapped in a velvet cloak. His eyes were closed and thickly lined with kohl, his mouth downturned, and he had an air of gothic tragedy about him. Morrigan liked him instantly.

'Afternoon, Frank.'

'Ah, Jove,' said the little man, cracking open one mournful eye. 'There you are. I was just thinking about death.'

'Of course you were.' Jupiter sounded unimpressed.

'And the songs I want to sing at the Hallowmas party this year.'

'It's almost a year away, and I said you could sing *a* song, singular, not *songs, plural*.'

'And the scarcity of fresh towels in my room.'

'You get a fresh towel every morning, Frank.'

'But I want two fresh towels every morning,' Frank said with a note of petulance. 'I need one for my hair.'

Morrigan stifled a giggle.

'Talk to Fenestra about it. Splendid job last night, by the way – our grandest Eventide yet.' Jupiter leaned down to whisper to Morrigan. 'Frank's my official party planner. Roof-Raiser-in-Chief. Best in the business, but we mustn't tell him that or he'll look for a job somewhere fancier.'

Frank smirked drowsily. 'I already know I'm the best, Jove. I'm still here because there is no place fancier – you're the only hotelier in the Free State who'd never impose a budget on my genius.'

'I *do* impose a budget on your genius, Frank, but you always ignore it. Speaking of which, who approved the booking of Iguanarama?'

'You did.'

'No, I said to book *Lizamania*, the Iguanarama tribute band. They're a quarter of the price.'

'Naturally. They have a quarter of the talent,' huffed Frank. 'Why are you here, anyway? Can't you see I'm in recovery?'

'I've brought someone special to meet you. This' – Jupiter clapped a hand on Morrigan's shoulder – 'is Morrigan Crow.'

Frank sat up very suddenly, his eyes narrowing at Morrigan. 'Ah. You've brought me a gift,' he said. 'Young blood. This pleases me.' He snapped his teeth. Morrigan tried not to laugh. She suspected he aimed to terrify, and it seemed sporting to go along with it.

'No, Frank.' Jupiter pinched the bridge of his nose. 'Honestly, between you and Fen . . . look, she's *not for biting*. *No one* in the Deucalion is for biting. We've been over this.'

Frank closed his eyes and lay back down, looking sullen. 'Then why bother me?'

'Thought you might like to meet my candidate, that's all.'

'Candidate for what?' asked Frank, yawning.

'For the Wundrous Society.'

Frank's eyes flew open. He sat up, observing Morrigan with renewed interest. 'Well. Isn't *this* a curious turn of events? Jupiter North, sworn lifelong non-patron. Taking a candidate at last.' He rubbed his hands together, looking gleeful. 'Oh, won't people *talk*.'

'People do love to talk.'

Morrigan looked from Jupiter to Frank and back again. 'Talk about what?'

But Jupiter didn't answer.

Had he really sworn never to become a patron? She couldn't help feeling pleased by that. Jupiter North, apparently beloved and admired by all, had chosen *her* as his first-ever candidate. She wished she knew why.

Frank was eyeing her suspiciously, as if he too had his doubts. 'Delighted, Morrigan. May I ask you a question?'

Jupiter stepped in. 'No, you may not.'

'Oh, please, Jove, just one.'

'Just none.'

'Morrigan, what's your—'

'You won't even get *one* fresh towel tomorrow if you keep this up.'

'But I only want to know—'

'Lie down and enjoy the sage, Frank.' The walls had started rolling out fresh clouds of green smoke. 'Martha will be around soon with the tea cart.'

Frank harrumphed and, turning his back on them, threw himself down sulkily onto the love seat.

Jupiter guided Morrigan through the opaque fog to the door, speaking quietly into her ear. 'Frank's a bit dramatic, but he's a good egg. Only dwarf vampire in Nevermoor, you know.' Morrigan detected a note of pride in his voice.

She looked back at Frank through the greenish haze, feeling slightly alarmed — had she *really* just been talking to a vampire? 'Not very popular in the dwarf community *or* the vampire community, sadly, mostly on account of—'

'Vampire dwarf,' Frank corrected him from the other side of the room. 'There is a difference, you know. You might think about getting some sensitivity training if you're going to run a hotel.'

'—mostly on account of his moodiness, I expect. Imagine being *too moody* for other vampires,' Jupiter finished in a whisper, and then called over his shoulder, 'Their loss, Frank. Their loss.'

Outside the Smoking Parlour they passed Martha the maid pushing a cart full of tea things and delicious-looking treats. With a wink, she slipped a pink iced cake into Morrigan's hand as she went by, and Jupiter made a great show of pretending not to notice.

Morrigan had just taken a large, heavenly mouthful when a young man in a driver's cap and uniform burst through the elevator doors. He had dark brown skin and wide, worried eyes.

'Captain North!' he shouted, running down the hall. Morrigan froze; an unhappy effect of her curse was that she knew *exactly* what bad news looked like. 'Kedgeree sent me, sir. There's been another messenger from the Transport Authority. They need you to come at once.' The driver took off his cap and ran his fingers nervously along the brim.

Martha abandoned her cart and dashed over to join them, looking stricken. 'Not another accident on the Wunderground?'

'Another—' Jupiter began, shaking his head. 'What do you mean, *another* accident?'

'It was in the news this morning,' Martha replied. 'A train derailed on the Bedtime Line shortly after dawn and crashed into the side of a tunnel.'

'Where?' demanded Jupiter.

'Somewhere between Blackstock and Fox Street stations. They said dozens were injured.' Martha stood perfectly still, clutching her throat, and added quietly, 'No deaths, thank goodness.'

Morrigan felt something twist in her centre. Here it was – the catastrophe she'd been awaiting. *Hello, Nevermoor,* she thought, biting her lip. *Morrigan Crow has arrived.* She watched Jupiter, waiting for an accusation, for him to turn on her with suspicion.

But her patron only frowned. 'The Wunderground doesn't derail. It's never derailed.'

'Martha's right, sir,' said the driver. 'It's all over the papers, on the wireless. Some people are saying . . . they're saying it could be the work of' – he stopped to swallow, dropping his voice to a whisper – 'of the *Wundersmith*, but . . . but that's . . .'

'Nonsense.'

'That's what I said, sir, but . . . it's such a nasty accident, people are bound to think—'

'Could it really be the Wundersmith?' Martha interrupted, her face draining of colour.

Jupiter scoffed. 'Given that he's been gone for more than a hundred years, Martha, I rather think not. Don't let the scaremongers get to you.'

'What's the Wundersmith?' Morrigan asked. Could there be someone else to blame? Someone who wasn't *her*, for once? She was ashamed of how her heart lifted at the thought.

'Fairy tale and superstition,' Jupiter told her with a resolute nod, and turned back to his driver. 'Charlie, the Wunderground is self-propelling, it's self-maintaining. It's driven by *Wunder*, for goodness' sake. Wunder doesn't *have* accidents.'

Charlie lifted one shoulder, looking equally baffled. 'I know. The Transport Authority wouldn't say what you're needed for, sir, but I've sent word to the coach house to fuel a motor. We can be ready to leave in four minutes.'

Jupiter looked dismayed. 'Very well, then.' He turned to Morrigan while Charlie ran ahead. 'Sorry about this, Mog. Rubbish timing. I didn't even get to show you the duck pond or the Things-in-Jars Room.'

'What's the Things-in-Jars Room?'

'It's where I keep all my things in jars.'

'You were going to tell me about the Wundrous Society . . .'

'I know, and I will, but it'll have to wait. Martha—' He waved the young maid closer. 'Could you give Morrigan a little tour? Just the highlights.'

Martha brightened. 'Of course, sir. I'll take her to meet Dame Chanda Kali, she's rehearsing in the Music Salon.' She put one arm around Morrigan's shoulders, giving her a friendly squeeze. 'Then we'll go out to the stables and peek in on the ponies, how about that?'

'Perfect!' Jupiter said enthusiastically, running to where Charlie was holding the elevator doors. 'Martha, you're a treasure. Mog, I'll see you later.'

Then the doors closed, and he was gone.

Morrigan recognised Dame Chanda Kali at once. Not by the powerful soprano voice that was echoing in the rafters of the Music Salon when Martha and Morrigan arrived, nor by the deep reddish-brown colour of her skin or the glossy black hair rolling down her back in thick waves, flecked with silver. It was Dame Chanda's robe she recognised – long, flowing silk in bright pink and orange, encrusted with tiny glittering beadwork all over. It was almost identical in style to the purple silk gown the woman had worn at the rooftop party. Dame Chanda, Morrigan realised, was that first valiant soul to have leapt from the balustrade in celebration of Morningtide.

Now she stood in the centre of the Music Salon, performing an aria for an unlikely audience: two dozen fluttering bluebirds, a mother fox with her two babies and several bushy-tailed red squirrels, all of whom appeared to have wandered in through the wide-open windows and were gazing at the singer with deep adoration.

'Dame Chanda is a Grand High Soprano and Dame Commander of the Order of Woodland Whisperers,' Martha whispered loudly to Morrigan over the music and birdsong. Morrigan spied a golden *W* pin, just like Jupiter's, hidden amongst the beadwork of Dame Chanda's gown. 'She's a member of the Wundrous Society herself, but she lives here at the Deucalion. She's performed in all the grand opera houses of the Free State, although some of them aren't very pleased when this lot turn up – they can make a dreadful mess,' she said, indicating the woodland creatures who were apparently helplessly drawn to the sound of Dame Chanda's voice.

The music ended, and Martha and Morrigan burst into applause. Dame Chanda took a bow and smiled warmly, shooing the wildlife out the window. 'Martha, my angel, I should have you perform all my introductions. You do it so charmingly.'

The maid blushed. 'Dame Chanda, this is Morrigan Crow. She's—'

'Jupiter's candidate, yes, I've heard,' said Dame Chanda, turning her dazzling gaze on Morrigan. It felt like being caught in the beam from a lighthouse. Like speaking to royalty. 'News travels fast at the Deucalion. Everybody's talking about you, Miss Crow. Is it true, then, darling? You're to take the trials?'

Morrigan nodded, fidgeting with the hem of her dress. Standing before this remarkable woman, she felt like a street urchin.

This is what a Wundrous Society member looks like, she thought. Beautiful and stately, like Dame Chanda. Interesting and admired, like Jupiter. What must they think of her, she wondered – Martha and Dame Chanda and Fenestra and Frank? Were they already whispering about what a terrible choice Jupiter had made?

'How extraordinary,' the opera singer breathed. 'Our Jupiter, a patron at last! I'm glad to know you, Miss Morrigan, for you must truly be somebody wonderful. Are you excited about your first trial, sweet girl?'

'Er. Yes?' Morrigan lied, unconvincingly.

'Of course, you'll have the Wundrous Welcome first. Has Jupiter arranged a fitting?'

Morrigan looked at her blankly. What in the world was a Wundrous Welcome? 'A . . . a fitting?'

'With his seamstress? You must have a new dress, my dear. First impressions are important.' She paused. 'I think perhaps I'll have my own costumier see to this.'

Martha beamed at Morrigan, wide-eyed, as if this were truly the greatest honour Dame Chanda could bestow and not a mysterious, terrifying prospect.

'Naturally Jupiter gets away with his own . . . *interesting* sartorial choices, because he's so handsome,' Dame Chanda continued. 'But we cannot inflict his dreadful taste on you. Not for such an important event.

'The Wundrous Welcome isn't just a garden party, Miss Morrigan. It is, most unfortunately, a garden full of people judging everything about you. The other candidates and patrons will be sizing you up as their competition. It is *very* intense.'

Morrigan's insides were shrivelling. Competition? Judgement? Jupiter's letter had mentioned that her entry into the Society wasn't guaranteed, and that she had to make it through the entrance trials.

But . . . deep down, Morrigan had thought after everything she'd been through to get to Nevermoor, after escaping the Hunt of Smoke and Shadow and getting past border control and – and *cheating death*, for goodness' sake – that perhaps the hard part was over. Nobody had mentioned a *very intense garden party*. (Morrigan could think of at least twelve disasters she and her curse could bring to a garden party, not even counting bumblebee stings and hay fever.)

Dame Chanda seemed to sense that she had hit a nerve. She affected a breezy air, waving off the topic as if it were a fly. 'Oh, no need to worry, darling. Just be yourself. Now, if I may ask – we're all dying to know' – she leaned in, her eyes twinkling, and spoke quietly in Morrigan's ear – 'what's your knack? What *marvellous* talent do you possess?'

Morrigan blinked. 'My what?'

'Your knack, child. Your clever little skill. Your *talent*.'

Morrigan didn't know what to say.

'Ah, but I bet our Jupiter has a dramatic reveal planned, doesn't he?' said Dame Chanda, touching a finger to her nose. 'Say no more, my dear. Say no more.'

'What did she mean?' Morrigan asked Martha as they left the Music Salon and headed down the spiral staircase towards the lobby. 'I don't have a . . . a knack, or a talent, or anything.'

Martha laughed, not unkindly. 'Course you've got a knack. You're a candidate for the Wundrous Society. You're *Jupiter North's* candidate. He can't bid on you unless he's sure you've got one.'

'He can't?' This was news to Morrigan. 'But I don't—'

'You do. You just don't know what it is yet.'

Morrigan said nothing.

She thought of the night before – of the wonderful moment when Jupiter had shown up at Crow Manor, the joy she'd felt at the break of dawn when she'd landed safely in the forecourt of the Hotel Deucalion. She'd believed a whole new world had opened up to her. Now she felt as though she were looking at her new life through a wall of unbreakable glass.

How would she ever get into the Wundrous Society if she had to have some sort of *talent*?

'You know, he's never had a candidate before,' Martha said gently. 'He should have by now. They're all supposed to, once they reach a certain age. And it's not as if he didn't have plenty of parents banging on his door, offering him money and favours and all sorts, if he'd only choose their little darlings. You should see the sad cases we get sniffing around here come Bid Day! But he's always said no. Nobody was ever special enough.' She smiled brightly, reaching out to tuck a lock of black hair behind Morrigan's ear. 'Until now.'

'There's nothing special about me,' Morrigan said, but it was a lie. She knew the thing that made her special. It was the same thing that made people in Jackalfax cross the street to avoid her. The thing that would have killed her on Eventide, if Jupiter hadn't shown up in his mechanical spider and swept her away to Nevermoor.

The curse made her special.

Was being cursed a talent? Was *that* why Jupiter had bid on her? Because she had a *knack* for ruining everything? Morrigan grimaced. What a horrible thought.

'Captain North is a little odd, Miss, but he's no fool. He sees people the way they really are. If he chose you, that means—'

But Morrigan didn't find out what it meant, because Martha was interrupted by a deafening crash and the sound of shattering glass. A ghastly scream echoed all the way up the stairs.

Martha and Morrigan ran the rest of the way down to the lobby and were met by a dreadful sight: the pink sailing ship chandelier had crashed down onto the black and white chequerboard floor. Glittering rays of shattered glass and crystals sprayed across the marble. Wires dangled from the ceiling like entrails from a carcass.

Guests and staff stood open-mouthed, staring at the giant mess.

Martha held both hands to her cheeks. 'Oh . . . Captain North will be so upset. That ship's been there forever, it's his favourite thing. How could this happen?'

'I don't understand it,' said Kedgeree, emerging from the concierge desk. 'Maintenance only checked the old girl last week! She was fit as a fiddle.'

'And to happen on Morningtide, of all days!' Martha cried. 'What awful luck.'

'I'd say we've had splendid luck,' said Kedgeree. 'A lobby full of people, and not a soul hurt? We can thank our lucky stars.'

But Morrigan privately agreed with Martha. It was awful luck, and she ought to know. That was her specialty.

Martha gathered up some of the staff and began giving directions for the cleanup, while Kedgeree spoke to the guests, smoothly ushering them away from the mess.

'Ladies and gentlemen, I apologise on behalf of the Deucalion for the terrible fright you've suffered,' said the concierge. 'If you'll make your way to the Golden Lantern cocktail bar on the sixth floor, a special happy hour will begin at once. Drinks on the house for the rest of the evening! Enjoy yourselves.'

The dozen or so guests who'd witnessed the chandelier crash seemed happy to wander upstairs for their free drinks and forget it had ever happened. But Kedgeree, Martha and the rest of the staff looked as troubled as Morrigan felt.

She edged around the scene of the disaster. 'Can I help?'

'Oh! Don't you dare trouble yourself, Miss Morrigan,' said Kedgeree, guiding her away. 'In fact, I think it's best if you scuttle upstairs too – away from all this loose wiring and broken crystal. We don't want you getting hurt.'

'I won't get hurt,' Morrigan protested. 'I'll be careful.'

'Why don't you head up to the Smoking Parlour? I'll call ahead and have them pop on some chamomile smoke to soothe your wee little nerves. You've had a nasty shock. There's a good lass, off you go now.'

Morrigan paused at the landing, looking back to watch Kedgeree, Martha and the other staff scurry to and fro, sweeping the remains of the chandelier into sad piles of sparkling rose-coloured dust.

Nobody glared at her or muttered under their breath about the cursed child being to blame. None of them knew why this awful thing had happened.

But Morrigan knew why.

And she knew why that train had crashed on the Wunderground.

The curse had followed her. She'd survived it, lived through it . . . then somehow brought it all the way to Nevermoor anyhow, smuggled it through border control and given it a nice cosy home at the Hotel Deucalion.

And it was going to ruin everything.

CHAPTER EIGHT

Interesting. Useful. Good.

Something woke Morrigan in the night. A sound – like the fluttering of wings or the riffling of pages. She lay awake, waiting for it to return, but the room was silent. Perhaps she'd been dreaming, of birds or books.

She closed her eyes and willed herself to fall into a deep and dreamless sleep, but it never came. The patch of sky in her bedroom window lightened from darkest black to inky predawn blue, the stars extinguishing one by one.

Morrigan thought of the pink sailing ship, smashed on the chequerboard floor, its light gone out forever. Jupiter's favourite thing, Martha had said. When Morrigan went to bed Jupiter still hadn't returned from the Transport Authority. What would he say, she wondered, when he saw the gaping cavity in the ceiling where his *favourite thing* used to be?

Logically, Morrigan knew she wasn't responsible for a giant light fixture falling to its sparkly death – especially as she hadn't even been in the room at the time. Still, she couldn't shake the feeling that she'd gotten away with a terrible crime.

But this hotel must be over a hundred years old, she thought. She rolled over and punched her pillow into a comfier lump, resenting her own accusation. *Old things break!* The chandelier probably had faulty wires that had worn away or – or the plaster in the ceiling was crumbling!

Morrigan sat up in bed, suddenly determined, and threw her blanket off. She'd examine the damage for herself. She'd see it wasn't her fault. She'd go back to sleep and live happily ever after. The End.

Of course, the lobby was rather dark without the glow of the chandelier. The concierge desk was empty. It was spooky being down here all on her own in the small hours, her footsteps echoing in the emptiness.

This was stupid, Morrigan thought with a flash of regret. A stupid idea. The mess had all been cleared away anyway, and the lobby was so dimly lit that from where she stood, the hole in the ceiling was just a vague black smudge up high – she couldn't see any worn-away wires. She wasn't even certain they were still there.

Morrigan was ready to give up and go back to bed when she heard a sound.

Music. Humming?

Yes – somebody was there, in the shadows, *humming*.

It was a strange little tune. One she vaguely recognised . . . a nursery rhyme, or a song she'd heard on the wireless. Her pulse quickened.

'Hello?' she said quietly – or she meant to say it quietly, but her voice resounded and bounced off the walls. The humming stopped. 'Who's there?'

'Don't be afraid.'

She turned towards the voice. It was a man – sitting half in shadows, legs crossed, coat folded neatly across his lap. Morrigan stepped closer, trying to see his face. He was shrouded in darkness.

'I'm just waiting for the front desk to open,' he said. 'My train was late, so I missed last check-in. Sorry if I frightened you.'

She knew that voice. Soft and clipped, all crisp *T*s and sharp *S*s.

'Haven't we met before?' she asked.

'I don't believe so,' the man said. 'I'm not from here.' He

squinted at her, leaning forward, and a beam of moonlight crossed his face.

'Mr Jones?' There wasn't much about him that was memorable – ash-brown hair, grey suit. But she recognised his voice and, looking closer, his dark eyes and the thin scar that sliced through one eyebrow. 'You're Ezra Squall's assistant.'

'I – yes, how did you – *Miss Crow*?' He stood, taking two swift steps towards her, his mouth opening in surprise. 'Can it really be you? They told us – they said you were . . .' He trailed off, looking uncomfortable. 'What in the world are you doing in the Free State?'

Uh-oh. 'I . . . I'm just . . . well, actually . . .' Morrigan could have kicked herself. How could she explain all that had happened? Would he tell her family? She was scrambling for something to say when an odd thing occurred to her. 'Wait . . . how do *you* know about the Free State?'

Mr Jones looked slightly shamefaced. 'Point taken. You keep my secret and I'll keep yours. Deal?'

'Deal.' Morrigan breathed a sigh of relief.

'Miss Crow, I don't know how you came to be here, or even how it is you are still alive when every newspaper in the Republic reported your death yesterday.' Morrigan looked away. Mr Jones seemed to sense her discomfort and chose his words with care. 'But whatever your . . . circumstances

. . . I can assure you my employer's offer still stands. Mr Squall was most disappointed to lose you as his apprentice. Most disappointed.'

'Oh. Um, thanks. But I already have a patron. Actually, I . . . I thought you were playing a prank on me. On Bid Day, I mean. You disappeared, and—'

'A prank?' He looked surprised and a little offended. 'Absolutely not. Mr Squall doesn't play pranks. His offer was genuine.'

Morrigan was confused. 'But I turned around and you were gone.'

'Ah. Yes. I must apologise for that.' He looked genuinely sorry. 'Forgive me, I was thinking of Mr Squall. If word got out that he was offering an apprenticeship, he'd have been inundated with parents trying to foist their children on him. That's why he bid on you anonymously. I did intend to return and speak with you, but Eventide took me by surprise.'

'Me too.'

'I'm afraid I handled things rather poorly. I appreciate that you have another arrangement, but . . . I'm certain Mr Squall would be thrilled if you were to consider changing your mind.'

'Oh.' Morrigan didn't know what to say. 'That's . . . nice of him.'

Mr Jones held up his hands, smiling. 'Please, there's no pressure. If you're content, Mr Squall will understand. Just know that the door is never closed.' He folded his coat neatly over one arm and sat down again, settling into an armchair. 'Now, I hope you don't mind my asking, but – why in heaven's name are you roaming the lobby of the Hotel Deucalion at this hour?'

There was something about Mr Jones that felt trustworthy and familiar. So instead of coming up with a story, Morrigan told the ridiculous truth. 'I came to look at the chandelier.' She pointed to the ceiling. 'What's left of it.'

'Good lord,' said Mr Jones, his eyes widening at the spot where the ship used to be. 'I thought something wasn't quite right. When did it happen?'

'Yesterday. It fell.'

'It *fell*?' He made a tutting noise. 'Chandeliers don't just fall. Certainly not at this hotel.'

'But it did.' Morrigan swallowed, looking sideways at Mr Jones, trying to gauge his reaction. Trying not to sound too hopeful. 'Unless – do you mean – do you think someone could have done it deliberately? Like maybe . . . someone cut the wires, or—'

'No, not at all. I think it grew out.'

She blinked. 'Grew out?'

'Yes. Like a tooth. See that?' He pointed, and Morrigan squinted up into the darkness. 'There – see the little glint of light? It's growing back in, replacing itself with something brand-new.'

She *could* see it now. A tiny speck of light, blooming out of the shadows. She'd missed it before, but there was no mistaking the little thread of crystal and light curling downward from the ceiling. Her heart lifted. 'Will it look just the same?'

'I shouldn't think so,' Mr Jones said, sounding wistful. 'I'm no expert on the inner workings of the Hotel Deucalion. But I have been coming here for many years, and I don't believe I've ever seen her wear the same dress twice.'

They stood in silence for several minutes, watching the newborn chandelier grow slowly, emerging from the safe cocoon of the ceiling just like an adult tooth from healthy pink gums. At this rate it would take weeks or maybe months to reach the size of the gigantic sailing ship, but Morrigan was so relieved, she could wait as long as it took. She wondered what it would look like in the end. Something even better than a sailing ship? An arachnipod, perhaps!

When Mr Jones spoke again it was in a gentle, hesitant voice, as if he was worried he might offend her. 'This patron of yours . . . I presume he or she has put you forward for the Wundrous Society?'

'How did you know?'

'Educated guess,' he said. 'There aren't many other reasons to bring a child all the way from the Wintersea Republic to Nevermoor. May I ask you something impertinent, Miss Crow?'

Morrigan felt her shoulders tense. She knew what he wanted to ask.

'I don't know what my knack is,' she said quietly. 'I don't even know if I have one.'

He frowned, looking puzzled. 'But . . . to get into the Wundrous Society—'

'I know.'

'Has your patron discussed—'

'No.'

He pressed his lips together. 'Don't you think that's strange?'

Morrigan turned her face upward. She watched the little stem of light on its glacial descent for a long, silent moment before answering.

'Yes. I do.'

Jupiter's hand was still hovering in the air, mid-knock, when Morrigan threw open her bedroom door to greet him later that morning.

'What's my knack?' she demanded.

'Good morning to you too.'

'Good morning,' she said, stepping aside to let him in. She'd been waiting for ages, pacing the floor as she brooded over her conversation with Mr Jones. The curtains were thrown wide, and buckets of morning sunlight streamed in through a window that had grown from a small square into a floor-to-ceiling arch overnight. Which was weird – but not, Morrigan thought, their most pressing matter to discuss. 'What's my knack?'

'Mind if I nick a pastry? I'm famished.'

Martha had come ten minutes earlier with a breakfast tray. It sat untouched in the corner. 'Help yourself. What's my knack?'

Jupiter stuffed his mouth full of pastry while Morrigan watched him and fretted. 'I don't have one, do I? Because you've got the wrong person. You thought I was someone else, someone with some big talent – that's how it works, isn't it? That's how you get into the Wundrous Society. You have to be talented, like Dame Chanda. You have to have a knack for something. And you thought I did, and now you know I don't. I'm right, aren't I?'

Jupiter swallowed. 'Before I forget – my seamstress is coming to fit you for a new wardrobe this morning. What's your favourite colour?'

'Black. I'm right, aren't I?'

'Black's not a colour.'

She groaned. *Jupiter!*

'Oh, all right.' He leaned against the wall and slid all the way down to the floor, stretching his long legs out on the rug. 'If you want to talk about boring things, we'll talk about boring things.'

Jupiter's long red hair, streaked with gold in the sunshine, was slightly tangled and fuzzy. It was the most dishevelled she'd seen him. He was barefoot and wore a wrinkled, untucked white shirt over blue trousers with braces that hung down untidily against his hips. Morrigan realised they were the clothes he'd worn the day before. She wondered whether he'd slept in them, or hadn't slept at all. His eyes were closed against the light, and he looked as if he'd happily sit there all day, letting the warmth soak into his bones.

'Here's how it works. Are you listening?'

Finally, Morrigan thought. With a curious mixture of relief and dread, she sat on the edge of the wooden chair, ready for some answers at last, even if they weren't good ones. 'I'm listening.'

'All right. Now don't interrupt.' He reluctantly sat up straight, clearing his throat. 'Every year, the Wundrous Society selects a new group of children to join us. Any child in the Free State can apply, so long as they've had their eleventh birthday before the first day of the year – you *just* scraped in, well done you – and provided they are selected by a patron, of course. The catch is . . . your patron can't be just anyone. It's not like other schools and apprenticeships, where anyone with more money than brains can sponsor your education. Your patron *must* be a member of the Wundrous Society. The Elders are very strict about it.'

'Why?'

'Because they're rotten snobs. Don't interrupt. Now, I'll be honest, Mog—'

'Morrigan.'

'—I've chosen you for my candidate, but that's just the beginning. Now you have to go through the entrance exams – we call them trials. There are four, spread out over the year. The trials are an elimination process, designed to separate the Society's ideal candidates from those who are . . . not so ideal. It's all very elitist and competitive, but it's tradition, so there you have it.'

'What sort of trials?' Morrigan asked, chewing her fingernails.

'I'm getting there. Don't interrupt.' He stood up and began pacing. 'The first three are different every year. There are many kinds of trials, and the Elders like to switch them around to keep things interesting. We won't know what each one will be until we're told. Some of them aren't too bad – the Speech Trial's fairly straightforward, for example. You just have to give a speech in front of an audience.'

Morrigan swallowed. She could think of nothing worse. She'd rather face the Hunt of Smoke and Shadow again.

'. . . and the Treasure Hunt Trial is fun, but I won't lie to you – some of them are horrendous. Be grateful they got rid of the Fright Trial two Ages ago.' He shuddered. 'They should have called that one the Nervous Breakdown Trial – some candidates never recovered.

'But, the fourth trial. That's the one you're concerned about. It's rather dramatically called the Show Trial, but honestly, it's very straightforward. Same thing every year. Each candidate who's made it through the first three trials must stand before the High Council of Elders and show them something.'

Morrigan frowned. 'Something . . . ?'

'Something interesting. And useful. And good.'

'Interesting and useful and good . . . you mean a talent, don't you?' She braced herself. 'They want to see a talent.'

Jupiter shrugged. 'A talent, a skill, a unique selling point . . . whatever you want to call it. We call it a knack. Silly Wundrous Society–speak, of course; it merely refers to the marvellous and unique gift you possess which the Elders will deem extraordinary enough to grant you a lifelong place in the Free State's most elite and prestigious institution.

That's all.' He grinned through his ginger beard in what he obviously thought was a charming fashion.

'Oh, is that all?' Morrigan choked out a hysterical little laugh. 'Well. I don't have one, so—'

'That you know of.'

'And what do *you* know of?' There was an edge to her voice. What was he hiding?

'I know lots of things. I'm very clever.' It was infuriating, the way he talked in circles. 'Really, Mog—'

'Morrigan.'

'—you needn't worry. Just get through the first three trials. The Show Trial is *my* problem. I'll take care of it.'

It all sounded . . . impossible. Morrigan slumped in her chair and sighed the deep, discontented sigh of someone who'd got quite a lot more than she'd bargained for. She cast Jupiter a sidelong look. 'What if I don't want to join the Society anymore? What if I've changed my mind?'

Morrigan expected him to be shocked or outraged, but he just nodded. Like he'd known she'd say that. 'I know it's scary, Mog,' he said quietly. 'The Society asks a lot. The trials are hard, and they're only the start.'

Terrific, she thought. *It gets worse.* 'What happens after the trials?'

Jupiter took a deep breath. 'It isn't really like a normal school. Scholars in the Wundrous Society are never coddled.

People think Society members are given a free ride, that once you get this little golden pin' – he tapped the *W* on his lapel – 'the world will smooth itself out for you, and your path will always be free and easy. And they're sort of right – the old gold spikes certainly open doors. Respect, adventure, fame. Reserved seats on the Wunderground. Pin privilege, people call it.' He rolled his eyes. 'But within Society walls you're expected to *earn* that privilege. Not just in the trials, not just once, but over and over again, for the rest of your life, by proving that you're worthy of it. Proving you're special.'

He paused, looking at her seriously. 'That's the difference between the Wundrous Society and a normal school. Even when your studies are over, you'll still be a part of the Society, and it will be a part of you. *Forever*, Mog. The Elders will hold you to account long after your years as a scholar, into adulthood and beyond.'

Morrigan's face must have betrayed how deeply unappealing all of this sounded, because Jupiter hurried to mend the damage. 'But I'm saying the worst bits first, Mog, because I want you to have the full picture.

'Look – the Wundrous Society is more than just a school. It's a *family*. A family that will take care of you and provide for you your entire life. Yes, you'll have a brilliant education, you'll have opportunities and connections that people outside the Society could never dream of. But *much* more important than that – you'll have your unit.

'The people who go through these four trials with you and come out victorious . . . they will become your brothers and sisters. People who will have your back until the day you die. Who will never turn you away, but will care for you as deeply as you care for them. People who would give their life for yours.' Jupiter blinked furiously and rubbed a fist against the side of his face, looking away from her. Morrigan was startled to realise that he was blinking back tears.

She'd never known someone could feel so strongly about their friends. Probably because she'd never had a friend. Not a real one. (Emmett the stuffed rabbit didn't really count.)

An instant family. Brothers and sisters for life.

It made sense to her now. Jupiter carried himself like a king, like he was surrounded by an invisible bubble that protected him from all the bad things in life. He knew there were people in the world – somewhere out there – who loved him. Who would always love him. No matter what.

That was what he was offering her. Like a bowl of hot, meaty stew to a hungry pauper, he held in his hands the thing she most craved.

And suddenly Morrigan's hunger burned. She wanted to join the Society. She wanted brothers and sisters. She wanted it more than she'd ever wanted *anything*.

'How do I win?'

'You just need to trust me. Do you trust me?' Jupiter's face was earnest and open. Morrigan nodded without hesitation. 'Then let me worry about the Show Trial. I'll tell you when you need to start worrying. I *promise*.'

It was an odd feeling to trust a stranger she'd met two days ago. But Morrigan felt somehow it was hard *not* to trust Jupiter. (He had, after all, saved her life.)

She took a fortifying breath before asking the question she dreaded to ask. 'Jupiter. Is my talent . . . my knack . . . is it to do with . . . you know.'

He frowned. 'Hmm?'

'Is being cursed my talent? Do I have a knack for . . . making things go wrong?'

Jupiter looked as if he was about to speak, then snapped his mouth shut. Thirty seconds passed during which he seemed to have a brief but lively argument inside his head.

'Before I answer that question – and yes, I will answer it, don't roll your eyes – I'm going to tell you about *my* talent,' he said finally. 'I have a knack for seeing things.'

'What sort of things?'

'True things.' He shrugged. 'Things that have happened, things that are happening right now. Feelings. Danger. Things that live in the Gossamer.'

'The Gossamer. What's that?'

'Ah. Okay.' Morrigan could almost see Jupiter mentally backtracking as he remembered how little she knew of his world. He spoke rapidly. 'The Gossamer is an invisible, intangible network that . . . hmm. Imagine a *web*. Imagine a vast and delicate spider's web laid over the entire realm, like . . . no. You know what, forget the Gossamer, all you need to know is that I see things other people don't.'

'Secrets?'

He smiled. 'Sometimes.'

'The future?'

'No. I'm not a fortune teller. I'm a Witness. That's the name for it. I don't see the way things *will be*, I see the way things *are*.'

Morrigan gave him a sceptical look. 'Doesn't everybody?'

'You'd be surprised.' He crossed the room in four enormous, lanky-legged strides and picked up the still-warm teapot from the breakfast tray. 'This. Describe it to me.'

'It's a teapot.'

'No, tell me *everything* you know about the teapot, just by looking at it.'

Morrigan frowned. 'It's a green teapot.' Jupiter nodded for her to continue. 'It's a mint-green teapot with little white leaves all over it. It has a big handle and a curvy spout.' Jupiter raised an eyebrow. 'It has . . . matching teacups and saucers . . .'

'Good.' Jupiter poured tea and milk into two cups and handed one to Morrigan. 'Very good. I think you've covered everything you can, which is to say virtually nothing. Shall I have a go?'

'Please,' said Morrigan, stirring a sugar cube into her cup.

He set the teapot down on the tray. 'This teapot was made in a factory in Dusty Junction – that's easy to know because most of the Free State's ceramics are made in Dusty Junction, so it doesn't really count, but I can see it anyway, the factory positively *oozes* out of it – and its first owner bought it seventy-six – no, seventy-seven years ago from a tea shop in Nevermoor's market district. Most of its early years have faded a bit, but it remembers the factory and it remembers the lady in the market district.'

Morrigan screwed up her face. 'How can a teapot *remember* something?'

'It's not a memory like yours or mine. It's more like . . . how shall I put this? There are . . . events and moments in the past that attach themselves to people and things, and cling to them through time simply because they have nowhere else to go. Maybe they eventually fade or get torn away or just die. But some things never die – the especially good memories or the especially bad ones can hang around forever.

'This teapot has soaked in some good memories. The old lady who owned it made tea every afternoon when her sister came to visit. They loved each other very much, the lady and her sister. That sort of thing rarely fades away completely.'

Morrigan eyed him suspiciously. 'You couldn't know all that just by looking at it. You must have known the old lady.'

Jupiter gave her a look of mock outrage. 'Just how old do you think I am? Anyway, hush, I'm not finished. It's been handled by four different people this morning – someone who made the tea, someone who moved the tray, someone who brought it to your room and . . . oh, of course, me. The person who made the tea was cross about something, but the person who brought it upstairs was singing. Someone with a sweet voice; I can see the vibrations.'

He was right about that – Martha had been singing the Morningtide Refrain. But then, he might have spotted her on her way up. Morrigan shrugged, sipping her tea. 'You could make up anything. How would I know the difference?'

'Good point, well made. Which brings me back to my own point.' Jupiter knelt on the floor in front of Morrigan, bringing his head level with hers. 'Let me tell you about *you,* Morrigan Crow.'

His eyes drifted across her face, darting here and there and back again. He studied her as if he were lost in the wilderness and her face was a map that would show him the way home.

'What?' she said, leaning backwards. 'What are you staring at?'

'That haircut.' He smirked. 'The one your stepmother made you get last year.'

'How did you know—?'

'You hated it, didn't you? It was too short and too modern and you grew it out as fast as you could . . . but you hated it with such a passion that it's still hanging around, I can see it.'

Morrigan smoothed her hair down. Jupiter couldn't possibly still see the asymmetrical pixie-like bob with the jagged fringe that Ivy had insisted Morrigan get because her limp, boring, unfashionable hairstyle was 'an embarrassment'. She'd hated that haircut, but it *had* grown out. Now it was limp and boring again, and down past her shoulders.

'You know what else I can see?' he continued, grinning as he picked up her hands and gave them a little shake. 'I can see the pinpricks in your fingers from when you cut up her favourite dress in revenge, sewed the pieces together and hung them as curtains in the living room.' He closed his eyes, and a deep laugh rumbled up from his chest. 'Which is *brilliant*, by the way.'

Morrigan smiled in spite of herself. She *was* proud of those curtains. 'Okay. I believe you. You see things.'

'I see you, Morrigan Crow.' He leaned forward. 'And I'll tell you this: your stepmother was wrong.'

'Wrong about what?' asked Morrigan, but she knew the answer. Her stomach did a little flip.

'She said you were a curse.' Jupiter swallowed and shook his head. 'She said it in anger. She didn't mean it.'

'Of course she meant it.'

He paused, considering that. 'Maybe. But that doesn't make it true. It doesn't make her right.'

Morrigan felt her face colour and looked away, reaching casually for a pastry from the breakfast tray. She ripped a piece off but didn't eat it. 'Forget it.'

'You forget it,' he said. 'You forget it, from this moment on. Do you understand? You are not a curse.'

'Yeah, okay.' Morrigan rolled her eyes and tried to turn away, but Jupiter took her face in his hands and held on fast.

'No, *listen to me.*' His wide blue eyes burned into her black ones. Righteous anger rolled off him like heat from the pavement in summer. 'You asked me if your talent is being cursed? If you have a knack for ruining things? Hear me when I tell you this: *you are not a curse on anyone*, Morrigan Crow. You never have been. And I think you've known that all along.'

Tears stung Morrigan's eyes, threatening to drop. She steeled herself to ask one final question. 'What if I don't get in?'

'You will.'

'But say I don't,' she persisted. 'What then? Will I have to return to the Republic? Will they . . . will they be waiting for me?' Morrigan knew Jupiter understood that she didn't mean her family, but the Hunt of Smoke and Shadow. If she closed her eyes, she could still see them – fiery red eyes in dark, swirling shadow.

'You are going to join the Wundrous Society, Mog,' Jupiter whispered. 'I *promise* you that I will see it done. And I never want to hear a word about this curse nonsense ever again. Promise me.'

She promised.

She believed him.

She felt braver, knowing that he was so staunchly on her side.

But still. Later that day, when Morrigan tried to count all the questions Jupiter had so far avoided answering, she would run out of fingers.

CHAPTER NINE

Wundrous Welcome

'Here it comes. Get ready to jump.'

Jupiter had decided they'd ride the Brolly Rail to the garden party so Morrigan could try out her birthday present. However, the problem with the Brolly Rail was that it never stopped or even slowed down to let passengers on and off. The circular steel frame hung from a cable that ran all over the city in a loop. You were supposed to jump on as it whizzed past the platform and hook your umbrella onto one of the metal rings suspended from the frame above, holding on for dear life, legs dangling in the air, until you reached your destination.

'Remember, Mog,' said Jupiter as they watched the circular frame speed towards them. 'When it's time to get off, just pull the lever to release your brolly. Oh, and when you land, try to aim for a soft bit of ground.' Morrigan's apprehension must have shown, because Jupiter added, 'You'll be fine. I've only broken a leg on this thing once. Twice, max. Ready . . . *Go!*'

They leapt for the rail, Morrigan holding so tight to her umbrella she thought she might crush it. The bone-shaking terror she'd felt watching the platform speed towards her was washed away by a wave of adrenaline, and she let out a triumphant shout as they hooked onto the rail. Jupiter grinned, throwing his head back to enjoy the ride. They zoomed through the Deucalion's neighbourhood and into the cobbled streets of Old Town, crisp spring air biting at Morrigan's face and stinging her eyes, and finally jumped off at their destination – both, miraculously, landing on their feet. Not a broken leg between them.

The Wundrous Society campus was surrounded by high brick walls. There was a stern security guard checking names against a list, but she recognised Jupiter immediately and waved the pair of them through, smiling.

Something changed when they stepped through the gates. It was as if everything was slightly different, as if the air itself had shifted. Morrigan breathed in deeply. The air smelled of honeysuckles and roses, and the sun felt warmer on her skin. It was strange, she thought. Outside the gates the sky hadn't looked quite as blue, and the flowers were still only tiny buds, the barest hint of spring's arrival.

Jupiter said something that sounded like 'one-sock weather'.

'One sock . . . Sorry, what?' asked Morrigan, puzzled.

'*W-U-N-S-O-C*: Wunsoc. Short for *WUN*drous *SOC*iety – it's what we call the campus. Inside the walls of Wunsoc, the weather's a bit . . . more.'

'A bit more what?'

'Just a bit *more*. More of whatever it's like in the rest of Nevermoor. Wunsoc lives in its own little climate bubble. Today it's a bit warmer, a bit more sunny, a bit more spring-like. Lucky us.' He nabbed a sprig of cherry blossom from a branch in passing and secured it in his buttonhole. 'Double-edged sword, though. In winter it's a bit more windy, a bit more frozen and a bit more miserable.'

The driveway stretching up to the main building was lined with gas lamps and – out of place amongst the colourful flowerbeds and pink cherry blossoms – two rows of dead, starkly black trees, untouched by the Wunsoc weather phenomenon.

'What about those?' Morrigan asked, pointing.

'Nah, they haven't flowered in Ages. Fireblossom trees – lovely, once upon a time, but the whole species is extinct, and impossible to chop down. Bit of a sore spot with the gardeners, so don't say anything – we all just pretend they're very ugly statues.'

Patrons and their candidates hurried along, chatting and laughing as if they were off to a birthday party, while Morrigan was twisted up in one big, nervous knot.

She couldn't have felt more distant from them if she'd been walking on the moon.

The main building on campus, signposted PROUDFOOT HOUSE, was five storeys of cheerful red brick covered with climbing vines of ivy. Candidates weren't allowed inside Proudfoot House today, but the gardens were glorious; the picture of a spring afternoon, filled with people in light linen suits and pastel dresses. Jupiter had allowed Morrigan to choose her own outfit – a black dress with silver buttons, which Dame Chanda declared 'smart, but utterly lacking in spectacle'. Morrigan thought Jupiter's lemon-yellow suit and lavender shoes provided enough spectacle for both of them.

A string quartet played on the steps of a sweeping terrace above the lawn. Inside a white marquee there was a table piled high with cream cakes, pies and towering, wobbly jelly sculptures, but Morrigan couldn't think of eating. It felt like mice were gnawing her stomach from the inside.

As they weaved through the crowd, Morrigan noticed people turning to look at them with expressions ranging from polite surprise to open-mouthed shock.

'Why is everyone looking at us?'

'They're looking at you because you're with me.' He waved merrily at a pair of women who were staring. 'And they're looking at me because I'm very handsome.'

The candidates were mostly huddled in groups. Morrigan edged closer to Jupiter.

'They won't bite,' he said, as if reading her mind. 'Well, most of them won't. Avoid the dog-faced boy over by that tree; he mightn't have had all his injections yet.'

There was indeed a dog-faced boy loitering near one of the large ferns that dotted the lawn. There was also a boy with arms twice the length they ought to have been, and a girl with metres and metres of glossy black hair that she'd piled up in braids and was pulling behind her in a little wagon.

'I don't think it's the year for interesting physical features, unluckily for them,' Jupiter mused. 'Nobody's quite gotten over the girl with sledgehammer hands a few years back. Huge repair bill after she graduated. I believe she's a professional wrestler now.'

Jupiter walked Morrigan around the garden paths, making comments under his breath.

'Baz Charlton,' he murmured, nodding discreetly towards a long-haired man in leather trousers and a wrinkled suit jacket. 'Odious man. Avoid him like the pox.'

A group of girls stood near Baz Charlton. One of them, with thick chestnut hair and a sparkly blue dress, glanced at Morrigan and whispered to her friends. They turned to stare. Morrigan smiled forcefully, remembering what Dame Chanda had said about first impressions, and the girls laughed. Morrigan wondered if this was a good sign.

Jupiter took two glasses of purple punch from a passing waiter and handed one to her. She peeked inside; there were pink things floating in it. No – *wriggling* in it. There were pink, squishy, wriggling things in her purple punch.

'They're supposed to wriggle,' said Jupiter, noticing her look of disgust. 'Wriggly things taste better.'

Morrigan took a hesitant sip. It was delicious – an explosion of sweet, rosy light. She was about to admit as much when the man in leather trousers appeared. He slapped Jupiter on the back and threw a heavy arm around his shoulders.

'North! North, me old mate,' he slurred. 'Lost the plot, have you, North? Hamish over there tells me you've gone and bid on a child. They not paying you enough at the League of Explorers? Or have you decided to hang up your compass and let someone else be the big adventurer? Quiet life now, is it?'

The man guffawed into his brandy. Jupiter grimaced, his nose crinkling unpleasantly.

'Afternoon, Baz,' he said, with a very small amount of forced politeness.

'This her, is it?' Baz squinted down at Morrigan. 'Famous Jupiter North's first ever candidate. Won't the tabloids be aflutter.'

He waited for Jupiter to introduce him, but Jupiter did not.

'Charlton. Baz Charlton,' the man finally said. He gestured grandly to himself, waiting for a spark of recognition from Morrigan. When no spark came, his face soured. 'What's your name, girl?'

Morrigan's eyes met Jupiter's. He nodded. 'Morrigan Crow.'

'Bit miserable-looking, North, if you ask me,' Mr Charlton whispered loudly into Jupiter's ear, ignoring her altogether. Morrigan bristled. Was she supposed to walk around constantly smiling like an idiot? 'She foreign? Where'd you find her?'

'Nunya.'

'Nunya? Never heard of it.' Baz leaned in close, his eyes gleaming, and whispered conspiratorially, 'That in the Republic, is it? Smuggled her in, did you? Go on, tell your old friend Baz.'

'Yes,' said Jupiter. 'A town called Nunya Business, in the Keep-Your-Nose-Out Republic.'

Baz Charlton chuckled humourlessly, looking disappointed. 'Oh, very clever. What's her knack, then?'

'Also nunya,' said Jupiter, extricating himself smoothly from the man's grip.

'Playing that game, are we? Fine, fine. Makes no difference. You know me, I don't push.' He looked Morrigan up and down. 'Dancer? No, legs aren't long enough. She's not a boffin either, not with that vacant look in her eyes.' He waved a hand in front of her face. Morrigan was tempted to slap it away. 'One of the arcane arts, perhaps. Sorceress? Oracle?'

'I thought you said it made no difference,' said Jupiter. He sounded bored. 'Where's your parade of candidates? Big haul this year?'

'Only eight, North, only eight. Three girls,' Mr Charlton said, waving vaguely towards the group who had laughed at Morrigan earlier. He sniffed and took a large swig of brandy. 'And the boys are around somewhere. Small group, but not a loser among 'em. Terrific pickings this year. That one's the real star, though. Noelle Devereaux. Don't want to give too much away, but – *voice of an angel*. Never met a stronger candidate. She'll rank number one, you mark my words.'

Morrigan watched the girl and her friends. Pretty, well-dressed Noelle was talking nonstop while the other girls listened avidly. She was poised and confident, with an easy smile. Morrigan couldn't help feeling a little jealous. Why *wouldn't* the Wundrous Society want someone like Noelle Devereaux?

'Congratulations,' Jupiter said blandly.

'But this one, North,' continued Mr Charlton, waving a hand at Morrigan. 'I don't understand. What's the appeal? I mean, those *eyes*, North, those awful black eyes. The Elders don't go for the mean-looking ones. This one would as soon kill you as look at—'

He was cut off by a sharp look from Jupiter, his mouth left hanging open.

'Consider your next words carefully, Mr Charlton,' Jupiter said in the low, cold voice that Morrigan had heard from him only once before, on Eventide at Crow Manor. She shivered.

Baz Charlton closed his mouth. Jupiter stepped aside, releasing the long-haired man from his gaze and allowing him to stumble away. He sighed as he smoothed down his yellow suit and gave Morrigan's shoulder a quick squeeze. 'Told you. Odious man. Pay no attention.'

Morrigan took a sip of punch, Mr Charlton's words ringing in her ears. *The Elders don't go for the mean-looking ones.*

'Baz is what we call a Spaghetti Patron,' Jupiter explained. He continued to guide Morrigan through the garden, waving to people here and there. 'He scours the Free State for potential candidates every year and enters about a dozen into the trials, regardless of whether they're truly ready, just to increase his chances of a placement. Like throwing strands of spaghetti against a wall and hoping one sticks, you see?'

'Does it work?' Morrigan asked.

'Maddeningly often.' He steered Morrigan left to avoid a boisterous group of teenagers who were trying to get his attention. 'Ah, here's young Nan.'

A towering, broad-shouldered woman approached and shook his hand. 'Captain North, in the flesh! I'd heard rumours you were taking a candidate, but I never believed it. "Jupiter North," I said, "not on your nelly." Here you are, though, candidate and all. Hello there,' she finished, with a smile at Morrigan.

'Nancy Dawson, meet Morrigan Crow.' Jupiter nodded at Morrigan, and she shook Nan's proffered hand. She was younger than Jupiter, with an earnest, dimpled smile that made her burly frame less intimidating.

'Pleasure, Miss Crow. I'd like to introduce my own candidate, Hawthorne, but he disappeared soon's we arrived. Probably setting something on fire.' Nan rolled her eyes, but she looked pleased. 'It's not his official knack, trouble-making, but it's a close second.'

'What's his official knack?' Morrigan asked. Jupiter's gaze flicked to hers and his eyes narrowed slightly. She mumbled under her breath, 'What? Is that a rude question?'

Nan chuckled. 'I don't mind. Don't go for all that secret squirrel rubbish, me.' She drew herself up. 'I'm proud as punch to tell you that Hawthorne Swift is, in my humble opinion, the finest dragonrider in Nevermoor's junior league.'

'Ah, of course.' Jupiter grinned. 'What else? A fine choice of candidate for the five-time Dragonriding Champion of the Free State.'

Nan's smile faltered, but only for half a second. 'Former champion,' she corrected. She tapped her right leg, and Morrigan was surprised to hear a hollow knock. 'Won't be competing again soon, not with this old thing.'

'Is that a false leg?' asked Morrigan. It took all her self-restraint not to reach out and tap it herself. Jupiter cleared his throat loudly, but Nan didn't seem bothered.

'Aye. A marvel of modern medicine and engineering, that is: cedar, Wunder and steel.' She lifted her trouser leg to reveal a limb of wood and metal that somehow, miraculously, seemed to move and flex almost like the muscles and tendons of a real leg, as though the wood itself were alive. 'That's good old-fashioned Wun ingenuity, Miss Crow. You wouldn't believe the things they can do at the Wundrous Society Hospital. Proper miracle workers, them.'

'What happened to the real leg?'

'Chomped off and swallowed by my opponent's dragon in the annual tournament two summers ago. Ugly, vicious thing he was.' She took a sip of wriggly punch. 'His dragon weren't very nice either.'

Morrigan and Jupiter laughed.

'Still, mustn't grumble.' Nan's face broke into a bright, sincere smile. 'I'm coaching full-time for the junior league now. It's steady work, and I couldn't ask for a better student than young Swift. He's been riding since he could walk, and he'll make a first-rate competitor when he's old enough to enter the tournament. If he decides to give up his lifelong commitment to being a boofhead.'

There was a sudden tinkling sound as patrons all around began gently flicking the rims of their glasses. The string quartet stopped playing. Three people – or rather, Morrigan noted with some confusion, one man, one woman and one shaggy bull in a waistcoat – had assembled on the balcony.

'That's our newest High Council of Elders,' Jupiter whispered to Morrigan. 'At the end of every Age, the Society elects three members to guide and govern us for the next Age. They're the best and most brilliant of us.'

'Okay, but why is one of them a bu—'

'Shh, listen.'

A reverent hush descended as one of the Elders approached a microphone stand. A thin, stooped woman with wispy grey hair, she seemed unbalanced by the enormous flowery hat on her head. Morrigan worried for a moment that she might topple over the balcony onto her face. One of the other Elders stepped forward to steady her, but the old woman slapped his hands away, clearing her throat imperiously.

'As many of you will know,' she began, 'I am Elder Gregoria Quinn. Beside me are Elder Helix Wong and Elder Alioth Saga.' She gestured first to the man, and then the bull. 'We, the High Council of Elders, would like to welcome you to Proudfoot House on this important day. I know that for all of you children this is your first real experience of the Wundrous Society. And for most of you, it will be your last.'

Morrigan winced at those stark words, and she wasn't the only one. All around her, candidates shot furtive looks at their patrons, seeking reassurance. Could they possibly be as nervous as she was? Morrigan doubted it. What if it *was* her last time here? Jupiter still hadn't said what would happen if she failed the trials.

'My esteemed colleagues and I,' Elder Quinn continued, 'wish to thank you, young candidates, for your bravery, optimism and trust. To face the challenges you are about to face, with no promise of a place in the Society at the end of it all . . . That takes no small amount of gumption. We applaud you.'

She paused to beam at the guests, and she and Elder Wong, a grey-bearded man with colourful tattoos covering his arms and neck, applauded enthusiastically. The bull, Elder Saga, stamped his hooves. Morrigan took a nervous sip of punch; her mouth had gone dry.

'I've been told our candidates this year number more than five hundred! With so many talented young people in our midst, I feel certain we will find nine new Society members who will impress us, make us proud and make us glad to know them for the rest of their lives.'

Morrigan looked at Jupiter, but he was watching the old lady with rapt attention.

Nine? They were only accepting *nine* new members? From *more than five hundred* candidates? Jupiter had failed to mention that small detail.

Her heart sank. She didn't have a hope. How could she possibly compete with Noelle, who had the voice of an angel, or Hawthorne, who'd been riding dragons since he could walk? Even the dog-faced boy stood a better chance than she did. At least he had a gimmick! Morrigan didn't know what she had, but she strongly suspected it was a big fat nothing.

'In the months to come you will be put to the test –
physically and mentally – beginning with the Book Trial at
the end of spring,' continued Elder Quinn. She paused to
look sternly over her glasses. 'We suggest you use your time
not only to make new friends and form valuable alliances
with your fellow candidates, but also to build strength of
mind in preparation for what lies ahead.

'Joining the Wundrous Society is a privilege granted to
the few and the special. Among our members are many
of the Free State's supreme thinkers, leaders, performers,
explorers, inventors, scientists, sorcerers, artists and athletes.
We are the special ones. We are the great ones. And there are
times when some of us are called upon to do great things,
to protect these Seven Pockets against those who would do
us harm. Against those who would seek to take away our
freedom, and our lives.'

Murmurs rippled through the crowd. A boy standing
nearby whispered '*The Wundersmith*', and the handful of
children who were close enough to hear him all looked
stricken.

The Wundersmith again, thought Morrigan. Whoever or
whatever he was, it seemed the spectre of the Wundersmith
loomed so large over Nevermoor that he needn't even be
mentioned by name to strike fear in people's hearts. Perhaps
it was because she was a Free State outsider, but Morrigan

couldn't help thinking it was a bit silly, given that Jupiter had said he hadn't been seen for over a hundred years.

'But,' continued Elder Quinn more brightly, 'it must be said that the benefits of joining our ranks rather outweigh the challenges.' There was a ripple of knowing laughter across the garden. Elder Quinn smiled and waited for silence before continuing. 'Children, look at your patrons. Look around you, at the members of our Wundrous family, and your fellow candidates.

'You all have one thing in common. There is something in you that makes you different. A gift that separates you from your peers, from your friends. Even from your own family.'

Morrigan swallowed. There were hundreds of people hanging on Elder Quinn's every word. But somehow, she felt the old woman was speaking only to her.

'I know from experience, that can be a lonely path to tread. Oh! How I wish we could fold each and every one of you under our wings. But to the nine of you who join us at the end of the year, I promise this: a place to belong. A family. And friendships to last a lifetime.

'From today, you are official participants in the trials for Unit 919 of the Wundrous Society. The road will be long and difficult, but perhaps – just perhaps – something wonderful awaits you at the end of it. Good luck.'

Morrigan clapped hard, along with everyone else. *Family. Belonging. Friendships to last a lifetime.* Were Elder Quinn and Jupiter reading from the same brochure? Or had they peered into her heart and read a wish list she'd never known was there?

For the first time, the Wundrous Society felt *real* to Morrigan.

After a round of applause, most of the patrons and candidates returned to the dessert buffet. Jupiter hung back, leaning down to speak in Morrigan's ear.

'I'm going to catch up with some old friends,' he said. 'You should go make some new ones.'

He twirled her around and gave her a gentle shove towards a group of children wandering around the other side of Proudfoot House.

You can do this, Morrigan thought, galvanised by Elder Quinn's extravagant promises. *Family. Belonging. Friendship.*

She lifted her chin in the air and followed the other children, practising in her head what she would say. Was it best to start with a joke? Or perhaps a more direct approach? Could she simply say, 'My name's Morrigan, would you like to be my friend?' Did people actually do that?

At the front of Proudfoot House the children were milling on the steps. Baz Charlton's candidate, Noelle, was addressing a plump, sweet-faced girl with rosy cheeks.

'So you're a nun, Anna?' said Noelle.

'No, *I'm* not a nun. I live with nuns – the Sisters of Serenity.' The girl's cheeks turned even rosier. 'And it's Anah, not Anna.'

Noelle looked to her friends with barely stifled laughter. 'Actual nuns? Nuns that dress like penguins?'

'No, no.' Anah shook her head, and golden ringlets danced around her face, settling prettily on her shoulders. Noelle twitched. Her hand shot straight up to her own lustrous, long hair, a lock of which she began curling feverishly around one finger. 'They mostly wear normal clothes. Black and white habits are only for Sunday chapel.'

'Oh, they only dress like penguins on *Sunday*,' said Noelle. She laughed, looking around to see who else found her hilarious. A few others joined in, but the tall, wiry girl with dark brown skin standing next to her seemed to find it funniest. She was doubled over with giggles, covering her mouth with both hands, her long black braid flipped over one shoulder. 'And the other days they just wear cheap, ugly dresses, like yours? Did the penguins give that dress to you when you became a nun?'

Anah's blush had crept across her entire face. Morrigan cringed in sympathy. Had Anah been trying to make friends too? Had she approached Noelle, just as Morrigan had intended to do, only to be teased in front of a bunch of strangers? Risky business, this friend-making thing.

'I'm *not* a nun,' insisted Anah. Her chin wobbled. 'Not that there's anything *wrong* with being a nun,' she added quietly.

Noelle cocked her head to one side, radiating false sympathy. 'But that *is* something a nun would say, isn't it?'

'Oh, shut up,' Morrigan snapped.

Everyone turned to look at her with mild surprise. She was a bit surprised herself.

Noelle's top lip curled. 'What did you say?'

'You heard me,' Morrigan said, raising her voice a little. 'Leave her alone.'

'Are you from the convent too?' Noelle said, raising her eyebrows at Morrigan's black dress. 'Don't you penguins have a curfew? Why don't you waddle off?' Her friend snorted in a most unladylike fashion.

Morrigan was beginning to miss the old days in Jackalfax, when everybody had been terrified by her mere presence. She thought of Jupiter and drew back her shoulders, saying in a voice as low and cold as she could muster, 'Consider your next words carefully.'

Silence. And then—

'*Ha!*' Noelle exploded with laughter, followed by her friend and all the other candidates. As they fell over themselves laughing, Morrigan realised how utterly unterrifying she had become. She didn't know if she was pleased or disappointed.

The laughter died down. Noelle glared at Morrigan. Anah, meanwhile, had taken the opportunity as a divine reprieve and disappeared. *You're welcome*, Morrigan thought, feeling a tiny bit resentful.

'It's rude to eavesdrop.' Noelle put her hands on her hips. 'But I wouldn't expect good manners from an illegal.'

'A what?'

'My patron says your patron smuggled you into the Free State. He says nobody's ever heard of you before so you must be from the Republic. Do you know that's against the law? You belong in jail.'

Morrigan frowned. Was she in the Free State illegally? She wasn't stupid . . . she knew Jupiter had done something funny at border control, that holding up a chocolate wrapper and a used tissue as their 'papers' definitely wasn't normal procedure.

But did that mean he'd smuggled her in? Were they *criminals*?

'You don't know what you're talking about,' Morrigan said, arranging her face into a convincing sneer. 'And your patron is an odious man.'

Noelle faltered, blinking momentarily. 'Is that your knack? Using big words? I thought it must be wearing horrible clothes or being as ugly as a gutter rat. You're obviously *very* good at those two—*Ugh!*'

An enormous green jelly sculpture had fallen from the sky and plopped straight down onto Noelle's head. The sticky green ooze trickled down her face and hair and sparkly dress. She looked like she'd been dunked in radio-active sewage.

'Want some dessert, Noelle?' called a voice from above. There was a boy dangling from a window by one hand. He held an empty platter in the other and waved it at the children below, grinning happily.

Noelle shook with anger. Her chest heaved in great gasping breaths.

'You – I'm – you'll never – you are in *so* much—*Ugh! Mr Charlton!*' She stormed down the front steps in search of her patron, the other children close behind, her friend with the braided hair still giggling.

The boy landed with a thud next to Morrigan. He flicked his head back, pushing a mop of thick brown curls out of his eyes, and adjusted his oversized jumper – a huge blue knitted thing with a glittery cat picture on the front. The cat had a pink ribbon sewn onto its head and a jingling silver bell attached to the collar. Morrigan wondered what in the world had possessed him to wear it.

'I liked that thing you did too. You know, "Consider your next words carefully" and all that,' he said, mimicking her low, angry voice. 'But I reckon the only language some people understand is the language of the surprise jelly attack.'

She didn't know how to respond to this unusual advice. The boy nodded sagely and they stood in silence for a few moments. Morrigan couldn't stop staring at his jumper.

'D'you like it?' he said, looking down at his chest. 'My mum bet me I wouldn't wear it today. She bought it from a catalogue. She gets loads of them for me, it's called the Ugly Jumper Company. She's pretty funny.'

'What do you get?'

'For what?'

'For winning the bet.'

'I get to wear the jumper.' He frowned, looking genuinely confused for a moment until his face lit up with some new idea. 'Hey – could you help me with something?'

Twenty minutes later they returned to the garden party, deep in conversation and carrying a heavy wooden barrel between them. They'd dragged it from an empty corner of the grounds all the way around Proudfoot House to the back lawn.

The boy was pretty strong for somebody so gangly, Morrigan thought. Despite his knobbly legs and skinny arms, he was carrying most of the weight.

'It's nice, yeah,' he puffed. 'All the flowers and statues and stuff. But I'm telling you – massive vermin problem. My patron knows the groundskeeper. Reckons they get all sorts. Mice, rats, even snakes. They've just had a toad infestation. Only so many the Sorcery Department can use in one week, the groundskeeper says.'

'I don't care,' said Morrigan, puffing with the effort of dragging the barrel up the steps, past the bemused players in the string quartet. 'Proudfoot House is still the nicest place I've ever seen. Except for the Deucalion.'

'You've got to let me visit,' he enthused. He'd been excited to learn that Morrigan actually *lived* in a hotel. 'Do you order room service every day? I would order room service every single day. Lobster for breakfast and pudding for dinner. Do they leave chocolates on your pillow? My dad says all the fancy hotels leave chocolates on your pillow. Does it really have its own smoking parlour? And a dwarf vampire?'

'Vampire dwarf,' she corrected.

'Wow. Do you think I could come this weekend?'

'I'll ask Jupiter. What's in this, by the way? It's so heavy.'

They'd reached the top of the steps and dropped the barrel at its final destination – the balcony railing.

The boy flicked his hair out of his eyes and grinned. He opened the barrel and, without a word, tipped it over the balcony. Dozens of slimy brown toads poured out like a disgusting waterfall and spilled in a wide arc across the pavement, croaking and leaping madly around the feet of the now screaming party guests.

'Told you. Massive vermin problem.'

Morrigan's eyes widened. She'd just helped to smuggle toads into a garden party. A slightly hysterical laugh escaped her; this probably wasn't the sort of first impression Dame Chanda had in mind.

The garden below was in chaos. People were falling over each other in their desperation to get away from the toads. Somebody shouted for a servant. A table was knocked over and a punch bowl shattered on the ground, the purple liquid spilling out and splashing Elder Wong.

Morrigan and the boy sidled away from the crime scene, then broke into a run. They made it down the balcony steps and around the side of Proudfoot House before doubling over, breathless with laughter.

'That—' Morrigan panted and pressed one hand to a stitch in her side. 'That was—'

'Outstanding. I know. What's your name, by the way?'

'Morrigan,' she said, holding her hand out. 'What's—'

'Enjoying yourselves?' Jupiter wandered over with a placid smile, ignoring the stream of servants rushing past with nets and brooms.

Morrigan chewed the side of her mouth guiltily. 'A bit.'

Nan Dawson ran up behind him. 'Captain North, have you seen—' She stopped short at the sight of Morrigan's new friend giggling helplessly. Her face turned red. *'Hawthorne Swift!'*

The boy gave his patron a sheepish grin.

'Sorry, Nan.' He did not sound remotely sorry. 'Couldn't waste a perfectly good barrel of toads.'

They took a carriage home, and there was silence for most of the journey. Finally, as they turned onto Humdinger Avenue, Jupiter spoke.

'You made a friend.'

'I think so.'

'Anything else of interest?'

Morrigan thought for a moment. 'I think I made an enemy too.'

'I didn't make my first proper enemy until I was twelve.' He sounded impressed.

'Maybe that's my knack?'

Jupiter chuckled.

Instead of taking them to the Hotel Deucalion's grand forecourt, the carriage stopped at the entrance to Caddisfly Alley. Jupiter paid the driver, and he and Morrigan made their way through the twisting narrow backstreet to the modest wooden door of the service entrance. Before he could open it, she put a hand on his arm.

'I'm here illegally, aren't I?'

Jupiter chewed the side of his mouth. 'A bit.'

'So . . . I don't have a visa.'

'Not exactly.'

'Not exactly, or not at all?'

'Not at all.'

'Oh.' Morrigan thought about that for a moment, trying to find the best way to ask her next question. 'If I don't . . . if they don't let me in, you know, to the – to the Society . . .'

'Yes?' he prompted.

She drew in a deep breath. 'Can I stay anyway? Here at the Deucalion, with you?' When Jupiter said nothing, she rushed ahead. 'Not as a guest! I meant you could give me a job. You wouldn't even have to pay me or anything. I could run errands for Kedgeree, or dust the silverware for Fen—'

Jupiter laughed loudly at that idea, pushing through the arched wooden door into the gaslit hallway with its faint smell of damp. 'Oh, I'm sure you'd *love* working for cranky old Fen. But I suspect the Federation of Nevermoorian Hoteliers frowns on child labour.'

'Promise you'll think about it?'

'Only if you promise you'll stop thinking about *not* getting into the Society.'

'But if I *don't* get in—'

'We'll blow up that bridge when we come to it.'

Morrigan sighed. *Just give me a straight answer*, she thought. But she said no more.

Jupiter ushered Morrigan down the hall ahead of him. 'Now. Tell me more about your resourceful new friend. Where in the Seven Pockets did he find a barrel full of toads?'

CHAPTER TEN

Illegal

Room 85 on the fourth floor was slowly becoming Morrigan's bedroom. Every few days she noticed something new and brilliant, something she loved instantly. Like the mermaid bookends that showed up on her shelf one day, or the black leather armchair shaped like an octopus that curled its tentacles around her while she read.

One night several weeks earlier, the bed had changed from a plain white headboard to an ornate wrought-iron frame while she slept in it. The Deucalion obviously thought it had made a mistake, though, because two days later she woke up swinging in a hammock.

Her favourite thing of all was a small framed painting of a bright green jelly sculpture, which hung above the toilet.

At first she thought it was Jupiter or Fen changing things in secret, testing her gullibility. Until once, in the middle of the night, she stepped into her bathroom for a drink of water only to see the bathtub growing four talon-shaped silver feet before her eyes.

Strangest of all, the size and shape of the room were changing. Where once was a single square window, she now had three arched ones. One day her bathroom was the size of a ballroom and had a tub like a swimming pool. The next day it was no bigger than a closet.

Soon there were window boxes full of red flowers, a skeleton hat stand wearing a grey fedora in her size, and thick vines of ivy twisting halfway up a stone fireplace – and for the first time ever, Morrigan Crow felt that she was in exactly the right place.

Midway through spring, a man in a mud-brown uniform came to the Hotel Deucalion. His moustache curled all the way to his cheekbones, and the light glinted off a silver badge on his chest. He stood at the concierge desk, his hands stiffly behind his back, appraising the hotel foyer with undisguised contempt.

Kedgeree had fetched Jupiter and Morrigan from the Smoking Parlour, where they sat in a cloud of forest-green vapour (rosemary smoke: for sharpening the mind), playing a game of cards. Neither was certain of the rules, but Frank whispered advice in Morrigan's ear, and Dame Chanda did the same for Jupiter, and every now and then someone would yell '*Huzzah!*' and the others would scowl or throw something, and all things considered Morrigan thought it was a pleasant way to spend an afternoon.

They both felt a bit put out when Kedgeree insisted they hurry to the foyer, and Morrigan was even more annoyed when she saw the moustachioed man sneer disapprovingly at the small, misshapen chandelier, which was still regrowing.

Rude, she thought. *It's not ready yet!*

The chandelier was creeping back to health day by day, but it still had a long way to go. At this stage it was impossible to see what form it would take. Fenestra had opened a betting pool. Frank swore up and down it would be a magnificent peacock, but Morrigan was still hopeful it might come back as the same pink sailing ship Jupiter had loved.

'What's the Stink doing here?' Jupiter murmured to Kedgeree, who shrugged as he scooted off behind the concierge desk.

'Who's the Stink?' whispered Morrigan.

'Ooh – ah, I meant the Nevermoor City Police Force,' Jupiter said under his breath. 'We, er – probably shouldn't call it the Stink. Not to his face. Actually, just let me do the talking.'

Jupiter approached the man and shook his hand amiably. 'Good afternoon, Officer. Welcome to the Hotel Deucalion. Checking in?'

The man scoffed. 'Not likely. You're the proprietor, correct?'

'Jupiter North. How do you do?'

'Captain Jupiter Amantius North,' said the man, consulting a notebook. 'Esteemed member of the Wundrous Society, the League of Explorers and the Federation of Nevermoorian Hoteliers. Secretary of the Wunimal Rights Commission, volunteer bookfighter for the Gobleian Library and chairman of the Charitable Trust for Decommissioned Robot Butlers. Discoverer of seventeen previously undocumented realms and *Snazzy Man Magazine*'s Snazzy Man of the Year four years running. Very impressive, Captain. Anything I've missed?'

'I also give tap-dancing lessons to underprivileged hoodlums, and I'm on the judging panel for the annual blackberry pie bake-off at the Nevermoor Maximum Security Rehabilitation Centre for the Criminally Insane.'

Morrigan laughed out loud at that, although she wasn't sure whether Jupiter was joking.

'Well, aren't you just a saint?'

'I'm only in it for the pie.' He winked at Morrigan.

The officer sneered. 'Think you're funny?'

'I often do think that, yes. Is there something I can help you with, Inspector?' Morrigan followed Jupiter's gaze to the man's badge, which read INSPECTOR HAROLD FLINTLOCK.

Inspector Flintlock sucked in his paunch and tried to look down his nose at Jupiter, which was difficult as Jupiter was several inches taller than him. 'I'm here acting on an anonymous tip-off. One of your Wundrous pals has dobbed you in, North, for harbouring an illegal refugee. That's big trouble, that is.'

Jupiter smiled serenely. 'It certainly would be big trouble, if it were true.'

'You're entering a candidate for the Wundrous Society trials this year, is that correct?'

'Correct.'

'And this is the candidate, is it?'

'Her name is Morrigan Crow.'

Inspector Flintlock narrowed his eyes at Morrigan and brought his face down close to hers. 'And where exactly are you from, Morrigan Crow?'

'Nunya,' replied Morrigan.

Jupiter tried to turn his snort of laughter into a cough. 'She meant to say she's from the Seventh Pocket of the Free State, Inspector. She just . . . pronounces it funny.'

Morrigan glanced at her patron. He had the same cool,

confident air as when he'd spoken to the border control guard on her first day in Nevermoor.

Inspector Flintlock slapped his notebook in the palm of his hand. 'Now listen here, North. The Free State has strict border laws, and if you're harbouring an illegal refugee you're breaking about twenty-eight of them. You're in a lot of trouble here, sonny. Illegals are a plague, and it's my solemn duty to guard the borders of Nevermoor and protect its true citizens from Republic scum trying to weasel their way into the Free State.'

Jupiter turned serious. 'A noble and valiant cause, I'm sure,' he said quietly. 'Protecting the Free State from those most in need of its help.'

Flintlock scoffed, smoothing his oily moustache. 'I know your type. You bleeding hearts, you'd let anything in here if we gave you half a chance. But I think you might find this scummy illegal of yours is more trouble than she's worth.'

Jupiter looked him dead in the eye. 'Don't call her that.'

A chill crept up Morrigan's spine. She recognised the cold wrath in Jupiter's voice, the ice in his hard blue eyes. Flintlock, however, wasn't so quick to catch on.

'I'll call her what she is, which is a dirty, stinking, rotten *illegal*. You can't fool me, North. Either hand over her papers – her *legitimate* citizenship papers – or hand yourself over for arrest, and this filthy illegal for immediate deportation!'

The inspector's words echoed in the lobby, bouncing off the high ceilings. A few of the staff wandered in, drawn by Flintlock's raised voice.

'Everything all right here, Captain North?' asked Kedgeree, leaving the concierge desk to stand beside them with Martha.

'What a terrible ruckus,' said Dame Chanda. She put her arm around Morrigan and glared at Flintlock.

'Did somebody call for security?' Fenestra said from the staircase, where she sat casually cleaning her enormous claws as if preparing for a meal.

'Shall I bite his kneecaps, Jove?' asked Frank the vampire dwarf, sticking his head through Jupiter's legs.

'That won't be necessary. Everything's fine, thank you. You can all go.' They all reluctantly left, except for Fen, who stayed just where she was. Jupiter was silent for some time, while Flintlock shot nervous looks in the Magnificat's direction.

When Jupiter finally spoke, it was in a quiet, measured voice. 'You have no right to demand the papers of someone who falls under the jurisdiction of the Wundrous Society, Flintlock. We deal with our own lawbreakers.'

'She's not *in* the Society—'

'You need to brush up on your Wun Law handbook, Flinty. Article ninety-seven, clause F: "A child who is participating in the entrance trials for the Wundrous Society shall for all legal purposes be considered a member of the Wundrous Society for the duration of said trials or until he or she is removed from the trial process." *All* legal purposes. That means she's already ours.'

A feeling of righteous relief coursed through Morrigan. *Already ours.* She glared up at Flintlock, emboldened by the knowledge that Wundrous Society law was on her side.

Flintlock's face coloured bright red, then purple, and finally white, contorting with rage. His moustache quivered. 'For now. She's yours for now, North. But as soon as she fails the trials I'll be wanting to see those *papers* of hers.' He stroked his moustache and straightened his mud-brown uniform, looking down at Morrigan as if she were something disgusting on the bottom of his shoe. 'She'll be back to her filthy Republic before you can say please-Inspector-have-pity. And you, my friend, will be in so much trouble that even your precious Society won't be able to help you.'

Flintlock marched out of the Deucalion's foyer, down the steps of the forecourt, and was gone. Morrigan turned to Jupiter, who looked as tense as she'd ever seen him.

'Can they really kick me out?' she asked, a lump forming in her throat. She thought of the Hunt of Smoke and Shadow, of its black shapeless form looming in the darkness.

The back of her neck felt prickly and cold. 'What happens if I have to leave Nevermoor?'

'Don't be silly, Mog,' Jupiter said bracingly. 'That's never going to happen.'

He left the foyer without looking at her.

When Morrigan went to bed that night, her hammock had changed again, this time into a wooden bed frame with stars and moons carved into the legs. She slept restlessly and dreamed of the Show Trial. In her dream she stood silently before the Elders, unable to speak, until finally she was dragged away by the Stink and handed over to the Hunt while the audience jeered and booed.

By morning, her bed was a futon. Perhaps the Deucalion hadn't made up its mind about her after all.

CHAPTER ELEVEN
The Book Trial

'Wassyoornackthen?' said Hawthorne through a mouthful of cheese toastie.

Jupiter had allowed Morrigan's new friend to visit her at the Hotel Deucalion on the condition that he help her study for the upcoming Book Trial. So far they hadn't studied anything but the Deucalion itself. Hawthorne especially loved the Smoking Parlour (chocolate smoke this afternoon: to promote emotional well-being), the Rain Room (though he hadn't brought any wellies and his trousers were now soaked to his knees) and the theatre. Actually, not the theatre itself but rather the dressing room backstage. The walls were lined with hanging costumes, and each one came with an accent and a funny walk that took ages to fade. Hawthorne was still skipping down the corridors half an hour after he'd taken off his Goldilocks costume.

Now they sat at a corner table in the Hotel Deucalion's busy kitchen, which was full of steam and noise and chefs scrambling to fill orders. Not the best place to study for a test, in Morrigan's opinion, but Fen wouldn't let them eat their lunch in the library and Kedgeree had earlier announced that gravity had been suspended in the dining room until further notice.

'Wass . . . what's my knack?' Morrigan had learned to dread this question. 'Um, I don't know.'

Hawthorne nodded, chewing and swallowing loudly. 'You don't have to tell me. Loads of candidates keep it a secret. Gives 'em an edge at the Show Trial.'

'It's not that,' said Morrigan in a rush. 'I don't think I have one.'

'You must do,' he said, frowning as he chugged half a glass of milk. 'Your patron can't put you in the trials unless you've got a knack. It's the rules.'

A thought still niggled at the back of Morrigan's mind. Did her knack have something to do with the curse? She longed to ask Hawthorne's opinion, but she wasn't even supposed to *mention* the curse anymore. She'd promised Jupiter.

'I think I'd know if I did.' Morrigan picked at her sandwich. She'd lost her appetite. It had been nice, she thought miserably, to have a friend for five minutes. Hawthorne would be better off befriending the dog-faced boy.

'S'pose you would.' Hawthorne shrugged. He polished off the last of his sandwich and opened up one of the textbooks Morrigan had borrowed from Jupiter's study. 'Should we start with the Great War?'

She looked up. 'What?'

'Or do you want to save that until we've covered the boring stuff?'

Morrigan tried to keep her voice light, to cover her surprise. 'So you . . . you still want to be friends?'

'What? Yeah. Duh.' He made a face. Morrigan felt her mouth twitch into a smile. Hawthorne was giving his friendship as if it meant nothing. He couldn't know that it meant everything.

'But we're supposed to be . . . making valuable alliances and . . . and all that stuff they said at the Wundrous Welcome.' Morrigan carried their empty plates to the sink, narrowly dodging the sous chef as he rushed past with a dish of steaming mussels. She felt duty-bound to make sure Hawthorne understood. 'I doubt I'm a valuable alliance.'

'Who cares?' he said with a laugh, turning back to his book. Morrigan felt a surge of relief as she sat down again. 'I think we should start with the Great War, because there's loads of blood and guts. First question: how many heads got chopped off at the Battle of Fort Lamentation in the Highlands?'

'No idea.'

He held up a finger. 'Trick question. The highland clans don't chop off heads in battle. They chop off torsos, hang their enemies upside down and shake 'em until their guts fall out.'

'How nice,' said Morrigan. The Free State really was a *very* different place from the Republic. Hawthorne rubbed his hands together, his eyes shining. He was only getting started.

'Next question: which famous Sky Force pilot was roasted to a crisp by an enemy dragon during the Battle of the Black Cliffs? Ooh – and a bonus question: which tribe of cliff-dwelling savages gobbled up his toasty remains when they fell out of the sky?'

A week later Morrigan walked up the long driveway to Proudfoot House for the second time, once again fighting the urge to turn and run. The bare, black-trunked trees lining the drive seemed even more menacing this time. Against the pale sky their spindly branches were like spiders looming above her, ready to pounce.

'Nervous?' asked Jupiter.

Morrigan's only answer was a raised eyebrow.

'Right. Course you are. You should be nervous. It's a nervous sort of day.'

'Thanks. That makes me feel loads better.'

'Really?'

'No.'

Jupiter laughed, looking up at patches of grey sky through the tree branches. 'I meant it in a good way. Your life is about to change, Mog.'

'Morrigan.'

'In a couple of hours you'll be one step closer to getting your little gold pin. And when that happens, the world will open up to you.'

Morrigan wanted to take heart from his confidence, she really did. She wanted desperately to feel that she could do this. If even a fraction of Jupiter's belief in her was justified, she would have colonised the moon and cured every disease in the realm by summertime.

But it was no good, because she still hadn't figured out whether or not he was a madman.

'The written part's the hardest,' said Jupiter. 'Three unseen questions, total silence, nothing but a pencil, paper and a desk. Just take your time, Mog, and answer honestly.'

'You mean correctly?' Morrigan asked, confused. Jupiter didn't seem to hear her.

'Then there's the oral component, but it's nothing to worry about – just a little quiz. More of a conversation, really. Again, *take your time*. Don't be afraid to make them wait. The Elders want to see what you're like. Just be your charming self and you'll be fine.'

Morrigan wanted to ask what charming self he was talking about, and whether he'd perhaps confused her with some other Morrigan Crow he'd met somewhere, but it was too late. They'd reached Proudfoot House, and patrons weren't allowed into the examination hall. She was on her own.

'Good luck, Mog,' Jupiter said, punching her lightly in the arm. Morrigan joined the stream of candidates climbing the marble steps. Her feet felt leaden. 'Go forth and conquer.'

The examination hall was the biggest room Morrigan had ever been in, filled with row after row of rectangular desks and straight-backed wooden chairs. Hundreds of candidates filed in, one after another, and sat silently as Wundrous Society officials handed out booklets and pencils. Morrigan craned her neck trying to spot Hawthorne, but no luck – the desks were allocated alphabetically, and she supposed he was all the way back in the *S* section somewhere. She gave up and read the front of her booklet.

Wundrous Society Entry Examination
Book Trial
Spring of One, Third Age of the Aristocrats
Candidate: Morrigan Odelle Crow
Patron: Captain Jupiter Amantius North

When every child had the exam paper, a Society official at the front of the hall sounded a glass chime. With a chorus of rustling, they opened their booklets. Morrigan took a deep breath and turned to the first page.

It was blank. As was the second page, and the third. She flipped through the rest of the booklet and found that there were no questions anywhere.

She raised her hand and tried to catch the eye of an official to tell them there'd been a mistake, that she'd been given a blank exam, but the woman at the front of the room was oblivious.

Morrigan looked at the first page again. Words appeared.
You're not from here.

Why do you even want *to join the Wundrous Society?*

Morrigan glanced around to see if any other candidate's booklet had grown a brain and started asking impertinent questions. If they had, nobody seemed surprised. Perhaps their patrons had warned them.

She remembered what Jupiter had said to her – *Just take your time, Mog, and answer honestly.* With a sigh, Morrigan picked up her pencil and began.

Because I want to be an important and useful member of soc—

Before she'd finished writing it, the sentence was scratched out by some unseen pen. She gasped.

Nonsense, said the book. *Why do you really want to be in the Wundrous Society?*

Morrigan chewed on her lip.

Because I want a little golden W pin.

The words scratched themselves out again. A corner of the page began to blacken and curl in on itself.

Nope, said the book.

A tiny tendril of smoke coiled up from the smouldering edges of the page. Morrigan tried stamping it out with her hand, but it wouldn't stop. She looked around frantically for a glass of water or an adult to help her, but none of the officials seemed disturbed. In fact, they seemed to be tranquilly ignoring the fact that not only Morrigan's, but several other candidates' exam booklets were in various stages of combustion.

One boy's paper burst into flames and burnt out completely, leaving nothing but a pile of ash on his desk.

An official tapped him on the shoulder and motioned for him to leave. The boy slumped out of the hall.

Honest answers, thought Morrigan quickly, and grabbed her pencil again.

Because I want people to like me.

The paper paused in its journey to self-destruction. It hovered in a flickering, smouldering state that usually preceded the *whoosh* of flames.

Go on, said the book.

Her hand shook a little.

I want to belong somewhere.

More, the book prompted her.

She took a deep breath, thought of the conversation she'd had with Jupiter the day after Morningtide, and wrote:

I want brothers and sisters who will stand by me forever, no matter what.

The damage began to slowly reverse itself, the clean white paper creeping back and reclaiming its burnt corners. Relieved, Morrigan loosened her death grip on the pencil a little. After a moment, the second question appeared.

What is your biggest fear?

Morrigan didn't even have to think about that one. Total no-brainer.

That dolphins will learn to walk on land and shoot acid out of their blowholes.

The words violently scratched themselves out and the paper once again began to char. Nearby, a girl shrieked as her own booklet conflagrated. She was sent out of the examination hall with singed eyebrows.

Morrigan racked her brain as the corners of her booklet turned to ash. She'd told the truth! Land-dwelling acid dolphins *were* her biggest fear, they had *always* been her biggest fear, except – well, no. She'd always *said* they were her biggest fear. Probably because her *biggest* fear, the real one, was too awful to talk about. She bit her lip and committed a new answer to the page.

Death.

The book continued to smoulder.

Death, she wrote again. *Death! It's obviously death!*

And then, a brain wave—

The Hunt of Smoke and Shadow.

But the book kept burning. Morrigan grabbed it, wincing as it scorched her fingers, and wrote in the last tiny patch of white space left:

Being forgotten.

The book unburnt a little.

Go on, it said.

That nobody will remember me. That my family won't remember me because

Morrigan paused, her pencil hovering above the smoky page—

because they'd rather forget that I ever existed.

The book smoothed and whitened, uncurling its pages until they were once again pristine. Morrigan waited patiently for her third and final question. She glanced around the room and saw that roughly a quarter of the desks were now empty but for little piles of ashes.

And how, asked the book, *will you ensure that people remember you?*

Morrigan thought for a long time. She leaned back in her chair and watched silently as small fires broke out all around her and a few dozen more candidates were made to leave the hall. Finally, she wrote the most honest answer she could think of.

I don't know.

And after a moment's hesitation, she added one more word:
Yet.

In an instant, all three questions and answers disappeared from the pages and were replaced with a single word in large green letters.

PASS.

Morrigan paced back and forth in an antechamber of Proudfoot House. Around a third of the candidates had failed the written examination. The rest were put into smaller groups and shepherded into rooms to await the next part of the Book Trial.

In Morrigan's group there was a boy hugging his knees to his chest and rocking back and forth, an energetic pair of twins firing questions at each other and high-fiving aggressively, and a girl slumped on a chair with her arms folded.

Morrigan recognised her; it was the friend of Noelle's from the Wundrous Welcome, the one who couldn't stop laughing at how hilarious Noelle wasn't. Her black hair was twisted into a thick braided knot at the back of her head. She watched the twins through hooded brown eyes.

'What are the three major exports of Upper Zeeland?' shouted one of the twins.

'Jade, dragon scales and wool!' shouted the other. They high-fived. Noelle's friend scowled.

A woman with a clipboard entered the room, her heels click-clacking on the wooden floor as she bustled over to the group of children. 'Fitzwilliam? Francis John Fitzwilliam?' she read from her list. The boy in the corner looked up at her and swallowed. Sweat beaded on his brow. He rose unsteadily to his feet and followed her out of the room, tapping his fingers on his thighs and staring at the ground.

'Who was the first Nevermoorian to walk on the moon?' shouted one of the twins.

'Lieutenant-General Elizabeth Von Keeling!' shouted the other. They high-fived. The girl with the braid breathed fiercely through her nose.

Morrigan closed her eyes and concentrated on naming the twenty-seven boroughs of Nevermoor. 'Old Town,' she whispered to herself, 'Wick, Bloxam, Betelgeuse, Macquarie . . .'

She could do this. She was prepared. She'd read every history and geography book she could get her hands on, and she'd made Kedgeree quiz her over and over the night before. She might not know much about the exports of Upper Zeeland (wherever that was), but she felt sure she knew enough now about Nevermoor and the Free State to get through to the next trial.

'Delphia,' continued Morrigan, looking up at the ceiling. 'Groves and Alden, Deering, Highwall . . .'

'They're not going to ask about the boroughs,' said Noelle's friend. Morrigan was surprised to hear her voice – it was lower, huskier than she expected. At the Wundrous Welcome she'd sounded like a giddy hyena. 'Every idiot knows what the boroughs are called. We learned that in nursery school, for goodness' sake.'

Morrigan ignored her. 'Pocock, Farnham and Barnes, Rhodes Village, Tenterfield . . .'

'Are you deaf or stupid?' asked the girl.

'Where do the time zones of the Unnamed Realm intersect?' shouted one of the twins.

'Centre of Zeev Forest, Fifth Pocket of the Free State!' shouted the other. They high-fived.

Morrigan squeezed her eyes shut and resumed pacing. 'Blackstock . . . um . . . Bellamy . . .'

She was stopped by a soft wall of person. She opened her eyes in surprise and found the woman with the clipboard looking down at her. 'Crow?'

Morrigan nodded gravely, straightened her dress and shoulders, and followed the woman to the interview hall. Halfway there she glanced back and saw Noelle's friend talking to the twins.

'You're going to fail,' she was saying to them in her husky voice. 'You're completely unprepared. You're not going to remember a single thing. You'll never get into the Society. You might as well just go home now.'

Morrigan looked up at the woman with the clipboard to see if she would go back and say something, but the woman's face was blank and uninterested, as though she hadn't heard a word.

'Go on,' she said, giving Morrigan a little push. 'They're waiting for you. Stand on the cross.'

The High Council of Elders sat at a table in the centre of an empty hall. As Morrigan approached they murmured amongst themselves, taking sips of water and shuffling through papers.

'Miss Crow,' said the spindly, wispy-haired Elder Quinn, adjusting her spectacles. 'Who is the leader of the Free State?'

'Prime Minister Gideon Steed.'

'Incorrect. The leaders of the Free State are innovation, industry and thirst for knowledge.'

Morrigan's stomach dropped as though she'd missed a step on a staircase. In that instant she knew that she was not prepared for the sort of interview the Elders had decided to give. Any scrap of confidence she might have felt earlier had now abandoned her, and she felt suddenly seized by fear.

'Who is Gideon Steed?' asked the bull, Elder Alioth Saga.

Morrigan faltered. 'He's . . . he's the p-prime minister. Isn't he?'

'Incorrect,' boomed Elder Saga. 'Prime Minister Gideon Steed is a democratically elected steward of the Free State, a sentry who has been appointed by the people to protect the values, standards and liberties that we hold dear.'

'But he *is* the prime minister,' Morrigan insisted. This wasn't fair. She'd answered the question correctly. 'You just said so yourself.'

The Elders ignored her protest.

'How does one tell a true incendiary botanical from a tree that has merely been set on fire?' asked Elder Helix Wong.

She knew this one. 'The flames of an incendiary botanical never produce smoke.'

'Incorrect,' said Elder Wong. 'Incendiary botanicals are extinct; *any* tree that appears to be an incendiary botanical *is* a tree that has merely been set on fire, and should be extinguished immediately.'

Morrigan groaned inwardly. She should have seen that coming. Of *course* fireblossom trees were extinct; Jupiter had told her that! Plus, she'd read in *A Vegetal History of Nevermoor* that nobody had seen a fireblossom burning in over a hundred years. She felt a twinge of annoyance at the trick question.

'How old is the great city of Nevermoor?' asked Elder Quinn.

'Nevermoor was founded one thousand, eight hundred and ninety-one years ago, during the Second Avian Age.'

'Incorrect. Nevermoor is as ancient as the stars, as new as powder snow and as mighty as thunder.'

'Well, this is impossible! How am I supposed to—'

'When did the Courage Square Massacre occur?' asked Elder Quinn.

Morrigan had started to answer (Winter of Nine, Age of the East Winds) when something came into her mind. She stopped and took a moment to let her brain form the answer before her mouth did. The Elders watched her expectantly.

Don't be afraid to make them wait.

'The Courage Square Massacre,' she began haltingly, 'occurred on . . . a dark day.'

The Elders said nothing.

'One of the darkest in Nevermoor's history,' continued Morrigan. 'A day when . . .' She paused while her brain scrambled for words. 'A day when fiendishness triumphed over goodness. A day when evil took hold of Nevermoor and . . . and . . . shook it until its guts fell out.'

The Elders continued to stare. Morrigan's heart hammered in her ears. What more did they want?

'A day never to be repeated,' she said finally. That was it; she had no more nonsense left in her.

Elder Quinn smiled. It was a tiny smile, but Morrigan saw it. It was like a very small flower in a bed of hopeless weeds.

The hunched little Elder looked as though she might be about to ask a follow-up question, and Morrigan felt suddenly terrified. She didn't actually know very much about the Courage Square Massacre. She and Hawthorne had stopped for a tea break halfway through that chapter of *The Encyclopedia of Nevermoorian Barbarism* and forgotten to get back to it.

Morrigan held her breath, hoping she'd done enough. Elder Quinn looked to her colleagues, who nodded curtly and returned to their papers.

'Thank you, Miss Crow. You may go.'

Morrigan emerged, blinking, into the sunshine. She walked in a daze down the steps of Proudfoot House to where Jupiter stood waiting.

'How was it?'

'Weird.'

'Obviously.' He shrugged, as if she should have realised that weirdness was standard procedure for the Wundrous Society. 'Your mate with the toads came out earlier, by the way. Said to tell you he got through to the next trial, and that you'd better get through too, or else. Then he and Nan had to rush off to a dragonrider training session, and I had to pretend not to be completely jealous of an eleven-year-old boy who gets to ride dragons. So, did you, er . . . did you get through?' he asked casually.

Morrigan held up the letter she'd been given, still not quite believing it herself.

'"Congratulations, candidate,"' Jupiter read aloud. '"You have proven your sincerity, reasoning and quick thinking and may proceed to the next round of trials for Unit 919. The Chase Trial will take place at noon on the last Saturday in Summer of One. Details to follow." I told you. Didn't I tell you you'd do it? Well done, Mog. I'm chuffed.'

Morrigan wasn't paying attention. She'd spotted the high-five twins leaving Proudfoot House. They ran, wailing, to their patron.

'We c-can't do it!' sobbed the first twin. 'We're c-completely unprepared!'

'We don't remember a s-single thing!'

Somewhere in amongst the relief she felt at her own success, Morrigan felt sorry for the twins. That awful girl, Noelle's friend, had obviously got inside their heads and knocked their confidence. She wanted to say something, to give them some sort of hint about what the Elders wanted, but Jupiter was already steering her away from Proudfoot House.

The sun had come out, making the bare black branches of the tree-lined drive seem somehow less sinister than before. She lifted her face, letting it warm her, and absently reached out to touch one of the dead trees as she and Jupiter strode down the drive. A flash of searing heat and tiny purple sparks met her fingertips, and she snatched her hand back.

'Ow!'

'What?' Jupiter stopped short. 'What's wrong?'

'That tree just burned me!'

He stared at her a moment, then chuckled. 'Very funny, Mog. I told you, fireblossoms are extinct.'

Jupiter carried on ahead of her, and Morrigan examined her unblemished fingers. She reached out, cautiously, to touch the tree again. Nothing happened.

She shook her head, giving a confused little laugh. Apparently her imagination *did* have a bit of nonsense left in it.

CHAPTER TWELVE

Shadows

Summer of One

With her first trial over and the next months away, Morrigan was free to enjoy summer at the Hotel Deucalion. Days of splashing in the sun-drenched Jasmine Courtyard pool gave way to balmy nights of ballroom dancing lessons, barbecue dinners and long lounging sessions in the Smoking Parlour, relaxing in vaporous clouds of vanilla smoke ('to soothe the senses and bring happy dreams'). If occasionally her thoughts drifted back to Crow Manor, if she remembered how Grandmother was always slightly nicer in the summer, or wondered whether Ivy had yet had her baby, the thought was always quickly chased away by an invitation to help Charlie groom the horses, or to taste-test the menu for Frank's next party.

Sometimes Dame Chanda, who famously had six suitors ('one for each night of the week, except Sundays,' she explained nonchalantly), would enlist Morrigan's help to choose her outfit for the evening. Together they would dive through the thousands of beautiful gowns, shoes and jewels in the soprano's wardrobe (which was nearly as big as the hotel lobby) to find the perfect ensemble for dinner and dancing with the man Jupiter had dubbed 'Monsieur Monday', a stroll in the park with 'Sir Wednesday of the Midweek', or a night at the theatre with 'the Honorable Lord Thursday'.

Life at the Deucalion brought fresh curiosities daily – like the time Kedgeree summoned the Paranormal Services men to remove a pesky ghost that'd been walking through walls on the fifth floor. Kedgeree said he didn't mind ghosts, on the whole, as long as they didn't have any annoying habits. But this one kept coming back, he said – they were already on their third visit from Paranormal Services – and while he'd never seen the spectre himself, the stories and rumours had so frightened some guests that he'd had to move them to another floor. Morrigan was allowed to watch the exorcism, but it wasn't as impressive as she'd imagined. She'd been hoping to see a real ghost fly out of the building, but there was just a lot of sage-burning and weird dancing, and then the Paranormal Services men handed Kedgeree a bill for four hundred and fifty kred and left.

The most disappointing thing about the summer, however – *much* more disappointing than the exorcism – was that Morrigan saw less and less of Jupiter. He was always being called away on business for the League of Explorers, or dashing off to endless meetings, dinners and parties.

'Bad news, Mog.' Jupiter slid down the curved marble banister one Thursday afternoon and landed in the foyer, where Morrigan and Martha were folding napkins into swans. Martha's swans looked perfect, like they could fly off in formation at any moment. Morrigan's looked like drunk, angry pigeons. 'Can't take you and Hawthorne to the bazaar tomorrow night. Something's come up.'

'Again?'

Jupiter ran a hand through his bright copper hair, hastily tucked his shirt into his trousers and snapped his braces in place. ''Fraid so, old girl. The Nevermoor Transport Authority has sent—'

'*Again?*' Morrigan repeated. The NTA had been sending messengers to fetch Jupiter from the Deucalion all summer long. They usually only needed his help with 'echoes on the Gossamer Line' – whatever that meant – but three weeks ago there'd been another derailment, and this time two people had been killed. It was front-page news for a week, and the Deucalion had gone wild with rumours about who was responsible and what it might mean. Some of the staff got into such a state of panic that Jupiter had to ban anyone from uttering the word *Wundersmith*.

'I could take Morrigan,' offered Martha. 'Tomorrow's my night off, and Charlie's taking me – I mean, Mr McAlister and I – well, he's going to the bazaar and he asked – I thought I might pop along too.' A crimson blush spread across Martha's face. It was common knowledge at the Deucalion that she and Charlie McAlister, the hotel chauffeur, fancied each other. They were the only ones who still thought it was a secret.

'That's all right, Martha. You and Charlie will have enough on your minds.' Jupiter smirked. 'We'll go soon, Mog – promise.'

Morrigan tried to hide her disappointment. The Nevermoor Bazaar was a famous market festival that ran every Friday night, all summer long. People came from all over the Seven Pockets just to see it, and lots of them stayed at the Hotel Deucalion. Every Friday at dusk, excited guests ventured out in carriages and on trains, and every Saturday morning they'd compare thrilling stories and photographs and purchases over brunch. But the summer was half finished and Morrigan still hadn't been. 'Next week?' she asked hopefully.

'Next week. Definitely.' He grabbed his long green coat and threw open the front door, then paused to look back. 'Wait – not next week. I'm scheduled on a gateway to Phlox II. Terrible realm. All the bloodsucking insect swarms of Phlox I, but none of the charm.' He scratched his ginger beard and gave a helpless chuckle. 'We'll sort something out. Hey, Jack will be home from orchestra camp next weekend. He'll be here for the rest of the summer. So we can go together, all three of us. Four of us – Hawthorne too.'

Morrigan had almost forgotten that Jupiter's nephew lived at the Deucalion when he wasn't at boarding school. Martha said he sometimes came home on weekends, but so far there'd been no sign of him.

Jupiter stepped back inside to grab his umbrella and paused to look at her strangely. 'Have you been having bad dreams?'

'What? No,' Morrigan said hurriedly, glancing at Martha. The maid suddenly got very busy counting her swans and pretending not to hear.

Jupiter waved his hand around Morrigan's head as if brushing away invisible flies. 'Yes, you have. They're hanging around you. What have you been dreaming about?'

'Nothing,' she lied.

'It's the Show Trial, isn't it? I told you not to worry about that.'

'I'm not worried about it.' *Lie.*

'All right.' Jupiter nodded slowly, then leaned over her chair and whispered, 'I'm really sorry about the bazaar, Moggers.'

'Morrigan,' she corrected, reaching up to fix his collar, which had flipped in on itself. 'Never mind. Hawthorne and I can do something else.'

Jupiter nodded once, aimed a playful punch at Morrigan's arm, and was gone.

Next morning, there was a boy at Morrigan's breakfast table in the dining room. Sitting in her chair. Eating her toast.

He was taller and older – perhaps twelve or thirteen – and though his face was mostly hidden behind a copy of the *Sentinel*, the top of his thick black hair was visible over the masthead. Flipping the pages of his newspaper and sipping blood orange juice, he leaned back in his chair as if he owned the place.

Morrigan cleared her throat quietly. The boy didn't look up from his newspaper. She waited a moment and then coughed loudly.

'Go away if you're ill,' he commanded. Another page flicked over. A slender brown hand emerged, took a piece of toast and disappeared again behind the newspaper.

'I'm not,' she said, taken aback at his rudeness. 'Guests aren't allowed down here. Are you lost?'

He ignored her question. 'If you don't have anything contagious, you can stay. But don't talk while I'm reading.'

'I know I can stay.' She stood up straight, making herself taller. 'I live here. You're sitting in *my* chair.'

At this, the boy finally, slowly, lowered his newspaper to reveal a long face and a look of extreme displeasure. One eyebrow arched smoothly and his mouth curled into a scowl as he looked Morrigan up and down.

Being accustomed to this reaction when meeting new people, Morrigan was less surprised by his disdain than by the black leather patch covering his left eye. She instantly recognised him from the school photo in Jupiter's study: John Arjuna Korrapati.

So *this* was Jack.

He folded the paper and placed it in his lap. '*Your* chair? You've lived here all of five minutes and you've claimed the furniture? I've lived here five years. This *happens* to be where I eat my breakfast.'

'You're Jupiter's nephew.'

'You're his candidate.'

'He told you about me?'

'Obviously.' He snapped open the newspaper and buried his face in it once again.

'I thought you weren't coming home until next weekend.'

'You were misinformed.'

'Jupiter's away on Phlox II.'

'I'm aware of that.'

'How come you're early?'

He sighed heavily and the newspaper dropped. 'Uncle Jove wouldn't tell me what your knack is. I can only guess you have the gift of annoying people while they're trying to read.'

Morrigan sat across from him. 'You go to that Greypants School for Clever Boys, don't you?'

'Graysmark School for Bright Young Men,' he snapped.

Morrigan smirked. She knew the real name. 'What's it like?'

'Just dandy.'

'How come you're not in the Wundrous Society, like Jupiter? Did you try out?'

'No.' Jack folded his paper again, shoved a piece of toast in his mouth and snatched his half-full teacup from the table before stomping out of the dining room and up the stairs.

Morrigan wondered where his bedroom was, and what it looked like, and where his parents lived, and what happened to his eye, and how come he didn't try out for the Society, and how she was going to make it through half a summer of his not-very-delightful company.

As she reclaimed her favourite chair and a piece of toast, she made a mental note to wake up earlier tomorrow and get there before Jack did.

⸻

'Someone probably gouged it out with a hot fire poker,' said Hawthorne that night as he and Morrigan dragged out the board-game chest in the Smoking Parlour (rose smoke tonight, hazy and pink – 'to encourage sweetness of temper'). 'Or stabbed it with a letter opener. Or put flesh-eating insects under his eyelid and they ate it all up. Something like that.'

'Ugh.' Morrigan shuddered. 'Who would do that?'

'Someone with a reason not to like him,' said Hawthorne.

'So it could be anyone he's ever met.'

Hawthorne grinned and then, surveying the contents of the chest with a look of dismay, he asked, 'We're not *actually* doing this, are we?'

'We are,' said Morrigan, pulling out a colourful box. She was determined to have a good night so that when he asked, she could honestly tell Jupiter it didn't matter in the slightest that he'd cancelled their promised trip to the Nevermoor Bazaar for the fifth week running. Not in the slightest.

'*Happy Housewives*? Oh, come on . . . I haven't played this since I was ten.'

Morrigan ignored Hawthorne and began setting up the pieces. 'I'll be Mrs Fuddledump, the kindly grandmother. You can be Ms Fierceface, the unsatisfied career woman. Not terribly modern, is it? I'll go first.'

She rolled the dice and moved her piece, picked up a card from the centre of the board, and read, 'You have won a flower-arranging contest. Collect your prize: an embroidered apron, the perfect thing to wear while cooking dinner for your hardworking husband. Don't forget to freshen your lipstick and fix your hair before he gets home.' She put the card down immediately and began packing away the pieces. 'Fine, then, what do *you* want to do?'

'What do you think? Go to the Nevermoor Bazaar, of course. My brother Homer's going with a bunch of his friends; I bet he'll let us come if we promise to pretend we don't know him.'

'Can't. I'm not allowed to leave the hotel without Jupiter.'

'Is that a rule, though?' Hawthorne asked. 'Did he actually *say* that? Because if he didn't *say* it's a rule, it's probably . . . more of a suggestion.'

Morrigan sighed. 'There are three rules. I had to learn them by heart. One: if a door's locked and I don't have the key, I'm not allowed in. Two: I mustn't leave the Deucalion without Jupiter. Three . . . I forget three. Something about the south wing. Anyway, it doesn't matter. I can't go.'

Hawthorne looked thoughtful. 'Does that first rule mean if any door's *un*locked you're allowed in?'

'S'pose so.'

He raised his eyebrows. 'Cool.'

They spent the next hour running up and down hallways rattling door handles, trying six floors before it got boring. The only unlocked rooms in the Deucalion seemed to be rooms they'd already visited a million times, but finally, on the seventh floor of the west wing, just as a game of *Happy Housewives* was looking inevitable, inspiration struck.

'This looks familiar.' Morrigan rattled another locked door. It was different from the others on this floor. Instead of solid brass, the doorknob was made of twisted silver filigree and had a tiny opal bird on the top, its wings outstretched. 'This looks like . . . Oh. Oh! *Wait here.*'

She ran all the way to the fourth floor and back, arriving out of breath but clutching her umbrella triumphantly.

Hawthorne tilted his head. 'Expecting bad weather?'

The silver tip fit the lock. Morrigan twisted the oilskin brolly and turned the handle. The door opened with a satisfying click, and she smiled. 'I knew it.'

'How—'

'Jupiter gave me this for my birthday,' she explained, her excitement growing. 'Do you think he knew this would happen? Maybe he *meant* for me to figure it out!'

'Yeah.' Hawthorne looked bewildered. 'He'd do something nutty like that.'

The room was large, echoing and entirely empty but for a glass lantern in the centre of the floor. It held a single lit candle, bright enough to cast a warm golden glow around the darkened room.

'Weird,' muttered Hawthorne.

It was an understatement. Morrigan was pretty sure there wasn't meant to be a lantern burning unattended in a locked empty room on the seventh floor. For one thing, it was probably a fire hazard. For another, it was spooky.

As they got closer to it, the light from the lantern made their shadows huge and monstrous. Hawthorne cracked himself up by hunching his back and doing a zombie walk, groaning loudly for effect. He shuffled towards the candle and his zombie shadow grew enormous on the wall behind him.

Then something strange happened. Hawthorne stopped moving. But his shadow did not. It continued its zombie walk without him, taking on a life of its own and lumbering across the far wall, until it melted into a dark corner and disappeared.

'Creepy,' breathed Morrigan.

'Very creepy,' Hawthorne agreed.

'Let me try.' She made a snake shadow puppet with her arm. It coiled away from her and slithered along the walls, striking angrily at the poor shadow-bunnies Hawthorne sent hopping towards it.

Morrigan's slightly rubbish attempt at a cat became a roaring lion that stalked and ate every one of those bunnies. Hawthorne made a bird, which turned into a bat that swooped down on his own shadow as if trying to scratch his eyes out.

Their creations became more elaborate as they tried to out-spook each other. They didn't even have to work very hard – it was as if the shadows were *trying* to be as scary as possible. A fish became a shark, became a circling school of sharks, became a swirling hurricane of giant sharks with Hawthorne and Morrigan's shadows at the centre. It was terrifying and thrilling and so, *so* cool.

'I'm . . . gonna make . . .' Hawthorne said, his tongue sticking out the side of his mouth as he bent his fingers into a complicated, unrecognisable shape, '. . . a *dragon*.'

And suddenly, his blobby shadow became a great reptilian beast. It loomed large on the wall, its black wings beating monstrously as it took flight. It soared and swooped around their heads and shot shadowy black flames from between its terrifying jaws. Hawthorne made a shadow-horse, and the dragon burned it to a crisp and gobbled it down in three sickening bites.

Morrigan and Hawthorne screamed as they watched it dive down and pick up Hawthorne's shadow in its talons, flying into the distance while Shadow-Hawthorne's black limbs flailed. Their screams turned to laughter.

'I think I just won,' said Hawthorne with a smug grin.

'Firstly, it's not a competition,' said Morrigan. 'And secondly – *I'm* going to win.'

They sat on the floor with the lantern between them, and Morrigan flexed her fingers. If Hawthorne thought he could out-scare Jackalfax's scariest citizen, he had another thing coming. 'Let me tell you a story.'

She twisted her hands into something that looked roughly like a person. 'Once upon a time, a little boy was walking alone in the woods.'

She made some tall, waving trees, and the shadow-boy walked obediently among them.

'His mother always told him not to walk in the woods alone. There was a witch who lived there, and her favourite thing to eat was chopped-up little boys on toast. But the boy didn't listen, because he liked to pick the berries that grew in the forest.'

Morrigan hunched over into what she thought was a suitably witch-like shape, her fingers bent into claws. Her shadow did the rest, transforming into a spooky old woman complete with hooked, warty nose and pointed hat. The shadow-witch stalked the boy through the trees.

'He thought he knew the forest, but he got lost and couldn't find his way out. He walked for hours and hours. Night fell, and the forest grew dark.'

Morrigan made an owl that suddenly took flight, shaking the branches of a tree. The shadow-boy looked over his shoulder and shivered, and so did Hawthorne.

'Suddenly, he heard a croaky old voice from behind him. "Who's that walking in my woods?" called the witch. "Who's been picking my berries?"'

'The boy tried to run, but the witch plucked him by the scruff of his neck and carried him home to her chopping board, cackling all the way.' (Morrigan was particularly proud of her witchy cackle.) 'As she lifted her knife high in the air, a howl pierced the night.'

Morrigan made a dog shadow puppet, which turned into a wolf, then a pack of wolves. They circled the witch and the boy, growling viciously. She hadn't meant to make so many of them, but the shadows had ideas of their own; they were too good at this. Morrigan needed to take control before the story got away from her.

'Finally,' she said, grasping for a hasty ending, 'the boy, um . . . the boy heard his mother calling for him in the distance. She came riding to his rescue on their trusty old horse, Sergeant Clop, and . . . and the boy cheered as he saw them galloping over the hill!'

Morrigan's shadow-puppet horse did indeed gallop towards the boy, the witch and the wolves. But there was no heroic mother on its back, coming to save the day. There was no mother at all. Only a towering, skeletal man holding a long black rifle.

'I didn't make that,' whispered Morrigan, cold fear rising up in her throat. The shadows had hijacked her story.

A brigade of horses swelled up behind the first, each bearing a ghostly hunter at the reins. The shadow-witch and the shadow-boy faded into darkness, and the wolves loomed larger and larger as they surrounded Morrigan and Hawthorne.

Morrigan screamed.

She ran for the door with Hawthorne close behind, and only when they emerged in the bright light of the hallway did Morrigan realise they weren't being chased.

'What's wrong?' said Hawthorne. 'That was getting good.'

She shook her head, trembling. 'That wasn't meant to happen. The Hunt of Smoke and Shadow wasn't meant to be in the story.'

'The Hunt of – what?'

Morrigan took a shaky breath and told Hawthorne the story of her eleventh birthday. Once she started, it all came tumbling out – about the Eventide curse and how she was meant to die but then Jupiter came and they were chased by the Hunt of Smoke and Shadow and went through the clock and that was how she ended up at the Hotel Deucalion, and how she really, *really* didn't have a knack, or even a clue what she was doing there. She even told him the most painful, scary part – about Inspector Flintlock, and how if she didn't get into the Society she'd be forced to leave Nevermoor and face the Hunt again.

Hawthorne stayed quiet until she'd finished, and for a little while afterwards. He looked dazed. Morrigan watched him, biting her lip, worried she'd said too much. Perhaps she should have left out the bit about coming from the Republic and being in Nevermoor illegally. And the bit about the curse. And all the other bits.

'No offence,' he said finally, 'but that story's *way* better than the one you made up.'

The air left Morrigan's lungs in a low *whoosh*. It was typical of Hawthorne to take the strangeness of her life in his stride, but she was deeply relieved nonetheless.

'Hawthorne, you *have* to keep it a secret,' Morrigan said. 'I wasn't supposed to tell. If anybody finds out – if Inspector Flintlock—'

Hawthorne held out his little finger. 'Morrigan Crow,'

he said solemnly. 'I pinkie promise to keep your secret and not tell another soul.'

Morrigan raised an eyebrow. 'You pinkie what?'

'Pinkie promise.' He pushed his little finger closer to her face. 'I've never broken a pinkie promise in my life. *Never.*'

She hooked her pinkie in his, and they nodded.

'Now,' he said, frowning. 'Please tell me that bit about getting chased through the clock by hunters with guns while driving a giant spider again.'

But she didn't get a chance, because suddenly Morrigan noticed two things:

1. They'd left the door to the Creepy Room of Creepiness open.
2. One of her shadow-wolves had escaped and was stalking down the hallway.

'Maybe it faded away,' Hawthorne moaned as they searched the kitchens for the third time. They'd looked all over the hotel, but the shadow-wolf eluded them. 'All the others did.'

'But what if it didn't? What if it comes across a guest? They'll be scared to death, their family will sue the Deucalion and Jupiter will kill me. We have to find it before someone sees it.' Morrigan didn't know how she was going to get rid of the wolf if she ever did catch it, but she couldn't think about that now.

'Before someone sees what?'

It was the last voice she wanted to hear. Jack stood in a corner of the kitchen, pouring a glass of milk.

'Nothing,' she said quickly. 'None of your business.'

He rolled his good eye. 'If there's something wandering around scaring people to death, it is my business. I don't want to stumble over any dead bodies on my way to bed. What is it?'

'You wouldn't believe it.'

'Try me.'

They told him. Jack listened with increasing annoyance. 'For goodness' sake! If you're going to leave a pack of killer wolves in the Hall of Shadows, at least shut the bloody door behind you. It's locked for a reason. How did you even get in?'

'I . . . we . . . well, I realised that—'

'Forget it!' Jack held up a hand to stop her. 'Don't make me your accomplice. Jupiter's going to be *furious.*'

As much as Morrigan didn't want to admit it, it was a stroke of good luck that Jack was there, because he knew an awful lot more about the hotel than she did. He led them to a maintenance closet and pulled out three battery-powered torches.

'Right, we're going to have to split up. I'll take the east wing, you' – he pointed at Hawthorne – 'take the west wing, and Morrigan, you take the north wing. If you find the wolf, shine your torch *directly* on it, at the highest setting. Don't let it get away, keep shining the light on it until it fades.

'It won't be in places like the hallways and kitchens, it'll be someplace darker, with other shadows to hide in. If you corner it in a room and you can get to a light switch, flick it on and flood the room with light. If not, your torch should do the job. Now, this is important – *do not* stop searching until you find it. Even if it takes all night.'

Morrigan didn't like the idea of splitting up. The last thing she felt like doing was wandering around in the dark looking for a giant ravenous shadow-wolf on her own, but what could she do? It was her fault the thing was out there. She had to find it.

The north wing was surprisingly dark. She crept down black stairwells and through unlocked rooms, unsure whether a shadow could hear her coming but unwilling to take the risk. It was hard to know what to look for in the dark. How do you find a shadow in the shadows?

After what felt like hours of searching, Morrigan was ready to give up when she heard a sound from the moonlit balcony of a fifth-floor drawing room. Somebody was out there, looking up at the sky and singing quietly. The sound drifted inside, and though Morrigan couldn't quite make out the words, she recognised the melody. And the man.

She held the gauzy white curtains aside and stepped onto the balcony, into the bluish light of a full moon. The beam of her torch fell across the man's face. 'Mr Jones?'

He was jolted out of his reverie. 'Miss Crow! Hello again.'

'Another visit,' Morrigan observed. 'You must come to Nevermoor a lot.'

'Yes, I have business here on occasion. And I like to visit friends.' He smiled a little sheepishly, holding up a hand to shield his eyes. Morrigan lowered her torch. 'I don't believe the Wintersea Party would approve, but what they don't know won't hurt them. Our deal still stands, I hope? You won't tell on me?'

'As long as you don't tell on me.' Morrigan shivered. The evening breeze had a bite. 'What are you doing out here?'

'Oh, just . . . looking for the Music Salon. I thought it was somewhere near my suite, but I suspect I'm a bit lost – the Deucalion still baffles me, after all these years. I passed this charming spot and couldn't resist a moment of reflection under the stars.' His voice was wistful. 'Such a beautiful evening.'

'Yes, it's—' From the corner of her eye, Morrigan saw something move in the drawing room. She threw back the curtains and swung her torch around, but it was only the branch of a small potted tree, swaying in the breeze from the open door. 'Where *is* it?' she whispered.

'Are you looking for something?'

'Um . . . yeah. But you probably wouldn't believe me if I told you.'

He smiled gently. 'I'm certain I would.'

She told him about the Hall of Shadows. He barely raised an eyebrow. 'And then one of the shadows I made escaped and now it's running around the hotel, and I have to find it before it scares somebody to death and Jupiter loses all his business and goes bankrupt. Jack says the only way to kill it is to shine a light on it until it fades away.'

Mr Jones didn't laugh at her, or call her a liar, or even express the smallest amount of surprise. 'You created this shadow on your own?'

'Sort of. And it sort of . . . created itself.'

He looked oddly impressed by that. 'Hmm. It's a scary shadow, you said?'

'They're all scary. Even if you make a nice one, like a kitten, it'll turn into a man-eating tiger or something. It's like they're *trying* to be scary.'

'That makes sense.'

Morrigan was surprised. 'Does it?'

'Shadows are shadows, Miss Crow.' His eyes reflected the moonlight. 'They want to be dark.'

Morrigan swung her torch wildly about the room, hoping to catch the wolf by surprise if it was there. The beam began to stutter and fade. She whacked the side of the torch. 'I think my batteries are dying.' With one last flicker the light went out. She groaned.

'I doubt it matters,' said Mr Jones. 'Miss Crow, I suspect your friend – the one who told you how to kill the shadow—'

'He's *not* my friend—'

'—was merely having fun at your expense.' He smiled, not unkindly. 'Your rogue shadow has almost certainly faded away on its own.'

Morrigan frowned. 'How do you know?'

'I've been staying at the Deucalion for many years; I hope I've learned a *few* of her secrets in that time. As I understand it, anything made inside the Hall of Shadows is nothing but an illusion – just a bit of theatre. It can't harm anyone.'

'Are you sure?'

'Quite sure.'

Morrigan felt relief wash over her, followed by cold fury. Had she really just wasted a bazillion hours chasing *nothing*? '*Jack*. I'm going to kill him.'

Mr Jones chuckled. 'Pity you can't send a real wolf to teach him a lesson. Now I'm afraid I must get myself to bed. I'm checking out in the morning. Goodnight, Miss Crow. And remember – my employer's offer is always open.'

He was well and truly gone by the time Morrigan realised she'd never told him the shadow was a wolf.

'What are you – you were meant to be looking in the north wing!'

The cavernous foyer was dim and empty but for Jack, lounging on a love seat and reading a clothbound book. The chandelier – growing, slowly growing – twinkled feebly overhead, still in its infancy. Jack shone his torch in Morrigan's face, nearly blinding her as she emerged from the hall.

'I was, you *rat*.' Morrigan glanced back the way she came. 'That is the north wing.'

'No.' He looked slightly panicked. 'That's the south wing. It's closed for renovations. It's unsafe. You're not supposed to enter under any circumstances. Can't you read?'

He pointed at a sign that said CLOSED FOR RENOVATIONS. UNSAFE. DO NOT ENTER UNDER ANY CIRCUMSTANCES. Morrigan had walked right past it. *Whoops.*

'Well, it's your fault!' she sputtered. 'You lied, Jack. We didn't need to chase that stupid wolf around the hotel at all.'

'Did anybody see you in there? Fenestra would kill—'

'Who cares about the south wing? You knew the shadow would disappear on its own, didn't you? You're a liar.'

Jack didn't look remotely guilty. 'It's not my fault you're gullible. Try having a brain next time.' He scowled and shook his head, muttering, 'I can't believe my uncle thinks *you* belong in the Wundrous Society. Can't even read a sign.'

'Are you jealous? Is that it?' Morrigan threw the torch down beside him. 'Jealous he chose me as his candidate and not you?'

Jack's eyes narrowed. 'What – did you just – *jealous*? Of *you*? Why would I be jealous of *you*? You don't even have a knack! You said so yourself, outside the Hall of—'

Morrigan gasped. 'You were *spying on us*!'

At that moment, Hawthorne bounded into the foyer, shining his torch into his face and laughing maniacally. '*Mwa-ha-ha*, I am Hawthorne, killer of shadows, *fear me, shadow-wolf, for I am your doom.*'

'You're too late, shadow-killer,' said Morrigan, grabbing his torch and tossing it at Jack. 'The shadow's already dead.'

'Oh.' Hawthorne's shoulders slumped. 'But I've just made up a victory song for when I vanquish it. I was gonna teach you the dance bit.'

Morrigan led him to the gold and glass elevator, speaking loudly enough for her voice to echo in the foyer. 'Maybe you can rewrite the words to be about Jupiter's weasel of a nephew, who spies on people and tells lies and makes everyone hate him.'

'Or about Jupiter's talentless candidate, who's too stupid to know how shadows work and runs around a hotel making an idiot of herself,' called Jack, settling back into the love seat with his book.

Morrigan jabbed the button for her floor, still seething. Hawthorne hummed, turning to her as the doors closed.

'What rhymes with *weasel of a nephew*?'

CHAPTER THIRTEEN

The Chase Trial

Summer was dying, but it refused to go down without a fight. The last weeks of August brought a heatwave to Nevermoor, with blazing temperatures and blazing tempers to match.

'Can we *please* take this seriously?' Morrigan said irritably. 'The second trial is only three days away.'

She'd been trying to talk to Jupiter for an hour, but his attention span had evaporated in the heat. He sat in a shady corner of the Palm Courtyard, drinking glasses of peach sangria and waving a handheld fan. Fenestra was sunbathing nearby, while Frank snored quietly under an enormous sombrero. Jupiter had given all staff the afternoon off. It was much too hot to work, and they'd been sniping among themselves all morning.

Jack, mercifully, was nowhere to be seen. Morrigan thought he was probably tucked away in his bedroom practising the cello, which was where he'd spent most of the summer – at least, when he wasn't kicking Morrigan out of the best spot in the Smoking Parlour, or criticising her table manners during dinner, or scowling in her general direction. Morrigan couldn't wait for him to go back to school so the Deucalion could feel like *hers* again. He'd reached heights of unbearable smugness when he'd been allowed to go to the Nevermoor Bazaar with his school friends. Morrigan had waited the whole summer for Jupiter to take her, but every week something more important would call him away. Now the bazaar was over for the year, and Morrigan had missed out. All things considered, she was happy to see the last days of summer . . . even if that meant it was time for her next nerve-racking trial.

'Do you think he's okay under there?' Jupiter asked, cracking one sleepy eye open to look at Frank. 'He's not going to burn down to ashes, is he? I don't know how dwarf vampires work.'

'Vampire dwarves,' Morrigan said. 'And he's fine. Can we please focus on the Chase Trial? I need a steed. And it can't have more than four legs – that's in the rules.'

'Right.'

'And I can't fly.'

'You certainly cannot,' said Jupiter, taking a sip of sangria, 'for you are Crow in name only.'

Morrigan huffed. 'No, I mean – the rules say—'

'Lighten up, Mog,' Jupiter snorted. 'I know what the rules say: you can't ride a flying animal. There was some kerfuffle a few years back with a dragon and a pelican. Poor bird got burnt to a cinder three seconds after take-off. More of a pelican't, in the end. Eh? Peli*can't*?' He grinned lazily at Morrigan, but her sense of humour had also evaporated. 'Anyway. They banned the whole lot, and now everyone goes on the ground.'

The rules for the Chase Trial had arrived by messenger the day before, sending Morrigan into a spin. It shocked her to realise that all these weeks, she'd barely given the Chase a thought. Perhaps Jack's annoying presence all summer had been a blessing as well as a curse. They'd been so busy arguing and getting in each other's way, it hadn't left any time for Morrigan to dwell on the upcoming trial.

'So,' she prompted Jupiter. 'Steed. Four legs or less.'

'Fewer.'

'Four legs or fewer. Could Charlie teach me to ride a horse?'

'Not sure that's the way to go, Mog,' said Jupiter. He waved away a buzzing insect. 'I've never seen a Chase Trial myself, but I've heard they get pretty wild. You'll need more of an all-terrain beast. Let me think on it.'

All-terrain beast. What in the world was an all-terrain beast? It was useless trying to get him to talk sense in this ridiculous heat. Morrigan vented her feelings by kicking at a tuft of grass growing out of the sandstone. 'This is hopeless. What's the point of the Chase Trial, anyway? Why do the Elders care who can win a race? It's stupid.'

'Mmm, that's the spirit,' said Jupiter distractedly.

She gave up and went to perch on the edge of a little pool, dipping her feet in as she pulled the Wundrous Society letter from her pocket and read it for perhaps the hundredth time.

> *Dear Miss Crow,*
>
> *The Chase Trial will take place this Saturday at midday, in the heart of Nevermoor, inside the walls of the Old Town district. The United Nevermoor Councils and Guilds has granted us permission to evacuate the streets of Old Town temporarily, ensuring the event will be undisturbed by the public.*
>
> *The remaining candidates have been divided into four groups. You are in the West Gate group. Please make your presence known to Society officials at Old Town West Gate no later than 11:30 on Saturday morning.*
>
> *There are three rules:*

*1. Every candidate must ride a living steed.
This can be any creature of transport with no
fewer than two legs, and no more than four.*

2. Flying creatures are strictly prohibited.

3. Candidates must dress in white clothes <u>only</u>.

*Any candidate found in breach of these rules
will be instantly disqualified.*

*The successful candidate in this trial will show
daring, tenacity and an instinct for strategy.
Further instructions will be given immediately
prior to the Chase Trial.*

Warmest regards,

Elders G. Quinn, H. Wong and A. Saga

Proudfoot House

Nevermoor, FS

A map was enclosed. Roughly circular and surrounded by medieval stone walls, Old Town was the smaller original city from which the rest of Nevermoor had grown outward in organic, misshapen swells, like a fungus. (This was according to Dame Chanda, who said she took an interest in the city's history because the Honourable Lord Thursday – an amateur historian himself – had given her a membership in the Nevermoor Historical Society two Christmases ago.)

There were four entrances to Old Town: through the

enormous stone archways of the North Gate, South Gate, East Gate and West Gate, like points on a compass.

The map showed Courage Square at the centre of town. Morrigan had only whizzed through Courage Square on the speeding Brolly Rail, but she remembered a broad, bustling plaza surrounded by shops and cafés and filled with people.

The square sat at the intersection of two streets stretching the length and width of Old Town. Lightwing Parade ran from north to south, with Proudfoot House at the far northern end and the Royal Lightwing Palace (home to the Free State monarch, Queen Caledonia II) to the south. Grand Boulevard ran from east (starting at the Temple of the Divine Thing) to west (ending at the Nevermoor Opera House).

The map highlighted other landmarks too – Dredmalis Dungeons, the Houses of Parliament, the embassies, the Garden Belt (a ring of green spaces circling the middle of Old Town, just like a belt), the Gobleian Library and perhaps a dozen others. Morrigan tried to memorise them, in case it turned out to be important.

'Dredmalis Dungeons,' she whispered, closing her eyes to test her memory. 'East Quarter, Rifkin Road. Houses of Parliament: North Quarter, Flagstaff Walk. Gobleian Library: East Quarter – no, South Quarter – no, I mean—'

'West Quarter, dummy,' came a languid voice. Fenestra lay in a nearby patch of sunshine, licking her fur in long, listless strokes. 'Mayhew Street. Do shut up.'

'Thanks,' Morrigan muttered.

She noticed Jupiter watching the Magnificat from the corner of his eye and turned to see what had him so fascinated. The combination of sunlight and saliva made Fen's shabby grey fur look like molten silver. Her muscular legs juddered as she stretched out in a sudden, toothy yawn. She really was beautiful, Morrigan thought grudgingly. In her own terrifying way.

'Do you two mind?' Fen asked, her voice oozing derision. 'I'm trying to have a bath. Creeps.'

Morrigan woke on the day of the Chase Trial feeling peaceful. For about five seconds, obviously, until she remembered what day it was and her peace turned to panic.

She still had no idea what creature of transport Jupiter had arranged for her. He'd spent the past three days having increasingly heated debates with the other staff on the merits of ponies versus camels, and whether a tortoise actually could win a race against a hare in real life, and if they should try it just in case (Frank's idea), and whether an ostrich counted as a flying animal even though it couldn't fly, since it technically had wings. None of these arguments ended well, and none of them put Morrigan at ease.

As she dragged herself out of bed, the door swung open and Fenestra strutted in, tossing some clothes onto the chair with a shake of her massive head.

'Wear that,' she said. 'New boots out in the hall. Martha's bringing your breakfast. Be downstairs in five minutes ready to go.'

And just like that, she was out the door without so much as a 'good morning'.

'Yes, I'm feeling super this morning, Fen, thanks for asking,' muttered Morrigan as she dressed in the white trousers Fen had left for her. 'Nervous? Just a little.' She pulled on a shirt and socks – all white, as the rules stipulated. 'Oh, thanks for the good wishes, Fen, you're too kind. Yes, I'm sure the Chase will go just fine, and won't at all end with me being trampled into the ground, arrested and kicked out of Nevermoor.'

'Who are you talking to, Miss Morrigan?' Martha was standing in the doorway with a breakfast tray. Morrigan took a piece of toast and ran out the door, grabbing her boots on the way.

'Nobody, Martha,' she called. 'Thanks for the toast.'

'Good luck, Miss. Be careful!'

In the foyer, Jupiter and Fen inspected Morrigan for a long time before either of them spoke.

'She needs to tie her hair back,' said Jupiter.

'She needs to keep her mouth shut,' said Fen.

'She's in the same room as you, so you needn't speak about her as if she's not here,' said Morrigan.

'See what I mean?' Fenestra growled. 'I'll not have her going on like that during the Chase. I'll lose my concentration.' The Magnificat turned to Jupiter, her huge grey ears perking up hopefully. 'Can we tape her mouth shut?'

'I rather think the Elders would frown on that sort of thing.'

Morrigan folded her arms, suddenly suspicious. 'What are you talking about?'

'Ah,' said Jupiter, rubbing his hands together in excitement. 'I've found you a noble steed.'

Morrigan, Jupiter and Fen arrived at the West Gate at eleven o'clock to find a clamour of children, patrons and animals. At the registration table, Morrigan and Jupiter both had to sign a waiver stating that if the Chase resulted in death or injury they wouldn't sue the Society.

'Comforting,' muttered Morrigan as she scribbled her name. Her stomach did a funny little somersault.

She was surprised to see the steeds some candidates had chosen. Most were riding horses or ponies, but she also saw a lot of camels, a few zebras and llamas, an ostrich (so that answered *that* question), two haughty-looking unicorns and one large, ugly pig. Morrigan gasped and grabbed Jupiter's arm when she saw the unicorns, her terror momentarily giving way to delight, but Jupiter was unimpressed.

'Mind the pointy bit,' he said with a worried look at the magical creatures.

Fen was in a strange mood. She hadn't made a single sarcastic remark all the way to the trial, and now she was pacing up and down the West Gate starting line, glaring at the competition. Jupiter approached her with caution.

'Fen?' She ignored him. He spoke up a little. 'Fen? Fennie? Fenestra?'

Fen was muttering to herself in a constant low growl, her amber eyes narrowed. A large leathery-skinned rhinoceros had caught her attention.

'Fen?' prompted Jupiter again, gingerly tapping her on the shoulder.

'That one,' she said with a toss of her head. 'That horned oaf with the funny ears. He'd better not get in my way. Better watch his big pointy nose, or I'll let him have one.'

'One . . . one what?' asked Jupiter.

'Headbutt. Him and that little demon on his back.'

Jupiter and Morrigan exchanged a look. What had gotten into Fen?

'You . . . you do know that demon is a child?' said Jupiter carefully.

Fen snarled in response and pointed one paw at a small boy nervously clutching the reins of a pony. 'And I'll give him one, too, him and his hell-beast.'

Jupiter snorted into his hand, trying to cover it up as a cough. 'Fen, that's a pony. I think you're—'

Fen shoved her face right up close to Jupiter's and spoke in a low growl. 'Him and his fat little half-horse come clip-clopping anywhere near me and they're done for. Got it?'

The Magnificat then swept off towards a throng of candidates milling around the registration table and proceeded to pace threateningly before them.

Jupiter smiled uneasily at Morrigan, who was waiting for an explanation as to why Fen the Magnificat had transformed into Fen the prison-yard gangster. 'She's . . . competitive,' he offered. 'Goes back to her days as a cage fighter.'

'A *what*?'

'Oh yeah. Fen was big on the Ultimate Cage Fighting circuit. Free State champion three years running, until she had to quit because of that scandal with the former prime minister's son.'

'Scandal with the—'

'He started it. And he's got a new nose now, so no harm, no foul. Oh, look – they're calling you over.'

As she drew near the starting line, Morrigan wondered what sort of steed Nan Dawson had found for Hawthorne. (Last they'd spoken, he'd sworn his patron had a cheetah lined up.) She knew it was pointless searching for her friend in the crowd; he was in the South Gate group.

However, she did find someone else she knew – the one person she absolutely did not want to see.

'Honestly, they'll let *anything* through these trials, won't they?' Noelle Devereaux said loudly, leading a beautiful brown mare by the reins over to where Morrigan stood. She looked Morrigan up and down. 'Is it still called the Wundrous Society? Or have they changed it to the Stupid, Ugly Society?'

Noelle's friends laughed, and she flicked her hair over her shoulder, basking in their attention. She was flanked by her usual gaggle of followers, minus her friend with the long braid – Morrigan wondered if the other girl had made it past the Book Trial.

'That would explain why you're still here,' said Morrigan.

Noelle's face turned a splotchy red. Her hand clenched tighter around the reins of her horse. 'Or perhaps it's called the Illegal Society now,' she snapped, glaring at Morrigan. 'And that's why *you're* still here.'

Morrigan's stomach did that funny little flip again. It was Noelle and her patron, the odious Baz Charlton, who had sent Inspector Flintlock to the Hotel Deucalion. She just *knew* it. In that moment Morrigan hated Noelle, really hated her, for making her feel so afraid and desperate. Had Noelle *any* idea of the trouble she and Baz had caused? That they were putting Morrigan's *life* in danger if she went back to Jackalfax? She wanted to lash out, to shout at Noelle, but she couldn't. Not here.

'You could be disqualified for that, you know,' she said instead, pointing at Noelle's hair.

Noelle was dressed, like the other candidates, all in white – from her smart ivory jodhpurs to her leather saddle and riding crop. Everything *except* the tiny gold ribbon poking through her thick chestnut curls. Morrigan knew it was a petty thing to mention, but she couldn't resist.

However, instead of looking worried or tucking it away, Noelle curled the ribbon around her finger and looked even more smug. She moved closer and spoke quietly so that only Morrigan could hear. 'Oh, this? Just my little message to the Elders. It was Mr Charlton's idea. He says it shows that I'm serious about winning the Chase. I want the Elders to know that I'm going for gold and I'll see them at the secret dinner.'

'Secret dinner,' said Morrigan, scowling. It sounded like Noelle was making things up now, just to mock her. 'What secret dinner?'

Noelle gave an incredulous giggle. 'Your patron doesn't tell you anything, does he? It's like he doesn't even *want* you to win.'

Turning to leave, she called back over her shoulder, 'By the way, is that your steed?' She pointed at the pig Morrigan had spotted earlier, which was now snuffling around the ground looking for food. 'How nice – you have matching faces.'

At the West Gate, a Wundrous Society official climbed up on a platform to address the candidates.

'Over here, please! No, leave your steeds for the moment, thank you. Quiet, please. *Quiet!*' she shouted into a megaphone. 'Now listen carefully, because you will only hear these instructions once.'

Morrigan's heart beat so loudly she thought it would drown out the official's voice.

'The Chase Trial is not a race,' said the woman, her voice booming. 'Not exactly, anyway. It's a game of strategy. You are not looking for a finish line; you are looking for a target.'

The woman signalled another official, who took his cue to unveil a large map of the Old Town, propped up on a wooden easel. It was just like the map enclosed with Morrigan's letter, but much bigger, and with dozens of coloured targets marked all over, like rainbow sprinkles on a cake.

The targets were scattered across Old Town in nine very loose concentric rings, like the inside of a tree trunk, each ring a different colour of the rainbow. Close to the outer stone walls, the first ring of purple targets circling the town was densely plotted – there must have been one every twenty or thirty metres. But the closer you got to the centre of town, through sections of blue, teal, green, yellow, orange, pink and red, the sparser the targets became, until finally in the last section – a golden circle that covered massive Courage Square – Morrigan counted only five golden targets, right in the middle of the square.

'This is your sole task,' the woman with the megaphone was saying. 'Hit one target – and *only* one target – firmly, with the flat of your hand.' She demonstrated. 'Once you hit a target, you've won. You're through to the next trial.'

The candidates mumbled amongst themselves, looking unsure. It all seemed too easy. Morrigan waited for the catch.

'Now,' continued the woman. 'The question is: which target will you try to hit? There are three hundred candidates remaining, but only one hundred and fifty targets. Will you go for the first one you see, in the outer rings of Old Town? That makes sense – there are more targets there, and in nice, easy spots.'

Yes, thought Morrigan. *Of course I'll go for one of those! Get in, hit an easy target and get through to the next trial.* She could see from some of the other candidates' confused faces that they were thinking the same – why *wouldn't* they go for the easiest targets?

'Or,' said the woman, 'you could challenge yourself.' She smiled widely, pointing to the centre of the map. 'Here, in Courage Square, there are five golden targets. Hit one of these and not only will you win your place in the third trial, you'll also win a ticket to a very private, very special event – the Elders' secret dinner, inside the Proudfoot House Elders' Hall itself.'

A shock of excitement rippled through the candidates. '*Inside* the Elders' Hall?' whispered a boy standing near Morrigan. 'Only Society members are allowed in there!'

Morrigan glanced at Noelle, who was near the front. So that was what she meant by *going for gold*. Noelle curled her gold ribbon around one finger again, looking unbearably smug. *How had she known?* Morrigan wondered. All the other candidates seemed just as surprised by the news as Morrigan. Why was awful Noelle the only one with insider information?

The Society official held up her hands for quiet. 'In addition to these five golden targets, there are five more, scattered at random throughout the Old Town. However, there's a twist – these five will look like ordinary coloured targets. It's a lottery – you won't know you've got a gold target until after you've hit it.'

'How will we know?' shouted a girl with red hair.

'You'll know.'

A boy in the front put his hand up and called out, 'Why're we dressed in white?'

The Society officials smirked at each other. 'You'll see,' said the woman with the megaphone. 'Only ten candidates – and their patrons – will attend the Elders' secret dinner. This is a unique opportunity to meet the Elders personally before your third and fourth trials.' Morrigan could see now why Noelle was so determined to hit a golden target. What an advantage it would be at the Show Trial, to have already met the Elders and made an impression. She was certain Noelle would charm them, just as she'd charmed her simpering band of followers. The thought of it made Morrigan queasy.

The Society official continued. 'Remember, you can only hit *one* target. Will you bypass the coloured targets for an uncertain chance at hitting gold and winning a special advantage? Or will you hit the very first target you see, to guarantee your spot in the next trial? Are you an ambitious risk-taker? Or cool-headed and efficient? We're about to find out. Please gather at the starting line. The Chase Trial will begin in precisely five minutes.'

Morrigan's nerves were undercut by a twinge of annoyance that odious Baz Charlton's odious candidate had known so much about the trial before she even arrived. Had Jupiter known too? And if so, why hadn't he told her? Noelle's words echoed in her head: *It's like he doesn't even want you to win.*

Jupiter and Fen approached, but there was no time for questions.

'Mog, listen,' Jupiter said in a low, urgent voice as he led her to the starting line. 'Forget the secret dinner. It doesn't matter. Just hit a target and get through to the next trial – don't worry about *anything else*. Go straight past – Fen, are you listening too? – go straight past the purple and blue targets. They'll be chaos; most candidates will go for the first targets they see, and you don't want to get caught up in that mess. Better to make a beeline straight down Grand Boulevard, then turn left onto Mayhew Street – that's where the green section starts. There'll be fewer targets there, but much less competition if you get there quick enough. Yes?'

Morrigan nodded. *Straight down Grand, left onto Mayhew.* At that moment Jupiter was ushered away by a Society official. He looked back and mouthed the words, '*Good luck,*' and though Morrigan couldn't bring herself to open her own mouth just in case her heart fell out of it, she hoped a grim nod and a shaky thumbs-up would get the message across.

Nearby, Noelle was having a final word with her patron as well, but Morrigan could only make out the words *gold* and *Roderick* (*Who's Roderick?* she wondered) before Fen sidled up close and spoke in her ear.

'You don't need to do anything, understand? I'll get us to the target, just be ready to hit it when I say so. You don't steer, or brake – and if you kick me in the sides even *once*, I'll hide raw sardines in your room. You'll never find them, but the stench will seep deep into your skin and clothes and invade your dreams at night until you go mad. Got it?'

'Got it,' said Morrigan. A big clock above the West Gate was counting down: sixty seconds to go. It suddenly occurred to Morrigan that she had no idea how she was going to climb up on Fen's enormous back. 'Fen, how do I—'

Before she could finish, she felt Fen's hot breath on her neck and the tickle of whiskers and fur as the Magnificat lifted Morrigan up with her sharp yellow teeth and tossed the girl effortlessly onto her back. Morrigan tried to adjust her position as if she were riding a horse – which, as she'd never ridden a horse, was mostly guesswork – and found she had no way to steady herself. She clutched two handfuls of soft grey fur.

As the final seconds counted down, she threw her head down onto Fen's neck, feeling the sudden rise of panic.

'Fen, what if I fall off?'

'You'll probably get trampled and die. So don't fall off.'

Morrigan tightened her grip and swallowed a whimper.

Fenestra turned back and said, a little more kindly, 'All right, dig your heels into my sides if you have to. It'll help you balance. And whatever you do, don't let go of my fur.'

'What if I accidentally rip some out?'

'As you can see, I have plenty. Now shut up, it's time.'

The clock hit zero and a deafening klaxon went off, and suddenly Morrigan's world lurched into a chaotic melee of clattering, pounding footfall and the roar of cheering patrons somewhere behind her. She squeezed her eyes shut and held on tightly to Fen, who was keeping a good pace. Chancing an upward glance, Morrigan saw that Jupiter was right; straight ahead, on the marble steps of the Nevermoor Opera House, was a purple target about the size of Morrigan's head, and half the candidates were barrelling straight towards it. It was sure to end in a nasty collision, but Morrigan wouldn't be there to witness it – Fenestra was taking a wide circle around the opera house and emerging onto Grand Boulevard. The commotion was already behind them.

BANG!

BANG!

BANG!

Morrigan turned back to see purple targets exploding all over the place as candidates hit them. Each one blasted a cloud of brightly coloured powder all over the candidate's face and clothes, staining them purple. The air filled with dust and colour and noise.

So *that* was what the white clothes were for. At the end of the trial there would be a rainbow of a hundred and fifty winning candidates . . . and a hundred and fifty sad kids still in pristine white.

Not me, thought Morrigan fiercely, leaning into Fen. *I'll be green.*

They passed through the sea of purple and blue targets – some hanging from trees and street signs, some stuck on the sides of easy-to-reach buildings, some just sitting on the cobbled ground – and quickly made it to the teal section. The targets here were harder to spot but still scattered generously across the landscape.

Fen was so fast they'd left half the crowd in their dust, but a number of tenacious souls were keeping up – including, Morrigan saw to her displeasure, Noelle Devereaux on her left and Fen's apparent sworn enemies, the rhinoceros and its rider, on her right. Noelle's brown mare flew like the wind.

Meanwhile, Fen had been right not to trust the rhinoceros. He was trouble. He charged wildly, veering left and right with no regard for whom he trampled, or for where his swinging head landed its dangerous horn. He wasn't just trying to get a golden target; he wanted to knock out the rest of the competition before *they* reached Courage Square.

That was smart, Morrigan thought. Nasty, but smart. There'd be other candidates from the East, North and South Gate groups headed for those five targets too, and probably reaching the square at the same moment. There weren't enough golden targets for everyone; Courage Square would be a chaotic free-for-all. Morrigan was glad she and Fen were going for green.

But Fen didn't slow down in the green section. They didn't turn onto Mayhew Street, as Jupiter had instructed. They blew straight past, into the yellow section. The targets were getting fewer and farther between; if they didn't hit one soon they might miss out. But Fen kept going, straight through the yellow targets, then the orange, showing no sign of stopping.

'Fen!' Morrigan finally shouted. 'Fen, stop! Where are you *going*?'

'Courage Square,' Fen yelled back. 'I'm getting you a gold target!'

Morrigan felt the blood drain from her face. What was Fenestra *thinking*? She'd gone mad; her cage-fighter competitive streak had taken over.

'No – Fen, Jupiter said—'

'Jupiter says lots of things. It's all background noise to me. *Hold tight.*'

Fen went into turbo-gear, weaving and dodging through the candidates with a grace of which Morrigan hadn't thought her capable. She leapt over three, four heads at a time, landed elegantly in the tiniest patches of ground, and without missing a beat, bounded off again. She was absolutely the 'all-terrain beast' Jupiter had hoped for – launching from ground to trees, rebounding off the sides of buildings. Morrigan could only cling on for dear life.

She looked over her shoulder and saw, with no small amount of glee, that Noelle and her mare were gone – disappeared completely, as if they'd been swallowed back into the crowd or had shot off down a side street.

A tiny tendril of hope blossomed in Morrigan's heart. Maybe Fen was right – maybe they *could* get a golden target!

But the stampeding rhino was gaining speed. Morrigan could see his rider properly now, and was surprised to find she recognised her – it was Noelle's awful friend.

Only she wasn't laughing like a hyena, as she'd done at the Wundrous Welcome. Nor was she smug and superior, like she'd been at the Book Trial. She looked . . . terrified. Her long black braid had fallen half-loose and wild, and she was shouting and pulling hard on the reins to no avail; she'd lost all control of her steed. (Morrigan knew the feeling.)

The rhino, on the other hand, was fierce and determined. He had sussed out who his biggest competition was and was aiming right for them, horn first.

Morrigan tugged hard on Fen's fur and yelled into the Magnificat's ear the only words her brain could force out of her mouth: *'Fen! Rhino!'*

CHAPTER FOURTEEN

A Most Noble Steed

'They're coming right for us!'

Fen didn't look back, but instead picked up speed and began weaving left and right, trying to throw the rhino off. The great horned oaf kept pace but much less gracefully, ramming into other candidates and knocking them over with a series of bellows and crashing noises. Morrigan looked over her shoulder, watching Noelle's friend stare ahead with wide-eyed terror, unable to steer or slow down, unable to do anything but clutch at the reins for dear life.

Fen ran faster and faster, widening the gap between her and the crowd; the rogue rhinoceros alone stayed close on her tail.

'Just let him past us!' Morrigan shouted, but Fenestra didn't hear, or perhaps didn't listen. She was a mad thing, single-minded and possessed . . . but she was also panting heavily now, beginning to lose stamina.

Suddenly the rhino was thundering alongside them, shaking his enormous head.

'Watch out, Fen!' yelled Morrigan as the beast shoved violently into them from the side. The girl on the rhino screamed. Morrigan threw herself down onto Fen's furry neck and clung on tight. The Magnificat lost her balance but quickly recovered, taking a defensive swipe at the rhinoceros. She sliced him right across the face with her long, sharp claws, and he bellowed in pain.

Morrigan lifted her head at the sound of another piercing scream behind them. She turned just in time to see the rhinoceros stumble, throwing his rider off. The girl fell to the ground with a sickening thud. The rhino tumbled horn over hooves and then, struggling upright, charged away down the nearest side street, his greed for a golden target apparently forgotten. He bawled loudly as he fled, the deep gashes in his leathery face weeping blood, all fierceness and aggression vanquished by just one slash of Fen's mighty claws. Fenestra hurtled onward, finally free of her pursuer.

The rider, Noelle's friend, was left in the middle of Grand Boulevard. She shook her head, looking dazed. The rest of the candidates were catching up and would soon be upon her. Here and there targets exploded in the background, sending clouds of bright pink and red dust into the air, coming closer to where the girl sat unmoving on the ground.

Morrigan looked ahead. A hundred metres away, Grand Boulevard opened up into the enormous cobbled plaza of Courage Square, and at the centre she could see them – four golden targets, placed evenly around the edge of an elaborate fountain. Morrigan could just make out the fifth target in the fountain's centre, at the top of the statue. It gleamed gold in the sunshine, held aloft in the mouth of a concrete fish.

They were close – *so close*. There was nobody ahead of them. Courage Square was empty. She could really *win* this, she could get a golden target—

But Morrigan looked over her shoulder again.

The girl was still there. She seemed frozen in time, staring back at the wall of hooves and coloured dust that was barrelling towards her with no sign of slowing down.

Morrigan's heart sank.

'Fen, we have to go back!' she shouted. 'They'll trample her.'

Fen didn't hear, or if she did she was ignoring her. Morrigan tugged roughly on her ears. *'Fen!* She'll be killed!'

Fenestra growled. 'You do realise this is a *competition*?' But even as she said it, Fen was turning back, racing to where the girl sat helplessly, clutching her leg.

'Faster, Fen!'

Fenestra put on a burst of speed, making it to the rhino girl just in time to scoop her up in her teeth and jump clear of the oncoming crowd, down a side alley off Grand Boulevard. The other candidates stampeded over the empty spot where the girl had sat seconds earlier.

With a fierce shake of her head, Fen threw the girl onto her own back to land in front of Morrigan, where she sat shaking and crying. 'Oh, stop your snivelling,' growled the Magnificat.

Morrigan guided the girl's trembling hands to the thick fur on Fen's neck and helped her get a hold of it. She flinched as the last few candidates and their steeds barrelled past, kicking up clouds of dust and keeping Morrigan, Fen and the rhino girl stuck firmly at the margins of the race. It was hopeless. The golden targets would be gone within seconds.

'Maybe,' Morrigan said in breathless desperation, 'maybe we could go back to the green targets, or – or the yellow—'

'Get a grip,' said Fen.

'I can't just give up, Fen! There might be one left somewhere—'

'No, you idiot, I mean *get a grip on my fur*. And hold tight.' Morrigan did as she was told, and Fen reared backwards. 'We're still going for gold!'

The Courage Square fountain was like the scene of some apocalyptic battle. The four golden targets stationed around the fountain had already been hit . . . but that one final target remained, metres up in the air, still gleaming in the mouth of the fish statue, untouched. Water churned underneath the statue as dozens – maybe almost a hundred – children waded through it, waist-deep, having abandoned their steeds to go on alone. They shouted and gurgled, pushing each other under the water in their desperation to get to the target. A few had already reached the statue and were climbing up its fins and tail, kicking out at the candidates underneath who tried to pull them down. It was a nightmarish scene, and Morrigan hated the idea of joining in.

But Fenestra wouldn't be stopped. She reared back, took a running leap, and bounded over the backs of the abandoned horses and ostriches and zebras around the fountain, using them as stepping-stones. She launched from her powerful hind legs and soared through the air over the other candidates, landing at the top of the statue, wrapping her paws around the fish's head and digging her claws in.

'*Hit it!*' Fen shouted.

Morrigan reached up as high as she could, her fingertips nearly there . . . *nearly there* . . .

But Noelle's friend was closer. She seemed to have recovered from her fall and was climbing up on Fenestra's neck, shoving her knees right between the giant cat's shoulder blades. She reached up, and Morrigan reached up behind her, and at the very same moment they both hit the target.

BANG!

It exploded in a cloud of golden dust, coating the other girl's face, white clothes and long, swinging braid in the colour of victory . . .

. . . and missing Morrigan entirely.

'One at a time, please, *one at a time!*' shouted the harassed-looking Society official. 'Now, who hit the target? Who rode the big cat?'

'I did,' Morrigan and the other girl said together. They turned to glare at each other.

'*I did*,' repeated Morrigan. 'I rode the big cat.'

'And your name is?'

'Cadence,' interrupted the other girl. 'My name is Cadence Blackburn, and *I* rode the big cat. I hit the target.'

'No, *I* hit the target! I'm Morrigan Crow, and the Magnificat is *my steed*. Cadence fell off hers – she was on the rhinoceros – and we went back to—'

'I was sitting in front,' cut in Cadence. 'I was sitting in front, so you see I *must have* hit the target. Look at me, I'm covered in gold!'

The race official looked from Morrigan to Cadence and back again. 'Is that true? Was she sitting in front?'

Morrigan was flabbergasted. She couldn't deny that, in fact, Cadence had been sitting in front of her, and that was why she was covered in gold dust. But that was ridiculous! A silly technicality couldn't mean anything – it just *couldn't*. It wasn't fair.

'Well, yes, but . . . only because we turned back and picked her up. She would have been trampled otherwise!'

The official snorted. 'Think that's going to get you a place in the Wundrous Society, do you?' He shook his head. 'Why does everyone think *valour* and *sportsmanship* are going to win them any favours? We're testing for tenacity and ambition, not bloody niceness.'

'But that's not the point,' said Morrigan desperately. 'The Magnificat was my steed, and she climbed that statue for me, not Cadence. *I* hit the target! This is just—'

'Nonsense,' said Cadence in her low voice, like the hum of a wasp. She stepped closer to the official and looked up at him. 'That cat was *my* steed. I hit the golden target, and I *will* go through to the next trial.'

The official handed her a little golden envelope, which Cadence pocketed with a look of triumph as she ran off.

Morrigan could have screamed at the unfairness of it, but no sound would come out of her mouth. Instead she levelled her gaze at the race official, cold and accusing.

'That cat was her steed,' he said, shrugging. 'She hit the golden target. She will go through to the next trial.'

Morrigan deflated like a punctured bicycle tyre. She was out. Game over.

At that moment Noelle sauntered past, surrounded by friends. She too was covered in shimmering gold dust and held her gold envelope like a trophy. 'I saw a pink target on the corner of Roderick Street and just decided to go for it, I don't know why. Maybe because pink's my favourite colour,' she said breezily. 'Imagine my surprise when it turned out to be one of the hidden gold targets! Guess I'm just lucky.' She looked back at Morrigan, grinning at the sight of her still-white clothes.

Roderick Street, Morrigan thought bitterly, remembering what Noelle's patron had whispered to her at the starting line. *Roderick!* It wasn't a person; it was a direction to a golden target. Noelle hadn't been lucky at all – Baz Charlton had helped her cheat! He *told her* where the hidden gold target would be.

No wonder she'd been the only candidate to know about the secret dinner! Baz was telling her secrets, handing her everything she needed to win the trials.

Morrigan slumped on the edge of the fountain, overwhelmed by outrage at Cadence and Noelle's cheating, and by the crushing agony of her own defeat. She felt so foolish. Even worse, she felt terrified of what would happen next. She'd be kicked out of Nevermoor, of course, and then . . . and then . . .

The Hunt of Smoke and Shadow reared up in her mind's eye like a great black swarm, blocking out the sun and casting the day further into darkness.

When Jupiter heard the story, he was dumbfounded. Fenestra was furious.

'Where's that official?' she fumed, pacing back and forth and baring her yellow teeth. 'I'll take his clipboard and shove it right up—'

'We have to go,' said Jupiter suddenly, looking over his shoulder. 'We have to go right now. He's here.'

'Who's – oh.' Morrigan's stomach dropped somewhere south of her knees. Snaking through the crowd of candidates and patrons was a small brigade of brown-uniformed police officers, led by perhaps her third least favourite person in Nevermoor (after Cadence Blackburn and Noelle Devereaux).

Jupiter grabbed Morrigan's arm and started to march her in the opposite direction, only to find their way out blocked by yet more brown uniforms. They were surrounded by Stink.

'I'll be seeing those papers now, Captain North.' Inspector Flintlock, his face positively glowing with self-righteousness, held out his palm. 'Hand them over.'

Morrigan held her breath. Would she get a chance to go back to the Deucalion, she wondered, before they deported her? Would she be able to say goodbye to the residents, and pack her things, and – Hawthorne! They couldn't make her leave without saying goodbye to her friend, could they? She looked frantically around Courage Square, trying to see him one last time. *Had he hit a target?* she wondered.

And the Hunt of Smoke and Shadow, said a small, panicked voice inside. *Will they be waiting for me at the border?*

'To which papers do you refer, Inspector Flintlock?' said Jupiter, smiling pleasantly. 'The morning papers? They'll all be lining cat litter trays or wrapping fish and chips by now. I must say it is *marvellous* that you're trying to keep up with current events, Flinty. Good for you. Let me know if you need help sounding out the big words.'

Flintlock's jaw twitched, but the smile never left his face. 'Very witty, North. Very witty indeed. I refer, of course, to your . . . *former* candidate's Free State passport, her residential papers for the Seventh Pocket and her educational visa for Nevermoor. The papers which, with one look, will convince me once and for all that your *former* candidate has every right to reside here in the First Pocket of the Free State, and isn't in fact a dirty illegal smuggled from the traitorous Republic under cover of night.'

'Oh, *those* papers,' said Jupiter. 'Why didn't you say so?'

With a dramatic sigh, he made a show of patting down his jacket, pulling his pockets inside out and even feeling through his luxurious beard for the nonexistent papers. Morrigan might have laughed at him, if it hadn't been the least funny day of her life.

'I'm losing my patience, North.'

'Yes, sorry, they're right here – no, sorry, that's a hanky. Bear with me.'

Morrigan wondered if she should make a break for it. If she could sneak past the Stink while they were distracted, she might make it to the nearest Wunderground station.

She stepped sideways casually as an experiment. Nobody grabbed her. She looked around – the Stink were focused entirely on Jupiter and his paper-finding circus act. She took another step away, then another, remembering how

Hawthorne had sidled off from the scene of the crime after his toad-spilling episode. Just a few more steps and she'd be swallowed up by the crowd and could run for it.

'Morrigan *Crow*!' boomed a voice. Morrigan froze. This was it. She was going to be arrested. Goodbye, Nevermoor. *'Morrigan Crow! The girl on the cat! Where is she? Has anyone seen Morrigan Crow, the girl who rode the cat?'*

It was the race official. He spotted her and came waddling over, waving an ivory envelope in his hand. 'There you are! Thank goodness I found you. Here, this is yours.'

She took the envelope. 'What is it?'

'What's it look like? Your invitation to the next trial, of course.'

Morrigan's head snapped towards Jupiter, who looked as stunned as she felt. Flintlock's mouth opened and closed but no sound came out. He looked like a goldfish that had been turfed out of its bowl and lay gasping for air on the carpet.

Morrigan hardly dared to hope she'd heard correctly. 'But . . . but you said . . . but Cadence—'

'Well, yes, but there was . . . an incident. Bit embarrassing, actually. One of those blooming unicorns turned out to be a Pegasus with its wings tucked away and an upside-down ice cream cone glued to its head. Can't believe we didn't spot that earlier. Very cruel to the poor thing, of course, and totally against the rules. Even if they weren't *using* the wings, the rulebook clearly states that no flying animals may be used in the Chase Trial. Anyway, that candidate's been disqualified, which means a place has opened up, and, well . . .' He looked a little sheepish. 'Due to the, er, *unusual* circumstances surrounding your – er, well, we thought it was only fair. Congratulations.'

The man shuffled off, leaving Morrigan overjoyed, gazing at the precious envelope in her hands as if it were carved out of diamond. It wasn't gold – it wouldn't get her into the Elders' secret dinner – but she couldn't care less. 'I got through,' she whispered, then more loudly, 'I got through to the next trial!'

She ripped open the envelope and read the note inside aloud.

> *Congratulations, candidate.*
> *You have proven your tenacity and ambition*
> *and have won a place in the next round of trials*
> *for Unit 919 of the Wundrous Society. The*
> *Fright Trial will take place in Autumn of One*
> *at a date, time and location unspecified.*

Jupiter laughed – a loud, explosive, joyful laugh that reverberated in Morrigan's ears. Even Fenestra gave a wheezing chuckle. Morrigan felt like jumping up and down. She'd never been so happy, so relieved.

'*Brilliant*, Mog. Brilliant. Sorry, Inspector, you'll have to wait for those papers. At this time, the question of Morrigan Crow's citizenship remains a private matter for the Wundrous Society. Ha *ha*!'

Inspector Flintlock was practically foaming at the mouth. 'This isn't over,' he threatened, and in his rage he slammed his baton onto his own thigh for emphasis. Morrigan winced – that had to have hurt. 'My eyes are everywhere, Morrigan Crow. I'll be watching you – both of you. Very closely.'

The inspector turned on his heel and marched away, followed closely by his brown-coated brethren.

'Creep,' Fenestra called after him.

CHAPTER FIFTEEN

The Black Parade

Autumn of One

'I need a queen, please.'

'What for?'

'Just do. Hand it over.'

Heaving a great, put-upon sigh, Hawthorne shuffled through the pack of cards until he found the queen of diamonds. 'I don't think you're doing this right.'

After their Chase Trial success (Hawthorne had hit an orange target – riding a camel, definitely *not* a cheetah), Jupiter had promised that Morrigan and her friend could have a sleepover at the Deucalion on Hallowmas night – so long as they swore to ignore bedtime, eat lots of sugar and get up to no good. True to their word, they'd already demolished handfuls of sweets and were now teaching themselves to play poker in the Music Salon while they waited for Fen, who was taking them out to the Black Parade at midnight.

In honour of Hallowmas, the salon was lit entirely by candles and jack-o'-lanterns. Frank the vampire dwarf was singing an obnoxious song about beheading his fearsome enemies and drinking their blood. The guests clapped along, enchanted by the idea of the little man beheading anybody at all, fearsome or otherwise.

Morrigan arranged her cards in a fan on the table. 'Poker!'

Hawthorne examined them. 'That's not poker.'

'Yes it is, look: the Queen of Diamonds was out in the park one day, walking her dog, Jack of Diamonds. She met the King of Hearts and they fell in love. They were married six (of hearts) weeks later and had three (of diamonds) children and lived happily ever after.' She grinned triumphantly. 'Poker.'

Hawthorne groaned and slapped down his cards. 'That *is* poker. You win again.' He pushed the large pile of Hallowmas sweets over to her side of the table.

'Thank you, thank you, friends,' the vampire dwarf was saying loudly. 'And now, on this Hallowmas night, the night when we feel closest to those we have lost – in honour of my dear departed mother, I shall sing for you her favourite song.' His audience cooed sympathetically. Frank motioned to the pianist. 'Wilbur, if you please – "My Sweetheart Is a Garrotter" in D minor.'

'Where's Fen?' asked Hawthorne, shuffling the cards listlessly. 'It's almost ten-thirty! If we don't leave soon all the best spots will be taken.'

'My sweetheart is a garrotter, my sweetheart loves to strangle. Her hands are wrapped around my throat, but my heart is in a tangle . . .'

Hawthorne had talked of nothing but the Black Parade since autumn began, and as Jupiter was marching with the rest of the Wundrous Society, he'd persuaded Fenestra to accompany Morrigan and Hawthorne in his place. Fen had agreed under *extreme* protest, and only after she'd extracted a promise from Jupiter that if they misbehaved, she could put itching powder in Morrigan's bedsheets every night for a month.

'Fenestra does things on Fenestra time,' said Morrigan, biting into a sour skeleton.

'She grips me with her burly arms and the stars begin to shine. My scrawny neck is hers alone, her violent heart is mine!'

Frank finished his song with a grand flourish and a high note that made Morrigan and Hawthorne wince. The other guests broke into applause and the vampire dwarf took a deep bow.

'Any requests?' asked Frank.

'Sing something scary!' a young man shouted.

'Ah. Beheading and strangling not scary enough for you, eh?' There was a gleam in Frank's eye. 'Then perhaps you'd like to hear a song about . . . the Wundersmith?'

The guests gasped, then fell into nervous laughter. Across the card table, Hawthorne grew very still. 'Shall we go wait in the foyer?'

'Fen said to wait here,' said Morrigan. 'She'll be cross if we leave. What's wrong?'

'I just . . .' He swallowed and lowered his voice. 'I wish he wouldn't sing about the Wundersmith.'

'The *Wundersmith*.' Morrigan rolled her eyes. 'What's a Wundersmith, anyway? Why is everybody so scared of it?'

Hawthorne's eyes bulged. 'You *don't know about the Wundersmith*?'

On the other side of the room, the piano clanked to a halt. 'Can that be *true*?' called Frank. He was staring right at Morrigan. 'Can this really be a child who has never heard the stories of the *Wundersmith*?'

His audience turned to look at Morrigan with shocked faces. 'I mean,' she said, 'I've heard of him, but . . .' She shrugged and bit the head off a gummy ghost.

'Can it be,' Frank continued, his voice rising, 'that she knows nothing of the thing they call the Butcher of Nevermoor? The Curse of the Capital? That wicked devil with blackened mouth and empty eyes?'

Hawthorne made a strangled noise in the back of his throat. Morrigan sighed. 'So what is he?' she asked, exasperated.

'My child, my dear darkling child,' said the vampire dwarf, drawing his cape around him with a dramatic swish, 'perhaps it is best you don't know . . .'

The guests fell for his ruse. 'Tell her, Frank,' they cried, clapping their hands with savage delight. 'Tell her about the Wundersmith!'

'If you insist,' he said, affecting a reluctant air. The pianist hit a loud, dramatic chord, and Morrigan giggled. This was all rather silly, she thought.

'Who – or *what* – is the Wundersmith?' Frank began. 'Is he a man, or is he a monster? Does he live in our imaginations, or is he lurking in the shadows, waiting . . . to . . . *pounce*?' Frank lunged at a group of women, who shrieked, first with fright and then with laughter. 'Is he human, or is he a *savage animal* who will tear through the realm with talons and teeth *until he has consumed us all*?' Here he paused to bare his own impressive fangs, and there were gasps and giggles around the room.

'The Wundersmith is all of those things. He is a phantom that lives in the darkness, watching, always watching, biding his time until the day when we have let down our defences, when we are not expecting him, when we have almost forgotten he existed.' Frank grabbed a candle from its holder and held it under his chin so that his face was eerily lit by the glow. 'And that is when he will return.'

'Tosh,' said a quiet voice from the corner. Morrigan turned to see Dame Chanda playing chess with Kedgeree Burns, the concierge. They were staring at the board, deep in concentration and all but ignoring the musical goings-on at the opposite end of the room.

Kedgeree hummed in agreement. 'Aye, utter nonsense.'

'Is it?' said Morrigan. 'Then the Wundersmith isn't real?'

Dame Chanda sighed. 'Oh, the Wundersmith is real. But I wouldn't ask that sharp-toothed showboat about it,' she muttered, nodding towards Frank, who was now doing a tap dance in the instrumental break. 'He wouldn't know the real Wundersmith from a potted agapanthus. He thinks it's funny trying to scare people.'

Morrigan frowned. 'But why *is* everyone so scared of the Wundersmith? What is it?'

'That's a very good question,' said Dame Chanda. Kedgeree shook his head warningly, but she waved a hand at him. 'Oh, Ree-Ree, she's bound to find out sooner or later. Better to hear the truth from us, don't you think, than a load of hogwash from some other fool?'

Kedgeree held up his hands in defeat. 'All right, but I don't think North will like it.'

'Then North should have told her himself.' Dame Chanda took a moment to capture Kedgeree's knight and sip her brandy. 'Now. Frank *is* being silly, of course, but he poses an interesting historical question: is the Wundersmith a man, or is he a monster? Certainly he was once a man. He once *looked* like a man, although almost all photographs and portraits from his younger days have been destroyed. Some people say he has turned inside out, and the darkness within him is now on the outside, for everyone to see. They say he is hideously deformed, that his teeth and mouth and the whites in his eyes have turned black like a spider. That his skin is greyed and decaying like his decaying soul.'

'Is it true he was exiled from Nevermoor?' asked Hawthorne.

'Yes,' said Dame Chanda, her expression grave. 'Over one hundred winters he's been in exile, banned from Nevermoor, from all Seven Pockets of the Free State. To this day he is kept out by the force of this great and ancient city, by the combined efforts of the Royal Sorcery Council and the Paranormal League, by our protective borders, which are manned by the Ground Force and watched over by the Sky Force and patrolled by the Stink and spied on by the Stealth and probably by dozens of other secret organisations that exist only to protect us from the Wundersmith. Thousands of men and women all working constantly, twenty-four hours a day, seven days a week, for more than a hundred years, all to keep one man out.'

Morrigan swallowed. Thousands of people . . . just for *one man*? 'Why? What did he do?'

'He was a man who became a monster, lass, that's what he did,' said Kedgeree. 'A monster who made monsters of his own, who was so brilliant – so talented and *twisted* – that he decided to play God. He built a great army of fearsome creatures with which he planned to conquer Nevermoor, to enslave the people of our city.'

'Why?'

Kedgeree blinked. 'For power, I suppose. He sought to own the city, and by owning the city to own the entire realm.'

'Some people stepped up and tried to stop him,' added Dame Chanda. 'But they were massacred. Brave, selfless men and women, destroyed by the Wundersmith and his army of monsters. It happened not too far from here, in the Old Town. The place where they died was renamed for those brave people. Courage Square.'

'We've been there. That's where the Chase Trial ended,' said Morrigan, and Hawthorne nodded grimly. It was hard to imagine that cobbled, sunlit square awash with the blood of a massacre. 'And – oh! We read about the Courage Square Massacre, didn't we, Hawthorne? When we were studying for the Book Trial. *The Encyclopedia of*

Nevermoorian Barbarism didn't mention anything about the Wundersmith, though.'

'No, it wouldn't,' said Kedgeree, pointedly raising an eyebrow at Dame Chanda. 'Even history books don't like talking about the Wundersmith.'

'Nobody knows exactly what happened to the Wundersmith that day,' continued Dame Chanda, ignoring his comment. 'Some say he was weakened by the attack. Some say his monsters deserted him – that they'd got a taste for death and liked it, and so they melted away into the darkest corners of Nevermoor, where they lurk still, killing off its people one by one, waiting for the day when their master will return to conquer the city.'

'Chanda . . .' Kedgeree said, shooting her a significant look.

'What? That's what some people say.'

'It's not true, wee ones,' said the concierge. 'Just a scary rumour.'

'I never said it was true, Ree-Ree, I only said it's what people say,' said Dame Chanda, ruffled. 'Anyway, after that day, Nevermoor locked her doors to him forever. Of course, the ban is reinforced by sorcerers and magicians, the Stink and the Stealth and all the rest, but everyone knows it's Nevermoor herself who truly keeps the Wundersmith out.'

'How?' said Morrigan with a glance at Hawthorne, who swallowed hard. She thought he looked a little clammy. 'What if the Wundersmith finds a way back in?'

'This is an ancient and powerful city, children,' said Kedgeree, 'protected by ancient and powerful magic. More powerful than any Wundersmith, don't you worry about—'

'*Fen's here!*' shouted Hawthorne suddenly. He grabbed Morrigan's arm and ran to meet the Magnificat at the door, clearly eager to leave all talk of the Wundersmith behind him.

Nevermoor was full of ghosts.

Also vampires, werewolves, princesses and warty-nosed witches. Quite a few fairies. The occasional pumpkin. Thousands of people in costumes lined the high street, waiting for Nevermoor's Hallowmas festivities to begin.

Morrigan rubbed her hands together for warmth and pulled her scarf tighter around her neck. She and Hawthorne shared an excited grin, their breath turning to fog in the crisp autumn air. They'd managed to barge their way through the heaving crowd to what Jupiter had promised would be the best spot on the parade route, right on the corner of Deacon Street and McLaskey Avenue.

The Wundrous Society had started the parade hundreds of years ago, Jupiter had said. It was originally a silent procession of Society members, dressed in formal black uniforms with their gold *W* pins at the throat, marching to honour those Wuns who had died in the last year. They walked through the streets in rows of nine on Hallowmas night, when the walls between the living and the dead were thinnest.

As years went by, the people of Nevermoor started gathering to watch the procession in silence and pay their respects. It became one of the city's most sacred traditions, and they called it the Black Parade. Over the Ages it grew into something much louder and more colourful, but the Wundrous Society still upheld tradition by marching first.

The crowd was eerily quiet as the solemn rows of nine passed by, their footsteps on the cobblestones the only sound to be heard. Morrigan thought she spotted Jupiter's big ginger head at one point, but there were so many Society members going by so quickly that she couldn't be sure. They wore sombre expressions, their eyes straight ahead. Here and there were empty spaces, and some of the people marching carried candles – one candle for each of the departed, Jupiter had said. The youngest Society members, who looked only a little older than Morrigan, marched in the first row. She supposed this must be Unit 918.

Would she and Hawthorne march in next year's parade,

Morrigan wondered. It was hard to picture Hawthorne keeping a straight face for that long.

Another, unwelcome image entered her head: Hawthorne and Noelle marching side by side. *That's more likely*, she thought miserably. The dragonrider and the girl with the voice of an angel, joining the rows of talented Society members marching through the streets of Nevermoor. Her excitement dimmed a little.

Once the Wundrous Society reached the end of the route, the 'proper parade' (as Hawthorne called it) began at last. A wave of anticipation rolled through the crowd as music began to play.

'I've *never* been this close to the front before!' said Hawthorne.

'You've never had Fen to scare people away before,' said Morrigan, glancing up at the Magnificat, who loomed behind them drawing looks of alarm from passers-by.

Though she wasn't thrilled to be babysitting, Fen took her duties very seriously. When anyone came too close, she hissed and bared her teeth until they retreated, wide-eyed, and a small plot of empty space miraculously ballooned around Morrigan and Hawthorne. She was like a mean, furry force field.

The parade was led by a marching band dressed as demons, conducted by a flickering ghostly apparition. They were followed by a procession of what looked like garden hedges, trimmed into animal sculptures and brought to life by some mysterious combination of puppetry and mechanics. A hedge mammoth swung his enormous tusks to and fro, and a leafy green lion growled and roared at groups of squealing children.

Morrigan and Hawthorne made themselves hoarse screaming and laughing in turn as the parade floats went by. There was a terrifying three-storey-high puppet of a werewolf, controlled with long wooden sticks by a team of people below. They could even make it snap its jaws and blink its yellow eyes.

But the Alliance of Nevermoor Covens was Morrigan's favourite.

'They've embraced the cliché this year, haven't they?' said Fen, in a tone of grudging approval. The witches wore pointed black hats and had fixed fake warts to their noses. Some carried black cats, and others flew on motorised wooden broomsticks. Cackling filled the air. 'Normally they're all, "Oh, don't stereotype us, we're just normal people." This is better. Witch it up, ladies!'

The grown-ups in the crowd were just as excited as the children, cheering each float as it passed. With one exception: when an enormous puppet of an old man in a cape came into view, accompanied by screechy violins and spooky organ music, it was met with gasps and disapproving glares. It wasn't as big as the werewolf puppet, and in Morrigan's opinion, nowhere near as scary – but a lot of parents looked very unhappy as it lumbered past, and children hid their faces. Even Fen was frowning, although Morrigan couldn't tell if it was just her everyday-grumpy frown or her special-occasion-grumpy frown.

'Did they have to ruin the fun?' said a lady standing nearby, covering her young son's eyes. 'There is such a thing as *too* scary, even for the Black Parade. The Wundersmith! Honestly.'

'*That's* the Wundersmith?' Morrigan laughed and turned to Hawthorne, who was eyeing the puppet warily.

It didn't *look* frightening. Just a hunched old man with sharp black teeth, black eyes and a swirling cape, his fingers ending in long talons. Occasional sparks of fire shot from his hands and eyes, and a silly, maniacal laugh issued from a speaker in his mouth. Morrigan wondered how anyone could be frightened of something so daft, but then she remembered the story of the Courage Square Massacre, and Dame Chanda's words rang in her head: *He was a man who became a monster.*

'Here it is!' Hawthorne shouted, looking determinedly past the Wundersmith puppet. 'The Morden Cemetery float. It's the best one.'

Built to look like a real cemetery, the float was shrouded in white mist and swarmed with zombies. Morrigan knew it was only people dressed up as zombies – the green makeup gave it away – but they gave her chills, groaning and clawing their way out of freshly dug graves. They reached through the rails of the wrought iron fence that encircled the float, lunging at children who wavered between delighted squeals of laughter and terrified screams.

Hawthorne was right; it was the best float. The crowd seemed to agree, because people were pushing closer to the front and standing on tiptoes to see. A man in front of them lifted his son up on his shoulders, blocking Morrigan and Hawthorne's view completely.

Hawthorne groaned. 'Come on – there's a rubbish skip back there. If we climb up we'll be able to see.'

Morrigan hesitated. 'But Fen—'

'We won't be long. Quick, while she's distracted!' said Hawthorne, nodding at Fen, who was swiping at the zombies as they reached through the rails.

'Fine,' Morrigan grumbled, 'but I swear, if I get itching powder in my sheets . . .'

The alley was dirty and the skip smelled awful. Hawthorne struggled up first, then offered Morrigan a hand.

'Help me.' The voice came from the end of the alley. There was nobody there.

'Please – somebody please help. I've fallen down.' It sounded like an old lady, frail and frightened. Morrigan and Hawthorne exchanged a glance. Hawthorne took one last longing look at the Morden Cemetery float before jumping down from the skip.

'Hello?' said Morrigan. 'Who's there?'

'Oh, thank goodness! Please, I need your help. I've fallen down here and . . . it's dark and wet, and I've hurt my ankle.'

They stepped cautiously down the alleyway.

'Where are you?' said Hawthorne. 'We can't see you.'

'Down here.'

The voice came from beneath their feet. Morrigan stepped back.

'It's a manhole, Hawthorne.' A feeling of unease crept upon her. Was somebody actually *stuck* down there?

They pried the manhole cover up with their fingers and heaved it to the side. Peering down into the hole, Morrigan saw only darkness. 'Hello? Are you down there?'

'Oh! Thank goodness you heard me. I tripped and fell, and . . . I think I've broken my ankle. I can't climb up by myself.'

'Okay, don't – don't panic!' Morrigan shouted. 'We'll climb down and help you.'

Hawthorne pulled her aside, whispering anxiously, 'I'm no expert, but do you reckon maybe if you hear a voice from the sewer asking you to climb down inside, you should consider . . . *not* climbing down inside?'

'She's just an old lady.' Morrigan was trying to convince herself as much as Hawthorne. There *was* something weird about it. 'Since when are you scared of old ladies?'

'Since they started shouting at me from sewers.'

'She needs a doctor.'

'Maybe we should get Fen—'

'Oh yeah, let's go tell Fen we ran off down a dark alley without her,' hissed Morrigan. 'Brilliant idea.'

Hawthorne growled. 'Fine. *Fine.* But if we get eaten alive by giant rats or torn to shreds by the Nevermoor Scaly Sewer Beast, my mum will be *really* cross.'

They decided it was best for Morrigan to go down and help the old lady climb onto the ladder so that Hawthorne – who had more upper-body strength, thanks to all his dragonriding – could pull her up from above.

Morrigan stepped onto the ladder feeling nervous, but by the time she'd gone two or three steps down into the dark, she was downright terrified. She looked up to check that Hawthorne was still there.

'You sure about this?' he asked.

A cry came from below. 'Please hurry – I can barely stand.'

Morrigan swallowed. Her pulse throbbed in her neck. She took another step, then another, concentrating only on putting one foot down after the other, and at last stepped onto solid ground.

It was darker than she'd imagined. She blinked, waiting for her eyes to adjust.

'H-hello? I can't see you. Where are you?'

No reply. Morrigan's heartbeat quickened. '*Hello?*' she said. Her voice echoed. 'Are you all right?'

She looked up. The light from the alleyway above was gone, as was Hawthorne. She gasped and reached for the ladder, grasping all around in the dark, but it had disappeared too.

'What's going on?' demanded Morrigan. She tried to sound tough, but her voice came out squeaky. 'This is *not funny*.'

The old lady cackled with laughter.

Morrigan heard the unmistakeable sound of a match being struck. The darkness yielded to glowing yellow light, and Morrigan blinked into the sudden glare. When her eyes adjusted, it was clear that she and the old lady were not in a sewer at all.

And they were not alone.

CHAPTER SIXTEEN
Follow the Glow

They surrounded her in a tight circle, their faces eerily lit by candlelight.

Morrigan wanted to scream, to run, to yell for Hawthorne, but she was frozen with fear.

'We are the witches of Coven Thirteen. We are the eyes that have seen the unseen. We are the voices of those who don't speak. We will distinguish the bold from the meek.'

They were seven but they spoke as one. A mix of young and old, with not a pointed black hat or warty nose among them. They wore long-sleeved black dresses buttoned all the way up to their necks with their hair pulled back tightly and netted black veils over shadowed, cruel faces. This, Morrigan realised, must be what *real* witches looked like. She didn't like them much anymore.

'What do you want?' She turned in a circle, scared to take her eyes off any one of them for too long.

'Two frights befall you this All Hallows' Eve,' they said in unison. 'One to be seen and one to believe. Flee if you must. Charge if you dare. Or follow the glow and you might have a prayer.'

One of the witches handed Morrigan a small ivory envelope. The card inside read:

> *Welcome to the Fright Trial.*
> *You may turn back now and withdraw from*
> *the Wundrous Society entrance trials if you wish.*
> *If you continue, we accept no responsibility for*
> *the consequences.*
> *Choose wisely.*

'Fright Trial,' Morrigan whispered. She didn't know whether she was relieved or terrified. On one hand, the witches evidently weren't here to boil her in a cauldron or turn her into a newt. On the other hand . . . what had Jupiter called it? The Nervous Breakdown Trial? *Some candidates never recovered.* He'd been appalled to learn that the new High Council of Elders had reinstated it.

Morrigan swallowed. Coven Thirteen stared down at her with cold, dark eyes.

'We are the witches who'll settle your fate,' they chanted. 'We know the terrors and dread that await. Be wise and turn back, before it's too late. Or if you dare – open the gate.'

The candles blew out, as if in a gust of wind, and the coven disappeared.

Two lights appeared in the darkness. To Morrigan's right, the ladder had returned, illuminated by ambient street light from the open manhole above. Looking up, she heard the distant, celebratory noise of the Black Parade and longed to return to it.

'Hawthorne?' she called hesitantly. 'Are you there?'

But her friend was gone. Morrigan's stomach twisted. Had he gone to find Fen? Or was he somewhere else, in the midst of his own Fright Trial?

To her left, farther into the darkness, an arched wooden gate stood half-hidden in shadow. A single, melted-down candle stub burned dimly above it, inviting her inside. *Follow the glow and you might have a prayer.*

Morrigan desperately wanted to take the ladder.

But how could she quit the trials now? She thought of Jupiter, and Inspector Flintlock, and Hawthorne and the Hotel Deucalion, and most of all, she thought of having to face the Hunt of Smoke and Shadow again if she was kicked out of Nevermoor. Surely nothing in the Fright Trial could be more frightening than that.

Scrunching her hands into fists, Morrigan forced herself to push open the gate before she could change her mind.

Night air sent a chill down her neck. She was outside again.

But not in the alley.

A full moon shone over rolling hills covered with jagged tombstones, concrete angels and hulking mausoleums. An engraved stone archway above Morrigan's head read MORDEN CEMETERY.

This was no parade float, with cardboard headstones and crepe-paper trees. It was the real Morden Cemetery . . . wherever *that* might be.

That was the bad news.

The worse news was that, once again, Morrigan was not alone.

A groan rose from the ground beneath her feet. She was standing on a grave, and the grave had a corpse, and the corpse had a head, and the head was emerging from the sodden earth with an eerie, rasping moan.

Morrigan screamed. Struggling to free itself from the dirt, the corpse grabbed her ankle with one decaying skeletal hand. She fell and tried to crawl away on her hands and knees, but the hand kept its grip.

There were more – Morrigan could hear them all around, rising from their rest. She kicked hard and wildly, clawing at the grass to get away. With one wrenching kick, she dislodged the zombie's arm from his body and sent his skull flying halfway across the cemetery. She stumbled to her feet and, feeling a wave of revulsion, pulled off the disembodied hand that still gripped her ankle.

'Ugh, disgusting,' she muttered, wiping remnants of glistening grey flesh from her hands.

There were dozens now, coming fast like a tidal wave, their hungry white eyes fixed on Morrigan. Skin and muscle hung loose, rotting on their bones. Burial clothes, all shredded and greying with age. These were nothing like the costumed zombies on the Black Parade float, with their artfully torn clothes and caked green makeup. These were the rising dead. And they were coming for her.

'Arrrrrrrrgggggghhhhhhhhhh!'

A curly-haired, gangly-limbed storm of fist and flame tore through the horde, screaming itself hoarse. The corpses stumbled away, if not in fear, at least in mild alarm.

'Take *that*, death-breath!'

Hawthorne's clothes were torn, and he had leaves and bits of twigs tangled in his hair. He held a burning torch with both hands and swung it at the zombies in wild, haphazard blows. Morrigan had to duck to avoid getting a faceful of embers, but it seemed to keep the dead at bay.

'Where have you *been*?' She'd never been so happy to see anyone in her life.

'Me?' said Hawthorne. 'Where have *you* been? I was shouting for you and I tried to climb down, and then the alley went dark, and these witches showed up—'

'Coven Thirteen!' said Morrigan. 'I met them too, and they were awful, and they said we're going to get—'

'Two frights each, I know.' His eyes wide as dinner plates, Hawthorne lunged forward and swept the torch back and forth like a sword. *Whoosh, whoosh.* The dead kept crawling from their graves like rats from a sewer.

Morrigan shuddered. 'How do we get out?'

'No idea.' *Whoosh.*

'Well, how'd you get here?'

'Dunno. It's like I was in a tunnel, and at one end I could see the Black Parade, and at the other end there was just this candle, and I knew if I went back to the parade' – *whoosh, whoosh, whoosh* – 'I'd be kicked out of the trials, so I just . . .'

'*Followed the glow*?' Morrigan gasped, grabbing his shoulder. 'Hawthorne – the candle! *Follow the glow,* that's what the witches said. I followed a candle through the gate and—'

'They're getting closer!' Hawthorne shouted breathlessly, still swinging. *Whoosh, whoosh.* 'Let's make a run for it.' *Whoosh.*

'And how exactly – *will you be careful!*' Morrigan ducked again, narrowly missing a torch to the head. 'Where'd you get that thing?'

'It was hanging outside a crypt. Up there, beneath . . .' Hawthorne trailed off, his eyes suddenly alight. Morrigan followed his gaze to a marble tomb, the biggest in the cemetery, at the top of a gently sloping hill. '. . . Beneath the angel. The angel statue – above the crypt – it was holding a candle, I'm *sure* it was.'

Morrigan's heart leapt with a giddy mix of hope and fear as they bolted across the cemetery. *Follow the glow and you might have a prayer.* Angel – prayer – it was a clue! If there was any way out of this, she thought, it *must* be through that crypt. They were either about to escape this nightmare or be trapped inside a fancy marble box with an undead army battering down the door.

Hawthorne led the way, using the torch to beat a path through their attackers like an explorer hacking through thick jungle with a machete. The zombies ducked and stumbled, melting away from the fire in fear.

There was a flicker of light at the crest of the hill – a

small, glowing beacon, drawing them onward. They were going to make it! The crypt was close, it was *so close*, it was—

'Locked,' puffed Hawthorne. He dropped the torch, pulling at the iron door with all his might. Morrigan joined in, but even with their combined strength the door wouldn't budge.

A renewed chorus of groans rose up behind them, the rasping scrape of flesh and bone dragging across pebbled ground as the unhappy residents of Morden Cemetery closed in. Hawthorne snatched up the torch again and, in his panic, swung a bit too enthusiastically. With one last arcing *whoosh* through the air, the flame blew out.

That's it, thought Morrigan. *We're done.*

In despair, she lifted her face to the statue above the crypt. The angel looked down mockingly, a melted-down candle stub in its pudgy angel hand.

But . . . *wait.*

Morrigan blinked. The angel's other hand, she saw, was pointing to the ground on their left. At a freshly dug, unfilled, open grave. A six-foot-deep hole in the ground.

A new variety of dread crept into Morrigan's bones.

Hawthorne continued to swing his burnt-out torch at the zombie horde, but without the threat of fire they didn't seem that bothered. In a last, desperate attempt, he threw it at the head of a finely dressed corpse, succeeding only in knocking off its top hat. 'Any other ideas?'

'Just one.' Morrigan grabbed Hawthorne's arm and started inching towards the grave, one eye on the zombies.

'Is it a good one?'

'Yes,' she lied. It was a terrible idea. Truly awful. But it was the only one she had.

'Are you going to tell me what it is?'

'Nope.'

Morrigan jumped into the grave, pulling Hawthorne down with her. She braced for impact, for the moment she would land in the dirt at the bottom and realise she'd made a dreadful mistake and was about to have her brain chewed by zombies.

But that moment didn't come. The two friends fell – screaming all the way – through the cold and dark, seemingly forever. When they finally landed, it was on soft, damp grass. They sat for a full minute, catching their breath and grinning stupidly with relief.

'How' – Hawthorne puffed – 'did you know that would work?'

'Didn't. Guessed.'

'Good guess.'

Morrigan got up and dusted herself off. They were in a garden courtyard, surrounded by twenty-foot-tall hedges.

Tiny golden lights twinkled amongst the foliage. At one end of the courtyard, a pond burbled pleasantly. At the opposite end, an apple tree had dropped its mottled red harvest on the ground. To their left, a natural archway in the hedge led to a dark, foggy path. To their right, a wooden gate was ajar, shining a beam of pale, silvery light into the courtyard.

'Where are we?' Hawthorne asked.

The air was richly autumnal. It smelled of rain and chimney smoke and decomposing leaves. Of apples and beeswax. The moon seemed brighter and yellower here. It was as if someone had taken the autumn night and turned it up several notches. Everything was just a bit . . . *more*.

'Wunsoc weather,' murmured Morrigan. 'Hawthorne, I think we're in the Wundrous Society gardens.'

'Oh!' he said, surprised. 'Is that it, then? Did we pass?'

'Not sure. Aren't we supposed to have *two* frights?'

Hawthorne screwed his face up. 'I was hoping the witches counted as one.'

Morrigan frowned. Was it really going to be that easy? The witches *were* creepy, and she'd be happy never to set foot inside Morden Cemetery again, but even so . . . she couldn't see why anyone would call this the Nervous Breakdown Trial. Perhaps she had a higher threshold for scariness than most people.

It felt peaceful and safe in the courtyard. Morrigan was in no rush to leave. Maybe somebody was about to come and congratulate them, to tell them they'd got through to the final trial. *Perhaps*, Morrigan thought, *I'll just wait here awhile . . .*

She drifted as if in a dream, drawn by the pleasant tinkling sound of the pond. It felt like the water itself was beckoning her on, pulling her on a string.

Then she saw it. A golden light on the broken surface of the water. On a stone in the centre of the pond sat a single candle, dripping tiny rivers of melted wax into the water. She had opened her mouth to call for Hawthorne when—

'Morrigan, look!' he shouted from the opposite end of the courtyard. 'I found it! I found the next candle!'

Morrigan ran to where he stood beneath the tree, pointing up into the branches. Sure enough, right at the top of the uppermost branch sat a burned-down candle stub in a pool of molten wax. A quick investigation revealed a third candle melted onto the handle of the wooden gate, and a fourth dripping into the grass beneath the shadowy archway.

'Which are we supposed to follow?' said Morrigan.

'It's obvious, isn't it?' said Hawthorne, looking puzzled.

'The pond,' said Morrigan, at the exact same moment Hawthorne said, 'The apple tree.'

'No, the *pond*,' she insisted. 'Don't you see, we're supposed to jump in! How can you *follow the glow* when it's stuck up a tree?'

'Climb it! Duh.'

'And what, break our legs on the way down?'

How could he *possibly* think they were meant to follow the apple tree candle? It was obvious the pond candle was the right one. Morrigan could feel it, deep inside her bones. It called to her.

'We can't stay here all night,' said Hawthorne. 'Let's draw straws.'

'We don't have straws.'

'Rock-paper-scissors, then.'

Morrigan groaned, exasperated. *'Fine.'*

'Are you two completely stupid?' said a voice from the shadows.

They followed the sound to a girl sitting on the ground, leaning against the hedge, her legs stretched out. Her long, thick hair was in two braids, and she wore flannel pyjamas, a dressing gown and striped woollen socks. The witches of Coven Thirteen must have pulled her straight out of bed.

Morrigan felt an unpleasant jolt of recognition.

'What are *you* doing here?'

'What do you think?' said Cadence Blackburn, rolling her eyes. 'Fright Trial. Same as you.'

Morrigan scowled. 'You're a cheat, Cadence.'

'You—' The girl's sour expression faltered, and surprise flickered briefly across her face. 'You remember me?'

'Of course I remember you,' said Morrigan, feeling her anger rise. 'You stole my place in the Chase Trial, *and* my ticket to the Elders' secret dinner.'

Cadence stared silently, her mouth slightly open. Morrigan wondered if she was going to apologise, but then she seemed to snap out of it. 'So? You're here, aren't you?'

'Hope the dinner was worth cheating for,' Morrigan said resentfully. 'S'pose you and Elder Quinn are best mates now, are you?'

'No, actually.' Cadence stood, pulling her dressing gown tight around her. It was streaked with dirt, and she had twigs and leaves in her hair. Morrigan wondered what her first fright had been, if she'd been chased by zombies too . . . but couldn't bring herself to ask. 'If you must know, it was rubbish. Noelle wouldn't shut up about herself. Nobody could get a word in. The Elders barely noticed I was there,' Cadence finished abruptly. Morrigan was surprised to hear her talk about her friend that way. The girl walked to the edge of the pond. 'Anyway, have you figured it out yet, idiots?'

'Figured what out?' asked Hawthorne.

'You're not *supposed* to pick the same one.' Cadence made a face as if it were obvious. 'The others all just ran straight through the arch or climbed the stupid tree or whatever. You're the only two idiots who've decided to *draw straws*.'

'Others?' said Hawthorne. 'How many people have been through?'

'Loads. We all get dumped here and everyone goes gaga over one of the candles. It's part of the test. You're meant to pick the one you're drawn to. At least,' she said with an indifferent shrug, 'that's what I think.'

'Why haven't you gone through, then, if you're so brilliant?' asked Hawthorne. 'You scared?'

Cadence made a face at him. 'Course I'm not *scared*. I just – nobody's jumped in the pond yet. They've all gone for the other three. I was waiting . . .'

Morrigan groaned. 'Oh, of *course* – you were waiting to see what happens! You don't want to jump in first yourself in case it's something bad. You're a cheat *and* a coward. Well, I don't care, I'm not afraid,' Morrigan lied. She stepped to the edge of the pond, clutching the hem of her dress to stop her hands from shaking. 'Hawthorne,' she said, squeezing her eyes shut, hoping she sounded more confident than she felt. 'You climb the tree. I'm jumping in the water.'

'Are you sure you don't—'

'Count of three,' she continued, before he could talk her out of it. 'One—'

'*Three!*' shouted Cadence, and pushed Morrigan from behind.

Morrigan splashed face-first into the pond and sank down, down, down until there was no more breath left in her lungs. She kicked and struggled upward, opening her eyes in the dark water. There was no candlelight above. Everything was black. Her lungs burned. She was going to drown, she was going to die, and then—

Still.

Dark.

Dry.

Land.

Morrigan gulped mouthfuls of sweet, cold air into her empty lungs.

The ground was bumpy and hard. She struggled to her knees, then stood, staggering slightly as she regained her balance.

All was quiet. A cool breeze brushed her neck.

Morrigan spotted a street sign; she was on the corner of Deacon Street and McLaskey Avenue. A single golden gaslight above her head beamed a circle of light around her onto the empty cobbled road, which earlier – what was it, hours ago? Days? – had been filled with costumed revellers and silly parade floats.

Where was Fen, she wondered. Where was *Hawthorne*?

The street was empty of life.

'Hello?' she called softly, afraid of what she'd hear in reply. Afraid she'd hear nothing at all.

But there was something – a gentle fluttering.

Looking up, Morrigan saw a black thing, like a small bat or a large moth. It winged its way down through the glow of the gaslight, quivering on the breeze before landing precisely at her feet.

A black envelope with her name on it.

She bent to pick it up.

Inside, a note.

> *You have failed.*
> *They are coming.*
> *Get out.*

Morrigan felt all the muscles in her legs tighten, but somehow she couldn't make them move. *They are coming.* The words echoed in her head.

It was over. She'd failed the Fright Trial. She'd outrun her curse all year long, and it had finally caught her.

The quiet was shattered by the bellow of a hunter's horn.

The clattering of hooves on cobblestones. The note fell from Morrigan's hand, floating to the ground in slow motion and landing with the back facing up. It bore only one word:

RUN.

But there was nowhere to run. The Hunt of Smoke and Shadow was suddenly all around her, creeping out of the darkness, swallowing the edges of her circle of light. It shrank, growing dimmer and dimmer . . .

An unexpected voice spoke, somewhere in the back of her head.

Shadows are shadows, Miss Crow.

They want to be dark.

'Light,' Morrigan whispered shakily. 'Stay in the light.' She forced herself to look away from the glowing red eyes of the Hunt, to look up, to gaze into the golden lamp above her. She reached up, grabbing hold of the gaslight's metal post, and began to climb. She might have failed the trials. She might be kicked out of Nevermoor. But she couldn't let the Hunt take her now. She wouldn't.

'Stay in the light,' she whispered again, feeling stronger, putting one hand in front of the other. Her foot slipped but she held on for dear life, wrapping her legs around and shimmying up. Drawing closer to the light. Blocking out the growling wolves below, and the sounds of rifles being cocked. Closer to the light, closer and closer, one hand after the other, up one rung and then one more, to the top of the ladder . . . the *ladder* . . . towards the circular light from the manhole above. Out of the sewer, up, up, up, into the alley, and at last . . . at *last* . . . to safety.

Morrigan leaned against the alley wall, catching her breath and gazing out to the street beyond. There it was. All the life and colour of the Black Parade, as if she'd never left it. The Hunt of Smoke and Shadow was nowhere to be seen. Her nightmare had ended. She sighed and closed her eyes.

It had all been part of the Fright Trial. She was so relieved she could have cried.

'I don't need legs to fight you!' came Hawthorne's frenzied voice. Morrigan opened her eyes to see him crawling up from the sewer, using only his upper body. 'Come back here, you coward! I'll fight you legless!'

'Hawthorne!' Morrigan yelled, jumping up to help him out of the manhole. 'Hawthorne, it's not real. The trial's over. You've got legs!'

Hawthorne stopped flailing but still breathed heavily, his eyes darting left and right as if searching for his opponent. After a moment he looked down and seemed to come to himself, patting down his legs all the way to the toes. 'I've got – I've got legs!' he shouted, jumping up with a gleeful laugh. '*Ha!* I've got legs!'

Morrigan laughed too. 'What did you think happened to them?'

'Dragon bit 'em off.' He was smiling, but his face was still white, his hands still shaking as he ran them through his hair. 'Big ugly thing.'

'So you were going to . . . fight a dragon?' she asked, grinning. 'Legless?'

Before Hawthorne could respond, the night went dark and silent again, as if all the noise and light of the Black Parade had been swallowed up. As if the moon itself had gone out.

A match was struck in the darkness, and suddenly Morrigan and Hawthorne were surrounded by the veiled, candlelit faces of Coven Thirteen.

Hawthorne dug his fingernails into her arm. 'I thought it was over?' he whispered.

'So did I,' she whispered back.

Their seven voices rose as one.

'We are the witches of Coven Thirteen. Abigail, Amity, Stella, Nadine, Zoe, Rosario, Sweet Mother Nell. (That's the old bat who pretended she fell.) You have been chosen, young Swift and young Crow. You will proceed to the Trial of Show. Your courage and daring whilst facing a fright have served you both well on this Hallowmas night. So go with our blessing, go without fuss, and enjoy ten per cent off at Cauldrons 'R' Us.'

The witches handed them each a voucher for a magic supplies shop and an ivory envelope, inside which was an invitation to the final trial – the Show Trial – to take place at the Trollosseum arena on the fifth Saturday in Winter of One.

Coven Thirteen blew out their candles and disappeared. The sights and sounds of the parade returned slowly, rising up around them as if someone was turning a dial, and finally – *finally* – the Fright Trial was truly over.

Morrigan's legs had turned to jelly. She'd done it. She'd made it through the first three trials, as Jupiter had said she must. Now she only had to trust her patron to do as he'd promised: to get her past the Show Trial and into the Wundrous Society.

It sounded so easy in her head.

The parade was ending just as they got back, much to Hawthorne's disappointment. He and Morrigan made their way through the dispersing crowd to find Fenestra, who was nowhere to be seen.

'She's going to murder us,' groaned Morrigan. 'Come on, let's get to the Wunderground, maybe she's looking for us there.'

'It's not our fault, is it?' said Hawthorne, picking up the pace. 'I can't *wait* to tell my mum about the zombies, she'll be so jealous.'

'I wonder if Cadence ever left the courtyard.'

'Who's Cadence?'

'The girl who pushed me in the pond – that's her name, Cadence Blackburn.' Morrigan ducked as a bat swooped overhead, its last hurrah for Hallowmas. 'I wonder if she ever jumped in. Probably still sitting there, the chicken.'

Hawthorne looked puzzled. 'What are you talking about?'

'What happened after I left? Did you see her jump in, or—'

'See who jump in?'

'Very funny, Hawth—*oof!*' A woman in a pumpkin costume knocked into Morrigan and sent her sprawling to the ground, then hurried past without noticing.

'Dear me, how rude,' said a voice from above. 'Are you all right? Let me help you.' Morrigan looked up, slightly dazed, to see a man in a grey overcoat with a silvery scarf wrapped around his neck and half his face. He made to reach out a gloved hand, but Hawthorne was already helping her up off the cobblestones.

'I'm fine. Thanks.'

'Oh, it's you,' the man said, pulling down the scarf to reveal a familiar pale face and bemused smile. 'Hello again, Miss Crow.'

'Mr Jones!' said Morrigan, dusting off her hands and trousers. 'What are you doing back in Nevermoor?'

He blinked. 'Just visiting some old friends. They were in the parade, I thought I'd lend my support.'

'I haven't seen you at the Hotel Deucalion. Are you staying somewhere else?'

Mr Jones looked faintly surprised. 'Goodness, no. I'd never stay anywhere but the Deucalion. I'm afraid my employer couldn't spare me for long this time; I'm only here for the evening's festivities.'

'It's a long way to come just for one night. You must really love the Black Parade.'

He chuckled. 'I suppose I do.'

'Well . . . Happy Hallowmas.' She looked over his shoulder towards the Wunderground station and thought she could see Fen's fluffy grey ears poking up out of the crowd. 'We should go. It was nice to—'

'Are you here with your patron?'

'No, my friend. This is Hawthorne.'

Mr Jones turned to Hawthorne with an amiable nod, his eyes very slightly narrowed in appraisal. 'How do you do?'

Hawthorne glanced up at him distractedly. 'Thanks. I mean – you too. I mean, good. Morrigan, we've got to go, Fen'll be mad.'

'Right. Nice to see you again, Mr Jones.'

'Wait – I've been meaning to ask how your Society trials are going.'

'Good, actually!' Morrigan couldn't keep the surprise out of her voice. 'We just finished one now – the Fright Trial.'

'And you made it through?'

'Just,' said Morrigan, grinning. Suddenly she remembered that strange moment when she'd heard Mr Jones's voice in her head as the Hunt was closing in. *Shadows are shadows, Miss Crow.* Would it be weird to tell him?

'Congratulations!' He returned her smile. 'Three down, one to go. You should be very proud. And I presume you know by now what your knack is?'

Morrigan's heart turned over. Her smile faltered, and she was about to admit that no, actually she didn't, when—

'Morrigan,' Hawthorne said pointedly. *'Itching powder.'*

'You should go, Miss Crow. I think your friend is in a hurry. Good luck at the Show Trial.' Mr Jones tipped his hat. 'Both of you.'

To Morrigan's great surprise, Fen waved off their harried explanations and apologies with a careless flick of her tail. 'I know, I know. Fright Trial. Jupiter said.'

'You *knew*?' said Hawthorne.

'Course I knew.' Fen rolled her eyes. 'Why do you think I pretended to be distracted while you tiny reprobates scurried away? Now hurry up, if we miss the last train you two are carrying me home.'

They were following Fen through the station's stuffy, unfathomable maze of stairways and tunnels when Hawthorne finally turned to Morrigan and asked, 'Who was that weirdo in the grey coat?'

'Mr Jones,' she said, pulling off her scarf and shoving it in her pocket. 'He's not a weirdo, he's nice.'

'He asked eleventy billion questions. I thought he'd never leave. How d'you know him, anyway?'

'He offered me an apprenticeship on Bid Day.'

Hawthorne's eyebrows shot upward. 'You got two bids? I was excited to get *one*.'

'I got four,' said Morrigan, her face turning scarlet. She hurried on, 'But two were fakes. It was a prank or something.'

Hawthorne's face grew thoughtful, and he was silent until they got to their platform. The three of them ran for the last train and leapt on board just before the doors closed.

'Do you know what it is yet?' he asked Morrigan as they settled into the last two seats. Fenestra sat on her haunches nearby, giving the other passengers her trademark glower.

'What?' She knew exactly what he meant.

'Your knack. It must be a really good one. To get four bids.'

'Two bids,' she corrected him, staring resolutely at her shoes. 'And it can't be that good if I don't even know what it is.'

They sat in silence through the remaining seven stops, although Morrigan knew Hawthorne was dying to ask more questions. When they emerged into the cool night air, he finally cracked.

'So,' he said, nudging Morrigan with his elbow, 'what school did the grey weirdo come from?'

Morrigan frowned. 'He's not from a school, he's from a company called Squall Industries. And don't call him that.'

'He wanted you for an apprenticeship, this Jones bloke?'

'No,' said Morrigan. 'It was his boss who bid on me. Ezra Squall.'

'Ezra Squall,' repeated Hawthorne, his brow creasing deeply. 'Where have I—'

'Will you two *please* stop dawdling?' Fen shouted from nearly a block ahead of them. They ran to catch up. 'What were you whispering about back there?'

'Nothing,' puffed Morrigan, just as Hawthorne said, 'Ezra Squall.'

'*Ezra Squall?*' Fen nearly choked. 'Haven't heard those two words in a long time. How do you two know the name Ezra Squall?'

'How do *you* know Ezra Squall?' asked Morrigan. 'Is he a friend of yours?'

Fen looked deeply offended. 'Is that supposed to be funny? No, the evillest man who ever lived isn't a *friend of mine*, thanks very much,' she snapped.

'"The evillest man who ever lived?" asked Morrigan. 'What are you—'

'Just shut up about Ezra Squall, will you?' Fenestra said, lowering her voice and glancing around. She was more serious, more agitated than Morrigan had ever seen her. 'It isn't funny to joke about being friends with the Wundersmith. If anyone heard you—'

'The . . . the Wundersmith?' Morrigan stopped walking. 'Ezra Squall – the *Wundersmith*?'

'I said *shut up* about him.' Fen stalked down Caddisfly Alley ahead of them, leaving Morrigan and Hawthorne stunned into silence.

Only when they'd reached Morrigan's room and settled into bed (two hammocks tonight, swinging side by side) did the two friends finally speak.

'It might be a different Squall.'

Morrigan snorted. 'Yeah. I bet there are loads of Ezra Squalls around.'

They were quiet for several minutes, and then—

'I'm an idiot,' said Morrigan quietly. 'Mr Jones told me – he *said* Ezra Squall was the only person alive who knew how to control Wunder. That's it, isn't it? That's what a Wundersmith is.'

'S'pose it must be.'

'Of course. I'm so *stupid*.' She sat up and hung her legs over the side of the hammock. 'Why does the evillest man who ever lived want *me* as his apprentice? Does he think . . .' She paused to swallow. 'Does he think I could be evil too?'

'*Now* you're being stupid,' said Hawthorne, sitting up as well. 'You'd be rubbish at being evil. You don't have the stomach for it. *I* could be evil. My evil laugh is brilliant. *Mwa-ha-ha-ha-ha!*'

'Shut up.'

'*Mwwwaaaaaa-ha-ha-ha—*' He broke off, spluttering. 'Oh, that one hurt my throat a bit, actually. *Mwa-ha-ha—*'

'Hawthorne, *shut up*,' Morrigan snapped. 'Do you . . . do you think I could be . . .'

'What, evil? You're serious, aren't you?' He leaned forward to look at her in the moonlight. 'No! Morrigan, of course you're not evil. Don't be ridiculous.'

'It has to do with the curse, I know it does. They were right.'

'Who?'

'Everyone. My father. Ivy. The Registry Office for Cursed Children – everyone, the whole Republic! I'm cursed, so maybe—'

'But you told me Jupiter said the curse wasn't—'

Morrigan wasn't listening. '—maybe that makes me evil.'

'You're *not* evil!'

'Then why does the evillest man who ever lived want me for his apprentice?'

Hawthorne thought for a moment, chewing his lip, then said quietly, 'Maybe Jupiter will know.'

'Jupiter.' Morrigan's heartbeat quickened. 'So you think . . . you think I should tell him?'

Hawthorne frowned at her. 'Well – yeah. Yeah, of *course* you should. You've got to! It's the *Wundersmith*.'

'But I haven't even met him!' Morrigan protested. 'I've only met his assistant. You heard Dame Chanda and Kedgeree – the Wundersmith himself can never come back to Nevermoor. The city won't let him.'

'What if he finds a way?' asked Hawthorne. Morrigan hated the growing dread on her friend's face. She hated that she was responsible for it. 'What if that's why Mr Jones is here? This is *serious*, Morrigan.'

'I *know* it's serious!' she said, swinging forward in her hammock so violently that it nearly tipped her out. 'Didn't you hear Fen? "It isn't funny to joke about being friends with the Wundersmith." What if Jupiter thinks I'm *friends* with Ezra Squall? What if he doesn't want to be my patron anymore? And if the Stink found out . . .' She paused, thinking of Inspector Flintlock. As if he needed another reason to ship her back to the Republic. 'Hawthorne, if I don't get into the Society, they're going to kick me out of Nevermoor.' *And the Hunt of Smoke and Shadow will be waiting*, she thought, but she couldn't bring herself to say the words out loud.

Hawthorne looked aghast. 'Do you really think they'd . . . do you really think Jupiter would—'

'I don't know,' said Morrigan honestly. Jupiter had chosen her, rescued her and defended her, even though she was cursed. But if he knew that the evillest man who ever lived had chosen her too . . . would that finally be enough to change his mind? Morrigan didn't want to find out.

Hawthorne stood up and began pacing the floor, a bundle of nervous energy. 'We can't let them kick you out. I won't let them. But we need a plan.

'How about this: if you see Mr Jones again, we'll tell Jupiter everything. *Everything.* If not, we'll just wait until *after* the last trial, once we're both members of the Wundrous Society and nobody can possibly send you back to the Republic. *Then* we'll tell him. Okay?'

'Okay,' said Morrigan. She felt guilty about keeping such a big, terrible secret from Jupiter, and even worse about dragging Hawthorne into it, but it was extremely comforting to hear her friend say *we* instead of *you.* She breathed deeply. 'Okay, fine. And until then—'

'I won't tell a soul.' Hawthorne stuck out his pinkie finger, looking worried but determined, and Morrigan hooked it with her own. 'Promise.'

CHAPTER SEVENTEEN

The Battle of Christmas Eve

Winter of One

December was the hotel's busiest month. The foyer buzzed constantly with guests checking in from all over the Free State, coming to experience Christmas in the big city.

Morrigan awoke one chilly morning at the beginning of winter to find that her new home had transformed into a Christmas wonderland overnight. The halls were decked with ribbons and evergreen boughs, the foyer lit up by shining, shimmering fir trees dotted with silvery baubles. The Smoking Parlour rolled out emerald-green waves of pine-scented smoke in the morning, red-and-white-striped candy cane smoke in the afternoon and warm, spicy gingerbread smoke at night.

Even the chandelier was embracing the season. It had slowly grown all year long and finally was full size again, but for the past two months it had shifted and changed every few days, as if the Deucalion couldn't settle on a final shape yet. So far this month it had been a shimmery white polar bear, an enormous green holly wreath, a sparkly blue bauble and now a glittering golden sleigh.

Back in Jackalfax, Christmas had meant decorating a modest-sized tree and hanging the odd string of fairy lights (if Grandmother was feeling particularly festive, which she usually wasn't). Occasionally Corvus would drag Morrigan along to the annual Chancery Christmas party, where she'd be whispered about by boring politicians and their boring families.

But Christmas in Nevermoor was a month-long celebration that didn't stop, with festive parties and themed suppers to attend almost every night. Choirs and brass bands performed carols in Wunderground stations all over town. The River Juro froze over completely, turning into a traffic-free highway snaking through the city, and scores of people began ice-skating to school and to work.

There was a pervasive feeling of goodwill, but the season also inspired a competitive spirit between friends and neighbours, many of whom went to great lengths to out-Christmas each other. Houses were lit up in almost every neighbourhood, each one brighter than the last, each street an extravaganza of tackiness and wasted Wundrous energy, flashing and twinkling and blinding anyone within a mile radius. It was garish and absurd. Morrigan loved it.

But the most intense rivalry of all was between the two public figureheads of Nevermoor's holiday season.

'I don't get it,' said Morrigan one afternoon as she and Hawthorne sat stringing popcorn and cranberries onto fishing line. 'How can he get around the entire realm in one night? That's impossible.'

Hawthorne had invited her over to his place to show her how to make traditional Christmas tree decorations. Outside, it was a chilly, wet December day, but here in the Swift family living room there was hot chocolate, carols on the wireless and a saucepan full of corn kernels on the woodstove, popping merrily away.

'It's not impossible – ow,' said Hawthorne, sucking blood from the finger he'd just pricked with his needle. 'It's Wundrous.'

'But really, a flying sleigh? Powered by deer?'

'Reindeer,' Hawthorne corrected her.

'Sorry, *rein*deer. How do they even fly? They don't have wings. Has he bewitched them?'

'Dunno. Why are you so bothered?'

Morrigan screwed up her face, trying to pinpoint exactly what was so strange about the whole thing. 'It's just . . . perverse, that's why. What about the one with the glowing red nose? What happened to it?' She finished off her fourth garland and reached for the roll of fishing line to start another. 'Was it an *experiment*? That's sick.'

'I think he was born that way.'

'What about this Yule Queen lady? I've never even heard of her. At least Saint Nicholas is on all the soft drink and chocolate adverts.'

Hawthorne popped another piece of popcorn into his mouth. He'd finished making his garlands and was now working on unmaking them, one morsel at a time. 'Dad reckons people really underrate the Yule Queen, 'cause she's never in any Christmas plays or anything. But Christmas would be rubbish without snow, and where do you think snow comes from? It doesn't just float out of the sky on its own.'

'You're telling me the Yule Queen makes snow?'

'Course she doesn't. Don't be daft.' Hawthorne spoke as if to a simpleton. 'The *Snowhound* makes the snow. But he wouldn't bother if the Yule Queen didn't tell him to.'

Morrigan was completely lost. 'So . . . these two, Saint Nick and the Yule Queen, they have to kill each other?'

'What? No. You're so bleak.' He laughed. 'They battle each other on Christmas Eve to see who has the best Christmas spirit. If the Yule Queen wins, her promise is a blanket of snow on Christmas morning and a blessing on every house.'

'And if Saint Nick wins?'

'Presents in every stocking and a fire in every hearth. You'd better pick a side. We're a pro-Nick household, except for Dad secretly fancying the Yule Queen a bit. The Campbells next door are big-time Yule supporters, as you can see from all the green.' He pointed to the window; the house next door was decorated entirely with green banners, twisting ivy and twinkling green fairy lights.

'What's the green for?'

'Yule Queen supporters wear green, Saint Nick supporters wear red. Here, take this.' He pulled something out of the Swift family's decoration box and threw it at Morrigan, who fumbled to catch it.

'What's this for?'

'So you can support Nick, like me,' he said, shrugging. 'Presents and fire – what's not to like?'

It was a scarlet ribbon. Morrigan tucked it away in her pocket. 'I'll think about it.'

⌐═══▬

'Who do you support?' Morrigan asked Jupiter that night over dinner. 'Saint Nicholas or the Yule Queen?'

'The Yule Queen,' said Jack, spooning mashed potato onto his plate. 'Obviously.'

Morrigan scowled. 'I wasn't asking you.'

Jack had come home for the Christmas holidays a few days earlier, and had been doing his utmost to annoy Morrigan ever since.

'No, you were asking Uncle Jove, but you're simple-minded if you can't see that he's pro-Yule. Are you a *complete* idiot?'

'Take it easy, Jack,' warned Jupiter, shooting him a look.

'Why?' snapped Morrigan. 'He isn't wearing any green. He hasn't worn green at all this week. Are you blind in *both* eyes?'

'Bad form, Mog,' said Jupiter, and Morrigan was stung by the disappointment and surprise in his voice. Her insides writhing with guilt, she opened her mouth to apologise to Jack, but before she could speak he barrelled on, apparently unfazed by Morrigan's unkindness.

'Obviously he can't be *seen* wearing green,' said Jack. 'Important public figures should appear neutral at Christmas, that's just good manners. But if you had a brain you'd realise Uncle Jove and I prefer elegance and finesse over flashy displays of consumerism. Saint Nick is just a capitalist fat cat with a good publicity department. The Yule Queen has *style*.'

Morrigan had no idea what he was talking about, but in that instant, she knew who she would support. She took the red ribbon from her pocket and tied it in a tight bow around her ponytail, staring defiantly at Jack.

'Is that supposed to intimidate me?' said Jack, laughing. 'Are you going to challenge me to a duel over the dinner table? Dessert spoons at dawn?'

'Come on, you two . . .'

Morrigan considered throwing her dessert spoon right at his smug face. 'If the Yule Queen's so great, where are all the pantomimes about her? And why isn't she in any adverts? Saint Nick's the face of Holly Jolly Toffee, Dr Brinkley's Holiday Fizz *and* Tristan Lefèvre's winter collection of cashmere bobble socks. I've never seen the Yule Queen on a billboard. I wouldn't know her if I fell over her.'

Jupiter slumped down in his chair. 'Why can't we all just get along?'

'That's because she has integrity,' said Jack, pointing his fork at Morrigan and ignoring his uncle. 'Which is something your oversized friend and his gang of flying fleabags wouldn't know if *they* fell over it.'

'Saint Nick is the soul of generosity, charity and . . . and jolliness!'

'You're just parroting what you've heard on the wireless,' Jack muttered. (That was *almost* true – she'd read it in a newspaper advertisement for a sugary breakfast cereal with Saint Nick's picture on the box.) 'I suppose now you're going to tell me his sick experimentation with artificial bioluminescence only makes the reindeer more *magical*.'

Morrigan slammed her hand on the table. 'The reindeer *are* magical. Even the one with the nose.' She pushed her plate away with a clatter and stormed out, yelling over her shoulder, 'And anyway, he was *born like that*!'

From the hallway, Morrigan heard Jupiter sigh. 'Really, Jack, why are you and Mog always at each other? I hate having to umpire. Makes me feel like a grown-up.' He said the last word as though it tasted bad. 'Why can't you just be friends?'

'F-friends?' Jack spluttered. It sounded like he was choking on his dinner, which Morrigan found quite a pleasing mental image. 'With *that*? Not even if you paid me.'

Jupiter's voice went very quiet. 'She's a long way from home, Jack. You know how that feels.'

Morrigan frowned. Where *was* Jack from, she wondered. Where were his parents? She'd never thought to ask . . . but then, Jack didn't like nosy questions.

'But she's *infuriating*, Uncle Jove. And I don't know how you think she's going to get into the Wundrous Society, honestly, I mean, does she even have—'

Morrigan didn't want to hear any more. She covered her ears and ran down the hall, up and up the spiral stairs and into her bedroom, where she flopped down on the bed (a grand four-poster this week, wrapped in garlands of silver tinsel) and shoved her head under the pillows.

Morrigan awoke with a start. She'd been dreaming of the Show Trial again. This time she'd stood in front of the Elders trying to sing, but the only noise that came out of her mouth was the squawking of a parrot. The audience had pelted her with mashed potato.

She lay awake, listening to the sounds of the Deucalion. She could hear Frank's gentle snoring from the floor above, Fenestra's answering wheeze from across the hall, and the groaning of pipes from below. A fire crackled in the hearth; Martha must have lit it after Morrigan fell asleep.

It amazed her how she'd come to rely on these things, how normal this life felt to her now. When she thought about the prospect of failure in the Show Trial, of having to leave Nevermoor in just a few short weeks, she was surprised at how it made her chest ache.

But worse than being humiliated, worse than having to leave the Hotel Deucalion, worse than all of it was the thought of what might be waiting for her in the Republic.

Was the Hunt of Smoke and Shadow still there, biding its time? Would her family welcome her home if they knew she was still alive? Could they protect her if the Hunt returned to finish her off?

Noises from the hallway jarred Morrigan out of her brooding. The thump of someone tripping up the last step. A splash. A whispered curse word. She threw off her blankets and tiptoed over to open the door.

In the low lamplight of the hall she saw an empty glass and a puddle of spilled milk on the floor. Jack was on his hands and knees, trying vainly to mop up the mess with the end of his nightshirt. Without a word, Morrigan fetched a towel from her bathroom and brought it out, kneeling down to help.

'It's fine,' he mumbled. 'I can do it. You'll get your towel dirty.'

'You'll get your shirt dirty,' she countered, smacking his hands away. He leaned back on his heels and let her finish.

'There,' she whispered once it was cleaned up. 'You can put this in the laundry – what? What are you staring at?'

The look on Jack's face was familiar. She'd had a lifetime of looks just like it, back in Jackalfax. It was fear and mistrust, mingled with reluctant curiosity and just a touch of abject horror. However, that wasn't the most disturbing thing she noticed about his face.

'Your eyes are perfectly normal!' she cried, standing up at once, forgetting to whisper. He followed less gracefully, nearly falling over as he continued to stare, open-mouthed. His black leather patch was nowhere to be seen; both wide brown eyes were fixed on Morrigan. 'You fraud. You're not half-blind at all. Why have you been pretending all this time? Does Jupiter know?'

Jack said nothing.

'Stop staring, Jack, and answer me!'

Suddenly there were footsteps on the stairs and Jupiter's face appeared, rumpled with sleep. 'What's this racket? There are guests trying to—' He looked at Jack, who still hadn't taken his eyes off Morrigan. 'Jack?' he said quietly.

'Did you know?' demanded Morrigan. 'Did you know he doesn't need an eye patch?'

Jupiter didn't answer her. He gave his nephew's shoulder a gentle shake and Jack seemed to finally come to himself. He pointed at Morrigan with a shaking hand, which Jupiter took in his own.

'Cup of tea, I think. Come on.' He started to guide Jack down the stairs. 'Go back to bed, Mog.'

Morrigan's mouth fell open. 'Me? Why do I have to go back to bed? He's the one who's been faking half-blindness.'

Jupiter breathed in sharply through his nose, his face suddenly fierce. 'Morrigan!' he whispered hoarsely. 'Back to bed. I don't want to hear another word about this. Understand? Not a single word.'

Morrigan flinched. Jupiter had never spoken to her so severely. Part of her wanted to argue, to demand an explanation for Jack's behaviour, but one look at her patron's stormy face and the words died on her lips.

Jack got halfway down the stairs before looking back. His eyes were clouded with confusion.

You and me both, Morrigan thought miserably as she clicked her bedroom door shut, dumped her milk-soaked towel in the bathtub, and climbed back into bed.

Christmas Eve was crisp and cool, and there was a tremor of excitement in the air. The Hotel Deucalion seemed to vibrate with high spirits as guests and staff alike prepared for the battle that was to take place in Courage Square at the centre of the Old Town.

'Jolly Christmas, Kedgeree,' Morrigan said as she passed the concierge desk, dinging the bell twice.

'Jolly Christmas to you, Miss Morrigan. And a glad Yuletide, too!'

The foyer was filled with noise and warmth. Guests scoffed rum balls and eggnog as they waited for Jupiter's signal to leave.

'Only a ribbon, Miss Morrigan?' asked Chanda Kali. Dame Chanda wore her hair in green coils, with dangling emerald earrings, a matching emerald choker and a forest-coloured velvet cloak. She bit her lip as she surveyed Morrigan's black dress, black coat and black lace-up boots. 'I've a darling crimson chapeau that might fit your little head. Or a ruby necklace? I have twelve. You could keep one!'

'No, thank you, Dame Chanda,' said Morrigan, who considered her ribbon quite festive enough.

Not for the first time that day, she wished Hawthorne was coming to watch the battle. The Swifts spent every second Christmas in the Highlands, and Hawthorne had left Nevermoor the day before with one last promise to keep quiet about Ezra Squall. Morrigan had vowed to put the worrying mystery of the Squall apprenticeship out of her head and enjoy Christmas. Even so, in the back of her mind she cherished a hope that she wouldn't run into Mr Jones again before the Show Trial.

Watching the staff from her vantage point on the stairs, Morrigan had to admit they had festive style by the bucket-load. Frank the vampire dwarf had painted his fingernails red to complement his red-lined cape, and Kedgeree was bedecked in layers of red tartan and tinsel. Martha showed her allegiance to the Yule Queen with a smart green coat and matching scarf. Charlie the chauffeur wore a pea-green tweed jacket and driver's cap, even though he had the night off.

The clock began to chime and Jupiter ushered everyone out the front door to the forecourt, where a row of fancy carriages was waiting to take them to the big event. He winked at Morrigan and gave her a friendly nudge as she went by. Three days had passed since the incident with Jack, and Jupiter still hadn't mentioned it. Morrigan had followed his lead, even though she was dying to ask about Jack's eye patch.

Not tonight. She wouldn't spoil Christmas Eve.

Morrigan had expected Courage Square to be a swirling sea of red and green, but instead there were large pockets of each colour where pro-Nick and pro-Yule supporters gathered in droves, shouting slogans and trying to out-sing each other. Just as a chorus of 'Ode to a Jolly Old Fat Man' or 'Have Yourself a Jolly Little Christmas' exploded from a patch of red, a nearby patch of green would rise up with 'The Yuletide Hymn' or 'Green Is the Colour of My Cheer'. Jupiter found a spot between two groups, where Morrigan could stand with the reds and Jack could stand with the greens and Jupiter could station himself between them to discourage any fisticuffs.

'You look like broccoli,' Morrigan said to Jack, making a face at the elaborate green hat that towered over his head like a small, artistically designed explosion. Then, just to be clear, she added, 'Really stupid broccoli.'

'At least my support for the Yule Queen is obvious,' said Jack, adjusting his eye patch, which was once again covering his left eye. Morrigan had to bite her tongue to stop herself from asking why he wore it at all when he obviously had two perfectly functional eyes. She'd scarcely seen him since the hallway incident. It was hard to tell whether he was avoiding her or if Jupiter had been purposely keeping them apart. 'I notice you're only wearing that pathetic little ribbon. Is it because you're embarrassed to be seen supporting a morbidly obese home invader and enslaver of elves?'

'The only thing I'm embarrassed to be seen with is that revolting hat.'

'*Ding ding ding,*' said Jupiter, making a T with his hands. He gave Jack a meaningful look. 'Time out, please, for the love of—Ooh! It's starting.'

A hush descended. People pointed into the northern sky, where a hulking figure was emerging from the dark. Morrigan held her breath, the excitement properly kicking in at last. A cheer rose up from the red sections as Saint Nicholas swooped down into Courage Square, his nine flying reindeer performing an impressive loop-the-loop and coming to land neatly on a raised platform in the centre. A pair of elves jumped off the sleigh and began waving feverishly at the crowd, goading them like promoters at a troll fight to cheer more and more loudly for the jolly, white-bearded man as he heaved himself out of the polished mahogany and red velvet sleigh.

Morrigan grinned. She had to admit she was pleased with her decision to support Saint Nicholas. His magnificent reindeer stamped and shook their great antlers back and forth, clouds of frosty air shooting out of their nostrils. The elves jumped up and down as the crowd bellowed their support for Nick, who waved and pointed at random people in the crowd as if they were old friends of his whom he'd only just spotted. One man actually fainted at the acknowledgement. Saint Nick, Morrigan decided, was a rock star.

She turned to Jack, feeling self-satisfied, but Jack merely shrugged.

'Just wait,' he said, smirking as he gazed to the south of the square.

She didn't have to wait long. Seconds later, the sea of people parted for what looked at first like a small frost-covered mountain but was in fact the ten-foot-tall Snowhound moving through the spellbound audience. A beautiful woman stood proudly on his back, gazing out at the hushed square.

Morrigan had to fight the urge to say, *Ooooh*. It was true, what Jack had said about the Yule Queen, all of it. She was the most elegant woman Morrigan had ever seen. She had *style*.

The Queen's diaphanous pale-green gown fluttered delicately behind her, flowing like silk underwater. Her hair fell in soft, shimmering waves past her waist and, like the fur of the splendid hound, was the colour of freshly fallen snow. Her lips were pale and bloodless, her smile nothing less than a glowing expanse of white teeth and twinkling eyes that acted as a spotlight, casting everything around her into shadow. The masses gathered in Courage Square released a collective sigh of pleasure as she appeared to float towards the platform.

Morrigan didn't need to look at Jack. She could feel the smugness radiating from him.

The Yule Queen stepped onto the platform and nodded at Saint Nicholas, who bowed in return. For a moment, nothing happened. Then the Yule Queen lifted her face to the sky and grew very still.

'Here we go,' whispered Jupiter.

It was faint at first, just a distant tinkling sound, like wind chimes or glass. Morrigan watched in amazement as each of the brightly shining stars over Nevermoor grew even brighter, morphing and moving until they somehow,

327

impossibly, resembled billions of tiny silver bells reflecting the light of the city. A complex symphony of chimes filled the air. Morrigan gazed at the star-bells, breathless and enthralled, until each one jingled its last jingle and turned into a distant star once again.

Three seconds of awed silence followed this extraordinary display, and then every green supporter in the square erupted into passionate applause. Even some of the reds were clapping, albeit grudgingly. Morrigan felt like cheering out loud, so delighted was she by the Yule Queen's magic, but couldn't bear to give Jack the satisfaction. She stayed quiet.

All eyes were now on Saint Nick as he rubbed his hands together, turning in a circle to survey Courage Square. He began pointing erratically, and Morrigan at first thought he was doing his rock star thing again, until pockets of the audience began squealing and stumbling over each other. In each spot, a giant fir tree was sprouting rapidly from the ground, pushing people out of the way as they grew and grew – six feet, then twelve feet, then twenty, then forty, until there were a dozen evergreens towering sixty feet over the square.

Morrigan grinned and began applauding, but Saint Nick wasn't finished. With a click of his stubby fingers, great shiny baubles of red and gold popped out of the branches, and thousands of fairy lights sparkled among the needles. The red supporters went mad.

Jack betrayed no reaction. His eyes were fixed on the Yule Queen, waiting to see her response.

The Queen smiled serenely at Saint Nick's handiwork and then gestured to each of the Christmas trees in turn. On her command, dozens of snow-white doves emerged from the branches and flocked together to form a massive, quivering cloud of wings. They flew in miraculous form-ation, making the shape of a snowflake, then a star, then a bell, then a tree, and finally a peace sign, before flying off into the distance to a thunderous roar of applause.

Saint Nick motioned to his elves, who jumped up onto the sleigh, where two large, dangerous-looking cannons were pointed at the crowd in opposite directions. Morrigan glanced up at Jupiter, wondering if this was legal, but he didn't seem at all disturbed. If anything, he looked bored.

'Didn't he do this one last year?' Jupiter said, nudging his nephew.

Jack snorted. 'Predictable. Pandering to the greedy masses.'

'Shush,' said Morrigan. She elbowed Jack in the ribs to drive the point home. They might have seen it before, but she didn't want to miss a single second.

The cannons went off with a loud bang, and again, and again, as the elves fired round after round of colourful foil-wrapped sweets over Courage Square. Children and adults alike scrambled on the ground and jumped to catch them in midair, and soon everyone was shouting approval through mouthfuls of toffee, including Morrigan.

The Queen turned to the Snowhound, who padded regally towards the platform with his head held aloft and his bright blue eyes fixed on his mistress. As she reached up to scratch him behind the ears, he lifted his head and bayed at the moon. It was a long and eerie howl soon echoed by every dog in Nevermoor, like an unearthly choir of wolves. Morrigan felt a fluttering of something in her hair.

'Snow,' she whispered.

Tiny frozen flakes of white danced and swirled through the air, coming to land gently on her nose and shoulders and upturned palms. Morrigan had never seen real snow before. She felt happiness expanding in her chest, filling her up like a balloon. She almost took hold of Jupiter's coat, worried she might just float away on her own delight.

For a long moment the audience was quiet but for soft gasps and whispers. Then the square exploded with whoops and applause, the reds and greens all cheering together, their rivalry forgotten.

Saint Nick applauded too, smiling and sticking out his tongue to catch a snowflake. The Yule Queen laughed.

'Time for the big finale,' said Jupiter. 'Candles out, you two.'

Morrigan and Jack dug in their coat pockets for the white candles Jupiter had given them earlier. Following Jack's lead, Morrigan held her candle high in the air. A murmur of excitement rippled through the square as everyone around them did the same.

They all seemed to know what was coming, and the younger children giggled and nudged each other as Saint Nick scratched his beard and hammed it up, pretending he'd been bested and didn't know what to do next.

Then an idea apparently occurred to him – he clapped his hands with delight and swept his arms out towards the crowd, spinning around and around. One by one the candles lit up, picking up speed in a spiralling outward pattern, a continuous roar of flame bursting spontaneously into life until Courage Square was filled with laughter and golden light.

Saint Nick and the Yule Queen embraced as old friends, smiling and kissing each other's cheeks. The reindeer gathered around the Snowhound, rubbing their necks against him as he playfully snapped at their antlers and licked their faces. The elves threw themselves at the Yule Queen's legs.

The red and green sections of the crowd merged in a flurry of movement. Nick and Yule supporters swapped items of clothing – a crimson mitten for a sage scarf, a fuchsia flower for an emerald beanie – until nobody was discernible as supporting one or the other. Martha knelt down and offered her scarf to Frank, who in return draped a length of tinsel around the maid's shoulders. Dame Chanda took Kedgeree's red tartan bow tie, and he blushed as she fastened her emerald choker around his neck.

Jack took off his ridiculous hat and offered it to Morrigan with a shrug. 'I suppose the candles were pretty good.'

'Yeah,' she agreed. 'But the snow was the best bit.' She pulled the scarlet ribbon from her hair and tied it around his wrist in a bow. He looked down at it and grinned. 'Wait,' said Morrigan. 'Who beat who?'

'It's *whom*. And nobody beat anybody,' said Jupiter as he led them out of the square. 'They declared a truce like they do every year, and now they're going to go about their business, delivering presents and making it snow all over the Free State. Job's a good'un. Sugarplums, anyone?' He ran ahead to the pickled sugarplum stand and ordered two dozen in a brown paper bag.

'So nobody wins?' Morrigan asked. She couldn't help feeling a little short-changed.

'You must be joking. Presents *and* snow?' said Jack, laughing as he threw a snowball at Jupiter's back. 'Everybody wins.'

The three of them decided to walk home, waving off the carriages and pelting each other with snowballs until they were too wet and exhausted to continue. Jupiter piggybacked Morrigan the rest of the way while Jack happily slipped and slid along the icy pavements. They demolished the whole bag of sweet-sour sugarplums between them, and arrived at the Deucalion forty minutes later with frozen fingers and purple tongues.

'Do you think Saint Nick's been yet?' Morrigan asked Jack as they trudged upstairs. She licked some purple sugar from the corner of her mouth.

'No. He only comes when you're asleep, because he's too busy to chat. So hurry up and get to bed.' He pushed her down the hall, smirking. 'Goodnight.'

'Goodnight, broccoli-head.'

Jack laughed as he disappeared into his room.

CHAPTER EIGHTEEN

An Almost Jolly Holiday

Morrigan woke on Christmas morning to the smells of cinnamon, citrus and woodsmoke. A fire roared cheerfully in the hearth, and hanging on her headboard was a fat red stocking, overstuffed with treats.

She tipped it upside down and into her lap spilled a treasure of chocolate, clementines and gingerbread, a shiny pink pomegranate, a knitted scarf that looked like a fox, a pair of red mittens, a gold and purple tin of Pakulski's Pickled Sugarplums, a small clothbound book called *Finnegan's Faerie Tales*, a deck of silver-backed cards and a wooden hairbrush with a ballerina painted on the handle. All this, just for her! Saint Nicholas had outdone himself.

Morrigan pulled on the soft woollen mittens and held them to her face, remembering much less satisfying

Christmases past. The Crows were never big on gifts. Once, long ago, she'd worked up the courage to ask Corvus if she might get a surprise at Christmas that year, and to her delight he'd said yes. After weeks of anticipation Morrigan jumped out of bed on Christmas morning, excited to see what had been left overnight, and found an envelope at the foot of her bed. Inside was an itemised bill for every cent Corvus had spent that year paying reparations to the Registry Office for Cursed Children on her behalf.

He hadn't lied, at least. It was a surprise.

As Morrigan worked the gold foil off a chocolate coin with her teeth, her bedroom door flew open and Jack strolled in carrying a piece of paper in one hand and his stocking in the other.

'Jolly Christmas!' Morrigan said. She almost added, *Now go back outside and knock*, but decided she was too full of Christmas cheer to really mind.

'Glad tidings of Yule to you.' Jack dropped onto her bed, handed her the note and made himself comfortable, pouring out the contents of his stocking in a pile. He picked out a gingerbread dog and tore off its head. 'Except not entirely glad, because Uncle Jove's been called away.'

'On Christmas morning?' asked Morrigan, reading the note.

Urgent business on Ma Wei. Back in time for lunch. Take Mog sledding for me.
J.

'What's Ma Wei?'

Jack swallowed a mouthful of gingerbread. 'One of the middle realms. Probably another explorer missed their scheduled gateway home. He always gets called in on Christmas Day to help some idiot. Ugh – here, you can have this.' He handed Morrigan the pomegranate from his stocking with a look of distaste, and she threw him a couple of her clementines in return.

'You don't have to take me sledding.' She bit into another chocolate and shrugged. 'I don't even have a sled.'

'What do you think that is, a pony?' said Jack, nodding towards the fireplace.

Morrigan peered over the end of the bed and saw a shiny green sled encircled with gold ribbon. The tag said *Jolly Christmas, Mog.*

'Wow,' she breathed, quite overwhelmed. Never in her life had she received so many gifts.

'Mine's red,' said Jack, rolling his eye. 'Thinks he's funny.'

C·━━

Jupiter didn't make it back in time for lunch or supper, instead sending his apologies with a messenger. Morrigan

336

might have been disappointed by his absence, except she was far too busy having the greatest Christmas of her life.

The day was marked by a thick, swirling snowfall, courtesy of the Yule Queen. Jack and Morrigan spent the morning sledding down nearby Galbally Hill over and over again and warring with the neighbourhood children in an epic snowball fight.

They trudged back to the Deucalion at midday just in time for lunch in the formal dining room. Long tables groaned under the weight of glazed hams, smoked pheasants and roast geese, dishes of fat green sprouts with bacon and chestnuts, golden roast potatoes and honeyed parsnips, boats of thick gravy, crumbly cheeses and braided breads, and bright red crab claws and glistening oysters on ice.

Morrigan and Jack were determined to try a bit of everything (except maybe the oysters), but they both gave up halfway through to lie down in the Smoking Parlour (peppermint smoke: to aid digestion), declaring they'd never eat another bite of food as long as they lived. Fifteen minutes later, however, Jack was dutifully ploughing through a heaped bowl of trifle and two mince pies, while Morrigan demolished a fluffy white meringue with cream and blackberries.

During Jack's third trip back to the dining room, while

Morrigan lay on a corner sofa and breathed in the soothing mint-green vapours, she heard someone enter the parlour.

'It's not that I don't trust him,' said a man's voice. 'He must know what he's doing. The lad's a genius.'

Morrigan opened her eyes sleepily. She could just make out two figures through the thick waves of smoke rolling out from the walls – elegant Dame Chanda dressed in flowing silks of red and green and spry, snowy-haired Kedgeree Burns in his Christmas kilt.

'Too clever for his own good,' Dame Chanda agreed. 'But he isn't immune to making mistakes, Ree-Ree. He's only human.'

Morrigan wondered hazily if she should let them know they weren't alone. She was about to clear her throat when—

'Why *Morrigan*?' said Kedgeree. 'Of all the candidates he might have chosen, why her? Where's her knack?'

'She's a dear girl—'

'O' course, o' course. Grand wee thing. Champion of a gal. But what makes Jupiter think she's *Wundrous Society* material?'

'Oh, you know Jupiter,' said Dame Chanda. 'He's always taking on challenges nobody else will. He was the first to climb Mount Ridiculous, you remember. And he went blazing into that troll-infested realm that no one else in the League of Explorers would touch with a hundred-foot pole.'

The concierge chuckled. 'Aye, and look at this place. It was a wreck when he found it. He took it on as a hobby and now it's the grandest hotel in Nevermoor.' His voice had a grave edge. 'But you cannae take on a child as a hobby.'

'No,' agreed Dame Chanda. 'At least if he'd failed with the Deucalion, it wouldn't have mattered so much. You can't hurt a hotel.'

There was a pause. Morrigan froze and held her breath, worried for a moment that they'd spotted her through the clouds of peppermint smoke.

After some time, Kedgeree sighed heavily. 'I know we should keep our noses out, Chanda, but I'm only worried about the poor wee thing. I think he's setting her up for a terrible disappointment.'

'It's worse than that,' added Dame Chanda in an ominous voice. 'If the Stink finds out she's here illegally, think of what Jupiter risks. It's *treason*. He could go to prison, Kedgeree. His reputation, his career . . . gone. And not only that, but—'

'The Deucalion,' finished Kedgeree solemnly. 'If he's not careful he'll lose the Deucalion. And then where will we all go?'

Morrigan was unsurprised to find herself wandering the halls of the Hotel Deucalion in the middle of the night, trying to banish her stomach-ache and bad dreams.

It was past midnight when she noticed that the door to Jupiter's office was ajar. She peeked inside. He sat in a leather armchair by the fire, and on the table beside him was a steaming silver teapot and two small painted glasses. He didn't even look up. 'In you come, Mog.'

Jupiter poured the tea – mint, with swirling green leaves – and stirred a sugar cube into Morrigan's glass. His eyes flicked up to her face briefly as she took the chair opposite. She thought he looked tired.

'Another nightmare.' It wasn't a question. 'You're still worried about the Show Trial.'

Morrigan sipped her tea and said nothing. She was used to it by now, the way he always knew these things.

Once again she'd dreamed of epic failure. But this time, instead of ending when the audience began to jeer and boo, the nightmare continued with a parade of vicious, slavering trolls filing into the Trollosseum with clubs, presumably to beat Morrigan to death and put her out of her misery.

'The trial's next Saturday,' she said pointedly, hoping it would prompt him to tell her, at last, what she was supposed to do, how she was supposed to perform.

He sighed. 'Stop worrying so much.'

'You keep saying that.'

'Everything will be fine.'

'You keep saying that too.'

'Because it's true.'

'But I don't have a talent!' she said, accidentally splashing tea down the front of her nightgown. 'Why am I even doing these trials when I'll never get into the Society? I can't ride dragons or – or – sing like an angel. I can't do anything.' Morrigan found that once she started naming her worries out loud, she couldn't stop. 'What if the Stink finds out I'm here illegally? They'll kick me out and put you in prison. They'll take the Deucalion away from you. You – your reputation – your career—' Morrigan's voice caught in her throat. 'You can't risk all that just for me! What about the staff? What about *Jack*? You can't look after him if you're in prison. And what about—' She faltered, losing her thread.

Jupiter waited for her to continue, smiling politely behind his glass of mint tea. That infuriated Morrigan even more. Was he even *worried* about whether she'd make it into the Society? Or was this just something he was doing for fun? Was Morrigan just his . . . *hobby*?

The thought made something swell up inside her, like a cornered animal rearing back, preparing to force its way out of her rib cage. She put her glass down. It rattled on the tray.

'I want to go home.'

The words were out of her mouth, low and dark, before she'd even thought of saying them. They hung heavily in the air.

'Home?'

'Back to Jackalfax,' she clarified, though she knew Jupiter realised exactly what she meant. He had become very still. 'I want to go back. Now. Tonight. I want to tell my family I'm alive. I don't want to join the Wundrous Society and I don't—' The words wouldn't come easily; they fought her at every syllable. 'I don't want to live at the Hotel Deucalion anymore.'

That last bit wasn't true, but she thought it would be easier if Jupiter thought so.

Morrigan loved the Deucalion, but no matter how many rooms and hallways and floors it had, it would never be big enough to contain her growing dread of the Show Trial. Her worry felt like a monster, like the ghost that haunted the Deucalion's walls, seeping into her bones like winter so that she could never feel truly warm.

She waited for Jupiter to speak. His face was impassive, and so very still that she thought it might crack, like a porcelain mask. He stared into the fire for a long time.

'Very well,' he said finally. His voice was soft. 'We'll leave at once.'

342

CHAPTER NINETEEN

The Gossamer Line

'How much farther?'

'Not much. Keep up.' Jupiter marched down the dingy tunnel with its off-white tiles and flickering overhead lights, keeping his usual pace while Morrigan jogged, trying to match it. She glanced up at his face now and then but couldn't read anything from it.

He'd barely spoken, other than to tell Fenestra where they were going. The Magnificat had looked at him with alarm and – to Morrigan's surprise – sorrow. She hadn't said a word, but when Morrigan followed Jupiter out the front door, Fen nudged her gently with her great grey head and emitted a quiet, mournful sound. Morrigan blinked fiercely, clutching her oilskin umbrella, and didn't look back.

They'd made their way through the darkened streets, hopping a Brolly Rail platform to the nearest Wunderground station, and then began their descent through the maze-like tunnels and staircases. They climbed through hidden doors into dark, dirty hallways, following a path Morrigan had never taken before but Jupiter seemed to know by heart.

Twenty minutes and countless blind turns later, they rounded a tight corner and came upon an empty platform. Posters lining the walls were faded, cracked and old-fashioned, advertising products Morrigan had never heard of.

A sign above their heads said it was the departure point for the Gossamer Line.

'Are you sure about this?' Jupiter's eyes were fixed on the tiled floor. Though he spoke quietly, his voice bounced around the cavernous space. 'You don't have to go.'

'I know,' said Morrigan. She thought of Hawthorne, of never getting to say goodbye to him, her best friend – and of Jack, sound asleep at the Deucalion, waking up to find her gone – and she felt a sudden sadness. She pushed it down, clamped a lid on it. She couldn't stay and watch Jupiter lose everything he had, because of her. 'I'm sure.'

Jupiter nodded and reached out to take her umbrella from her. Morrigan held on to it. 'Can't I keep—'

'It has to stay here. I'm sorry.'

Morrigan loosened her grip. As Jupiter hung the silver-handled umbrella over a rail on the platform, she felt a dull, resentful disappointment. It was supposed to be a birthday gift, after all, and she'd made so many good memories with it. Jumping off the Deucalion roof, zooming through Old Town on the Brolly Rail. Unlocking the Hall of Shadows. (When Morrigan had finally asked him about it, Jupiter had admitted he'd thought it would be a bit of fun, that he'd been waiting ages for her to figure out she had a secret key to a secret room. He said if only she'd been a bit nosier, she'd have found it much sooner.)

'Ready?' He took her hand and they stepped over the yellow line to the very edge of the platform. 'Close your eyes. Keep them closed.'

Morrigan closed her eyes. The air was still. A long moment passed in silence.

Then she heard a sound in the distance – getting louder and louder – of a train gaining speed very quickly. She felt a *whoosh* of cool air from the tunnel, heard the train stop directly in front of them and open its doors.

'Step boldly, Morrigan Crow.' Jupiter squeezed her hand and led her inside.

'Can I open my eyes now?'

'Not yet.'

'Where are we going? What's the Gossamer Line? Will it take us all the way to Jackalfax or do we have to change?'

'Hush.' He squeezed her hand again.

The journey was short – just a few minutes – but Morrigan felt nausea rising inside her as the train rocked from side to side. She wished she could open her eyes.

The train stopped. The doors opened. Morrigan and Jupiter stepped out into cold, sharp air that smelled of rain and mud.

'Open your eyes.'

With an aching dread deep in her heart, Morrigan found herself standing at the front door of Crow Manor. She was home.

This was what you wanted, she reminded herself.

In just minutes, the Gossamer Line had taken her all the way from Nevermoor to Jackalfax. Morrigan turned around; the train had disappeared. Behind her there was nothing but the tall iron gates separating Crow Manor from the woods beyond. She shook her head. It was impossible.

A familiar silver raven knocker glared down at her. She lifted her hand to knock, but Jupiter walked straight through the solid wooden door and disappeared.

'Impossible,' she breathed.

Jupiter's hand reached back through and pulled her into the dimly lit hallway of her childhood home.

'How did – how – what just happened?'

Jupiter looked at her sideways. 'Technically we're still in Nevermoor. At least, our bodies are. The Gossamer Line is supposed to be decommissioned, but as an interrealm explorer with a level nine security clearance, I have . . . certain privileges.'

Morrigan wondered if this was the sort of 'privilege' he could get arrested for. 'How can we still be in Nevermoor? We're standing in my grandmother's house.'

'Not exactly. We're travelling on the Gossamer.'

'What's that?'

'It's everything, it's . . . how can I explain?' He stopped and took a deep breath, looking up. Morrigan recalled that he'd tried to describe it to her once before and failed miserably. 'We're all part of the Gossamer, and the Gossamer is all around us. The things I can see – your bad dreams, for instance, or the history of a certain green teapot – they all exist on the Gossamer, like tiny invisible threads woven in a vast, hidden web connecting everything together. The Gossamer Line simply gives us a way of travelling through those threads with intent. It was a by-product of interrealm exploration – something the League created about thirteen or fourteen Ages ago. Your body remains safely in Nevermoor while your consciousness travels the Republic undetected. Very clever system, and *very* much a secret, so for goodness' sake don't tell anyone. It was never available for public use. Too volatile. These days even top-ranking military personnel are banned from riding it.'

'Why?'

Jupiter grimaced. 'This mode of travel doesn't suit everyone. Some people who rode the Gossamer Line came back sort of . . . wrong. Their bodies and minds, once parted, never perfectly reunited. They were permanently unsynchronised, and it drove them to madness. This is a very dangerous business if you don't know what you're doing.'

'I don't know what I'm doing!' said Morrigan, slightly panicked. 'Why'd you let me on it?'

He snorted. 'If anyone can ride the Gossamer Line, it's you.'

'Why me?'

'Because you're . . .' He stopped, seeming to catch himself. 'Because you're . . . with me.' He looked away. 'We can't be here long. Understand?'

She wasn't sure whether she felt disappointed or relieved. 'But I didn't want to visit. I wanted to come back for good.'

'I know this isn't what you were expecting. I just want you to be certain, before—'

'Jolly Christmas!' Ivy swept down the hallway towards them, smiling broadly. Morrigan stepped forward with an explanation on her lips, but her stepmother passed right by in a rustle of satin, leaving a cloud of sickly-sweet perfume in her wake. 'Jolly Christmas, everyone!'

Morrigan followed her into the sitting room. It was filled with people, each of whom raised a glass to their radiant hostess. Ivy gestured to a young man behind a piano, and he launched into a lively carol. Corvus – dressed in a tuxedo with a rose tucked into the lapel – beamed at his wife from across the room.

'They're having a party,' Morrigan observed. 'They never have parties.'

Jupiter said nothing.

She watched as Ivy and her father struck up an impromptu dance, spurred on by applause from their guests. One man said something to Corvus as he waltzed by, and Corvus threw his head back and laughed. Morrigan could count on one hand the times she'd seen her father laugh like that. In fact, she could count them on one finger. Including this time.

'Can't they see me?'

Jupiter hung back, staying close to the wall. 'Only if you want them to.'

Morrigan frowned. 'I want them to.'

'Apparently you don't.'

Ivy had redecorated. There were new curtains and upholstery (periwinkle blue) and flowery wallpaper. Every available surface was covered in photo frames, all of them housing pictures of Corvus, Ivy and the new baby – no, *babies*. Twins. An identical pair of rosy-faced boys with snowy-blond hair like their mother. A dual silver photo frame was engraved with the names 'Wolfram' and 'Guntram' in fancy lettering.

So Morrigan had brothers. She tried to digest this news as the party swirled around her, but her brain found it impossible to grasp at the idea. *I have brothers*, she kept thinking, over and over, *I have brothers*. But the words felt as light as air, with no weight or meaning at all, so she let them float away.

Morrigan wondered where her grandmother might be, before realising she already knew.

The Hall of Dead Crows was dark and still. It was just as Morrigan remembered it – cold, empty and musty-smelling. Only one thing had changed: her own portrait now hung there.

It wasn't really called the Hall of Dead Crows, at least not by anyone but Morrigan. Its actual name was, boringly, the Portrait Hall. But the only people who ever got their portraits in there were members of the Crow family, and only if they were dead. For some reason it was Grandmother's favourite place – she would sometimes disappear for hours at a time, and if you ever needed to look for her, you knew where she would be. Standing in the Hall of Dead Crows, gazing at the grand lineage from Carrion Crow (Morrigan's great-great-great grandfather – accidentally shot by his valet on a hunting trip) right down to Camembert Crow (her father's prize greyhound – chewed through a box of soap flakes and died foaming at the mouth).

Morrigan was surprised to see that Grandmother had cleared a premium space for her between venerable Great Aunt Vorona, who was killed when she fell off her racehorse, and Uncle Bertram, Corvus's brother, who had died young of a fever. Grandmother was notoriously particular about which dead Crows went where. Morrigan's late mother's portrait was all the way down at the far end of the hall, among the lesser-beloved pets and the third cousins twice removed.

The artist commissioned to paint Morrigan had been painting the Crows for more than sixty years. This meant that he was very old and painfully slow, and Morrigan had to stand still for hours while he tottered about with his paintbrush and occasionally shouted things like 'Stop moving!' or 'Where's that shadow coming from?' or 'I can see you breathing!' or 'Don't scratch your nose, you beastly child!'

Halfway through the last-minute portrait sitting on Eventide Day, Ivy had come in with a tape measure, holding the telephone between her ear and shoulder while she took Morrigan's measurements. 'One hundred and twenty centimetres long . . . yes, I should think so, at least . . . Oh no, wider than that, she's quite broad-shouldered . . . How much is the mahogany? The pine, then, I think. No – no, Corvus would want the mahogany, we mustn't look cheap. Pink silk lining, of course, with a ruffled pillow and a pink ribbon wrapped around the base. And I trust you'll deliver it to the house? What do you mean *when*? First thing tomorrow, obviously!'

Then she'd swept out of the room without a word to Morrigan or the artist. Once Morrigan realised what the conversation had been about, she'd spent the rest of the afternoon feeling annoyed that her coffin was to feature so much pink. The result was the portrait that now hung in the hall, of a scowling Morrigan with her arms folded defiantly across her chest.

It was the first time Morrigan had seen the finished artwork. She liked it.

'Who's there?'

Grandmother stood over by the window in the darkened room, lit only by the glow of lamplight from the hallway. She wore her usual formal black dress, with jewels at the neck and her dark grey hair piled high on her head. The air was fragrant with the familiar, woody scent of her perfume.

Morrigan approached her with caution. 'It's me, Grandmother.'

Grandmother squinted as she scanned the dark room. 'Is somebody there? Answer me!'

'Why can't she see me? I want her to see me,' Morrigan hissed at Jupiter.

'Keep trying,' he replied, gently pushing her forward.

She took a deep breath, squeezed her hands into fists, and thought with all her might – *See me. Please see me.* 'Grandmother? It's me. I'm right here.'

'Morrigan?' Grandmother whispered hoarsely. Her eyes widened. She stepped towards her granddaughter, shaking her head as if to clear it. 'Is that . . . can it be . . . ?'

'You can see me?'

Ornella Crow's milky blue eyes focused on her grand-daughter's face, and for the first time in Morrigan's memory, they were full of terror. 'No. *No.*'

'It's all right.' Morrigan held up her hands as if she were gentling a spooked animal. 'I'm not a ghost. It's really me. I'm alive. I didn't die, I'm not—'

Grandmother shook her head over and over. 'Morrigan. *No.* Why are you here? Why have you returned to the Republic? You shouldn't be here. They'll come for you. The Hunt of Smoke and Shadow. *They'll come for you.*'

Morrigan felt a sliver of ice cut through her. She looked at Jupiter, who was standing back with his hands thrust into his pockets, his gaze on the floor. 'How does she know about the Hunt—?'

But Grandmother turned on Jupiter, suddenly furious. 'You! You foolish man! Why did you bring her back here? You promised you would keep her in Nevermoor. You promised she would never leave the Free State. *You shouldn't have come.*'

'We're not really here, Madam Crow,' Jupiter said hurriedly, reaching out to run his hand straight through her body. Grandmother shuddered and stepped backwards. 'We travelled on the Gossamer Line. Our bodies aren't . . . it's a long story. Morrigan wanted to come; I felt she deserved—'

'You promised you'd never bring her back here,' Grandmother repeated, her eyes wild. 'You swore to me. It's not safe, it's not . . . Morrigan, you *must go*—'

'*Morrigan?*' A voice came from the doorway. Someone flicked a switch, and suddenly the Hall of Dead Crows was bathed in light. Corvus strode into the room, his blue eyes flashing. Morrigan opened her mouth to speak but the chancellor marched right past her, took hold of Grandmother's shoulders and shook her. 'Mother, what is this madness? Why are you acting this way? Now, of all times – it's a *Christmas* party, for goodness' sake.'

Ornella Crow glanced over her son's shoulder, her eyes flicking anxiously towards her granddaughter. 'It's . . .

it's nothing, Corvus. Just my imagination playing tricks on me.'

'You said the name,' Corvus whispered, his voice tight with fury. 'I heard it from the hallway. What if one of my colleagues had been walking past and heard it too?'

'It was – it was nothing, dear. Nobody heard a thing. I was just . . . remembering . . .'

'We swore we'd never speak that name again. We *swore* it, Mother.'

Morrigan felt as if her breath had left her body.

'The last thing I need is for people to be reminded of *all that*, just when I'm making inroads into federal government. If anyone in the Wintersea Party—' Corvus cut himself off, pressing his lips into a thin line. 'Tonight is important for me, Mother. Please don't spoil it with *that name*.'

'Corvus—'

'That name is dead.'

Corvus Crow turned on his heel, walked straight through the spot where his daughter stood, invisible to him, and was gone.

Morrigan was out of the house and all the way down to the gate before the cold air caught in her lungs. She leaned over, trying to catch her breath.

How could she feel it, she wondered. How could she feel the biting wind on her face and the hard ground beneath her feet, or smell the rain and the mud and her grandmother's perfume, while her father couldn't even see her standing in front of him?

She heard Jupiter's footsteps crunching on the gravel behind her. He stood there for a long time, waiting patiently for her to declare their next move, never giving advice or sympathy or saying *I told you so*. Just waiting, until at last Morrigan stood up straight and took a deep, trembling breath.

'She knew. My grandmother. She knew I wasn't dead.'

'Yes.'

'She knew about the Hunt.'

'Yes.'

'How?'

'I told her.'

'When?'

'Before Eventide. I had to find *someone* to sign your contract.'

Oh. So it had been her grandmother's signature, that unrecognisable name. Grandmother who'd slipped the envelope beneath her door on Bid Day. 'Why her?'

'She seemed to like you.'

Morrigan choked out a laugh, drawing her sleeve across her nose to hide a sniffle. Jupiter was polite enough to pretend, for a moment, to be very interested in the state of his shoes.

'Come back with me,' he said finally, in a quiet voice. 'Please? Your grandmother's right, it's not safe for you here. Come back to the Deucalion. It's your home now. We're your family – me, Jack, Fen and the others. You belong with us.'

'Until I fail the Show Trial and get deported.' She sniffled again. 'Until you get arrested for treason.'

'Like I said, we'll blow up that bridge when we come to it.'

Morrigan wiped her face until it was completely dry. 'Where do we go to catch the Gossamer Line?'

'Nowhere,' said Jupiter, his eyes lighting up with joy and relief. He clapped Morrigan on the back, and she gave him a watery smile. 'It will come to us. That's what the anchor is for. You must never ride the Gossamer Line without anchoring yourself first.'

'What do you mean – what anchor?'

'The one I left on the platform.' He grinned. 'A precious personal object left behind on departure, tethering you to Nevermoor with a single invisible Gossamer thread. Waiting to pull you back home. Can you picture it?'

Morrigan thought for moment. 'You mean . . . my umbrella?'

He nodded. 'Close your eyes and see it as clearly as you can, hanging on the rail. Every little detail. Hold that image in your mind, Mog. Have you got it?'

Morrigan closed her eyes and saw it: the shiny oilskin canopy, the silver filigree handle, the tiny little opal bird. 'Yes.'

'Don't let go of it.'

'I won't.'

She felt Jupiter's warm fingers close around hers. A train whistled in the distance.

The halls of the Hotel Deucalion were warm and familiar. Exhaustion crept into Morrigan's limbs as she shuffled to her room, thinking longingly of her many pillows and thick duvet, and hoping her fireplace was still alight, somehow knowing it would be.

As she reached out to open her bedroom door, a cold, bony hand grabbed her arm. She gasped and jumped backwards.

'Oh! It's you, Dame Chanda.'

'I didn't mean to frighten you, sweet girl,' said the soprano. 'I'm just heading off to bed myself. Aren't we a pair of night owls! All that rich Christmas food keeping you up too, I suppose?'

Morrigan smiled awkwardly. In her head she could still hear flashes of that mortifying conversation between Kedgeree and Dame Chanda. *At least if he'd failed with the Deucalion, it wouldn't have mattered so much.* 'Um, yeah.'

'Well, as I couldn't sleep, I've been doing a bit of digging through my old books and boxes of records.' Dame Chanda pulled out a crumpled piece of paper, unfolding and gently smoothing it. 'I thought you might be interested to see this. I knew I had a likeness somewhere. It's not recent, of course. He must have been in his twenties or thirties. He'd be well over a hundred now. Quite a good-looking young man, was the infamous Ezra Squall, as you can see – although I suppose that's an unfashionable opinion these days. For goodness' sake, don't tell anyone I called a mass murderer handsome – they'll come for me with torches and pitchforks.' She raised an eyebrow, smiling conspiratorially at Morrigan. 'You can keep this one, it's just a print of the original oil painting. I'm pleased you've taken an interest in Nevermoor's history, however ghastly this particular period may have been. Goodnight, Miss Morrigan, and a glad Yuletide to you, my dear.' She squeezed Morrigan's hand as she left, looking at her kindly, as though she'd wanted to do something nice for the poor girl who didn't have a chance of getting into the Wundrous Society.

But for once, Morrigan wasn't thinking about her chances in the trials.

She couldn't speak. Her throat felt like it was closing up.

The man in the painting smiled tranquilly. His ash-brown hair was slicked back, his old-fashioned suit immaculate and unmistakeably expensive. The dark eyes, the skin so pale it was nearly translucent, the thin pink smile and angular features, they were all exactly as she'd last seen them. And that scar, the thin white line that cut one eyebrow clean in half . . . she knew that scar. She knew this man.

It was Mr Jones.

CHAPTER TWENTY

Disappearing Act

The white blanket of snow over Nevermoor turned to miserable grey slush in the days after Christmas. Rain battered the windows of the Hotel Deucalion and jolliness quickly turned to post-holiday gloom, every hour of which brought Morrigan closer to the day she had been dreading all year long – the Show Trial.

But, unbelievably, the Show Trial was only her second-biggest problem now.

Morrigan had spent an agonising two days since Christmas working up the courage to tell Jupiter what she'd learned about Ezra Squall and Mr Jones. Every time she'd gone to knock on his office door, the picture of Squall clutched in her white-knuckled fist, her nerve had utterly failed her.

She desperately wanted to tell him. But how? What could she possibly say? *Guess what, Jupiter? The evillest man who ever lived thought I'd make a great evil apprentice. Oh, and he's been visiting me in Nevermoor for months. Oh, and I put the whole city in danger because I didn't want to tell you.*

More than anything, Morrigan wanted to talk to Hawthorne. Just when she thought the awful truth was going to bubble up and burst out of her like molten lava, her friend returned from the Highlands at last.

'Are you *sure*?' he said, squinting at the picture, a note of desperate hope in his voice. 'It could be his grandfather?'

Exasperated, Morrigan groaned and rolled her eyes for approximately the hundredth time that afternoon. She'd barely slept a wink and was now wearing a line in her bedroom floor from pacing back and forth (the bedroom seemed amused by this and kept stretching the walls farther apart so she had to walk longer distances each time).

'I'm telling you – it's him. It's the exact same man. He's got the same scar, the same freckle above his lip, the same exact nose, the same everything. If this isn't Mr Jones, I'm not Morrigan Crow.'

'But why would he pretend to be his own assistant?'

'Maybe because he hasn't aged a single day since this portrait was painted almost a *hundred years ago*.' Morrigan snatched the book from Hawthorne's hands and shoved the print an inch from his nose. 'Look. You saw him on Hallowmas – just *look*.'

Hawthorne pursed his lips, pulling the picture back and squinting at it. He took a long, deep breath and finally nodded reluctantly. 'It's him. Has to be. That scar—'

'Exactly.'

He frowned. 'But Dame Chanda said—'

'—that he's banned from the Free State, I know,' Morrigan interrupted. 'And Kedgeree said the city keeps him out with ancient magic.'

'Exactly. Plus, what about all those people guarding the borders? The Sky Force, the Royal Sorcery Council, the Magicians' League, and all that? Nobody could get past all that lot, not even the Wundersmith.'

Morrigan dropped into the armchair, hugging a cushion to her chest. 'But Mr Jones – Squall – he was *here*, Hawthorne. I saw him. We *both* saw him. It doesn't make any sense.'

They sat in silence for a moment, listening to the rain pelt against the glass. It was nearing dusk.

Hawthorne sighed. 'I have to go. I promised Dad I'd be home before dark. Show Trial's tomorrow – don't forget,' he added, half joking. As if either of them could forget their final trial for the Society. As if Morrigan could forget the day she'd been having nightmares about for months.

Hawthorne watched his friend for a long, solemn moment. 'Morrigan, I think it's time to—'

'I know,' she said quietly, turning to face the gloom outside her window. 'I have to tell Jupiter.'

Morrigan knocked tentatively on the door to Jupiter's study.

'What?' grumbled a voice that certainly didn't belong to her patron. She pushed the door open to find Fenestra stretched out on a rug in front of the fireplace. The Magnificat yawned broadly and fixed her sleepy yellow eyes on Morrigan. 'What do you want?'

'Where is he? I need to see him. It's urgent.'

'Who?'

'*Jupiter,*' said Morrigan, not bothering to hide her annoyance.

'Not here.'

'Yes, I can see that.' She gestured to his empty study. 'Where is he, the Smoking Parlour? The dining room? Fen, this is *important.*'

'He's *not. Here.* He's not at the hotel.'

'He – what?'

'He left.'

Morrigan's heart leapt into her throat. 'Left to go *where?*'

A shrug. A lick of her paw. 'No idea.'

'When will he be back?'

'Didn't say.'

'But – but it's the last trial tomorrow,' Morrigan said, her voice pitching upward. 'He'll be back before then, won't he?'

Fenestra rolled over and clawed at the rug, then rubbed her ears languorously.

Morrigan was suddenly terrified. When Jupiter left the Deucalion he was sometimes gone for hours, or sometimes for days, or sometimes for weeks at a time. Morrigan never knew when he'd be back, nobody ever knew, and the thought that he might not return in time for the Show Trial filled her with icy dread.

He'd promised her. He'd *promised*.

Just like he promised to take you to the Nevermoor Bazaar, said a little voice in the back of her head. *And look how that turned out.*

But this was different, Morrigan told herself. This was her *trial*. The big one – the one he'd sworn he'd take care of, the one he'd said she didn't have to even think about. She'd done her very best *not* to think about it, but now what? She couldn't do it on her own. She didn't even know what her talent was supposed to be.

'Fenestra, please!' she yelled, and the cat turned to glare at her. 'What's he *doing*, where did he *go*?'

'He said he had something important to do. That's all I know.'

Morrigan's heart sank. More important than being there for the most important day of her life? More important than keeping his promise?

She felt wrong-footed. Seized by the sudden terror of her predicament, she entirely forgot why she'd been looking for him in the first place.

She was on her own. She would have to do her Show Trial without him. She was *on her own*.

Morrigan slumped down into one of the leather armchairs by the fire. Her whole body felt as if it were made of lead.

Fenestra stood up suddenly and appeared above Morrigan's armchair, bringing her enormous squashed furry face down to the girl's eye level. 'Did he say he'd be here for your trial?'

Tears pricked Morrigan's eyes. 'Yes, but—'

'Did he tell you he'd take care of it?'

'Yes, but—'

'Did he promise you everything would be all right?'

A few hot tears spilled down Morrigan's face. '*Yes*, but—'

'That settles it, then.' With a placid blink of her huge amber eyes, Fen nodded once. 'He'll be here for your trial. He'll take care of it. Everything will be all right.'

Morrigan sniffled and wiped her nose with her shirtsleeve. She squeezed her eyes shut, shaking her head. 'How do you know that?'

'He's my friend. I know my friend.'

Fenestra was silent for a while, and Morrigan thought she'd fallen asleep standing up. Then she felt something warm, wet and sandpapery lick the entire right side of her face. She sniffled again, and Fen's big grey head rubbed her shoulder affectionately.

'Thanks, Fen,' Morrigan said quietly. She heard Fenestra padding softly to the door. 'Fen?'

'Mmm?'

'Your saliva smells like sardines.'

'Yeah, well. I'm a cat.'

'Now my face smells like sardines.'

'I don't care. I'm a *cat*.'

'Night, Fen.'

'Goodnight, Morrigan.'

CHAPTER TWENTY-ONE

The Show Trial

'Ooh, fairy floss,' said Hawthorne, waving over a uniformed Trollosseum worker selling treats. 'Want some? I've got Christmas money from my granny.'

Morrigan shook her head. There was only so much room in her stomach, and at present the entire space was taken up by nerves, nausea and the growing certainty that today was going to be the most humiliating day of her life. 'Aren't you nervous?'

Hawthorne shrugged as he tore off a huge strip of fairy floss with his teeth. 'A bit. I s'pose. I'm not doing any new tricks today, though. Nan thought I should stick with my best ones. I just wish I could pick which dragon I'm riding.'

'Won't you be riding your own?'

Hawthorne gave a short, sharp laugh. 'My own dragon? Are you mental? I don't have my own dragon. Whose parents can afford to buy them a dragon?' He licked remnants of sticky pink spun sugar from his fingers. 'I ride one of the Junior Dragonriding League's featherweights when I'm doing tricks. Usually either Flies Effortlessly Like a Discarded Sweet Wrapper on the Back of the Wind, or Glimmers in the Sun Like an Oil Slick on the Ocean. Oil Slick is definitely the best trained, but Sweet Wrapper's much braver. She's good at pulling out of steep dives.'

'Why can't you use one of them?'

'You know what the Society's like.' Morrigan didn't bother to remind him that no, being from the Republic, she didn't. 'They reckon their dragons are better than the League's dragons. Nan says it's best not to argue. I hope they don't give me a Highland breed, though – they're so bulky, I can never turn them properly. Ooh, look – it's starting.'

Finally, thought Morrigan as she watched the Elders enter the Trollosseum. A cheer rose from the stands. Elder Quinn held her hand up for silence and spoke into a microphone.

'Welcome,' she said, her voice booming from the speakers, 'to the final trial for Unit 919 of the Wundrous Society.'

Another cheer. Morrigan's ears rang. The stadium was packed not only with the remaining candidates, but also their patrons, other Society members who'd come to scope out the new talent, and of course friends and family. Hawthorne's parents were up there in the stands somewhere, as was Jack, who'd come home for the weekend specially to support Morrigan – which she found surprising and, actually, quite touching. There was an air of festivity in the Trollosseum, as if this was a normal day out and they were about to watch two trolls bash each other's skulls in.

'Welcome, esteemed members of the Society. Welcome, patrons. But most of all welcome to our candidates, the seventy-five brave young souls who have come so far, accomplished so much, and made my fellow Elders and me so very, very proud.

'Candidates, when you arrived today you each were randomly assigned a number to determine the order of your trials. A Society official will come to collect you from your seats in groups of five. Be prepared to move quickly when your number is called, and follow the official down to the gate, where your patron will meet you and escort you into the arena.'

'Yeah, if I'm lucky,' Morrigan muttered, and Hawthorne snorted, smiling at her sympathetically. He would be eleventh in the trials today, but Morrigan had been assigned number seventy-three . . . which at first she'd been unhappy with, as it meant a long, nervous wait ahead. But as Hawthorne pointed out, the later she was on, the more time Jupiter would have to get there.

'If, after your trial,' continued Elder Quinn, 'you have earned a place in the top nine candidates, your name will appear on the leaderboard. If not, well . . . we will wish you all the best for your future, somewhere else. Good luck, girls and boys. Let us begin.'

The first candidate to enter the arena was Dinah Kilburn of Dusty Junction. Before she began, her patron fussed about arranging chairs, tables and ladders in haphazard towers to create a sort of makeshift jungle gym.

Dinah was amazing. An agile climber, an extraordinary acrobat, and, Morrigan was shocked to discover—

'A *monkey*?'

Hawthorne laughed and then looked around guiltily. 'Morrigan! You can't call her that. She's not an *actual* monkey. She just has a tail.'

Dinah swung neatly from one tower to another, balancing on top or hanging upside down by her tail, and finished with a perfect landing. But the Elders took only a minute to reach their decision, waving her out of the Trollosseum without adding her name to the leaderboard. Dinah looked crushed.

'Ooh,' said Hawthorne, cringing. 'Tough start.'

Morrigan was flummoxed. Exactly *what* were the Elders looking for? What sort of person did they consider Wundrous Society material? She thought of the only Society members she knew – Jupiter, whose obscure knack was for seeing things nobody else could. Dame Chanda Kali, award-winning opera singer and gatherer of small woodland animals. When they were eleven years old, were they even *more* remarkable than Dinah Kilburn, the extraordinary monkey-tailed acrobat? Or was there something else the Elders were looking for, some other indefinable quality that made the perfect Wundrous Society member?

The performances only went downhill from there.

None of the next four candidates – a landscape painter, a hurdler, an illusionist and a boy who played the ukulele – ranked in the top nine. When they brought forward the second group of candidates, there were still no names on the leaderboard.

In fact, nobody ranked at all until the ninth candidate, Shepherd Jones – a boy who claimed he could speak to dogs. He performed an incredible series of tricks with a dozen canines, big and small. He barked commands to them and the crowd cheered as the dogs jumped through hoops, walked backwards on their hind legs, and danced with each other. The Elders remained sceptical, however.

'Send one of the dogs over to me,' commanded Elder Quinn. Shepherd barked at a blue cattle dog and it ran up into the stands to Elder Quinn, who showed it the contents of her handbag and sent it back to him. 'Now tell me what the dog saw.'

Shepherd knelt down to have a short conversation with the dog. 'A coin purse, a pork pie, an umbrella, a lipstick, a rolled-up newspaper, readin' glasses and a pencil.' The dog barked once more. 'Oh, and a piece of cheese.'

Elder Quinn nodded, and the audience applauded.

The dog barked twice. Shepherd glanced up at Elder Quinn shyly. 'Er – he says can he have the pork pie, please?'

Elder Quinn beamed and tossed the pie down to Shepherd. 'Here, he can have the cheese too.'

The cattle dog whined a little and barked three times. Shepherd's face turned red. 'I ain't tellin' 'em that,' he said quietly.

'What did he say, boy?' asked Elder Wong.

Shepherd Jones ruffled his hair, looking at the ground. 'He says cheese makes him constipated.'

Shepherd Jones was the first candidate added to the leaderboard, and the audience applauded as his name appeared on the big screens at either end of the Trollosseum.

The tenth candidate, however – a girl called Milladore West who made three extraordinary hats in eleven minutes and presented one to each of the Elders – was not awarded a place.

Next it was Hawthorne's turn. Morrigan wished him luck as he was ushered down to the arena with the next group of five. He was dressed head to toe in soft brown leather, and as Nan Dawson introduced him ('Hawthorne Swift of Nevermoor!'), Hawthorne fastened his shin guards, wrist guards and helmet. The audience gasped as a Wundrous Society dragon handler led in a twenty-foot-tall dragon with iridescent green scales and a long, jewel-bright tail.

Morrigan had seen pictures of dragons, of course. (They were considered both a Class A Dangerous Apex Predator and a Plague Proportions Pest in the Republic, and the Dangerous Wildlife Eradication Force often made headlines in culling season. Either for successfully destroying a nest, or for having their faces burned off.) But nothing compared to seeing the real thing. Hawthorne had offered several times to sneak her into a dragon stable under cover of night, since he wasn't allowed to invite her to training sessions. But Jupiter had said no, he'd prefer Morrigan kept all four of her original limbs, thanks.

The dragon emitted steaming-hot air in great bursts from slit-like nostrils as it swung its head from left to right. The crowd leaned back in their seats.

Hawthorne seemed entirely unfazed by his proximity to an ancient reptile that could burn him to a crisp if it sneezed the wrong way. He took a few minutes to acquaint himself with the animal, allowing it to get comfortable with his presence and patting its flank gently but firmly. The dragon watched him closely through one fiery orange eye.

Hawthorne walked around it in a circle, trailing his palm over the dragon's rough hide so that it knew where he was and wouldn't get skittish. Morrigan had seen a stable hand at Crow Manor do the same thing with her father's carriage horses. The Elders leaned forward, watching this interaction very closely. Elder Wong looked especially impressed and kept nudging Elder Quinn and whispering in her ear.

Hawthorne took a large piece of raw meat from the Wundrous Society handler and fed it to the dragon, patting it more roughly now on the neck until finally – without hesitation – he took a running leap and climbed up into the saddle that had been fitted between the dragon's shoulder blades. He snapped the leather reins and lurched forward in his seat as the enormous green reptile beat its wings and took off into the air.

Hawthorne and his dragon soared in a wide circle above the arena before beginning their show in earnest. Hawthorne yelled a command Morrigan couldn't quite make out, dug his heels into the animal's side, and they were off – rolling into tight somersaults, swooping over the stands and taking steep dives down to the ground only to pull back at the last second. They sped in a straight line with the dragon's wings outstretched as Hawthorne stood up on its back, mimicking the movement with his own arms out as if he were flying. Then he abruptly took his saddle and called out a command, and the dragon pulled its wings in tight and tumbled over in a 360-degree turn before outstretching its wings again without losing any height at all.

Morrigan had never seen Hawthorne like this – completely confident and in control, as if he was doing the thing he was born for. Shoulders back, eyes ahead. He commanded the dragon masterfully; it could have been an extension of his own body. Hawthorne was every bit the champion Nan Dawson had described.

The response of the audience confirmed it. Everyone – including the Elders – was in Hawthorne's thrall, gasping and screaming as he sped downward to the ground and cheering when he pulled out of a dive or glided around the Trollosseum stands, mere inches above their heads.

Morrigan was surprised by her friend's talent. It wasn't that she hadn't believed Hawthorne would be good, exactly. It was just that this poised, dazzling dragonrider was hard to reconcile with the boy who had once spent an afternoon showing her how he could make fart noises with his armpits.

As his final flourish, Hawthorne used the dragon's fire-breathing mechanism to write his initials in the sky with smoke before coming to land neatly in the arena.

The audience and the Elders leapt to their feet to cheer Hawthorne as he climbed down off the dragon's back and took a bow. Nobody cheered more loudly than Morrigan.

The Elders conferred briefly but seemed to be in perfect agreement; Hawthorne's name went straight to the number one spot.

But the quality of the trials stalled again after that, and nobody from the next three groups was added to the top nine.

Finally it was time for the candidate Morrigan had been waiting all year to see. When Baz Charlton announced 'Noelle Devereaux of the Silver District', Noelle entered the arena like a queen at court. After a minute of preening she opened her mouth to sing, and it was like a choir of angels had exploded and spewed stardust over the Trollosseum.

There were no words to the song. It was a cloud of melody – a clear, sweet lullaby that seemed to surround Morrigan like a bubble of perfect contentment. A quick look around told her she wasn't the only one; there were glazed eyes and tranquil smiles everywhere, as if Noelle's voice had cast a strange, blissful spell. Morrigan never wanted the song to end. She had to admit that Noelle's knack was truly, breathtakingly good.

How annoying.

The entire stadium – even Morrigan – applauded wildly as Noelle bowed and curtsied, blowing kisses into the crowd and beaming at the Elders. Hawthorne nudged Morrigan and made gagging noises, but it was too late for that. She'd already seen him wipe away a sneaky tear when the song ended.

Elder Quinn waved a fragile hand at the leaderboard and the names rearranged themselves so that Noelle the songbird was now in second place behind Hawthorne, with Shepherd the dog whisperer close behind. Noelle's face fell for the briefest moment, as though disappointed she wasn't number one, but she quickly recovered her poise and left the arena with her nose high in the air.

Morrigan's stomach dropped. Noelle was going to get into the Society. Popular, talented Noelle was going to be in Unit 919, and so was Hawthorne, and they'd become best friends. Hawthorne would forget all about Morrigan, and Morrigan would have to leave Nevermoor, and Jupiter, and all her friends at the Hotel Deucalion, and she'd never see them again. She knew it. The certainty of it took her breath away, just as if a big, depressed elephant had sat on her chest.

Hawthorne seemed to know what she was thinking. (Maybe not the depressed elephant bit.)

'It's easier to rank high near the beginning,' he said, elbowing her in the ribs as he took a long slurp of peppermint fizz. 'There are plenty of people left to knock Noelle off the board. They'll probably knock me off too.'

Morrigan knew he was just being modest, but she appreciated it all the same. 'You know you'll get in,' she said, elbowing him back. 'You were amazing.'

As the afternoon wore on, Hawthorne's prediction seemed unlikely. Although Shepherd quickly dropped out of the top nine, Noelle only went down two places. Ahead of her was Hawthorne, who'd dropped to second place, and in third was a boy named Mahir Ibrahim, who performed a long soliloquy in thirty-seven different languages with what Elder Quinn declared 'perfect intonation'.

Currently in first place was Anah – the plump, pretty girl with golden ringlets, whom Morrigan remembered from the Wundrous Welcome. With her faded yellow dress, patent leather shoes and hair tied back in a bow, Anah looked like she was off to Sunday school . . . which left Morrigan utterly unprepared for her unusual talent.

Anah's patron, a woman called Sumati Mishra, boasted that her candidate had a knack for knowing the human body. To prove this, she volunteered to lie down on a metal hospital gurney while Anah sliced her open with a scalpel, removed her appendix and sewed her back up again with neat, tiny stitches. Most extraordinarily, Anah did all this blindfolded.

Morrigan found it *tremendously* satisfying to watch Noelle Devereaux's face drop when Anah went straight to first place and bumped her down to fourth.

The trials continued with mixed results as candidate after candidate took the nerve-racking walk to the centre of the arena. Some were confident and brash, others looked like they were praying for the arena floor to open up and swallow them.

One frightened girl trembled so violently that she appeared to fade into the air, becoming incorporeal from the sheer terror of stage fright. Luckily, that was her knack – becoming incorporeal. She shimmered like a milky, pearlescent ghost in the sunshine and demonstrated her intangibility by walking straight through the Elders' table. The audience was impressed. Gradually the girl's confidence grew.

Unfortunately, it seemed her talent stemmed from her terror, because once she felt more comfortable and began enjoying the limelight, her body became substantial again. On her return journey through the Elders' table, she bumped right into it and sent a jug of water flying over Elder Wong. She didn't make it onto the leaderboard.

Meanwhile, Morrigan tried to quell the anxiety that had been growing in the pit of her stomach. Between each performance she scanned the rows of patrons.

'Where *is* he?' she muttered.

'He'll be here.' Hawthorne offered her some of his popcorn, which she refused. 'Jupiter would never miss your last trial.'

'What if he doesn't make it?'

'He'll make it.'

'What if he doesn't?' Morrigan repeated over the roar of the crowd as Lin Mai-Ling ran a speedy twelve-second lap of the Trollosseum, then stamped her feet in frustration when the Elders waved her away kindly. The audience groaned in sympathy. 'I don't even know what my knack is supposed to be! How am I supposed to do my trial without him?'

'Look, he'll make it, all right? But if he doesn't . . .' Hawthorne craned his neck, looking around the stadium. 'If he doesn't, I'll come down into the arena with you. We'll think of something.'

Morrigan raised one eyebrow. 'Like what?'

He chewed his popcorn and thought seriously for a moment. 'Can you make fart noises with your armpits?'

The sun set behind the Trollosseum grandstands and the floodlights turned on. In Morrigan's head they were like giant spotlights, designed to cast a very bright glow on her public humiliation.

The rankings shifted constantly, and the candidates in the top nine anxiously watched the leaderboard. Every time a new candidate was ranked, there were groans or tears or tantrums from the candidate who was bumped out of the top nine.

Morrigan glanced down at Noelle, two rows below, chewing her fingernails and glancing every five seconds at the leaderboard. She was now clinging to seventh position.

Just ahead of Noelle was a boy Morrigan recognised from the Book Trial, Francis Fitzwilliam, who'd whipped up a seven-course dinner for the judges. Each course took them on a roller coaster of heightened emotions that was bizarre to watch: from severe paranoia after a dish of grilled octopus, to gales of gleeful laughter brought on by a blueberry soufflé.

In fifth place was Thaddea Macleod, a brawny redheaded girl from the Highlands who defeated a full-sized adult troll in single combat.

Hawthorne had dropped to fourth place, just behind a small, angelic-looking boy called Archan Tate. Archan was a violinist, and as he played he moved nimbly all around the stadium and through the rows of seats without missing a note.

He was very good, but the Elders didn't seem inclined to add him to the leaderboard . . . until the very last moment, when sweet-faced Archan revealed his true talent. With a slightly sheepish grin, he emptied his pockets of what turned out to be quite a lot of jewellery, wallets, watches and coins that he'd managed to purloin *while playing the violin*. Morrigan was deeply impressed. He'd even swiped Elder Quinn's earring, right out of her ear!

Hawthorne didn't seem at all put out that a pickpocket had ranked above him. If anything, he was delighted by Archan's knack, even after realising his own leather dragon-riding gloves were among the pile of pilfered loot that the boy was now returning, piece by piece, to its rightful owners. 'How did he *do* that?' Hawthorne kept saying, grinning widely and examining his gloves as if they might give him a clue.

Morrigan was about to say for the twenty-seventh time that she didn't *know*, and would he *please* stop asking, when she saw Noelle's sidekick enter the arena with Baz Charlton.

'That's her.' Morrigan nudged Hawthorne. 'That's the girl we saw in the courtyard during the Fright Trial. Remember? Oh, what was her name . . . ?'

She was the eighth candidate Mr Charlton had presented that day; of his group it was Noelle who'd come the furthest. Morrigan looked at Noelle; she was watching her friend with a blank, disinterested expression – like she was just any other candidate.

Hawthorne shook his head. 'What are you going on about?'

'Do you *really* not remember her?'

'Remember who?'

Bored, distracted murmurs rippled through the rows of candidates when Baz Charlton announced his candidate as Cadence Blackburn of Nevermoor. His voice was nearly drowned out by the restless audience talking amongst themselves. But unlike everybody else, Morrigan was paying close attention.

'Cadence! That's her name. I forgot. How did I forget that?' Morrigan said to Hawthorne, who shrugged.

'Proceed,' said Elder Quinn, pouring herself a cup of tea. The Elders too were beginning to show signs of weariness; after several hours of judging there were glances at wristwatches, chins leaning in hands and long, open-mouthed yawns.

Baz Charlton gestured to somebody in a small windowed room at the top of the stands. The floodlights dimmed, throwing the audience into darkness, and a film was projected onto the big screens.

CHAPTER TWENTY-TWO

The Mesmerist

The scene that flickered into life was one Morrigan recognised: Proudfoot House gardens, on the day of the Wundrous Welcome. The camera panned shakily across the sunny lawn and bustling dessert buffet queue, before zooming in on two people: Noelle and Cadence. They stood near a huge green jelly sculpture, which Morrigan also recognised. Hawthorne was a few steps behind them, predictably piling his plate high with cake and pastries.

'Tacky,' Noelle was saying on the screen. She poked the jelly, making a face. '*Horrid*. Who serves this stuff at a *party*? We're not in *nursery school*.'

'Right,' Cadence replied. She had been about to grasp one of the miniature jelly sculptures surrounding the bright green behemoth, but she changed strategy at the last second and began spooning bread and butter pudding into her dish instead. 'Tacky. They're so stu—'

'Mummy would have a fit,' Noelle continued, talking over Cadence. 'Can you believe they're making us serve ourselves, Katie?'

'It's . . . Cadence,' said the other girl, her face falling. 'Remember?'

'Do you know how many servants the Wundrous Society employs?' Noelle continued as if she hadn't heard. 'And they put on a *buffet*? Don't they know buffets are for *poor people*?'

Something flickered in Cadence's eyes but was quickly gone. 'Yeah, exactly,' she said, her hand hovering over a serving spoon, suddenly unsure.

'Forget it. Come on.' Noelle dropped her own dish in the middle of the table, then snatched Cadence's pudding from her and tipped it upside down on top of a delicious-looking chocolate fudge cake. She flounced out of the marquee, evidently expecting her friend to follow.

Cadence took one longing look at her ruined pudding, breathed in deeply, and made an abrupt turn, coming face-to-face with Hawthorne, who'd overheard everything and was trying not to laugh.

Cadence leaned in close to Hawthorne and spoke in the same flat, husky voice Morrigan remembered her using on the twins at the Book Trial, and again on the Society official at the Chase Trial.

'Don't you think somebody ought to drop that big green thing right on her head?'

Hawthorne nodded solemnly.

Morrigan turned to the real Hawthorne sitting beside her. He looked deeply confused. 'I don't remember that,' he murmured.

The scene changed to show Noelle, Cadence and a group of children – including Morrigan – gathered on the front steps of Proudfoot House. The image was partially blocked by a blur of green leaves. Morrigan supposed that the camera – and the person holding it – had been hidden behind a tree.

'Is that your knack?' Noelle was saying to Morrigan on the screen. 'Using big words?'

Cadence giggled helplessly, but not – as Morrigan had thought at the time – at Noelle's cruelty. She kept glancing upward, to where Hawthorne was positioning himself in the window with the jelly sculpture. She was laughing at what was about to happen to Noelle.

'I thought it must be wearing horrible clothes or being as ugly as a gutter rat.'

The real Morrigan sitting in the Trollosseum stands felt her face flush. It'd been bad enough hearing that the first time, surrounded by a dozen strangers. Hearing it again in the presence of hundreds was close to torture. She slid down in her seat, trying to make herself invisible.

The scene unfolded as Morrigan remembered it, climaxing with Hawthorne's magnificent jelly drop, at which point the Trollosseum exploded with laughter. Hawthorne grinned at Morrigan.

'Might not have been my idea, but it was still brilliant.'

Several rows in front of them, Noelle was glaring at the screen and shaking her head, her eyes narrowed to slits. She seemed utterly shocked – obviously she'd had no idea about the knack of her so-called friend.

The next few minutes of film showed an incredible scene in which Cadence wandered down a posh street with a can of bright red spray paint in her hand, spraying rude words and pictures all along the immaculate white façades of the houses. By the time she was stopped by a brown-coated officer of the Stink, almost the entire street had been vandalised.

'*Stop right there!* What do you think you're doing, you little menace?'

'Art,' she said flatly.

'Oh, *art*, is it?' the officer asked, her eyebrows shooting up to her hairline. 'Looks like *crime* to me. Maybe I should slap you in handcuffs!'

'Maybe you should slap yourself in handcuffs,' Cadence suggested. And the woman did, tightening them around her own wrists without a second thought.

Cadence put the can of spray paint into her hands. 'Number twelve needs a bit more red. Have a nice day.'

'Have a nice day, ma'am.' With that final, dead-eyed statement, the officer's gaze slid past Cadence like oil over water and landed on the glossy white front door of number twelve, which didn't stay white for much longer.

It was extraordinary, the things Cadence could make people do. It wasn't nice, Morrigan thought, it wasn't decent or honest – but it was extraordinary.

Morrigan had the uncomfortable experience of watching herself on the big screen yet again when Cadence's film showed the debacle of the Chase Trial in its entirety, from the stampeding rhinoceros to Fen's daring rescue to the moment of devastation when Cadence convinced the race official that it was she who ought to go through to the Fright Trial and not Morrigan.

But the film went further. It showed another conversation, a very different one, in which Cadence convinced the official that one of the unicorns was in fact a Pegasus in disguise. She pointed to its glowing silver horn – the perfect specimen of a genuine unicorn horn – and said, 'See? Someone's glued an upside-down ice cream cone onto its head. I can't believe you didn't spot this earlier. And its wings have been tucked away.' She pointed to the unicorn's flawless white flank, which was decidedly wingless.

Morrigan was speechless. It was Cadence who'd gotten her through to the Fright Trial. She'd snatched away Morrigan's spot and then given it back to her – just like that. Why? Did she feel *guilty*?

Scene after scene of manipulation and trickery followed. The film showed that it was Cadence who had convinced the high-five twins, way back at their very first trial at Proudfoot House, to quit before they'd begun. She'd even persuaded Elder Wong to act like a chicken during her Book Trial (a scene that was received with uproarious laughter from everyone but Elder Wong).

In the end, though there were mixed reactions from the Elders and certainly a lot of disapproving faces in the audience, they had no choice. Cadence Blackburn didn't just have a knack, she had a *gift*. A weird, mean gift. But a gift nonetheless.

'Number one!' said Hawthorne as Cadence's name lit up on the leaderboard, bumping Anah down to second place, Hawthorne to fifth and Noelle to eighth.

There were only three groups of five to go. Morrigan had given up looking for Jupiter and started looking for an escape route. As soon as her failure and humiliation in the Show Trial were complete, she'd have to make a run for it.

She hadn't seen Inspector Flintlock, but she felt certain he was somewhere in the stadium, biding his time. Waiting for her to fall on her face so he could seize his moment and arrest her.

At last the final group was called. Morrigan made her way down to the arena gates with four other candidates. Hawthorne tried to go with her, but the ever-present clipboard-toting Wundrous Society officials shooed him back to his seat.

Morrigan was on her own.

She stood in silence as the first three candidates performed. The girl with very long hair stood in the arena and – to the horror of the crowd – chopped off the lot, just above her ears. Moments later the hair began to regrow itself, and in mere minutes had fully replenished to its former length. Morrigan, like everyone else in the audience, was amazed. But apparently not the Elders. As Jupiter had predicted all the way back at the Wundrous Welcome, the girl did not make it into the top nine. She heaped both piles of hair – the one on the floor and the one on her head – into her pull-along wagon and moped out of the Trollosseum.

A ballet dancer. No place on the leaderboard.

A boy who could breathe underwater. No place.

Then it was Morrigan's turn. The Wun official held the gate open for her.

She could leave now. The thought struck her like lightning – she could just turn and walk away. This was her last chance to avoid humiliation (followed by deportation from Nevermoor, followed by certain death), and she could do it – she could spare herself what was bound to be the worst moment of her life so far – if she just *turned and walked away.*

Do it now, she thought. *Just go.*

'Ready?'

A whisper in her ear. A squeeze of her shoulder. She looked up.

A ridiculous ginger head. A pair of twinkling blue eyes. A wink.

'Yeah. I'm ready.' She hesitated and then asked – one rushed, desperate, final attempt to get an answer before everyone else in the Trollosseum knew – 'What is it, Jupiter? What's my knack?'

'Oh, that.' He blinked owlishly at her, as if she'd asked the least important question in the world. 'You don't have one.'

Then he stepped boldly into the arena, expecting her to follow.

'Captain Jupiter North presents Morrigan Crow of Nevermoor.'

CHAPTER TWENTY-THREE

Foul Play

The mood in the Trollosseum shifted when Jupiter stepped into the arena. The hum of distracted chatter turned to whispers. People actually sat up straighter. One of the Wundrous Society's most celebrated sons had finally taken a candidate. They were dying to see what she had a knack for, this girl who had tempted the great Jupiter North into patronage.

Morrigan was also dying, but not from curiosity.

She was dying to run, dying to hide, dying for the arena floor to explode like a volcano and engulf the whole place in a wave of molten lava. Her heart was beating out of its cage like it wanted to attack something.

Not something. Someone.

How could Jupiter do this to her? All year long Morrigan had trusted him, certain that whatever her mysterious knack was, her patron knew about it. He'd told her not to worry, that he had the whole thing in hand . . . and now he'd gone and thrown her under a bus.

She didn't have a knack. She'd been right all along.

Angry tears stung her eyes, threatening to spill over. How *could* he?

'May I approach?' Jupiter asked the Elders. Morrigan knew, having sat through more than seventy of these by now, that this was an odd request. But Elder Quinn waved Jupiter forward.

Morrigan stood alone in the centre of the hushed arena as Jupiter spoke quietly with the Elders. She looked around at the curious faces in the stands, imagining how they'd laugh when they discovered it was all a joke, that Morrigan Crow of Nevermoor had no talent at all. Or maybe they wouldn't laugh. Maybe they'd be angry at Jupiter for wasting their time.

Not as angry as me, thought Morrigan.

Then Jupiter did something very strange.

One by one, he held Elder Quinn, Elder Wong and Elder Saga by their shoulders and pressed his forehead to theirs. They emerged from this odd exchange blinking and dazed, shielding their eyes, and stared at Morrigan for a long time in silent astonishment.

And then Morrigan's name went straight to number one.

The Trollosseum erupted. People leapt to their feet, shouting at the Elders, demanding an explanation for this madness, demanding to see a knack from Morrigan Crow, the wretched interloper.

Morrigan herself was so stunned that she forgot to be mad at Jupiter. She stood frozen, absorbing the deluge of fury.

Bellowed accusations of favouritism and cheating echoed in the stadium. Morrigan saw Baz Charlton running down the stands, taking the steps three at a time, shouting incomprehensibly. Everywhere Morrigan looked, people were glaring at her. She scanned the crowd for Hawthorne, wondering if he too was angry. Could her friend possibly think her a cheat?

Jupiter strode over and took her hand, sweeping her along with him through a door at the back of the arena.

'Come, Mog. Let us leave the stroppy masses to their strop.'

The green room backstage was blissfully empty. There was a single couch, a tray of sad-looking sandwiches and a jug of pale lemon squash. Here and there on the walls were posters for past troll fights and dragonriding tournaments. Inoffensive panpipe music played in the background.

The room's lone attendant, a young man in a Trollosseum uniform who appeared to be at least half troll (his knuckles dragged on the floor), offered them the tray as they entered. 'Sammich?' he grunted.

'No, thank you,' said Jupiter. Morrigan shook her head. The half-troll got bored and left.

Morrigan took a deep breath, clenched her hands into fists, and was just summoning the right words to express her rage when Jupiter spoke up. 'I know – I know. I'm sorry. Please, Mog, I'm so sorry. I know how confusing this is.' He was all remorseful eyes, appeasing voice and shielding hands – *Don't hurt me, don't shoot.* 'But listen. It's about to get even more confusing, and there isn't time to explain properly now. But I swear – I *swear* – when this is over, I will answer each and every one of your questions in *excruciating* detail. But I need you to be patient and trust me, even though you might not think I deserve it, just for a *little* while longer. Okay?'

Morrigan wanted to yell at him, to say no, no, of *course* it's not okay, it's the *opposite* of okay – but she didn't. Instead she hooked Jupiter's little finger forcefully with her own, looking him dead in the eye. 'Every question. Excruciating detail. Pinkie promise?'

'Pinkie promise.'

Seconds later the doors burst open and the Elders swept in, their faces schooled and emotionless, their cloaks billowing behind them. Each wore a golden *W* pinned at the throat.

'How long have you known?' demanded Elder Quinn. 'Obviously since before Eventide, but how long before? Days, weeks? Months? *Years?*'

Jupiter held up his hands. 'Elder Quinn, I understand you're surprised, but—'

'Surprised! *Surprised?*' The tiny old woman seemed to grow three inches as she squared off to Jupiter, pointing her finger in his face. Morrigan felt like cheering her on. *You tell him, old lady.* 'Jupiter Amantius North, I taught your patron. I taught your *patron's* patron! I've known you since you were eleven years old, saved you from expulsion on countless occasions – I even recommended you to the League of Explorers, and *this is how you repay me?*'

'Forgive me, but what difference would it have made?' Jupiter ran a hand through his hair, shrinking a little as the older woman paced angrily before him. 'What could you have done about it? Could you have changed anything?'

Elder Quinn sputtered and stopped in her tracks. 'Well – no, of course not, but a bit of *warning* would have been nice! I'm an old woman, North, you might have given me a heart attack out there.'

A heart attack? Morrigan's eyes found Jupiter's; what had he shown the Elders that was so shocking?

He looked guilty. 'I'm sorry, Elder Quinn. I just didn't want to do anything that might disrupt the gathering, I didn't know if – I mean, it's not exactly . . .' He trailed off with a helpless shrug. 'I've never done this before.'

'When did the gathering begin?' asked Elder Wong, staring at Morrigan.

'Hard to pinpoint,' said Jupiter. 'A year or two ago? Winter of Ten perhaps, or Spring of Eleven? I've been paying staff in the Crow household for information here and there – tutors, cleaners, that sort of thing. Trouble is, they're all so superstitious, it's hard to sort out actual Wundrous events from silly stories. The cook was convinced Morrigan had killed the gardener by sneezing on him. Ridiculous.'

'Were there others?' asked Elder Quinn.

'Others?' Jupiter looked at her in surprise.

She raised an eyebrow. 'You know exactly what I am asking you, North.'

'Right, others.' He cleared his throat. 'Yes. Three others registered.'

'And they . . . ?'

'Didn't show any signs,' Jupiter said resolutely. 'Not worth pursuing.' Morrigan frowned. *Three others registered* . . . Was he talking about the three other children on the Cursed Children's Register? Had he saved her and left them to the Hunt of Smoke and Shadow because they were 'not worth pursuing'? She didn't want to believe that.

'And aside from your superstitious household spies, North,' said Elder Wong, 'any hard evidence?'

'According to the Wintersea News Network, Wunder shortages in Southlight and Far East Sang began around eighteen months ago. Yet from Winter of Ten through Winter of Eleven, Morrigan's hometown experienced record highs in Wunder density and remained untouched by the Republic's energy crisis. Until Eventide, that is, when Wunder readings in Jackalfax showed a sudden drop.' He paused, his eyes flickering over to Morrigan. 'Eventide night, to be precise. Around nine o'clock.'

When you saved my life, thought Morrigan. *When we escaped Jackalfax through the Skyfaced Clock.* What did the Wunder shortages have to do with her?

'How in heaven's name did you get her into the Free State?' asked Elder Quinn, then changed her mind. 'Wait. Forget it – I don't want to know. I'm sure it's something illegal.'

Jupiter pursed his lips and breathed heavily through his nose. 'I'm sorry I didn't tell you, Elder Quinn. Truly I am. Like I said, I was scared to do anything that might disturb the gathering – I know it's stupid, I know it makes me just as silly and superstitious as the Crows' kitchen staff, but I worried that if I spoke of it aloud, I might . . . scare it off.'

'Well, perhaps that might have been for the best,' muttered Elder Saga, the great shaggy bull. Elder Quinn cut him off with a sharp look. Morrigan had to literally bite her own tongue to hold back the thousand questions that had been burning inside her since this conversation began.

'So I didn't tell a soul.' Jupiter looked at the ground. 'Not even Morrigan.'

The Elders went silent. Elder Quinn looked horrified, turning from Jupiter to Morrigan and back again. 'You cannot mean – are you saying the child *doesn't even know*—'

'Really, North, this is unacceptable, entirely against Society rules,' huffed Elder Saga. 'To enter a child into the trials without her knowing why – unheard of! If your patron was here—'

'What about a safeguard pact?' Elder Wong interrupted. 'We've just allowed a dangerous entity into the Society and nobody has thought to enquire about a safeguard.'

'I'm not dangerous,' Morrigan objected, while a tiny voice in the back of her head said . . . *Yes, you are. You're cursed.* Was that what the Elders were talking about? Jupiter had told her all those months ago that she wasn't cursed, that she'd never been cursed. Had that been a lie, too?

'Oh, this is absurd. Gregoria, Alioth – are we insane? What have we done?' Elder Wong threw his hands up. 'There isn't a citizen in the entire *realm* who would sign such a pact, let alone *three* reputable, upstanding—'

'Three?' boomed Elder Saga. 'Heavens, no. A three-signatory safeguard would be fine were the child merely a conjurer of hurricanes or a mesmerist or some *ordinary* dangerous entity. For this, I suggest five signatories.'

Dangerous entity. Morrigan wished they'd stop saying that.

'Nine,' said Elder Quinn. Saga and Wong looked at her in surprise. 'And that's non-negotiable, Captain North. We cannot accept fewer than nine signatories. Not for a—' she cut herself off, shooting Morrigan a fretful glance. 'Not for this.'

'We might as well take her name off the leaderboard now,' said Elder Wong. 'He'll never get nine.'

'I have seven so far.'

The Elders looked taken aback. Jupiter retrieved a scroll of paper from his coat and handed it over. Morrigan tried to catch a glimpse, but he was too fast.

Elder Quinn raised an eyebrow as she examined the scroll. 'Senator Silverback? *Queen Cal?* You do have friends in high places. And they don't know—?'

'They know enough to be sufficiently warned,' said

Jupiter. Morrigan thought she detected a tiny amount of doubt creeping into his voice. 'But . . . no, nothing specific.'

'But they *have* met the child?'

'They will,' Jupiter assured her. 'Soon. I promise.'

'They certainly trust you. And they appear to be qualified, at least,' said Elder Quinn, trailing her finger down the list.

'Qualified for what?' asked Morrigan, unable to keep quiet any longer. But if any of the adults heard her, they paid no attention.

Elder Saga turned to Jupiter. 'None of this matters, North, if you cannot find an eighth and ninth signatory.'

Jupiter sighed and rubbed the back of his neck. 'I'm trying, believe me. That's why I was late to the trials today, I thought I had an eighth but it fell through. If I could just have a few more days—'

'I will sign the pact,' said Elder Quinn. The other Elders looked at her with alarm. 'It's not against the rules.'

'This is highly unusual, Gregoria,' said Elder Wong. 'Are you certain?'

'Quite certain.' She pulled a pen from the folds of her cloak and signed her name briskly at the bottom of the scroll. 'At least *someone* on this list will know what they're getting themselves into. Send me the paperwork this evening, North.'

Jupiter was momentarily silent, his mouth hanging open in shock. 'I – th-thank you, Elder Quinn. Really – *thank you*. I promise you won't regret it.'

Elder Quinn sighed deeply. 'I doubt that very much, dear. Nevertheless, we shall give you until Inauguration Day to find your ninth signatory. If you cannot find one, Miss Crow's place in Unit 919 will be forfeit. That's the best I can do.'

⌐━●

They left the Trollosseum through labyrinthine halls plastered with old posters and photographs of famous troll fights, Morrigan fighting to keep up with Jupiter's urgent pace.

'I'm sending you and Jack back to the Deucalion with Fenestra, Mog,' he said, three or four steps ahead of her. 'I've got to get that last signature, and I'm running out of options. I have one last lead, but it's a long shot, and I need—'

'But you promised to tell me—'

'I know I did, and I will, but—'

'There they are! I found them!'

Baz Charlton stomped down the hallway, followed by a flouncing, furious Noelle Devereaux, a bored-looking Cadence Blackburn and the smuggest moustache in all of

Nevermoor – Inspector Flintlock. Behind them, at least a dozen brown-uniformed officers of the Stink.

'Foul play!' cried Mr Charlton, pointing at Jupiter and shaking with self-righteous rage. 'Arrest these people, Inspector! Foul play! What was that, eh? What'd you do to the Elders? Some sort of sorcery?'

Jupiter tried to push past. 'Not now, Baz, I don't have time for your blithering.'

'Oh yes you *do* have time for my blithering!' said Mr Charlton, moving to block him. 'You might have hood-winked the Elders, North, but you can't fool me. You two have stolen the rightful place of my candidate, Noelle.' He pointed fiercely at Morrigan, who was surprised – last she'd seen, Noelle was still in ninth place on the leaderboard. One of the last two candidates must have bumped her off. Morrigan tried not to smile. 'This little black-eyed beast doesn't belong in the Society, and I'll be going straight to the Elders to tell them that she's—'

'That she's a *filthy illegal*,' interrupted Inspector Flintlock, hitching his pants up and puffing out his chest. He looked back at the other officers, making sure he had their full attention. His moment had arrived, and he was going to savour it. 'Smuggled in from the Republic and enjoying *unlawful* refuge in the den of a *criminal element*.'

Jupiter looked pleased. 'I've never been called a "criminal element" before. How exciting.'

'Shut it,' snapped Flintlock. He pulled a piece of paper from his jacket and held it up for them to see. 'I've got a warrant here. Now, I want to see some hard, physical proof that she is who you say she is, that she belongs in the Free State and isn't just Republic scum trying to take advantage of our hospitality, or worse – *spy* on us for the Wintersea Party.'

'Come on, Flinty, this is embarrassing now,' Jupiter said impatiently. 'I told you already – Wundrous Society members are outside your jurisdiction. You could lose your badge for this, mate.'

'That would be true, *mate*, were it not for the fact that the trials have now ended,' said Flintlock, looking extremely pleased with himself. He pulled out a second piece of paper and read from it. 'You need to brush up on your Wun Law handbook, North. Article ninety-seven, clause H: "A winning candidate is not an official member of the Wundrous Society until receiving his or her golden pin on completion of the unit inauguration ceremony, and until that time his or her provisional membership may be revoked without due process if deemed necessary and appropriate by the High Council of Elders."'

Jupiter sighed and shook his head. 'We've been through this, Inspector. Article ninety-seven, clause F: "A child who is participating in the entrance trials for the Wundrous Society shall for all legal purposes be considered a member—"'

"'A member of the Wundrous Society for the duration of said trials or until he or she is removed from the trial process,"' Flintlock recited over the top of Jupiter's voice. 'For the *duration of said trials*, North. The trials are over. The leaderboard is full. The Elders have gone home.'

'And the unit inauguration is weeks away,' added Mr Charlton, barely containing his glee.

'I believe that puts your wretched little stowaway well and truly within my jurisdiction,' finished Flintlock. His eyes had taken on a manic shine. His moustache quivered. He held out his hand. 'I'll be seeing those papers now, Captain North.'

Jupiter had nothing to say. Morrigan could see him weighing his options, counting the surrounding officers, looking for an escape route. The silence stretched and Flintlock kept his hand out, waiting patiently, a triumphant glow lighting up his horrible face.

Morrigan slumped against the wall, utterly defeated. She'd come so close – *so close*. Now it was over. She'd die and not get any of her questions answered. She closed her eyes, waiting to be put in handcuffs and marched away.

'Here they are.'

Cadence Blackburn's voice echoed in the hallway. Morrigan cracked open one eye to see her holding out a worn piece of paper with one of the corners ripped off, right underneath Inspector Flintlock's nose.

'What's this?' said Flintlock, confused. 'What am I looking at?'

It was an old troll fight poster advertising an 'epically gory battle' between Orrg of Clorflorgen and Mawc-lorc of Hurgenglorgenflut. Orrg and Mawc-lorc, two spectacularly ugly trolls, were pictured snarling at each other, and in colourful fonts the poster promised two-for-one ales, a dazzling half-time show and free entry to anyone who could prove they had troll blood in them.

'It's her papers,' said Cadence in her low, flat voice. 'See? It says right there: Morrigan Crow is a citizen of the Free State.'

Flintlock shook his head woozily, as if trying to dislodge something that was stuck. 'It – what? Where does it—'

'Just there,' Cadence insisted, not even bothering to point at anything. She sounded bored. 'It says, "Morrigan Crow is a citizen of the Free State and wasn't smuggled in illegally so why don't you just get over it so we can all get on with our lives." There's a government seal on it and everything.'

Baz Charlton snatched the papers from her hand. 'Let me see that.'

Noelle and Flintlock crowded around him, putting their heads together and squinting at Orrg's and Mawc-lorc's pockmarked, drool-soaked faces.

Baz frowned, blinking repeatedly. 'This isn't – these aren't – this is a troll fight—'

'No it's not,' Cadence said. 'It's a passport. It's Morrigan Crow's Free State passport.'

'It's not, it's – it's a troll – it's . . . Morrigan Crow's Free State passport,' he repeated, his eyes glazing over.

'Everything appears to be in order,' said Cadence. Her voice hummed like a beehive. 'So you'll be on your way, then.'

'Everything appears to be in order,' echoed Flintlock. 'So we'll be on our way, then.'

He let the poster float to the ground as he trooped down the hall, Baz and Noelle following dumbly behind. The Nevermoor Police Force officers hovered uncertainly, completely mystified by this strange turn of events, before obediently trailing after their commanding officer.

Cadence turned to Morrigan. 'You owe me.'

'Why did you help me?'

'Because . . .' Cadence hesitated. 'Because I hate Noelle. I don't like you much either, but I *really* hate Noelle. And also because . . .' Her voice grew quiet. 'You remember me. Don't you? You remember me from the Chase.'

'You nearly got me kicked out of the trials.'

'And Hallowmas night. Do you remember that, too?'

Morrigan glowered. 'You pushed me into a pond. It's not something I'm likely to forg—'

'Nobody ever remembers me,' Cadence interrupted, speaking in a rush. She looked at Morrigan strangely. 'People forget mesmerists, that's the whole point. But you remembered.' She glanced up the hallway. 'Gotta go.' She ran to catch up with her patron and had disappeared around a corner before Morrigan could think of what to say.

'What an odd little girl,' said Jupiter, staring after Cadence with a puzzled frown. 'Who is she?'

'Cadence Blackburn.' Morrigan picked up the discarded poster, folded it, and put it in her pocket. 'She *is* odd, yeah.'

'Hmm?' Jupiter shook himself out of his reverie and focused his gaze on Morrigan.

'I said she *is* odd.'

'Who's odd?'

'Cadence.'

'Who's Cadence?'

Morrigan sighed. 'Seriously? Never mind.'

CHAPTER TWENTY-FOUR

Battle Street

Jupiter sent for Fenestra, who reluctantly met them at the entrance to the Battle Street Wunderground station. She was to escort Morrigan, Jack and Hawthorne back to the Deucalion while Jupiter attended to the mysterious business of the safeguard pact, whatever that was.

'Don't let them out of your sight,' Jupiter told Fen for the umpteenth time as he returned from the ticket desk. 'No detours, no distractions – straight home to the hotel, no side trips or delays of any sort, understand?'

Fen rolled her eyes. 'Oh, but I was going to stop to buy ice cream and puppies.'

'Fenestra . . .' he said warningly.

'All right, keep your beard on.'

He turned to Morrigan, Hawthorne and Jack. 'Right, you three. It'll be crowded down there. Stay close to Fen and don't wander off. Fen, best take the Rush Line to Lilith Gate and then change onto the Centenary Line. That'll get you to Island-in-the-River; you can catch the Brolly Rail from there straight to Caddisfly Alley. You lot – got your brollies?'

The children nodded.

'But the Viking Line goes directly to Island-in-the-River,' said Fen.

Jupiter shook his head. 'Chap at the ticket desk says there's a delay due to a Viking horde attack in one of the tunnels. They'll be hours sorting that mess out.'

'Rush Line it is,' she agreed. 'Come on, you three.'

They descended into the busy station and pushed through the turnstiles. Fen, who was too large to go the normal way, jumped over the top. An indignant ticket collector made to tell her off, but she hissed at him and he immediately went about his business.

As they traversed tunnels and stairwells, Hawthorne kept looking over his shoulder at Morrigan, desperate to ask about her trial, but it was too noisy. Morrigan caught his eye and shrugged, mouthing the words, *'I don't know.'*

When they finally got to the platform, Fen pushed through the crowd to the yellow line at the front, parting the commuters like wheat stalks in a field. Hawthorne,

Morrigan and Jack each grasped a tuft of her fur and tried to keep up, apologising to people as they elbowed past.

'Slow down, Fen,' said Jack. 'You're going to trample people.'

'If people are in my way they deserve to be trampled,' grumbled the Magnificat. 'This is just what I need, after the ridiculous day I've had – to babysit you three in a packed-out Wunderground. The Deucalion's been a mess all day, people coming and going and making noise. We've had the electricians in to sort out the wiring in the south wing, and Kedgeree's had those ridiculous ghost hunters back yet *again*.'

'Ghost hunters!' said Hawthorne, looking excited.

'I thought they got rid of the ghost,' said Morrigan. 'Back in summer, remember? They did that exorcism.'

'And yet despite their really top-notch sage-waving,' Fen said drily, 'our grey man is still hanging about the south wing, spooking people. Walking through walls and disappearing around corners. The staff have even given him some funny name – oh, what was it?'

'I haven't seen any grey man,' said Morrigan.

'So you shouldn't, you've no reason to be in the south wing while these damned renovations are going on.' Morrigan exchanged guilty looks with Hawthorne and Jack but said nothing. They still hadn't told anyone about Morrigan's accidental visit to the south wing on the night the shadow escaped. 'It's the builders who keep complaining about him, they say they hear him from the next room and when they rush in to see who's there, he just disappears into the Gossamer.'

'Hear him doing what?' asked Jack.

'Singing or – no, humming. That's what they call him. The Humming Man. Ridiculous.'

Morrigan felt a sudden lurch, as though she'd missed a stair. The grey man. *The Humming Man*. Walking through walls in the south wing, disappearing into the Gossamer. Like a ghost.

She knew instantly how Ezra Squall had been getting into Nevermoor. It was like a light had been switched on in her head and she could at last see clearly.

'The Gossamer Line!' she cried.

'The what?' said Hawthorne.

'The Gossamer Line – that's how he's doing it, that's how he's getting into Nevermoor,' she said.

'How who's getting into Nevermoor?' asked Jack. 'What are you talking about?'

'Mr Jones – Ezra Squall – he's the grey man, the man who hums! That's why people think there's a ghost – he's travelling here on the Gossamer Line, he can walk through walls!'

But her voice was lost beneath a high-pitched whistle and *whoosh* of steam as their train pulled up to the platform.

Scowling, Fen nudged Morrigan and the boys into the first carriage. They had no trouble getting seats, since the other passengers had huddled at the opposite end, happy to give the giant yellow-eyed Magnificat a wide berth.

When they were settled, Fen leaned in close, shoving her great grey head between them. 'Watch what you talk about in crowded Wunderground stations,' she growled. 'The Gossamer Line's supposed to be top secret.'

'But Ezra Squall is using it,' hissed Morrigan, glancing over her shoulder to make sure no one was listening. 'We have to tell Jupiter. There is no ghost, Fen, it's Ezra Squall – *he's* the grey man!'

'Ezra Squall?' Fen dropped her voice even lower. 'The *Wundersmith* Ezra Squall? Nonsense. He was banished from Nevermoor Ages and Ages ago.'

'It's not nonsense! I saw him myself. He was in the lobby the day the chandelier crashed, and I spoke to him in the south wing one night last summer—'

'What were *you* doing in the south wing?' Fen demanded.

'—and he came to watch the Black Parade on Hallowmas.'

'It's true,' said Hawthorne, nodding fervently. 'He was there, I saw him too.'

'Dame Chanda showed me a picture of Squall from a hundred years ago and it's *him*, Fen – he looks exactly the same, he hasn't aged a day! That's how he's gotten around the ban, by leaving his body in the Republic. The border guards, the Ground Force, the Royal Sorcery Council – none of them could detect him floating around Nevermoor, because technically he was *never here*.'

'If that's true,' said Jack, with a deep frown, 'if it really is the Wundersmith and he really is getting into Nevermoor on the Gossamer Line, then . . . why?' His wary eyes flicked over to Morrigan. 'What does he want?'

'Maybe he's trying to find a weak spot,' said Hawthorne. 'Somewhere he can break back into Nevermoor.' He gave Morrigan a significant look, silently encouraging her to tell them about Squall's apprenticeship bid. He was right, she thought. She had to tell *someone*, and who knew when Jupiter would return?

'Fen, I think I know what—' Morrigan began quietly, but the Magnificat cut her off.

'This is rubbish! Even if he *was* riding the Gossamer Line, he couldn't hurt anyone. He couldn't even *touch* anyone. It's impossible to make physical contact with anything through the Gossamer.'

'Fen, listen,' said Morrigan. 'I know what Squall—'

'He is the *Wundersmith*, Fen,' Jack interrupted. 'There must be plenty of stuff he can do that other people can't.'

'I'm telling you, it's *impossible*.'

'Fen, *listen to me*!' Morrigan shouted.

Suddenly the lights in the pod flickered and the train slowed to a halt. The passengers all groaned.

'Why have we stopped, Daddy?' asked a little boy halfway down the carriage. 'Why aren't the doors opening?'

'Just another ruddy delay, son,' said the man, sighing the defeated sigh of a seasoned commuter. 'Mouse on the tracks or summat.'

The lights flickered again, fading to black and then stuttering halfheartedly back to life. There was an electrical-sounding squeal and a voice spoke over the public-address system.

'Good evening, ladies and gentlemen. Seems we have some sort of signal interference up ahead. Shouldn't be long before we're moving again. Thank you for your patience.'

The lights flickered again. The seats vibrated and the handrails shook.

Morrigan looked around – nobody else seemed to notice. She heard a rumbling from the tunnel and moved to the back of the pod to press her ear against the wall.

'What *are* you doing?' demanded Fen.

'Can't you hear it?'

'Hear what?' asked Hawthorne.

'It sounds like . . . like . . .'

Hooves. It sounded like the rumble of hooves bearing down the Wunderground tracks, echoing in the tunnel – then the screeching bray of a horse, the baying of hounds. The sound of a shot being fired.

Morrigan stumbled backwards, falling over the seats. 'Run!' she yelled. 'Everyone get back, they're coming!'

But there was nowhere to go. The carriage was packed, and the train was stopped in the middle of the tunnel. Morrigan turned to see the crush of the crowd surrounding her, dozens of puzzled faces – including Hawthorne, Fenestra and Jack, all looking worried.

'Morrigan, what are you talking about?' said Hawthorne, but his voice sounded so distant, so quiet compared to the thundering rush of the Hunt of Smoke and Shadow. 'I can't hear anyth—'

And suddenly, nothing but smoke, nothing but a thick swirling mass of shadow and smoke surrounding her, filling her lungs. Her feet were swept from under her and she was lifted into the air, carried along by the Hunt, the triumphant sound of horns deafening. She held tight to her black umbrella, clutching it as if it might somehow anchor her to the ground.

Morrigan had never been in the ocean, had never even seen it in real life, but this, she imagined, *this* was what it would be like to drown, to be swept away by a violent wave and tumbled over and over and over until there was nothing, only darkness and shadow and black, black, black . . .

CHAPTER TWENTY-FIVE

Master and Apprentice

Morrigan awoke on an empty platform. She groaned quietly as she tried to sit up on the cold concrete, pain shooting down her side. Her stomach reeled.

Blinking to bring the world into focus, she found she recognised the old-fashioned posters and advertisements lining the walls. It was the Gossamer Line platform. She picked up her oilskin umbrella and rose unsteadily to her feet. Her eyes landed on an unwelcome bit of news: she was not alone.

Forty metres along the platform, sitting on a wooden bench, was Mr Jones.

No, Morrigan thought, *not Mr Jones. Ezra Squall. The Wundersmith.*

He stared across the rail tracks at the tunnel wall, lost in his thoughts, humming his strange little tune. It sounded like a nursery rhyme, but wrong.

Morrigan's heart drummed faster.

She heard a low growl. Wisps of black smoke feathered out from the gaping mouth of the tunnel, and pinpricks of red light peered through the blackness. Morrigan jumped as a high-pitched whinny cut the air. The Hunt of Smoke and Shadow waited patiently in the dark . . . for what? For an order from their master, the Wundersmith?

There was only one way out.

Morrigan walked slowly down the platform, her footsteps echoing. Ezra Squall was unnervingly still. He just kept humming, kept staring at the wall.

If she could just get past him, Morrigan thought, maybe she could run for it – up and up the maze-like stairwells and hidden pathways of the Wunderground until she found a Nevermoor Transport Authority officer or a friendly crowd of passengers, or until she stumbled outside into the bright, noisy safety of a Saturday night in Nevermoor.

She took another tentative step, and another.

'*Little crowling, little crowling, with button-black eyes,*' Squall sang softly. A smile crept across his features, small and slow, never quite reaching his eyes.

'*Swoops down into the meadow, where the rabbits all hide.*'

Morrigan paused. Hadn't she heard this song before? Perhaps she'd learned it in nursery school, before they'd kicked her out for being cursed. Squall's voice was high and clear. Sinister in its sweetness.

'*Little rabbit, little rabbit, stay by Mother's side.*' He turned to look at her and as he did, one by one the green and white tiles that lined the platform walls turned gloss-black, as if by some silent command.

'*Or the crowling, little crowling, will peck out your eyes.*'

He finished his song, but the terrifying smile remained. 'Miss Crow. You look like a person who's figured something out.'

Morrigan said nothing.

'Go on,' he prompted, his voice barely a whisper. 'Show me how clever you are.'

'You . . . you're Ezra Squall,' she said. 'You're the Wundersmith. There is no Mr Jones, it was all a lie.'

'Good.' He nodded. 'Very good. What else?'

Morrigan swallowed. 'The Courage Square Massacre – that was you. You murdered those people.'

He inclined his head ever so slightly. 'Guilty. What else?'

'It was you who sent the Hunt of Smoke and Shadow after me.' The lights on the station platform flickered. Tendrils of black smoke drifted from the tunnel, curling around the walls and the ceiling, choking out the light. Morrigan trembled. She felt the darkness might devour her too.

'Correct. You and every other child unfortunate enough to be born on Eventide. It was meant to be a mercy.'

'A *mercy*?' said Morrigan. 'You tried to kill me!'

He closed his eyes as if disappointed. 'Wrong. I don't *try* to kill people, Miss Crow. I simply kill them. You may have noticed you are still alive. Not, I assure you, because your Captain North made his daring rescue, but because *I intended for you to live.*'

'Liar!'

'I am a liar. Yes. But not always, and certainly not this time.' He rose from his seat and stepped closer. 'You were only half right. I sent the Hunt after you, but not to kill you.'

At the mention of their name, the black-smoke hounds emerged from the tunnel, stalking low to the ground, followed by a wall of hunters on horseback. They moved slowly, dream-like. Waiting for an order to attack.

Morrigan stepped backwards.

'Don't run,' Squall warned her. 'They love it when children run.'

She froze, unable to take her eyes off the Hunt. Her pulse was thrumming all the way down to her fingertips.

'Quite frightening, I agree,' he said, glancing back over his shoulder. 'Some of my best work. They are the perfect murder machine – ruthless, unfeeling. Unstoppable. Believe me, Miss Crow, if I had ordered them to kill you, you would not have lived past Eventide. You would be nothing but a pile of ash. The order I gave was not to kill. It was to *herd*.'

He smiled. The skin on Morrigan's neck prickled. For the smallest of moments, a brief flash, she could swear she'd seen the shadow of the Wundersmith on his face. Black eyes and black mouth and sharp, bared teeth. The hollowed-out face of a creature who was neither man nor monster, but something else Morrigan dared not imagine.

'They failed the first time, of course, allowing that abominable ginger to spirit you away in his ridiculous mechanical spider. But I knew they wouldn't fail again, not once I finally found a weakness to exploit on the Gossamer Line. It's taken most of the year and one or two minor Wunderground disasters—'

'That *was* you,' said Morrigan. Her voice was shaking. 'Those derailments. People kept saying it was the Wundersmith, and they were right. You killed two people!'

'Trial and error,' he said with a shrug. 'All in the name of rounding you up like a lost sheep. And now, little lamb, it is time to go home.'

He turned to her and held out his hand. A train whistled in the distance.

Morrigan took another step back. 'I'm not going anywhere with you.'

'I respectfully disagree.'

Morrigan heard the sound of an engine gaining speed. A silvery-gold light shone from the depths of the tunnel, growing brighter and brighter, piercing the wall of blackness that was the Hunt of Smoke and Shadow until it finally broke through, shimmering and pearlescent, too beautiful and too terrible to look upon.

The Hunt scattered, evaporating into thin air and reappearing on the platform like a tornado with Morrigan at its eye. The oilskin umbrella tumbled from her hands. They spiralled around and around her, binding her in black ropes of shadow and smoke, pushing and pulling her deep into the blinding golden light of the Gossamer train.

A whistle blew. The train departed.

There was a chill in the air, and Morrigan could feel it even through the Gossamer. It was cold outside Crow Manor. The lawn was covered in a layer of frost. Behind the tall iron gates, the house was a black silhouette against the darkening sky.

Squall stepped forward, gazing up at the house with manic, shiny-eyed anticipation. 'Let's pay a visit, shall we?'

The Wundersmith was no longer a bodiless entity, floating on the Gossamer and unable to affect the things around him. He was back in the Republic, back in his body, and relishing his freedom.

He cracked his knuckles and stretched out his arms, and with one precise flick of his wrists, the gates opened – but no, they didn't just *open*. They peeled back, rail by rail, the solid iron groaning as if bent by some giant invisible hand.

The dogs came running around the side of the house, barking viciously at the noise.

'Woof! *Woof woof!*' Squall barked back at them like a madman. The dogs flew backwards through the air as if thrown, landing with dull thuds on the lawn and then running away, yelping.

'You've no idea what agony it is,' he said, turning to Morrigan as he crunched up the gravel drive, 'to be there, right there in my city – *my* city, my beloved Nevermoor – and unable to *do anything*. Unable to use my talents, to affect the things around me . . . even to touch anything.' He swallowed, staring into the distance. 'The Gossamer Line is a wonderful thing, Miss Crow – I should know, I created it – but sometimes it's a prison.' His face brightened. 'Let me show you how that feels.'

He turned to the house, raising his arms in the air like a conductor ready to command an orchestra, and began.

The bricks and stones that made up Crow Manor began to shift, turning and scraping against each other, churning up clouds of dust, reassembling themselves until Morrigan's childhood home was unrecognisable. It groaned and stretched into a tall gothic cathedral, looming above her more frighteningly than ever.

'An improvement, no?' Squall said, coughing as he waved the dust away from his face.

'Stop,' said Morrigan.

'I'm only getting started.'

With a click of his fingers, the dark grey stone of the transformed house began to glow, lit by a million golden fairy lights. It was beautiful.

Well, that was unexpected, thought Morrigan, eyeing Squall suspiciously. He gave her a questioning look and held out both hands, as if seeking her approval.

'This is what you want, isn't it, Miss Crow?' Another click, and a flagpole sprouted from the uppermost spire, a black flag bearing Morrigan's face waving proudly in the breeze. 'This is why you chose that ostentatious fool, isn't it, with his Wundrous Society and his arachnipod and his jumping off the roof at Morningtide?'

A flick of Squall's wrist, and a bright neon sign on the rooftop said WELCOME TO MORRIGANLAND in enormous flashing letters.

Morrigan might have laughed if she hadn't been so frightened. Ezra Squall, the evillest man who ever lived, had just turned her childhood home into a Morrigan Crow theme park.

He turned to her. 'All style, no substance. That's what Jupiter North is. Has he even told you yet?'

'Told me what?'

'No, of course he hasn't. But you have a moderately functioning brain in that dear little head. You must have figured it out.' As he spoke, Squall fluttered his fingers and made jets of water shoot up from the fountain and freeze in midair, like ice sculptures. He wasn't even looking. Morrigan wasn't certain he even noticed he was doing it. 'Tell me, Morrigan Crow: why did I ask you to be my apprentice?'

Morrigan swallowed. 'I don't know.'

'Nonsense,' he said softly. He lifted his hand and made a pattern in the air. The neon sign and fairy lights stuttered and died. The spire began to crumble. A few grey stones tumbled down to the ground. 'Tell me.'

'I don't *know*,' she repeated. She jumped aside just as a large chunk of stone fell where she stood.

'*Think.*'

But she couldn't. Crow Manor was crumbling right before her eyes. The outer walls turned to piles of dust and debris, revealing the warmly lit rooms inside, untouched by Squall's destruction; a tableau of life as normal for the Crow family.

Closest to where Morrigan stood, her father, stepmother and grandmother sat in comfy chairs in the parlour, oblivious to the fact that Crow Manor was turning to ruins around them. Ivy fed one of the babies; Corvus rocked the other to sleep. Grandmother was reading. A fire burned in the hearth.

'Do I really need to tell you?' Squall said, coming to stand beside her with a look of puzzled amusement on his face. 'Miss Crow, you are a Wundersmith. Just like me.'

At those words, Morrigan grew cold. She felt a shiver down her spine, just as real and as chilling as if an icy finger was drawing on her back. Her skin turned to gooseflesh.

A Wundersmith. Just like me.

'No,' she whispered, and then, more firmly, 'No!'

'No, you're right.' He tilted his head. 'Not *quite* like me. But one day – if you work hard and pay attention – you might come close.'

Morrigan clenched her hands into fists. 'I'll never be like you.'

'It's perfectly charming that you believe you have a choice in the matter. But you were born this way, Miss Crow. You are set on a path from which you cannot diverge.'

'I'll never be like you,' Morrigan repeated. 'I'll never be a murderer!'

Squall chuckled. 'Is that what you believe a Wundersmith is? An instrument of death? I suppose you're half right. Destruction and creation. Death and life. All tools within your grasp, once you know how to use them.'

'I don't want to use them,' Morrigan said through gritted teeth.

'What a dreadful liar you are,' said Squall. 'You must learn to deceive more skilfully, Miss Crow. You must also learn what we shall call the Wretched Arts of the Accomplished Wundersmith, and I will gladly be your teacher. Let us begin with lesson one.'

Squall stepped into the room and whispered something Morrigan couldn't quite hear. The fire leapt from the grate and spread instantly, encircling the Crows. In moments, the parlour was ablaze from curtains to carpet. Morrigan's family sat still, completely unaware of the danger they were in.

'Stop!' Morrigan shouted over the roar of the flames. 'Please, leave them alone!'

'Why do you care?' Squall sneered. 'These people hate you, Miss Crow. They blamed you for everything that went wrong in their lives. When you died – when they believed you to be dead – they were *relieved*. And why?'

The fire crept closer, closing in on the Crows. A bead of sweat rolled down Ivy's forehead, but Ivy herself seemed to feel nothing. Morrigan tried to pick something up – anything, a pebble, a piece of crumbled stone – to throw at Ivy or Corvus or Grandmother, to warn them. But she couldn't grasp anything. Her hand went right through.

'Because of a curse,' Squall continued, 'that never even existed.'

Morrigan swallowed, watching him through the flames. 'What do you mean, never existed?'

He laughed. 'The "curse" was nothing more than a convenient way to explain why all you Eventide-born have such a nasty habit of kicking the bucket before you come of a troublesome age. Before you start attracting and absorbing too much of *my* precious Wunder, like the greedy little lightning rods some of you have the potential to become. I couldn't have anyone diluting the source of energy that's made me obscenely wealthy and powerful, could I? If I am the only conductor of Wunder, its power resides with me. Of course I had to eliminate any potential threats. You can't blame me for that. It's good business sense.'

'There's no such thing as the curse,' Morrigan said. She finally understood. Jupiter had told her, but she hadn't believed him. Not really. '*You're* the curse.'

Squall continued as if she hadn't spoken. 'Over the years, the curse took on a life of its own. People are so *dramatic*. Once upon a time you little wretches were a cause for pity and compassion, having your insignificant lives snatched from you at such a tender age. But somewhere along the way, the heinous true nature of humanity kicked in, and people began to see cursed children as convenient scapegoats. Someone to point the finger at when things went wrong. Why did my crops fail? Blame the cursed child. Why did I lose my job? Blame the cursed child. Soon the cursed child was to blame for all sorts of mischief and strife. The legend grew and grew until cursed children were not only the sorrow of their families, but the bane of everybody else's existence.'

Squall took the baby from Corvus's arms. Corvus remained still, his eyes glassy and unseeing, reflecting the bright orange glow of the fire. The parlour had become a furnace, and the flames were throwing up billowing waves of smoke. The smoke became swirling black shapes, weaving in and out of the fire. Morrigan heard a howl. She shuddered.

The baby tried to grab at Squall's nose with his fat little fingers. The Wundersmith made a funny face and the tiny snowy-haired boy squealed with laughter.

'So you see, Miss Crow, I didn't make your family despise you. They did that all on their own.' He made the baby wave his little hand at her. 'Shall I kill them for you?'

'*No!*' cried Morrigan. 'Please – no!' Squall dropped the baby in midair, but instead of falling, it floated slowly to the floor. She had to do something, had to stop him, but *how*? What could she possibly do, through the Gossamer? She was powerless.

'No? Are you certain? I'm not sure I believe you.' He watched her with a tiny, teasing smile on his lips. 'Tell me, little crowling. Why do you think I let you live?'

Morrigan said nothing. The Hunt of Smoke and Shadow was taking form around them. Snarling hounds and faceless men on horseback grew out of the flames and surrounded her unguarded family. Closer and closer, waiting for a command from Squall. Waiting to kill.

'I've destroyed so many others. Been so patient all these years, waiting for the right one. A lesser man would have given up, but I knew . . . I *knew* that you would come. That one day, a child born on Eventide would rise to take my place. A child filled with dark promise, in whose eyes I would see a reflection of my own. My true and rightful heir.' He knelt down to bring his face level with hers. His voice was so soft and his smile so sincere that for a moment Morrigan saw her friend, Mr Jones, in this madman's face with its lines etched in shadow. 'I see you, Morrigan Crow,' he whispered, his eyes glittering. 'There is black ice at the heart of you.'

'*No!*' Morrigan shouted. Something inside her reared away from Squall, as the ocean pulls back water from the shore to build a wave. Suddenly that was what she was – a living tidal wave of rage and fear. She was *not* like him, she would *never be like him*!

Morrigan stumbled backwards and instinctively threw up her arms, surrendering herself to the wave inside.

A bright, blinding light filled the room, obliterating the Hunt of Smoke and Shadow and dousing the flames with one booming golden-white pulse that lasted several seconds, or maybe several days, or maybe an entire lifetime, and then was gone.

In its wake, silence.

The Crows, still shrouded in blissful ignorance, staring but not seeing.

Squall, wide-eyed and lightning-struck, sprawled on the ground as if he'd been thrown there. Staring up at Morrigan as if he'd just now been given the gift of sight.

And Morrigan herself, trembling with the aftershock of . . . *whatever that was.*

She'd destroyed the Hunt of Smoke and Shadow. Or if not destroyed, at least sent them away. That was good enough for now. Morrigan had no idea how she'd done it, how she'd made the light come, but in those few blinding seconds she recalled once again Squall's words to her this past summer: *Shadows are shadows. They want to be dark.*

Picking himself up off the floor, Squall found his voice at last.

'You see, Miss Crow,' he said, eyeing her warily, 'you should have accepted my offer, but the truth is I don't need you to. You have already apprenticed yourself to me, simply by living past your eleventh birthday. The gathering is underway. Wunder has noticed you, and you are at its mercy.'

'What does that mean?' Morrigan asked. 'What's the gathering?'

'You were born a Wundersmith, but if you do not learn how to harness Wunder, it will harness *you*. If you do not learn to control Wunder, it will control *you*. It will burn you slowly from the inside, and eventually . . . it will destroy you.' He shook his head, one side of his mouth curving into a rueful smile. 'I told you – it would have been a mercy, letting the Hunt of Smoke and Shadow kill you. But, alas, you seem to have driven them away, at least for now. Never mind. I didn't bring you here this evening to harm you. Or your family.'

'Then why did you kidnap me?'

'Kidnap you?' He looked amused and perhaps a little offended by the idea. '*Kidnap* is just another word for *steal*. I'm not a thief. This isn't a kidnapping. It's your very first lesson in how to be a Wundersmith. A masterclass, from a masterful teacher. Lesson two will take place as soon as you request it.'

Morrigan shook her head. Was he joking? Or just insane? 'I won't ever request anything from you. There's nothing you can teach me.'

Squall laughed softly as he stepped through the dying embers, kicking up swirls of ash and sparks. 'I am the only person alive who can teach you anything worth knowing. One day, very soon, you will come to a deep understanding of that terrible truth. My monsters and I will make sure of it.' He tilted his head to the side, all traces of amusement gone from his black, fathomless eyes.

'Until then, little crowling.'

Without looking back, he walked down the long gravel drive, disappearing into the darkness. In his wake, the last remnants of the fire were gently extinguished, the curtains and furniture unburnt, the shattered windows unshattered, the stone walls of Crow Manor rebuilt themselves and the mangled iron gates unbent, closing with a soft *clang*.

Morrigan stood in the middle of the now-peaceful parlour. She watched the oblivious Crows and felt a strange, yearning homesickness blossom inside her. But it wasn't for this place. It wasn't for these people.

Morrigan closed her eyes. She pictured in her mind the silver-handled umbrella with the little opal bird, lying on the Wunderground platform where it had fallen from her hands.

She waited. She heard the whistle of the Gossamer train. And she went home.

CHAPTER TWENTY-SIX

W.

At first, Morrigan thought she had gone blind.

'I said *slowly*,' said Jupiter. She felt him release her shoulders, heard him take a step backwards. 'Open your eyes slowly.'

She knew she was in the Deucalion, knew she was standing in Jupiter's office, but . . . it could have been the surface of the sun. The world had washed out. Everything was a brilliant sun-bleached white, dazzling and bright. If she squinted, she could just make out her silhouette in the mirror. Was this really what he saw, every time he looked at her?

'Don't look too long,' Jupiter warned.

The brightness didn't come from one big light. It came from thousands and thousands – maybe millions – maybe *billions* – of tiny pinpricks of the same golden-white light she'd seen at Crow Manor. They gathered around her like microscopic particles of dust, catching the light of a sunbeam. No, not like dust – like something living. Moths gathering to a flame.

'Is that . . . ?'

'Wunder. Nice, isn't it?'

Nice was not the right word. It was beautiful, but it was not nice. There was something about it that was the opposite of nice. It made Morrigan feel some combination of awe and expectation and panic and joy and very large and very small and screaming and whispering and *something else*.

'What's it doing?' Morrigan asked.

'Waiting.'

'For what?'

'For you.'

'Waiting for me to do what?'

Jupiter was quiet for a long moment, and then – 'I guess we'll see.'

He took her shoulders and pressed his forehead to hers a second time, just as he'd done to the Elders at the Show Trial. Morrigan hadn't realised at the time what was happening – that he was able to share the gift of his sight with other people. To show them how he saw the world, if only fleetingly.

To Morrigan's great disappointment and relief, the world went dull again.

The girl in the mirror – black-haired, dark-eyed, crooked-nosed – looked normal. Ordinary.

'He said I'm like him.' It was the first time she'd voiced her fear aloud. 'It's true, isn't it? That's what the gathering is – it's this. Wunder, gathering around me. It means I'm a . . . a Wundersmith.' She swallowed. She could almost taste the word in her mouth.

'Yes,' Jupiter said gravely. 'But try to understand – the word *Wundersmith* didn't always mean something bad or evil, Mog.'

'It didn't?'

'Heavens, no. There was a time in Nevermoor, long ago, when to be a Wundersmith was a celebrated honour.'

'Like being in the Wundrous Society?'

'Even greater than that. Wundersmiths were wish-granters and protectors. They used their powers to bring good things to the world. *Wundersmith* doesn't mean *monster* or *murderer* – Squall *made* it mean those things. He did something unforgivable. He betrayed his people and his city. Abused his power. He made *Wundersmith* a dark and terrible word, but it wasn't always. You can change its meaning again, Mog.' He beamed at her. 'And you will. I know you will. I meant it when I said you don't have a knack. What you have is *so much more* than that. You have a gift. A calling. And you get to decide what that means. Nobody else.'

As Morrigan's sight adjusted, Jupiter's study slowly swam back into focus – the photographs on the walls, the books on the shelves. Jupiter's face, all shining blue eyes and bright copper tangle of beard. Morrigan dropped into a leather armchair, crossing her ankles on the footrest.

'You knew all along what I was, didn't you?'

Jupiter nodded.

'And Squall? You knew he bid on me, too?'

'Yes.'

Morrigan sighed. All that time she'd wasted, worrying whether she should tell Jupiter about Squall. She felt stupid. 'So why did you make me go through the trials?' she asked. 'Why didn't you just tell the Elders?'

'You're supposing that being a Wundersmith is the most important thing about you.'

'Isn't it?'

'Not at all. If it were the most important thing, Mog, wouldn't we hold the Show Trial first? Think about it. We had the Book Trial, to see who was honest and quick-thinking. The Chase Trial, to see who was tenacious and strategic. The Fright Trial, to see who was brave and resourceful. Don't you think there might have been some fascinating knacks that we lost in those first three trials? Of course there were! Who knows, maybe the most talented people of all were weeded out before the Show Trial even arrived.

'The point is – as far as the Society is concerned – if you are not honest, and determined, and brave, then it doesn't matter how talented you are. You had to go through all four trials, because I needed the Elders to know what sort of person you are, in the hope . . .' He paused, swallowing, and then quietly finished, 'In the hope they'll continue to see you as a person first, and a Wundersmith second.'

'You told me the Wundersmith was fairy tale and superstition.'

Jupiter nodded. 'I know. I'm sorry I lied. Although it is *sort of* true . . . Wundersmith history is so bound up in myth and nonsense, for most people it's hard to tell the difference. It was only half a lie, but still. I'm sorry.'

'Why'd you lie?'

'Because I thought it was the right thing to do. I didn't want you thinking too much about the Wundersmith. Just one more thing to worry about, isn't it? Thought it was best to get you into the Society first, then deal with it later.'

'And the others?'

'What others?'

'*Three others registered* . . . you were talking about

the Cursed Children's Register, weren't you? Are they Wundersmiths too?'

'No.'

She waited for Jupiter to say more, but he was a closed book. 'What happened to them?' she prompted. 'Did you save them too, or . . . ?'

He relented a little. 'They're fine. They're far away, safe and sound, blissfully unaware of Ezra Squall and his Hunt of Smoke and Shadow.'

Lucky them, Morrigan thought.

The last two days since her encounter with Squall had been utterly draining. The train had returned Morrigan to the Gossamer Line platform just as Fen and Jack and Hawthorne had arrived, breathless and panicked, having figured out where she'd disappeared to and run to fetch Jupiter.

Jack reached her first, white-faced and speechless with relief. Jupiter swept her up in a tight squeeze that nearly choked her, and Fen licked her hair until it could practically stand up on its own. Hawthorne begged her to tell the whole story again at least twelve times, gasping and cheering at all the right moments with each retelling.

The tale of Morrigan's close call with the Hunt of Smoke and Shadow went around the Deucalion, but Jupiter made Fen, Jack, Morrigan and Hawthorne swear to keep the

Wundersmith bit a secret. Jack had responded indignantly, 'I already promised, didn't I?'

That hadn't made any sense to Morrigan until just now. She suddenly remembered that night before Christmas, when Jack had stared at her in horror and wonder.

'Jack knew, didn't he?' she said, realisation dawning. 'He's known since Christmas. Because he's like you. He's a – what do you call it?'

'A Witness,' said Jupiter, taking the chair opposite. 'Yes. He hates it.'

'Why would he hate it?' Morrigan asked, astounded. 'It would be like knowing everything. I thought that was Jack's favourite thing.'

Jupiter chuckled at that. His face grew thoughtful as he looked at her. 'It is a bit like that, sometimes, I s'pose. But not always. Sometimes even the Gossamer can hide things.'

'I'd love to be a Witness.'

'I'm not sure you would,' said Jupiter, wincing. 'Seeing all those hidden things? All the time? Every time somebody lies, it's there on their face like a black smudge. Every time somebody's miserable, it hangs around them like flies on a corpse. Pain, anger, betrayal – it's all there, everywhere around us, all the time. Most Witnesses can't ever live in a place like this, it would drive them to insanity.'

'You mean a place like the Deucalion?'

'I mean Nevermoor. Or any place where millions of people converge every day, leaving invisible trails that criss-cross each other in a million billion trillion threads of a mad tapestry. People leave pieces of themselves everywhere, Morrigan – all the fights they've had, all the hurts they've suffered, the love and joy they've felt, the good things and the bad things they've done.' He rubbed his face tiredly. 'I've learned to filter it, to only see the things that are important. I can pull apart all the different layers and threads and make sense of the madness.

'But that took me years, Mog, years and years of training. Jack isn't there yet. He won't be for some time. For now, the patch acts like a filter. It disrupts his sight, so he only sees what you or anyone else would see. Otherwise he'd go mad.'

It hadn't occurred to Morrigan that having a talent like Jupiter's might have a downside. Perhaps that was why Jack was so bad-tempered.

'Why didn't he just say so?' she asked.

Jupiter looked down at his hands and shrugged. 'I think he's embarrassed. People tend not to like Witnesses. It's hard to be friends with someone who can see your secrets.'

'But that's ridiculous,' said Morrigan, thinking of Jupiter's many friends and admirers. 'Everyone in the whole world likes you.'

Jupiter laughed – loudly, joyfully – until there were tears in his eyes. 'Your view of the *whole world* is radically out of kilter, Morrigan Crow, and that's one of the many things I like about you.

'That reminds me – something arrived for you today.' He stood up and beckoned Morrigan to follow. Unlocking his desk drawer, Jupiter took out a small wooden box and gave it to her. 'I'm not supposed to give you this until your inauguration day. But it's been a rubbish week, and I think in light of that you probably deserve to open it now.'

Inside the box, on a red velvet cushion, rested a small golden pin in the shape of a *W.*

Morrigan gasped. 'My pin! Does this mean – did you get it? The last signature for that . . . that safeguard thing?'

Jupiter's face fell a little. 'Not . . . quite. No. But I'll sort it out. I promise.' He fastened the pin to her collar. 'There you are. Your ticket to a reserved seat on the Wunderground. Hope it was worth it.'

Morrigan laughed. It seemed insane to have gone through everything she had this year – cheating death, competing in the trials, facing Flintlock and Squall and the Hunt of Smoke and Shadow, and every other wretched thing she'd faced, just for a tiny thing like this pin.

But it wasn't tiny. It was big – a very big promise. The promise of family, and belonging, and friendship.

The funny thing was, Morrigan thought, reflecting on the past week, and her life at the Hotel Deucalion . . . it turned out she had those things already.

⌐•▬

The chandelier had settled in its permanent form at last.

Frank won the betting pool. At least, he was the closest – it wasn't a peacock, but it was a bird. A large black bird, shining iridescent from certain angles, its wingspan spread over the lobby as if protecting the Hotel Deucalion and its inhabitants. Or perhaps poised to swoop down on their heads. It depended on whom you asked.

Jupiter said he loved it even more than the pink sailing ship.

⌐•▬

A few days later, Jupiter and Nan took their candidates out for a belated celebration. They had lamb shanks and ginger beer in a cosy pub on Courage Square, toasting Morrigan and Hawthorne's success.

The patrons spent hours telling them thrilling tales of their own first years as scholars in the Wundrous Society. Most of Nan's stories involved dragonriding, and most of Jupiter's involved such outrageous rule-breaking that he finally had to change the subject when he saw Hawthorne taking notes.

On the way home Morrigan kicked flurries of snow up from the ground as she walked. Despite the bitter cold, she thought Nevermoor had taken on an extraordinary shine on this otherwise ordinary midwinter's day. She felt different.

Everything felt different.

People in the street smiled at them as they passed. Morrigan was no longer the cursed Crow girl, waiting for the next terrible thing to happen. Waiting to take the blame. And yet there was something dark, something dreadful, lurking still in the back of her mind.

Jupiter nudged her as they reached the Brolly Rail platform. 'What are you thinking about?'

'He'll be back, won't he?' she asked quietly. 'Squall. He'll come back. With his monsters.'

Jupiter's face was grim. 'I imagine he'll try.'

Morrigan nodded. She clutched her umbrella tight, touching her fingertips absently to the little opal bird on top. 'Then we'll just have to be ready.'

A nearby group of children whispered to each other and craned their necks to watch as Morrigan and Jupiter reached out confidently with their hooked umbrella handles and were swept away by the passing Brolly Rail. They weren't just looking at Jupiter but at the pair of them, with their golden *W* pins gleaming proudly on their coats.

Patron and candidate. The mad ginger and the strange little girl with black eyes.

Acknowledgements

Thanks to that nice public librarian who published *The Three Koalas by Jessica Townsend, age 7* in the library newsletter, even though the author had quite badly misused the word 'exaggerating' and also wouldn't have known a line break if she fell over one.

Mad props to Helen Thomas, Alvina Ling, Suzanne O'Sullivan and Kheryn Callender. I am the luckiest author in the world to have this editing dream team on my side. I might never get over how brilliant and lovely you all are, so get used to hearing it.

Everyone at Hachette/Orion/LBYR – Fiona Hazard, Louise Sherwin-Stark, Justin Ractliffe, Hilary Murray Hill, Ruth Alltimes, Megan Tingley, Lisa Moraleda, Katy Cattell, Dominic Kingston, Samantha Swinnerton, Lucy Upton, Thy Bui, Monika Mueller, Penny Evershed, Ashleigh Barton,

Sophie Mayfield, Nathan Grice, Julia Sanderson, Victoria Stapleton and so many others who have welcomed me to the family – thank you for your support, and for the incredible work you've done to help bring Morrigan into the world.

Thank you to the super talented Beatriz Castro and Jim Madsen for your beautiful artwork.

Thank you Jenny Bent and Molly Ker Hawn, you total legends, for working so hard to champion *Nevermoor* in Frankfurt and beyond. Thank you to everyone at The Bent Agency, especially Victoria Cappello and John Bowers. Also to the many brilliant TBA co-agents across the world, and all my wonderful foreign publishers.

Thank you to the amazing Dana Spector and everyone at Paradigm Talent Agency for your tireless work and passion. Also to Daria Cercek, Emily Ferenbach and the team at Fox – I'm overwhelmed by your excitement for Morrigan, and so grateful to know she's in the right hands.

Shout out to Team Cooper – you all amaze and inspire me. I feel lucky to be among you.

Huge thanks to two of my earliest readers, Chris How and Lucy Spence. Your enthusiasm for Morrigan & co. has meant the world to me.

Also to my friend and high school English teacher, Charmaine Rye, who made me feel like a proper writer long before I was one.

Jewels and Dean – early readers, top cheerleaders. Big love.

Gemma Cooper – agent, friend, Slytherin but in the best ways, all-round good egg. You are the secret ingredient in this whole weird, amazing thing. You're like my Jupiter North, but if Jupiter North was a responsible adult, and also a lady and not ginger. What would I do without you? Endless thanks, G-Coop.

Sally – best bud, first reader, lifelong sounding board, rather big head so I shan't say much more but you get the idea. Cheers, big ears.

I know everyone thinks they have the best and most supportive mum around but actually I do, soz. Thanks, Mum.